Hey ALICIA,

THANKS FOR
SUPPORTING ME
AT BARR!

HOPE YOU ENJOY
THE STORY!

SP

LIKE SWEET BUTTERMILK

— a Novel —

S.F. POWELL

In memory of my mother and father

CONTENTS

ACKNOWLEDGMENTS

Thanks and praise to God for the gifts of love and laughter.
Thanks to my husband, Larry, and our children. You are home base (and there's no place like home).

For support most-intangible, I extend special thanks to:

Kyana "Kee Na-Na" Bundy
Vicki "Meis" Kelliebrew

For inspiration most-intangible:

Pamela "Spike" Bundy
Erinn "Heather-Lynn" Bundy
Malik D. Brown
Shellie M. Jackson
Aletcia Skinner
Gia T. Knox
Patricia F. Durham
Tanya A. Powell

Debbie Smith Brown
Mr. Ron "Ronaldis" Brown
Patsy D. Ramsey
Shelonda Merrell Blair
Angela Douglas Conyers
Derrick A. Johnson Sr.
Geta McGill-Amos

"The course of true love never did run smooth."
—William Shakespeare, *A Midsummer Night's Dream*

CHAPTER 1

Dinner for Two

For whatever reason, the evening progressed miserably.

Dinner was only so-so. The Cajun catfish? Dry. The rice? Overcooked. And there was this awkward silence between the fits and starts of conversation.

Richard "Rick" Phillips rubbed his eyes with the thumb and index finger of his left hand; he had a headache. Not intense pain, but hammer-taps behind his right eye. He sat across from his wife, Vivian, staring past her into the night and movements of downtown Washington, DC.

He shifted his gaze to her. "So, a family vacation is out?"

"I'm saying we may have to postpone it. You always go to extremes, Rick. Did you hear me say a family vacation was out? No, you didn't." She rolled her eyes and then looked down at her plate, pushing around the food left uneaten.

And there it was again: that awkward silence.

Rick reached for his right ear. The scar there provided an odd comfort to him; he fingered it absentmindedly and stared at his wife.

Viv's new haircut proved more-flattering than he anticipated. He liked her below-shoulder-length hair, so when she hinted at getting it cut, he stopped short of getting caveman on her and saying it was out of the question. Styled in a bob, Viv's hair framed her face softly despite its blunt cut. The restaurant lighting gently kissed the natural auburn highlights in her chestnut hair.

Rick reached to stop Viv's hand from pushing her fork around, wanting her to look at him.

He didn't understand why the evening floundered. Couldn't understand why a normally-romantic occasion seemed forced and staged, as if they were going through the motions for some unseen director. "Look at me," he encouraged warmly.

Viv looked at him.

God, he loved her.

"Rick, I don't want—"

"I know. You don't want to get into a 'thing.' But we're not go'n get into anything because, first, you're the one upset, not me. Second, I, as far as I know, haven't done anything. But I know you, Viv: something's wrong."

Viv sighed. "I'm just tired. I told you I didn't want to eat here for our night out." She glanced around DeTante's.

Rick looked around, too, trying to find what she was looking for. He took another bite of dry fish. "That you did. But we've eaten at several places since we were here last. DeTante's is *our* place. Why so anti-DeTante's, lately?" This was the most they'd said all evening.

Their server, Jorge, approached. "Everything okay?"

"We're good. Can I get an Elijah Craig Twenty-three, neat?" Rick looked at his wife. "Viv?" Her mind was elsewhere. Something was up.

"Oh. An espresso, please. Thanks, Jorge." She smiled, sending Jorge away.

Viv's eyes were gorgeous: wide and round like a child's, but sultry—the irises so dark they appeared black. She had a pretty smile, too. The smile at Jorge was ordinary, but Viv possessed a certain smile that made his heart skip a beat. Rick hadn't seen that smile of hers for some time.

He called it her "best present" smile: a smile coming when one opens that "best present, ever." The smile wasn't too big, showing too many teeth, but it was sincere, winning Rick's heart every time.

Not this time, though. This time the smile appeared weak and somewhat sad, and Rick's concern edged into irritation. He hated solving problems indirectly.

"Vivian." He spoke pleasantly to camouflage his annoyance.

"Yes?" Viv's tone mimicked his.

"Look, let's get to it. It's obvious something's bothering you, but usually you're right out with it. So, tell me."

He knew his last sentence sounded more like a command than a gentle prodding, but this was getting old (and his headache worsened).

Viv sighed. "Okay, Rick, look. You know how much I love you—"

"What's up, Phillipses?! Long time, no see." Jonathan Rast, DeTante's owner, smiled as he reached their table.

Rick shook his hand. "Hey, man. Yeah, it's been awhile. How's it going?" He started to stand, but Jonathan gestured for him to stay seated.

Jonathan shook Viv's hand. "Pretty good. Can't complain."

Jorge returned with their drinks. "Anything for you, Mister Rast?"

"Nah."

With a nod, Jorge retreated.

Viv looked up at Jonathan with caring-worry. "How's your mom, Jonathan?"

Rick could tell she appreciated the interruption. He thought about Viv prefacing whatever she was going to say, with a declaration of her love. Now truly, what good could follow that?

"Guess I spoke too soon. The Alzheimer's is taking its toll; we don't expect her to be with us much longer." Jonathan shook his head as if to clear any sadness. "But, hey, I'm not here for the gloom and doom. Just passing through. It's been a minute since I saw you two in here, so I came over. All's well?"

Rick read genuine concern on his face.

"Everything's cool." Rick glanced at Viv. "Nothin' major going on."

Jonathan pulled a chair from a neighboring table and sat.

Rick released a quiet sigh. He was tired of looking up at him—the neck strain didn't help his headache.

Jonathan stretched out, resting his hands atop his head.

Rick guessed he'd decided to visit awhile. He didn't mind. He was in no hurry to get back to whatever was about to follow Viv's opening line, anyway.

They settled into general conversation, but Rick's attention wavered. Viv's mood appeared to change for the better. Watching her, Rick recalled how he and Viv came across DeTante's.

They found DeTante's by chance—a missed subway stop during a rendezvous for their twelfth wedding anniversary. He remembered the night stroll downtown with Viv: her wanting to stop in the deserted alcove of a photography studio for a quickie, and him, his erection straining as she caressed him, rejecting her. He couldn't ignore being in

3

public; taking things further wasn't an option. Viv couldn't have cared less. If things were tasteful, she wanted sex wherever.

Turned out the "photography studio" was DeTante's: an upscale three-tiered restaurant with southern cuisine and soul food, a photography-themed décor, and the ever-present sound of flutes playing overhead. They met Jonathan that first night when he stopped by their table in his effort to greet new patrons. Rick remembered being uncomfortable and oddly territorial over Viv that night.

Over the years, they returned to DeTante's at least monthly. The atmosphere and southern cuisine rarely failed them. In that respect, DeTante's became their place.

Rick came in and out of this reverie, offering what he could to the conversation topics. He enjoyed Jonathan's stops by their table, having grown less-territorial over Viv.

He particularly noticed Viv's improved mood; it was brighter (*Okay, Rick, look. You know how much I love you* …), but she still didn't smile much.

"Oh, by the way, the next time you two are here, you're going to be in for a surprise." Jonathan words brought Rick back to the discussion at hand.

Viv's eyes widened with recognition. "When will they be up?"

"I expect to add to the series during downtime this weekend, so, sometime next week." Jonathan stood and stretched.

"Then we'll be back next week with Alna. Right, Rick?"

Mentioning Alna clued Rick in. About a year ago, Viv had taken up photography again. Even Alna caught the photographer's bug. Some Saturdays, Viv and Alna would have a girls' day out, shooting pictures instead of shopping. Rick had an appreciative-eye for Viv's shots, and Alna's pictures showed talent for the art, too.

Shortly after New Year's, he suggested submitting the photos to Jonathan for display at DeTante's. It was March now. He hadn't heard any more about it. He smiled, thinking about his daughter. *Alna will be overjoyed.*

Rick nodded curtly. "Damn skippy."

The intimation behind Viv being in contact with Jonathan without him crossed Rick's mind but disappeared into thoughts of a family outing. Rick valued family time. Viv would say he 'obsessed' over it, but he welcomed any opportunity for the three of them to be together. Viv could get with the family-time thing, but she considered alone-time important, too.

"Next week, then." Jonathan grabbed his leather bag and jacket from the neighboring table. He gave Rick a power-handshake before turning to Viv. "I'll also have the shots we didn't use, okay?" He bent down and kissed Viv's cheek.

Now, for years, Jonathan gave him the power-handshake and Viv the customary kiss on the cheek. Rick never had a problem with it. Didn't have a problem now. The kiss was cool: a simple brushing of his lips, barely touching Viv.

The kiss was fine.

Viv's reaction was not.

She smiled. And given that she hadn't smiled much all evening, Rick initially welcomed the smile. But then the smile grew into her best-present smile; the smile that warmed him inside.

Viv smiled that smile, directed at Jonathan and not at him, and Rick was pissed.

"Okay, next week then," Viv confirmed, that smile fading as quickly as it had come. But it was too late.

Rick turned to Jonathan. "A'ight, Jonathan. Catch you later. Our prayers are with your family, man."

Jonathan nodded his thanks, signaled for Jorge to return to the table, and was gone.

Jorge arrived, inquiring about dessert.

Rick initially had a taste for DeTante's pecan pie. His taste for it was gone now. He ordered it anyway.

Jorge turned to Viv.

"I was gonna pass, but since Rick ordered something, I guess I'll have a scoop of vanilla to go with his pie." She winked at Rick.

"I could order the pie a-la-mode and bring two spoons, Ma'am."

"No, thanks, Jorge. We'll do the mixing ourselves. Right, baby?"

Her mood reflected a total 180-degree turn. "Uh, sure."

Excitement about the photos probably carried over from Jonathan's visit. But this bold flirting confused him. Forty-five minutes ago, Rick could practically guarantee sex was a no-go.

He knew Viv's signals; she wanted sex. But why?

Awkward silence ensued while they awaited dessert, but it lingered with a different air. Earlier, the silences stemmed from tension between two people trying to avoid some unpleasantness. This silence pulsed with sexual tension, putting Rick on edge. The smile Viv gave Jonathan bothered him, but her suggestive words and flirtatious looks still turned him on.

Viv reached for his hand and caressed it. She often said she loved his hands. When the desire to make love hit her, she sometimes let him know by taking his hand and caressing it seductively as she did now.

The muscles in Rick's groin twitched, but he pulled his hand away, pretending to need to scratch his shoulder.

Jorge served their desserts.

As he headed away, Viv dug in.

"So, what's up?" Rick couldn't take it anymore.

She uttered "Huh?" around a spoonful of vanilla.

"I could barely get two sentences out of you earlier, let alone interest you in any 'after-dinner activity.' Now you're acting more like you, so I don't get it. Before Jonathan came, you were trying to tell me something. What was it? You started saying something about knowing how much you love me, but you didn't get to finish."

Viv pointed her spoon at his plate. "You gonna eat your pie?" She ate another spoonful of ice cream.

The pie was warm: Jorge's special touch. "Yes, I am. What were you go'n say?"

"I don't know. I guess I wanted to say that, you know I love you and these nights out, but tonight I wasn't up for it. I told you I was tired, but sometimes good news can bring you around." She reached over, scooping a spoonful of his pie. "And you must admit: Jonathan was a bearer of good news, telling us our photos would be on display. So, I'm excited about next week, and at the same time I feel bad about how I acted toward you earlier. See? No big deal. Now eat your pie so we can go."

Rick didn't believe her.

The part about being excited over the pictures sounded plausible. But the rest of it? Nope. There were no telltale signs she was lying: no eye twitching, or stuttering, or eye-contact avoidance. Rick didn't have any historical basis for not believing her, either. He just didn't believe her. But he decided to wait it out.

They finished dessert in comfortable silence.

Rick retrieved his wallet.

"I got it this time."

"That'll work. I got the tip, though."

Viv looked at him. "So, you ready?" She liked using that double entendre sometimes.

The effect on him was instant. "Damn skippy." He winked at her, then stood to get Viv's coat, purposely letting her see his semi.

Viv's eyes lingered below his waist momentarily before meeting his eyes. She smiled. "Then let's go."

As they walked to the car, Viv took his hand.

After fifteen years of marriage, Rick understood that things changed—the honeymoon didn't last forever. Routine set in. Yet there were still many nights like tonight (minus the tension of the first hour or two), so on a whole, he and Viv were doing quite well.

Chuckling, Rick opened the passenger door for her.

"What's so funny?"

"Thinking about our college days."

She lightly brushed his hand with hers before getting in. "Yeah, and?"

"How you didn't want to be bothered at first."

Viv smirked. "Not with those jokes you kept telling."

Rick scoffed and closed Viv's door. He settled in the driver's seat. "Give me a break; it was the times," he offered, playfully-defensive. "It got you talking to me." He turned the ignition.

"Rick, please. Those jokes were so corny." Viv giggled.

"Yeah, but you finally agreed to go out—even after learning I was two-years younger." Rick pulled into traffic.

"Well, you were corny but cute. Your appreciation for music from the '70s put you over, though." She touched his cheek. "And I did have a problem with the age difference. Louise convinced me to date you anyway."

"'Age difference'? You make two years sound like twenty."

"When you're a senior dating a sophomore, two years can seem like twenty."

"And here we are eighteen years later. Two still feeling like twenty?"

Viv lowered her hand and turned to her window. "No."

"Hey, what's wrong?"

She shook her head in reply.

This moodiness was one of the post-honeymoon changes. He couldn't pinpoint exactly when her moodiness started; he just wanted it to end. They did fairly-well communicating with each other over matters good or bad. They weren't exactly Cliff and Claire Huxtable. There'd been a mistake (or three, if counting) on his part, but they were very good together.

Rick waited at a stoplight. Traffic was light, even for late-evening. He rolled the windows down partially, and then placed a hand on Viv's thigh.

She rested her hand on his but continued looking through her window.

They were married in a small, intimate ceremony soon after Rick graduated from George Mason. His brother David was best man. Not wanting to think about David, Rick turned his thoughts to Alna.

They'd been married five years when they were finally blessed with Alna. Viv wanted a boy, and Rick, so pleased at the prospect of being a daddy, didn't care what sex the baby was, fully adopting the view: "as long as it's healthy." Alna was a joy: a sweet and affectionate little girl with enough tomboy in her for Viv to appreciate.

Off and on (despite losing two babies), they entertained the idea of a sibling for Alna. But lately (as demonstrated during the early-part of their date), Viv avoided discussing subjects relating to family.

The brisk night air helped alleviate his headache ('sleeping weather,' his mother called it). Mistakes and moodiness aside, they weren't a statistic. His family meant everything to him. Even with the mistakes he'd made, his family meant absolutely everything. He'd do whatever it took to keep it together. Family was important.

A flash of Viv smiling at Jonathan came to him as he turned into their driveway on Bard o' Avon Court. Rick briefly pondered that smile, but Viv's hand moved, stroking him gently.

Once parked in their garage, Rick leaned over and kissed his wife, and all was right again.

But something in her kiss told him, not quite as right as it used to be.

CHAPTER 2

Ain't Love Grand?

Mixed emotions. Viv tried concentrating on responding to Rick's kiss. Ordinarily she loved kissing him (his kiss was like no other's), but her emotions interfered with giving in like she wanted.

He'd asked if two years felt like twenty.

In terms of their age difference? No. But the question made her think of other aspects of their life together, so she hesitated before answering.

There were reasons things faltered as of late, but she was caught between Rick's devotion to family and not wanting to hurt him, versus wanting out (if only for a little while).

Ambivalence aside, Viv pulled Rick closer. His kiss finally got to her. Kisses didn't lie; his kiss was all that, every time. Fuck the dumb stuff: she wanted him.

She prided herself with having a healthy sexual appetite; she had no problem letting Rick know what she wanted. There were times when she wasn't in the mood, but overall, she liked sex and wanted it often. This wasn't tied to any sexual peak associated with her age, either. She enjoyed sex in her twenties as well as her thirties. And as she approached forty, if healthy, she'd be so inclined into her senior years.

"Let's see if Cynthia got Al off to bed." Viv gazed into Rick's eyes as she played with his tie. His eyes were an alluring red-brown, more burnt-umber than anything, lightened with red and dark-gold tones: oddly-gorgeous when sunlight hit them. Looking in Rick's eyes was like gazing into a cozy fire. She tapped the cleft in his chin. "If not,

I'll get little Miss Missy tucked in, then meet you in the sunroom." She opened her car door instead of waiting for Rick to open it for her.

"So, the sunroom tonight. Should I open the windows?" Rick inquired softly. He didn't balk at the idea this time.

"That'd be best." Viv exited the car. She felt his eyes on her as she walked toward the door leading into their laundry room.

"You know Alna isn't asleep. Cynthia adores her, so Al gets to do pretty much as she pleases. Now, Tracie's a different story."

She turned back. "Oh, Tracie adores her, too, but she doesn't let Al get away with too much, because Tracie's older and can resist a lot of Alna's wiles. Now come on, so I can get this girl to bed. I know she's up."

He raised an eyebrow. "What's your hurry?"

Viv simply smiled at the handsome man and entered the house.

It was 10:48 p.m. Except for low sound emitting from the television in their sunken family room, the house was quiet. The only lighting came from the stove overhead-light and from the TV. Cynthia was asleep on the sofa, her schoolbooks stacked on the floor. The faint but distinct smell of burned food lingered.

Rick came in and stood behind her. "Well, this is different. Now if Al's asleep, I'll know we're in the Twilight Zone. You goin' up?"

"Yeah. I wonder what culinary masterpiece burned in my kitchen."

"Who knows? I'll get Cynthia." He kissed her temple softly.

Viv headed through the kitchen's other entrance into the hallway. From the bottom of the stairs, she saw light around the closed door of the hall bath. She went up.

The calm and quiet of the house spooked her.

When she and Rick came home from a night out, if Cynthia was the sitter, Alna normally greeted them with hugs and tales of the evening. Viv almost expected it. Tonight, however, equated more with a scene from when Tracie sat for them. Light came from Alna's bedroom to the right. The remaining three bedrooms were dark.

She knocked on the bathroom door. "Al?"

"Hi, Mommy." Alna sounded small, tired. "You can come in." The definitive whoosh of the toilet flushing followed.

Viv opened the door. "What's wrong, sweetie?" She watched her daughter put water on her face.

"I didn't want regular dinner, so Cynthia said I could fix something else as long as I was sure I was gonna eat it," Alna explained as she dried her face, "So, I fixed somethin' I knew I would eat—"

"Alna, you did not have a PB-and-J with sardines on the side again, did you?" Viv held back a gag just thinking about it. *Rick and his concoctions.*

"Uh-huh, but Cynthia said I couldn't have the whole can, so I only had two fishes." Alna held up two fingers, looking cute in her sports-gear pajamas. Cynthia put one large french braid down the middle of Al's head and added gold barrettes to each side.

"*Fish*, Alna, not 'fishes,'" Viv corrected.

"Oil or mustard sauce?" Rick stepped up behind them.

Alna grinned proudly. "Mustard."

Viv turned to him.

"That's my girl." Rick smiled and winked at his daughter.

Viv loved Rick's bond with their daughter. It rooted her ambivalent feelings. She turned back to Alna. "So now your stomach's upset. Is it number two? Number three?" Viv felt Alna's forehead and neck.

"Number three. But, Mommy, I was fine with my dinner. Smelling the burned cheese sauce made me sick." Alna dropped her eyes and studied her feet.

"Been messing with the microwave, Alna?" Rick's tone lost its playfulness.

Alna shook her head.

Viv put a hand to Rick's arm; she had this one. "What happened, honey?" Alna usually owned up to mistakes.

"Nothing. Cynthia had nachos, but she burned the cheese sauce by accident." Alna's eyes were wide.

Viv's heart tugged, but she kept a straight face, wondering if children were born knowing how to use that skill. "Okay, sweetie."

Alna looked at her father, reading his expression.

Viv did the same.

Rick didn't appear upset. He stood calmly, hands in his pockets. He looked good, too. Good enough to eat …

He must have picked up on her vibe. Without another word, he kissed Alna on the forehead and palmed her head affectionately. As he turned to leave the bathroom, he winked at Viv and air-kissed her.

Warm stirrings trembled low in Viv's belly. Ready for some 'after-dinner activity,' she turned back to Alna. "Feeling better?"

"Guess so. Daddy was right about putting cold water on your face when you feel pukey."

"Yeah, your daddy has lots of good ideas rolling around in that brain of his. Come on; time for bed." Viv turned out the light. She exited the bathroom for Alna's room—Alna right on her heels.

"Did you and Daddy have fun?"

"We just went to dinner, sweetie, not a wild safari or anything." Viv patted Alna's bed. "Come on; hop up."

Alna climbed in and snuggled down low. "Did you go where Mister Rast works?" A simple question, but it bothered Viv anyway.

"Yes," Viv answered politely. She decided to hold-off sharing Jonathan's good news.

"Daddy likes that place. I kinda do, too; you guys don't let me go enough." Alna wore a slight pout. For some reason, the expression made Viv think of her mother, whom she missed dearly.

"Well, that's our special place to be together, but we've taken you plenty times. Besides, we trek to Zibby's Fun-Palace regularly, and you have a ball. Shouldn't Mommy and Daddy go someplace for grownups where there are other foods besides pizza, and no noisy rides?"

"I guess. So, did you have fun?"

"What is it with you and this 'fun'? It was dinner, sweetie; that's all."

"But you went to a favorite place. Doesn't that make it fun?" Alna was genuine in her wanting to know.

"Honey, grownups and children have different ways of looking at things as being fun. But, yeah, we had a good time. How's that?" Viv wasn't sure where her daughter was going with this, but she hoped her answer quelled further pursuit.

"You mean, when I grow up things won't be fun anymore?" Alna asked, dashing Viv's quelling hopes.

"They'll be fun, honey, just different fun."

Alna folded her arms over her chest; her pout was serious. "Then I don't wanna grow up. I like fun the way it is now. Why does grownup fun have to be different? When Cynthia talks to her boyfriend on the phone, she sounds like she's having fun, and she's an almost-grownup." Alna rose from under the covers. "Is love fun? When does the different fun start?"

"Whoa there, Miss Missy; slow down." Viv stopped Alna from climbing out completely. "I don't know why or even if grownup fun should be different, it just is. And there is no set time for when it changes. One day you just find that it has. And, yes, love is fun or at least it should be." Viv could not believe she was having this discussion with her nine-year-old.

"Fun should be fun no matter how old you are," Alna concluded. "You love Daddy, right?"

"Of course. Very much."

"And you said love was fun. So, is love-fun different, too?"

Viv thought about Rick's Twilight-Zone comment and smiled. *Who let this child in here?*

"Sweetie, it's time for bed. Mommy just doesn't have any good answers for you now. But I'll think about it and try to explain it better, later. Okay?" Viv leaned close with a pucker.

Alna kissed her goodnight.

Viv turned out the light on Alna's nightstand. "Candy castles and ice cream rivers." It was her mother's version of "sweet dreams" whenever she put Viv and her sister, Patrice, to bed.

A lump rose in Viv's throat. She didn't know why thoughts of her mother kept surfacing.

"G'night, Mommy." Viv heard the distinct rustle of covers as Alna got more-comfortable.

Viv paused in the doorway. "Sure your tummy's better?"

"Uh-huh." Alna already sounded sleepy.

Viv closed the door.

They were home all of fifteen minutes, but it seemed much longer. Viv anticipated meeting Rick downstairs, but wanted to freshen first. She decided against wearing lingerie, opting for her silk robe—and nothing else.

Walking through the double doors, Viv lifted her dress over her head and tossed it onto the cedar chest at the foot of their king-sized bed.

I'm gonna miss this room.

Viv froze, wondering where the thought came from. She hadn't made up her mind about anything.

Is love fun?

Viv lounged across the bed, thinking about Alna's question. She told Alna that, at the very least, love should be fun. And Viv believed that to be true. Her marriage, however, declined in the fun department ever (since Jonathan) since Rick's last incident years ago. But Viv didn't care anymore now that she had (Jonathan) a different perspective on things.

Given her conversation with Alna, Viv questioned her marriage-happiness quotient. She stared at the African-print rug in the middle of their bedroom, reflecting on the one time she and Rick made hot love on it. The image of their brown bodies mingling with the backdrop of the rug's pattern remained an erotic memory. She wanted to make love on the rug often, but Rick was pretty much a bed man. For reasons unknown to Viv, he preferred sex in their bed.

There were a few exceptions. In the sunroom tonight would be one, the one time on the rug, and another time last Christmas when Viv insisted on making love in the sunroom with a view of the Christmas lights twinkling from the family room. She told Rick she wanted the windows opened if they ever did it in the sunroom in a warmer month. She was surprised Rick remembered (or even entertained the idea of getting busy in the sunroom again at all).

Viv turned over. Hands behind her head, she gazed at the ceiling fan. There may have been other occasions (like on the balcony off their bedroom), but overall, her husband preferred a bed for intimacy. Rick's reluctance to make love outside of their bedroom, however, didn't strike the heart of her discontent. It was a factor of the bigger problem.

She was growing, changing (bored). And at thirty-nine, she was tired of trying to get Rick to revisit his wild-side. His devotion to their family was wonderful (sometimes weird), but at what cost?

Viv sat up. She didn't want to think right now, but she did decide something. She needed time and a break to consider the future of her marriage. She'd tell Rick what was going on with her soon (tomorrow?), but not tonight. Rick was downstairs waiting. Regardless of her feelings about staying married, their sex was amazing; she wanted her husband.

She laughed at the irony of contemplating leaving her no-longer adventurous husband on a night he seemed most spontaneous, like his old self. Is love fun? No, love hadn't been much fun for some time. But it would be shortly. Removing her slip, Viv entered their en suite to get ready.

When she came downstairs, Viv expected to find Rick asleep in the family room. She found darkness. The only sound was the night, heard through the open sunroom windows as a breeze rustled the trees.

Rick stood off to the side of their sunroom, looking out the window. Except for shoes, he was dressed—so that she could undress him. He understood that removing his clothes spurred her excitement—especially loosening his tie and opening his pants.

He held a glass of something in his left hand down by his side—probably iced tea: his preferred beverage.

Even in silhouette, Viv appreciated her husband's good looks. Just under six feet three and around 165 pounds, Rick was slim but muscular. A fifth-degree black belt in karate, his martial-arts training showed. He didn't have broad shoulders (like Jonathan), nevertheless he had that masculine V. A breeze rustled again, carrying the scent of Rick's cologne to her: he wore John Varvatos Artisan Black.

Rick's fragrance and the sounds of the night enticed her. Her nipples hardened with a flow of cool air brushing the silk of her robe against them. She went to Rick and encircled him from behind. Peering around him, she followed his gaze, taking in the view.

Their house backed to deep woods bordering Route 301 on the other side of the trees. The clear night rendered moonlight shining through the skylights, near-perfection in its contribution to the evening. Essentially, it was dark, the yard below black. Plants adorned the windows. Viv didn't worry about being seen. Intermittent traffic echoed in the distance.

Viv hugged Rick tighter. He let out a deep sigh, but didn't move: this interlude belonged to her.

She rested her forehead on his strong back. "I love you, Rick."

"I know. I love you." Tension filled his husky reply. "Want music?"

"No ..." Viv guided Rick to face her. Holding his face in her hands, she kissed him. Their tongues blended tenderly, his mouth tasting of iced tea: sweet with a hint of lemon. Realizing he still held his glass, Viv broke their kiss and collected his glass, placing it on the table beside them.

Taking his hand, she led him to the more-spacious side of their sunroom. She moved into Rick's body and resumed their kiss.

Rick rested his fingertips at her waist. The light pressure of his touch radiated both masculine power and a gentleness that conveyed his sexual prowess.

Mouths locked, Viv backed him to the wall. She steadily increased the aggression of her kiss until Rick simply raised his hands in casual surrender. Nibbling Rick's soft lips and getting a thrill from the brush of hair above them, Viv slowly released the Diagonal knot in his tie and unbuttoned his shirt.

Having him against the wall made her want to abandon preliminaries altogether and just take what she wanted.

She also wanted to cradle her husband's head to her breast and let him suckle himself to sleep.

Viv drew her hands over Rick's shoulders, removing his shirt as she lowered his arms. She broke from his mouth just long enough for him to remove his A-shirt, then kissed his neck and chest, trailing hands down his hard torso.

Looking in his eyes as she opened his belt, Viv winked.

With this sexy smile, he tilted his head back.

Viv lowered to his crotch. She kissed her husband's powerful erection through his pants, grabbing his rear with both hands and squeezing before unzipping and freeing him. Rick moaned when her hand encircled him. He pushed fingers through her hair, caressing her scalp as she mouthed him, tasting lotion and mountain-fresh soap, faintly-tinged with his own oils.

Rick pulled back as she got into it: if she wanted something more, he couldn't let that continue.

Understanding, Viv stood. She gazed at the delightful reveal as he removed his pants and boxers.

She gripped his hardness again, gently stroking his length as he opened her robe. His breathing was low and shuddery (exciting her more). Viv ran eyes over his diced body: cinnamon-brown muscles rippled everywhere, something definitely-male jutted toward her. Rick was … Oh, yeah.

Power and aggression moved through her, fusing with anger and regret: knowing that, even with what was happening now, a part of her wanted to separate. Viv looked at her husband, loving him deeply—and then loved him not so much.

Rick's scents enticed her: his cologne, his soap, the rainforest-smell of his hair. Air from the open windows tickled her flesh. The cool breeze on her perspiring skin didn't suppress the heat within, so she took things further: she slapped him.

His head rocked with the slap because it was unexpected, but Rick only returned his gaze to her. Seconds passed. Clouds shifted over the moon briefly, making it harder to read his eyes.

Viv waited, anticipating defending herself if Rick struck back (she knew better), but also waiting to continue their lovemaking.

Rick grasped her throat and pulled her to him, slamming his mouth against hers and driving his tongue into the deep corners of her mouth, taking her arousal higher. He didn't choke her but held her to him firmly, his erection jabbing her abdomen. Rick used his right hand to knead her breasts, tweaking each nipple deliciously before moving his hand elsewhere, anywhere on her, his touch a continuous confirmation of his expertise with her body.

He spun her around and forced her over the arm of the settee, yanking her robe above her rear.

Cool night-air chilled the moisture of her very-wet parts. His hand slid forward, holding the back of her neck.

Viv tried to rise.

Rick held her down. He used his legs to spread her wider, and then teased the tip of his hardness against his possibilities. The sensation of such vulnerability made her climax.

Taking the path of least-resistance, Rick uttered a soft, masculine moan of her name that said everything. He entered her gently enough but held her down, thrusting forcefully.

Ignoring the faint twinges of pressure inside, Viv moved with him. Her husband (God bless him) held back his climax, giving her opportunity to have another. She wanted one with him. She concentrated her energies, working her muscles on him with a womanly-precision that pleased them both.

Rick moaned low and slowed his thrusts to savor the sensation; he often did before exploding inside her. Tingly warmth exuded from her thighs, rising to circle her sweet center. Her second release arrived with the warmth of Rick's. She couldn't have timed it better.

The urge to cry surfaced.

Viv shut that down.

They remained connected, Rick lightly caressing her hips and rear. She didn't like him pulling out immediately; it brought on a sense of loss. He waited until his erection subsided before stepping back, but the feeling of loss touched her briefly anyway; it always did.

Viv rose and faced him. She couldn't see his eyes very well, but she could see his teeth: he smiled. Viv smiled back and put her arms around his neck, sending a hand to caress the crinkly-soft coils of his hair.

They kissed deeply for quiet seconds before Rick pulled back with a grin and picked up his clothing.

Viv took his hand.

They headed upstairs in silence.

After showering, Viv lay across their bed, preferring to lounge and air-dry. She didn't feel like moisturizing.

Rick toweled-off in the bathroom doorway.

Interestingly, they had yet to speak. Viv enjoyed the unusual silence between them, accented only by the whir of the ceiling fan.

She propped on an elbow, watching her husband prepare for bed. Rick usually shaved at night to save time in the mornings, making for three o'clock rather than five o'clock shadow. He prepared to shave but stopped, apparently deciding to abandon the activity. Viv was pleased. She hoped the unusual night of lovemaking would also cause him to abandon his need for pajamas, but as Rick reached in his drawer and pulled out a T-shirt and lounge pants, she knew her luck had run out.

Viv sat up. What difference did it make? *If you're separating from him, it shouldn't matter if he was nude or wearing four layers of thermals.*

But she knew it wasn't that simple.

Chill-bumps prickled her arms. She needed to moisturize, but she didn't want to move. Her body was spent, but her mind raced (*Is love fun?*). Viv reluctantly entered their bathroom. She decided to lotion with a lavender scent: maybe it'll bring on the sleepiness that eluded her.

Rick's sound-breathing greeted her when she reentered their bedroom: sleep hadn't eluded him, apparently. She retrieved a nighttime-bra and satin nightshirt from her dresser and put them on (she didn't bother with panties). Viv went over to Rick and watched him sleep (he wasn't a snorer). "Come what may, Rick, I love you."

She went to the sitting room, where she lay down to think, pulling the afghan strewn across the loveseat around her. More thinking,

LIKE SWEET BUTTERMILK

however, didn't last long: she fell asleep. Somewhere in her dreams were photographs of children at play.

"… today?" Rick's voice.

"Huh?" Someone was shaking her foot.

"I said: think you'd like to rise and join the rest of the world today?"

"Huhnmm?" Viv sat up, grimacing at the pain jabbing her neck.

"I can't believe you slept in here all night. Gotta crick?"

"Yeah, I guess. Time izzit?"

"Quarter till eleven. Alna's already been in here wanting to wake you. We're supposed to be taking her to get new fish, remember?" Rick's reply carried a touch of excitement.

Viv loved his voice. He spoke with a mellow baritone that translated beautifully when he sang; something Viv wished he did more often (his singing turned her on). A faint Southern cadence flitted through his speech every so often. Rick sounded sexy as hell over the phone.

"How could I forget? She's been bugging us about it for a week." Viv shook-off the last vestiges of sleep. She'd dreamed of three women, void of eyes and noses, but with menacing smiles, screaming, "Ain't love grand?" as she bolted from a dark room.

"And we've been putting her off for three. I'm starting breakfast. Want eggs?" Rick had already showered, unfortunately had shaved, and wore black sweats. She didn't care too much for sweats on Rick. He usually wore his sweatpants baggy; she couldn't see his tight butt well enough.

"Sure."

Rick headed away.

"Rick?"

He turned back to her.

"We need to talk, okay?"

Rick nodded curtly and continued out the door.

Viv stood and stretched, turning her head left and right to work out the stiffness. She had no idea what she was going to say to him. She didn't think Rick would easily accept anything she said, given his love for her and Alna. Remnant images of those 'women' from that dream, however, settled it. She may not be leaving Rick for good, but she needed a trial-separation at least.

19

She debated showering. She'd hit the high and low spots and call it quits. Viv snatched a pair of panties and a bra from one drawer, pulled a T-shirt and jeans from another, and headed for the bathroom.

Viv showered anyway. She used the time to ruminate the few (impossible) ways she could tell her husband she was leaving him.

CHAPTER 3

Breaking News

Viv came out of the shower, starving. Her almond-scented lotion didn't help matters. Normally she preferred a light breakfast, but she was glad it was Rick's Saturday to cook. He usually served up a big country breakfast as opposed to her just-this-side-of-continental alternative. The smells of scrapple cooking and potatoes frying conjured a sense of home.

Unease settled in her belly. Rick wouldn't cook the eggs until everyone was downstairs. Muffled sounds of conversation drifted up from the kitchen. Alna and Rick were waiting for her.

She wasn't ready.

Sitting at her vanity, Viv brushed her hair into a ponytail. She missed being able to tie it back into a longer one, but the shorter ponytail, which swept up rather than back, made for an even fresher, carefree style. And with the summer months approaching, the carefree interested Viv very much. When she was sixteen, her father had been steadfast against her cutting her hair. She remembered Rick initially being opposed to the idea months ago.

Rick opened their drapes to allow extra light in, but Viv wanted fresh air to circulate, too. *You can take five showers, comb your hair nineteen times, and open all the windows on this floor, but you're going to have to go downstairs eventually.*

She opened the windows in their bedroom and paused in front of the bay window next to Rick's armoire. It was warm for March. A gentle breeze carried flower fragrances from their yard below. Rick and Alna planted jonquils, hyacinths, and two forsythia bushes last October, and all were in various stages of bloom (they loved gardening and messing in the dirt). She liked flowers as much as anybody, but she'd just as soon call a landscaper.

Viv breathed in, wanting the floral bouquet below to infuse her with the bravado from last night that escaped her now.

"Mommy?"

Viv turned to see Alna standing in the doorway. Alna replaced the gold barrettes with purple ones, and pinned her braid up. She experimented more with her hairstyles lately—a sign that soon, her tomboy days would be gone. She wore jeans and a purple sweatshirt, both of which would be too short by summer's end.

"Hi, sweetie. Why're you in the doorway like that?"

"Well, Daddy said he thought he heard you up here. When you didn't come down, I wanted to see if you were okay." Alna walked toward Viv, hands in her back pockets. Socks and shoes were probably somewhere in Alna's bedroom waiting to join the ensemble. Her daughter much-preferred being barefoot anywhere it was allowed.

"Uh-huh. In other words, you came up here to tell Mommy to hurry up?"

"Kinda. Mommy, where're you goin'? Why you not goin' with me and Daddy?"

"Alna, it's: 'Why aren't you going with Daddy and me?' You know how to speak correctly."

"Daddy says when I'm home, I can 'lax the rules."

"It's *relax*, Alna."

"Mommy, why aren't you going to the fish store with us?"

"Well, who said Mommy wasn't going?" *There he goes taking things to the extreme again*. It was a habit of Rick's Viv didn't like. Irritation set in.

"Daddy."

Trying to explain anything to Alna was pointless, so Viv let the big picture go and dealt with the matter at hand. "Well, I'm not sure why Daddy said that, but I'm going, too."

Alna smiled. "Then come on. Daddy's hungry. I had cereal, but I want some eggs." She headed for the door. "Can we go by Aunt Louise's? I wa—"

"Al, Mommy needs some Alna-love. You got any?" Viv opened her arms for a hug.

"That's, *do you have* any?" Alna said in a sweet way. She hugged Viv and kissed her cheek. "Now come on!" Alna grabbed her mother's hand, pulling her toward the door. They headed downstairs together.

Rick sat on a barstool at the island counter, reading the newspaper. Viv's habit of reading the newspaper faded over the years since graduate school; these days she barely looked at one. Rick encouraged Alna to read at least four articles of interest a week.

Sunlight poured into the kitchen from the huge windows in the adjoining family room and from the sunroom. Located toward the back of the house, their kitchen, decorated in a color-scheme of apple green, dark brown, and white, was bright and airy, yet picture-perfect in its coziness. The granite counters weren't cluttered with appliances: only a laptop, Rick's juice machine (that he insisted on having for Father's Day two years ago, but rarely used) and a Crock-Pot were visible. Miniature woodwork carvings, most of which Viv made herself, adorned the counters instead. After their workroom, it was her favorite room in the house.

The cozy atmosphere of the kitchen, however, didn't alleviate the tension created by Viv's earlier request to talk to Rick. Alna, spurred on by excitement over getting new fish, innocently served as facilitator at breakfast with her chatter.

Sitting at the breakfast table, Viv looked at Rick intently from time to time, but he gave no notice. She watched her daughter, too (as Alna switched from subject to subject), marveling over the miracle of human reproduction. Alna's hair, redder in her infancy and toddlerhood, was now a warm-brown like her father's. Alna's hair complemented her cinnamon-brown complexion (also her father's). A pang of sadness over the loss of her other babies with Rick passed through her core, but she pushed it aside, keeping focus on her 'baby' now nine. Viv saw that, even at nine, Alna inherited her 'pear' body frame: slender torso and round, shapely hips. Alna wouldn't be a string bean all her life; her father's genes lost that battle.

Smiling to herself, Viv sensed Rick's eyes on her. Awkwardness settled over her heart again as she looked at him, instantly and intensely attracted. She wanted to jump his bones right there.

She quickly changed her line of thinking. She was attracted to more than just his looks; his mind and heart greatly appealed to her, too. Other than the obvious, there wasn't a checklist of things wrong with her marriage, but there were aspects of Rick's personality that, over the years, no longer meshed with hers. Last night, he exposed a former wild-side she liked very much—but didn't know if she'd see again.

Alna started clearing the table.

"Mommy and Daddy need to talk, honey. Go put something on those stinky feet, then chill in your room awhile, okay?"

Viv expected her daughter to protest, but Alna shrugged and went on her way.

She sensed Rick staring at her again. She stared back.

Rick's hand came up to trace the scar on his ear. Irritation etched his handsome features. "So, is this where you finish what you were saying last night at dinner? For real this time?"

"What do you mean 'for real this time'?"

"Nothing, Vivian, just go ahead."

Viv took a deep breath. "Rick, you know how much I love you and Aln—"

"Leave Al out of this."

"Fine. Anyway, I think I need a break from us for a little while. I haven't been happy for some time now ..." Viv didn't know how to continue. She anticipated doing more hedging. Rick's combative posture provided the gumption she needed to get it out. "I figure Alna and I can stay with Louise and Tim for a few weeks until I find a place. They're close by, so Alna's routine won't be interrupted. And this way the two of us can maintain relatively-close contact while we sort this out."

Rick stared at her, rubbing his scar. His reticence hurt.

She wanted to hurt him. "I guess another part of this is: I've been seeing Jonathan for the last seven months."

Requesting a separation from Rick, coupled with revealing her involvement with Jonathan, should have sent him into spasms of anger. Rick never hit nor so much as grabbed her as a form of intimidation, but given his perception of family and loyalty to it, Viv expected a fist slammed against the table at the very least.

"Wanna go to Columbia Mall or Annapolis Mall? You feel like a ride? It's a good day for it." His warm tone didn't match the stony glint in his eyes. The red in his irises sharpened—something they tended to do when he was angry.

She sat in disbelief. "Columbia Mall is fine."

"Done." Rick nodded curtly. "At the truck in ten." He headed for the foyer.

"Oh, Rick, Al wants to stop by Louise's." She heard the timidity in her voice, but Rick's reaction threw her.

"Whatever. That's fine." Rick dashed up the stairs. It sounded like he took two at a time.

Viv needed to go upstairs, too, but waited. She mentally replayed their discussion and Rick's reaction before chalking up his response to simple shock. *He wants to finish enjoying this family time with Alna. If he's going to be this rational about it, maybe our separation won't be a final step, but a healthy break.*

* * * * *

A week later, Viv sat alone at a table on the third tier of DeTante's. She watched Alna, Jonathan, and others peruse the restaurant, viewing the new photos decorating the walls. Viv's enthusiasm about their pictures being on display waned, but watching the absolute joy on her daughter's face delighted her.

Alna looked a doll in her skirt and blouse—her hair styled with a bun atop her head. She appeared to be having a ball and acted quite the charmer, from what Viv could tell.

Viv wished Rick had attended, but she understood his position. She didn't have to make any excuses for him, but she wanted him there. *You just told the man that you're seeing somebody he knows and that you want out. Even Rick, devoted family-man that he is, has his limits.*

She returned her attention to the activity below.

DeTante's décor coincided with the change of season. Gone were the dark hues of fall and winter. Viv favored winter, but the restaurant was alive with the symbols of spring. It was early-evening. Although closed to the public, DeTante's bustled with Jonathan's friends and other photographers whose works were on display.

Viv moved to a vacant table after dinner, bringing her water and their belongings with her. Her seat allowed her to see everything—including everyone's gracious host.

Jonathan held Alna's hand while talking to two young men. He wasn't partial to suits (claiming they emphasized his height), but he wore one this evening: an olive-green suit with a cream-colored shirt and a gold and olive-flecked tie. His shirt and very-dark skin contrasted nicely. He caught her eye and smiled.

Viv smiled back.

Engrossed in the activity below, she suddenly felt a small kiss on her shoulder. Startled, the kiss instantly irritated (embarrassed?) her. She checked to see if anyone spied the kiss—especially Alna.

"You know better. Where's Alna? I saw her with you a minute ago." Viv looked around DeTante's for her daughter.

Jonathan sat opposite her, turning sideways to allow his legs to extend into the aisle. "Alna's fine. She's with Jo in the kitchens."

"This turned out well, Jon. Alna's gonna want to come here all the time now."

"Why are you up here, Viv? You might as well not have come."

"I know," Viv sighed. They were virtually alone on tier 3. The four people up there with them were preoccupied with watching the other guests. Subtle sounds of New Age music drifted around them.

"Having second thoughts?" Jonathan wore L'Eau d'Issey. Viv was used to smelling it on Rick; she didn't know why she bought the same for Jonathan.

"Yes and no."

"You wanna break that down for a brotha?"

"What do you think, Jon? I'm supposed to be gung-ho about all this? Well, I was at first. Ready to leave Rick and move on. Ready to do the whole sistah-empowered-with-attitude thing. Until I found myself explaining a very-adult situation to my nine-year-old daughter. So, I'm at 'yes and no.' Get it?"

"Got it." Jonathan's skin was dark, but his eyes were hazel. Even with eyeglasses, his direct gaze made him look alien under the new lighting. The smallest flicker of vulnerability in his eyes helped soften his gaze and lessen its intensity.

"So, there it is."

Jonathan sat back. "There it is."

"Your turn." Viv reached for her water. Water was about all she could stomach these days.

"My turn what?"

"I broke it down for you. Now tell me what's on your mind?"

"Well, I'm at 'yes and no,' too."

"You don't have any major decision-making to do. How can you be at 'yes and no, too'?" Viv sat forward. Since she told Rick she wanted a break, and he'd virtually said nothing to her about it (except for telling her Alna wasn't going anywhere, he'd given no argument whatsoever), Viv needed a fight. Jonathan, given their situation, was fair game. "Please break it down for a sistah."

Jonathan leaned forward, too. "So, since I'm the unattached-male here, then what, I should have no worries? I should be fine just hittin' that ass?" The intensity in his eyes returned. "You should know me better than that."

Viv did know better but said nothing. She gazed through the windows.

Late-evening crept in as the dusky blue-gray of day transitioned into the purple-blue of night. The lights dimmed gradually. DeTante's famous flutes began their aria.

"Viv?" Jonathan waved a hand in front of her face.

Viv ignored his hand a few seconds before returning her gaze to him. "Shouldn't you be saying goodnight to your guests?"

"My guests are fine." He sighed. "Look, Viv, I'm not married with children. Well, I'm divorced with a teenaged son, but he's with his mother, so I'm somewhat removed from the day-to-day aspect of raising him. So, no, I don't have the same considerations you do."

"Exactly."

"Hold on now. I do, however, like your husband, which doesn't make this easy. Not only that, I have, or thought I had, strong views about the importance of the black family."

"Meaning?" Viv knew these things about Jonathan, but the fight in her was gone now.

"Meaning, I don't want to break up what by most standards is a strong family relationship. Your daughter is an innocent here. Rick, too, for that matter; they haven't done anything to me. So, it's fucked-up because I've fallen in love with you nonetheless."

"I still have the bigger fish to fry, Jon."

"Yeah. But just understand that there are black men with hearts and feelings out here." Jonathan paused. "Can I ask something?"

"Sure." Viv finished her water. She detected a subtle aftertaste of copper. More nausea fluttered through her briefly.

"When your mind goes through whatever it thinks on when you try to figure this thing out, am I in the equation at all?"

Viv rolled her eyes upward with a sigh.

"No, come on now, hear me out. If I weren't a part of things, would you still be leaving Rick?"

"I guess."

"Not good enough."

"I'm sorry?"

"Don't you see? This can't be about you and me; only about you and Rick. And even that has to be an absolute—no guessing."

Viv contemplated Jonathan's words while checking the restaurant for her daughter. Alna now helped Jorge reset some of the tables on tier 2. Viv looked at Jonathan; they were now alone on tier 3.

"Let me ask you this, then, Viv. Do you love me?" His voice cracked on "me," but his gaze remained direct and purposeful.

"Sure." And she did—just not the way she knew Jonathan meant it. Viv shifted uncomfortably.

Their table was not in disarray. There wasn't much on the table: cloth napkins, Viv's empty glass, Alna's small purse, a previous occupant's half-full glass of water, and a DeTante's menu.

Viv smiled a small smile at Jonathan and started straightening the table. She placed Alna's purse beside hers in the chair next to her. She adjusted the menu and refolded the napkins, arranging them both just so. She moved the glass of water from her left to her right. Very busy work.

Jonathan kept quiet as she went about it.

"Look. You said that this can't be about you and me. That it has to be about me and Rick."

"Right."

"Well, this is about me. Rick is content, having no desire to, as he calls it, 'betray our family.' I, on the other hand, find myself wanting out—at least for a little while."

Jonathan slowly shook his head and sat back.

"What?"

"Nothing. Never mind. Finish."

"No. You're shaking your head for some reason."

"I'll tell you what's wrong with what you said, but first I'm going to ask something you never give a straight answer to. Why're you so unhappy with Rick? Why do you want to leave him?"

Viv suddenly grew warm.

Someone's glass of water rested on the table. Remnants of ice cubes, the size of dimes, floated in the water. The water looked good. Viv's throat clicked. She tried to picture who left the glass, trying the impossible and incredible task of determining if she should take a sip of the water. Jonathan's question unnerved her; she was that tempted to drink from a stranger's glass.

Viv cleared her throat. "If you want specifics, Jon, I can't give them to you."

"In other words, you don't know."

"No. I know." She just didn't want to get into a discussion about it.

Jonathan leaned forward again. "Okay, no specifics then. Try some general reasons, because frankly, I can't recall you giving any of those, either."

Viv folded her arms across her chest and sucked her teeth.

"Why is this so hard for you? You make it quite-clear that you want out of your marriage, but won't, or can't, pinpoint why. Do you still love the man?"

"Yes."

"Well, that was quick and definitive. Fine. Do you still want him?"

Viv checked that glass out again. "Most times."

Jonathan chuckled. "I need some help here, Viv, because I must be missing something. You definitely love him, you still want him, yet you're determined to leave him." He sat back.

Viv saw amusement in his hazel eyes. "Like I've said, it's no *one* thing, but for now, let's say I'm bored and need a change. Now, why were you shaking your head?"

"You're kidding, right?"

"About what? Needing a change? No."

"What're you doing with me, Viv?"

"Doing with you?" Viv eyeballed the glass again: the ice deserted her.

"You're too old to play games."

"I'm not playing any games."

"Yes, you are. Maybe not intentionally, but you are. And maybe 'games' isn't the best word here." Jonathan removed his glasses and swiveled his legs under the table. "You say you only want out, even if it's for a brief period. You love him, still want him—"

"I said *most times* I want him."

"'Mounts to the same. Anyway, all that says to me is that I'm a temporary diversion from your 'boring' marriage." Jonathan leaned forward, forcing his words between clenched teeth: "If that is how you see me, then we need to let this thing between us go, because my feelings for you aren't temporary."

"You're not a passing-fling, Jon. Why're you so angry?"

Jonathan sighed and sat back again. "Because the only reason you can give for leaving your marriage is boredom. What kind of shit is that? You're bored? Rick's boring? So, you need a change? That's weak, Viv. Weak and sad."

"Weak or not, it's the truth, Jon."

"Then stay with Rick. You don't break up a family because you're bored. You need to be telling me something about adultery, refusal to work and contribute to the household, verbal or physical abuse— something concrete. I mean, okay, you're 'bored.' Does that mean I'll be a distant memory once you're bored with me?"

She could have chosen now to tell Jonathan about Rick cheating, but didn't want to. Besides, she understood why Rick—

"I do love you," Viv said rather loudly, but she wanted him to hear her say it.

"And you love Rick?"

"I do. Yes."

Jonathan observed her in silence before brushing his slacks with his palms and straightening his tie. He stood and leaned over, kissing her lightly on the forehead. His cologne again reminded her of Rick. "Look. This is supposed to be a happy occasion. It's not like we're going to solve anything tonight. I need to touch base downstairs, being host and all."

Viv suddenly realized how tired she was. "Okay."

Jonathan nodded and started away, stretching his neck before heading down to the main level.

Viv reflected on her conversation with Jonathan, on the unsettled atmosphere in her home. The tension at home proved a bit much sometimes, but she didn't know what else to do. Admittedly, she and Rick were handling Alna's situation well; both were determined to keep her stress to a minimum. She and Rick remained, if not overly amiable, at least polite to one another during the only real time they spent together these days—dinnertime. Other than that, Viv saw little of her husband.

Rick was more of a homebody nowadays, primarily wanting to venture out as a family. She thought maybe recent developments would've sparked a change in him. That maybe he'd stay away from the house out of anger or, if nothing else, try to make her curious about his comings and goings.

If anything, Rick seemed bent on maintaining his presence at home. An unvoiced challenge of sorts, but Viv did what she knew best: ignored him.

Instead of going to Louise's, she moved into a spare bedroom while Rick stayed in the master. That wasn't the way she wanted things to be, but as Rick pointed out, she was the one who wanted out, so Viv supposed it was fair enough. Since she only half-heartedly looked for another place to live, the current sleeping arrangement served its purpose.

There'd been no confrontations since their argument about Alna going with her. In fact, aside from the staid (but cordial) ambiance at the dinner table, communication hovered around nil. Viv was relieved, but part of her wanted to say *something* to him. Although she'd never admit it out loud, the tension in the house was getting to her.

Viv gathered their things. Tired of thinking, she wanted to go home. Regardless of the disruption in her personal life, Viv loved her house and presently, wanted to be in it. She and Rick no longer shared a bedroom, but Viv made plenty use of the garden whirlpool-tub in their master bath. A relaxing session in that tub beckoned.

She looked through DeTante's upper windows, trying to "read" the time, as her husband would often do so well. After a minute or two of trying to determine the time like Rick, Viv found herself just looking through the window. Essentially, the purple-blue sky with its streaky clouds told her that it was night and later than six o'clock. *Rick would know the time within a fifteen-minute window.* It was one of his endearing quirks.

When Jonathan returned, they sat in silence.

"You ready to head down?" Viv added the last three words to that question with a barely-noticeable delay. Jonathan knew nothing about the double entendre of 'You ready?' that she and Rick shared, but still.

"Might as well. But let me say this: just because I want you to be sure of what you're doing has nothing to do with how I feel about you or change my wanting to be with you. Love doesn't work like that."

"You sure are tossing the love word around."

"Yeah. Ain't love grand?" Jonathan wore the biggest smile.

Viv smiled back.

She couldn't help it. How could she not smile back with him looking like that? She smiled warmly, but a small glacier eased into the pit of her stomach. Jonathan's comment instantly reminded her of that dream about the faceless women. Although every detail remained fresh, she never took time to analyze it. "I guess it is."

Catching movement out of the corner of her eye, she glanced over in time to see Alna walk into the kitchens. Viv gathered their things and headed down, giving a last furtive-glance at the stranger's glass of water.

When they reached DeTante's main level, Alna was behind her.

"Hi, Mommy!" Alna sat at a table—eating yet again.

Jonathan walked to the bar.

"Hey, Al. Ready to go?"

"Okay." Alna stood. With only a small spot on the collar of her blouse, she looked as neat and clean as she did before leaving home. *Yep, she's growing up.* They walked over to the bar to say their goodbyes to Jonathan and Rosie, who were talking quietly.

"Well, that's it for us. We're outta here." Viv was sure she sounded too nonchalant—and too loud given the restaurant's quiet atmosphere.

"Did you enjoy yourself, Alna?" Jonathan leaned on the counter, one foot resting on the brass foot-rail. He looked nice.

Is love fun?

Viv ignored the thought.

Alna nodded. "Yes."

Looking around at the new pictures, Viv noticed those belonging to her and Alna. "Thank you, Jonathan, for making us a part of this."

Jonathan smiled. "Oh, almost forgot." He leaned over the bar to Rosie's side, craning his neck to view the shelving underneath. He extended his right arm. Apparently, something wasn't within reach.

"Rosie, can you hand me that envelope?" Following Jonathan's reach and gaze, Rosie retrieved the envelope from under the bar and handed it to him. He handed a manila envelope to Viv.

Viv looked curiously at him as she accepted it.

Alna grabbed her forearm with both hands. "What is it, Mommy?"

Viv used her sense of touch to determine the contents. "I think these are our leftover pictures, sweetie." Viv peeked under the envelope's flap. "Yep. See?" She gave Alna a better look.

"Can we put these up at home?"

"Sure. We'll go shopping for frames this weekend. Now, tell Mister Rast and Rosie 'thank you,' so we can go."

"Thank you, Mister Rast. Thanks, Rosie," Alna recited, sounding much like the rote responses fourth-graders give their teachers in class.

Viv leaned to give Jonathan the customary oh-we're-just-platonic-friends kiss on the cheek. Jonathan turned toward her. The movement caused their faces to graze. Eight fifty-two p.m. shadow speckled his face; he needed to shave. The scent of his cologne and the roughness of his cheek made Viv think of more-intimate things. She pulled away from Jonathan quickly and waved goodbye to Rosie.

*   *   *   *   *

Once home, with Alna settled, Viv indeed pursued a deep, hot, bubble-bath. Once submerged, tension from her conversation with Jonathan, the awkward atmosphere at home, and the day's activity dissolved with the soft, crackly-sound of the bubbles popping as she waited for her skin to stop tingling from the water's heat.

The hot water soothed her body, but Viv's nerves remained on edge. She laughed to herself, thinking, in her current state, a cold shower would probably be better.

Usually, either a hot bath or good sex sufficed to take the edginess out of her irritable moods. The latter was out, but the bath wasn't doing its job, either. The whole predicament struck her as funny.

Although she was horny from interaction with Jonathan, she wanted Rick. Her husband's body, his skill with hers, always left her panting and moaning deep with satisfaction.

Viv squeezed a quarter-sized dollop of liquid soap onto her body sponge. She lathered and washed twice, trying her best to keep her mind occupied with what she was doing and thoughts away from what she wanted to be doing (with Rick).

If I continue with this situation much longer, I'll go nuts.

She was used to getting some whenever the mood struck her. But although she was "with" Jonathan, she wasn't *with* him, so he wasn't available on the regular. And although Rick was available, he wasn't "available," so her options, suddenly, had become rather limited.

After a while, she got out of the tub and toweled-off.

Pulling her robe around her, she tentatively opened the bathroom door and listened. The sound of something hitting the kitchen floor told her Rick was still downstairs.

Viv hurried back to 'her' bedroom.

Opting for lounge pants and one of Rick's T-shirts to sleep in, Viv climbed into the queen-sized bed, pulled the comforter over her shoulders, and fell asleep.

Her sleep wasn't peaceful, but it was dreamless, and that was good.

CHAPTER 4

Three's a Crowd

R ick sat on the hood of his black Range Rover, humming.
He'd been coming to the park, sitting on the hood of his truck, and humming oldies every day for the past week. He liked today's music well enough, but Soul and R&B from the sixties and seventies? Nothing like it. Right now, "Zoom" by the Commodores felt good in his throat.

Viv's announcement shattered his world almost two weeks ago, but he couldn't come to terms with it.

She hadn't left yet, and he didn't know if that was helping matters or hurting them. Oh, he nipped her idea of taking Alna with her in the bud, and left it up to Viv to explain everything to their daughter.

Mainly, though, he wanted to hit her.

Just punch her in the face with everything he had. That embodied the extent of his anger, but he would never hit her. Instead, he ventured to the park and hummed a few tunes until he felt better.

He slid off the hood and ambled toward the lake, gathering rocks along the way and stuffing them into his pockets. The late-afternoon sky was overcast, contributing to the slight-chill in the air. Only a handful of people milled about. He guessed there would be more activity after Easter, but the clouds and the relative-isolation complemented his frame of mind.

At the lake's ridge, Rick removed the rocks from his pockets, forming a pile by his foot.

He stood on the bank and watched the water, thinking about Alna's sad little face when she came in with Viv from their visit to Zibby's

Fun-Palace. Since he opted out, Viv chose that opportunity to broach the subject of the separation.

Rick hated her for it. Although Viv did the right thing by leaving Jonathan out of her explanation, she chose a time and place that should have been tied to pleasant family memories.

He was in the kitchen when they returned. Seeing Alna's face, he seriously considered striking Viv then. Instead, he immediately gathered his daughter in his arms while Viv stood in the doorway. Alna never cried, but asked one simple question, muffled by his shoulder: "What happened, Daddy?"

The silence after that question echoes in my home.

Because Viv wouldn't answer the question. And he couldn't.

Rick now hummed Earth, Wind and Fire's "Keep Your Head to the Sky." He threw rocks into the water, reflecting on the unwelcome turmoil at home. For his part, he said little to Viv about her request to separate. He knew it bothered her, but he didn't intend to say much, because truthfully, there wasn't much to say.

If she's decided to abandon their family, he wasn't go'n help her feel better about it.

He was surprised he wasn't as upset with Rast as he thought he'd be. Oh, Rast was a bastard for pulling up on his wife, and he intended to tell him so, but in the end, it rested with Viv and her decision to betray their family. The idea of her merely wanting revenge for his indiscretions surfaced.

Okay, whatever, but I would never leave my family.

Rick tossed stones harder and farther until they landed on the opposite bank. The force behind his throws wrenched his left shoulder. He ignored the pain. Each throw buoyed his resolve that Viv wasn't going anywhere, so with each throw he felt better.

A dark cloud of emotion—something stranger and more-comforting than anger—settled in his center.

He paused, surveying the sky: around 5:45p.m.—dinnertime. Regardless of recent developments, he and Viv maintained the routine. It was his turn to cook. Tired and achy, he headed home to his wife and child—his family.

Rick loved his neighborhood with its colonial homes perched on well-kept lawns. The glowing streetlights broadcast an unsettled luster as nightfall edged closer.

He pulled into the garage (parking next to Viv's pearl-gray Lexus GS350), killed the ignition, and waited.

He didn't know whether to enter through the laundry room as usual, or through the front door. Entering through the front door made it less-likely he'd interact with Viv if she was in the kitchen or family room.

Rick hated the whole idea of walking around on eggshells. He got out of his SUV and purposefully entered through the laundry room.

He braced himself for a curt "hello" and a dash toward the stairs, but when he entered the kitchen, Viv could be heard but not seen. The alarm was set to bypass, so it didn't beep. The television was off; the radio provided background noise instead. This level was mostly dark. A lamp in the sunroom was on, and the pilot flickered on the stove's right back burner, a large pot sitting on its eye.

Rick didn't know Viv's exact whereabouts, so he listened for several seconds. Her voice came from the sunroom. She apparently hadn't heard him come in.

He stood in the kitchen contemplating what to fix for dinner. He wanted to look in the pot but feared any sound the top made as he returned it might alert Viv to his presence; right now, he was glad she didn't know he was home.

We'll have baked chicken and seasoned wild rice. I'm not in the mood for anything elaborate.

For a vegetable, Rick decided on corn. He hated vegetables, but he downed them for Alna's sake. Corn, because of its sweet taste, proved easier to roll with than many of the other greens and yellows, so the kid in him preferred it.

Having decided on a quick-and-easy dinner, Rick wanted to shower first; hot water on his shoulder would help the tenderness. He turned to go into the hall and up the stairs but hesitated, listening to Viv's voice coming from the sunroom. She was on the phone.

Rick's heartbeat picked up. He rubbed sweaty palms on his jeans, feeling like a criminal in his own home. And like a criminal, he tiptoed from the kitchen into the family room, staying as close to the shadows as possible. He paused to eavesdrop on his wife's end of the conversation.

"Uh-huh," Viv said.

Silence.

"No, Friday is better. Being a dress-down day and all."

Silence.

"He didn't say."

Silence.

Viv sighed. "I haven't figured that part out yet."

Rick retreated, heading toward the front of the house and up the stairs, silently patting himself on the back for his proactive thinking.

That awful day, when Viv said she wanted to separate, Rick held his tongue, but his mind worked far ahead. After he asked Viv about the choice of malls for their outing, Rick went upstairs to the smallest spare bedroom and retrieved an old telephone from the walk-in closet. He was thankful he didn't get rid of it despite Viv's protestations. The royal-blue rotary-dial phone was a throwback from his college days.

That awful day (guided only by what he considered a sense of need wily in nature), Rick retrieved the phone, lifted the receiver, unscrewed the mouthpiece, and removed the circular voice-transmitter (a trick David showed him). He put the phone back in the closet, and then took his family to the mall.

Twilight coming through the windows of the bedrooms illuminated the upper floor. Rick entered the spare bedroom Viv didn't occupy and closed the door. He retrieved the phone from the closet and plugged it in the wall-jack. Rick cautiously lifted the receiver and listened.

"—times do I have to explain this?" Viv sounded hurt.

"I'm just wondering about your motives, Viv." It was Louise.

"My motives are fine, Lou. It's funny, I've been thinking about my mother a lot lately. Maybe she's letting me know I should go with how I'm feeling."

"Viv, I'm not trying to be mean. I didn't know your mom, but that sounds like a bunch of bull. Next week is the twenty-fifth anniversary of her death. That's why she's been on your mind."

Silence.

Rick half-expected Viv to hang up with an attitude.

"So, what's this, your Vietnamese-wisdom coming through?"

Both women chuckled.

"Maybe. Still, you have to get at why you're leaving Rick."

Rick gripped the phone tighter.

Louise continued, "If you're bored and want Rick to recapture how he was, until what? three, four years ago, say that. If it's worrying about him cheating again, then just say that. If you worry about having another baby, tell Rick that. Just quit with the abstract, mystical shit. After fifteen years of marriage, Rick deserves better—and so does your mother."

"I can't compartmentalize and sum my unhappiness into one reason, Lou. It's a combination of things."

Louise sighed. "I'm tired of talking about this. You know how I feel about what you're doing. But you're my girl, so I'm here for you. Anyway, what time Friday are you meeting Jonathan?"

"Around ten thirty."

"Why so early?"

"He has a meeting at one."

"What are you telling Rick?"

"I'm not 'telling' him anything. Why?"

"Well, what if he calls or something?"

"Rick rarely calls during the morning while we're at work. Besides, that's what voicemail is for."

"I'm not feeling this, Viv. Why can't you just be honest? You said he knows about Jonathan."

"I know, but … Anyway, Missus Louise Nguyen-Collins, get off my phone. I'm tired of talking about this myself. Oh, can you see Alna tomorrow afternoon? She's complaining about a toothache, but I think she wants to talk to you; especially since you checked her teeth three weeks ago."

"Yeah, Al needs to talk to somebody, you need to talk to somebody, and Rick probably needs to get some things off his chest. I've mentioned this before, but why don't you give Doctor Alexander a call? Naomi's a good family therapist, Viv."

Silence from Viv, but Rick, now intrigued, wanted to know more.

Louise sighed. "Tomorrow's fine. Any time after five, okay?"

"No problem. We'll talk tomorrow. Bye."

"Bye." Louise hung up first.

Viv hung up.

Rick made sure the ladies were disconnected before hanging up.

It pleased him knowing Louise wasn't entirely in Viv's corner. Using his shirttail, Rick wiped the receiver down (he had no idea why). He unplugged the phone from the wall and returned it to the closet, placing it next to the gun box on the shelf. He did all this calmly enough. He was that much more determined Viv wasn't breaking up their family.

Giving the gun box a final sideways glance, Rick walked into their bedroom for a shower.

At dinner, Viv didn't talk much, but Rick was a virtual chatterbox. While teasing Alna at the table, he sometimes glanced at Viv: a tentative smile played around of her mouth. He was pleased, but decided to call her Friday morning, anyway.

* * * * *

That Friday evening, Rick sat in the sitting room waiting.

A door slammed downstairs several minutes ago.

He didn't care if Viv was pissed. After what she'd done to their family, pissing her off was the least he could do. He picked up his tablet computer and reclined on the leather loveseat. He heard Viv coming up the stairs and wanted to be doing something, anything, when she entered their bedroom.

"Rick?!"

Yeah, she was pissed. "In here."

Viv entered their sitting room. "Was that necessary, Rick?"

He continued surfing the web. "Was what necessary?"

"Was calling my office and cell, leaving twelve messages necessary? You know what I'm talking about."

"Why didn't you call back?"

"I don't know. You didn't leave a message or text. I thou—"

"Yes," Rick interrupted, knowing the real reason she didn't call back but determined to keep his tone devoid of emotion.

"Yes, what?"

"Yes, calling that many times was necessary."

"Why?" She now sounded puzzled, her anger seeming to dissipate.

He put his tablet down but didn't look at his wife. "To talk. We've been together entirely too long for this to be over after one conversation. That's not happening, Vivian. You and Alna mean more to me than you'll ever understand."

"I do understand, Rick. But as much as I love Alna, this is for me. And I love you, Rick. I've tried—"

"Tried what, Viv?" He swung his legs around so that he faced her.

She looked lovely in her denim jeans and black form-fitting sweater. Her slender waist and those shapely hips said, 'female.' Thankfully, Viv limited her cosmetics to mainly shaded lip-gloss; she didn't need makeup. A whiff of her camellia-sandalwood body-oil came his way, creating subtle, arousing distraction. "Instead of coming to me when you first started having these feelings, you let them build until you wanted out. You didn't give me a chance to fix it." Rick shook his head. "No, Viv, you haven't 'tried.' You haven't tried at all." He got up and walked past her, gritting his teeth and fighting the desire to grab his gorgeous wife and kiss her deeply, making this horrible dream go away. He hadn't gritted his teeth in years.

"So now you're going somewhere to pout? After calling me twelve times within three hours today, now you just walk away?"

Rick looked at his wife. She looked close to crying, but he knew better. "That's pretty much what you did, isn't it? Just walked away." He continued toward the stairs without looking back. "But no, pouting is not what I intend to do. And I'm not giving up on our marriage either, Vivian. It's as simple as that."

"It's not like you haven't done your share o' shit!"

Rick continued down the stairs, letting the silence speak for him.

He reached the kitchen and continued down to the basement. Their furnished basement, nicely decorated with themes of learning and science, never became as cozy as other rooms in the house. *Because no one spends time down here.*

Rick headed back up the stairs. The basement wasn't where he wanted to be. He needed to think, and did his best thinking while in motion. The workroom would be his best bet; he could work on his cars.

Since both he and Viv pursued hobbies requiring special tools and space, they added the workroom adjoining the garage six years ago. Viv enjoyed woodwork and created anything from the decorative miniature pieces to the various pieces of furniture (mostly tables, chairs, and shelving) placed throughout their home.

His interest was model cars. The hobby was his brother's originally. When his father started boxing up David's things for charity, Rick claimed the model cars. He had a hard time accepting David's leaving, so the connection to his brother remained sacred.

He entered their workroom, immediately assaulted by smells of acrylic and smoky sawdust. He stood in the doorway, scanning the space: a sizable, almost-perfect square. The room was never officially divided into his-side-her-side, but a natural separation of territories made itself apparent. Viv performed her usual cleanup after working in the room a few days ago, but traces of sawdust persisted, even invading his side.

Rick went to his side and stared at the mess that was his worktable. As of late, he concentrated his efforts on a 1967 Ford Mustang. No surprise there. He loved Mustangs. David had been partial to Chevys, but since taking over the hobby, the number of Mustang models outnumbered everything else.

Rick sat on his stool, rotating side-to-side. The Mustang needed the excess glue and plastic trimmed before priming could begin.

He picked up his blade and got to work. He trimmed and thought about colors for his car. He trimmed and thought about giving the family therapist Louise mentioned a call.

What was her name again? Oh yeah, Dr. Alexander. Naomi Alexander.

Rick worked on the Mustang for an hour.

In the end, he decided metallic-brown would be best and that he would contact this Dr. Alexander by himself first before bringing his family to her. He needed to get with Louise anyway if he was to uncover any good information about Viv.

Louise would tell him. Her loving him in all the wrong ways for years would be enough to get her talking.

He also wanted to talk to Rast, but that could wait.

Rick stood and stretched. He looked down at his latest work.

She was ready for coat one, but later. He wanted to make a phone call and grab a snack, but first he needed to see a man about a horse.

Rick left the workroom for the bathroom, whistling his own rendition of Earth, Wind and Fire's "After the Love Has Gone."

He felt better than he had in weeks. And between Louise and Dr. Alexander, Rick hoped to be feeling even better real soon.

CHAPTER 5

Moody Blue

Dr. Naomi Alexander listened to the patient sitting across from her (a woman having serious issues with her sister), wanting nothing more than to go home and have some pineapple vodka over ice. Nevertheless, she assumed the concerned-and-attentive-psychiatrist pose and let the woman, Willette Hargrove, finish her session. Willette had twelve minutes left.

Naomi tried to give her full attention to those twelve minutes.

Willette didn't speak for eight long minutes. Her facial expressions changed with the apparent dialogue going on in her head.

Naomi leaned back in her chair.

Maybe white wine would be better. I have two reviews due tomorrow.

"Envious, I guess," Willette said, interrupting Naomi's thoughts.

Naomi purposely let Willette see her irritation. Eight minutes and that's all she comes back with? "Willette have you voiced anything *new* here? You've spent weeks trying to get across that you're not jealous of your sister." Naomi stood.

Willette took the hint and prepared to leave.

"Look, Willette." Naomi assumed her business posture once again. She usually put aside her professional mode with her patients; the stance wasn't conducive to getting them to open-up. But she was irritated now, and not as interested in Willette opening-up. "The session is over, but let's have a better answer next week."

Willette's eyes flickered before she nodded.

Naomi headed to her desk. "Then I'll see you next Monday. At three thirty rather than four. Okay?" She removed her eyeglasses, placing them on her desk with a click.

She watched Willette leave her office. The woman habitually wore very loose, ill-fitting clothes. Her charcoal-gray two-piece outfit hung about her like skin on an elephant having rapidly lost too much weight. Naomi was trained to mind the details, so she observed how Willette's rear-end rounded the sides of the skirt, how her breasts did the same for the top. *You'd truly have to wear a muumuu to cover all you want to hide, my dear girl; too-large outfits won't cut it.*

Naomi needed to call her daughter, Leslie. She reached for the phone, seeing her message light.

I'll talk with whoever that is tomorrow.

But Naomi didn't pick up the receiver to call Leslie. She stared at the tiny red rectangle winking at her.

Intuition. A hunch. Naomi called the sensation now passing through her, a "flash of truth." And at forty-four, she was virtually unaffected by its occurrence, having lived with the "flashes" for over twenty years.

She was a sophomore in college when she experienced her first flash. It helped her decide between astronomy and psychiatry as her major. She happened to be peeing at the time.

Her 'flashes' manifested as acute hunches somehow, someway, grounded in truth. And in the twenty-some odd years since her first one, the flashes occurred haphazardly at best. She could go weeks, sometimes months, without an occurrence. Naomi didn't question where her flashes came from; simply satisfied they didn't happen often. Although she didn't gamble, the haphazard nature of the hunches didn't provide a financial advantage in making the perfect wager, either.

Naomi grew still. Less than a minute passed; it was over. She picked up the phone and called her daughter. After leaving a voicemail message, she stared at the message light. "I'll speak with him tomorrow."

She knew the person who left the message was male and that her encounter with him and the woman he brought (his wife, no doubt) would upset her already-wavering principles, yet be interesting and entertaining, to say the least.

*   *   *   *   *

44

The clanging pots and pans rankled Naomi's nerves.

It was just shy of five thirty in the morning, and given that she hadn't fallen asleep until well after two (2:37 a.m. is what Naomi last remembered the clock reading), it meant she was beginning another day with less than three-hours sleep. Naomi was used to getting little sleep, but this morning the noise proved too much.

Someone clanged a frying pan on the stove. Someone else ran water into two huge pots in the sink, causing a loud whoosh. Naomi stiffened but smiled at Tammy, who filled the pots.

Wasn't it Tuesday two days ago?

Naomi wanted a drink. She immediately thought of the flask of Hennessy X.O. in her briefcase and just as quickly dismissed it. *A homeless shelter, where you've come to help people, is the last place you need to be (seen) drinking.* With a sigh, she steeled herself against the sounds of the kitchen and continued peeling potatoes and sending them through the slicer.

Every Tuesday for the past nine years, Naomi took on a volunteer project to help the less-fortunate. Apart from one occasion, she never missed a Tuesday. She changed her community-service effort every eighteen to twenty-four months. Last May she started working with Hardluck Rebound, a group of volunteer men and women who prepared breakfast for the local homeless on a rotating basis. The group Naomi signed-up for worked on Tuesdays.

This Tuesday, they were serving breakfast in the cafeteria of an aging elementary school in northwest DC.

With the potatoes peeled, sliced, and ready for frying, Naomi carried two bowls, heavy with potatoes, over to Merriam, who readied iron skillets. Naomi was a small woman, only five feet three and a drop above 110 pounds, but she carried the bowls effortlessly. Setting the bowls on the table beside the stove, she removed her Baltimore Ravens cap and ran a hand over her close-cropped hair, damp with sweat. She needed to contact her barber soon.

"Probably going to have an early summer," Merriam commented.

"You might be right on that one, Merriam." Naomi placed her cap back on her head, backwards this time. "For March, it's already warm outside, and it's only going to get warmer in here once we get rolling." She sensed someone approach before Merriam's gaze shifted. She turned around.

"Horace can't make it today." Leslie hugged her. "But he's sending a stand-in. Hi, Miss Merriam."

Leslie (twenty), inherited height from her father, Tyson. His height had whispered over six feet depending on who he stood next to, but, of course, standing next to Naomi, practically anyone looked taller than they were.

At five feet nine, Leslie easily drew attention. Her dignified walk only emphasized her height. Even in the sweatpants and T-shirt she wore now, Leslie looked regal. She had plain brown eyes, but her thick, shapely eyebrows complemented her small nose. With Naomi's mocha-brown complexion, Leslie didn't have a blemish: only the smallest of moles in front of her right earlobe.

She wished Leslie hadn't cut her hair: she wore it close-cropped, too. Naomi still waited for the look to grow on her.

Naomi looked up at her daughter. "I didn't think he would from the way he sounded last night. Visiting him later?"

Leslie nodded. "I thought I might."

"Mmm. Let him know we're thinking of him."

"What, Ma?"

"Not now, Les."

"Yeah, right." Leslie walked past Naomi to the stove, where she began pouring cooking oil into the skillets Merriam set aside.

Merriam cleared her throat. She was a large woman with pecan-brown skin, who possessed the softest and sweetest of voices. "Look, why don't you two finish the potatoes. I'll help Tammy with the grits." She spoke more to Naomi than Leslie, giving Naomi a conspiratorial wink before walking away.

Naomi watched the others work.

Like cogs in a well-oiled machine, everyone moved about the kitchen, gradually moving to a rhythm that would soon have a hot, hearty breakfast ready for about a hundred people in less than two hours. Naomi watched them with pride.

Somehow, she became the unofficial leader of the Tuesday group. That type of thing happened often enough she was used to it, but she had no problem removing the "leader" hat and letting it find another owner. Taking one last look at her team of ten (well, nine, until Horace's sub arrived), Naomi reluctantly turned around to prepare fried potatoes and onions with her daughter. "You wanna get the rest of the potatoes? I'll slice onion."

"Fine." Leslie walked away.

I truly am not in the mood for this.

Leslie carried two more bowls filled with potatoes and placed them on the table. "This should be plenty."

Naomi pulled a bag of onions toward them.

"No electric slicer?"

Naomi shook her head. "Not for this."

Leslie peeled onions. Naomi sliced them. They worked in silence.

"I don't see how you do it," Leslie said finally.

"My eyes don't water when I slice onion. So?" Cooking-talk was safe ground.

"Well, why didn't I get your impervious-to-onion gene? Or your southpaw one?" Leslie wiped a tear from her cheek.

"You'll have to take that up with a Higher Power. And being left-handed has its drawbacks." Naomi handed Leslie a two-handed scoop of sliced onions. "Here, start with these."

"Ma, the potatoes need to cook first. They take longer, remember?" Leslie gently pushed her hands back and reached for a bowl of potatoes.

Tammy turned on her portable CD player. Mahalia Jackson's "Upper Room" mingled with the clanging kitchen sounds.

"Got all turned around there for a sec. Probably tired."

Leslie gave her a sideways glance. "Still not sleeping?"

"It's getting better."

"For a psychiatrist, you sure don't lie very well."

"Shrinks are supposed to be expert liars?" Naomi hurried her slicing; they were falling behind schedule.

"No, but with all the mental-hijinks you get involved in, surely a white-lie or two comes into play." Leslie slid two handfuls of potatoes into the oil, and then added four more. She sighed heavily. "So why don't you want me seeing Horace?" The question was barely-heard above the noise of the kitchen.

"It's not Horace per se, Les. It's Horace, Gavin, Clarence. And, oh, what's his name? Adello. I don't understand why you have to see so many men."

"*Seeing* them, Ma, not sleeping with them. Well, not *all* of them." Leslie snickered at her correction.

Naomi smirked. "Cute. But I'm still your mother. There's sharing and then there is TMI."

"Uh-huh. Anyway, I thought you'd like Gavin: he's an artist."

Naomi hesitated. "What's that got to do with anything?"

"Lately it seems it has to do with everything."

Naomi did not want to have this conversation.

The women worked together quietly.

"… Sorry you feel that way."

Leslie scoffed. "No, you're just sorry I haven't followed your advice."

"Oh, so now you're the therapist?"

"No, but like you, I just calls 'em as I sees 'em."

"Then why can't you 'see' that art is your true calling, not international marketing?" Naomi pulled another bowl of potatoes toward them.

"Because I'm practical, like Daddy was."

Naomi stiffened. "And practicality kept your father miserable."

"You always say that, but I never saw it."

There was another quiet period of simply frying potatoes and onions, and transferring cooked potatoes into large aluminum trays.

"Les, children are often shielded from the negative."

"I was sixteen when Daddy left us, not six. I would have known if Daddy was unhappy."

"First of all, Les, your father died. He didn't 'leave us' the way you keep saying it. You should be stronger about that now."

"Should be, but I'm not. Second of all?"

"There were plenty signs you didn't notice."

"Such as?"

"Such as, you need to turn those potatoes: they're scorching."

"I got this, Ma. Finish." Leslie added more oil to the pan.

"Well, you know how he constantly complained of headaches and rarely wanted to do anything recreational."

"He was tired."

"Exactly. He worked hard and lost his enthusiasm for the goofy-stuff in life."

"The 'goofy-stuff,' Ma?"

"Yes, the goofy-stuff. Look, Les, I had conservative parents, so I appreciate your desire to have a conventional plan. But be happy, too."

Leslie added potatoes to a tray. "Studying marketing strategies from varying world views is interesting. I like it."

"Yeah, but when you sculpt, tell the truth, there's nothing like it. Is there?" Naomi was surprised this topic was going well; angry words were usually spoken by now.

Leslie didn't respond.

"Les?"

"When the police pulled in front of our house, what went through your mind?" Leslie stood motionless, both hands holding an aluminum tray filled with cooked potatoes.

"Sheer, unadulterated curiosity." It was the truth. Naomi avoided recalling that day, but memories have no expiration date.

That Tuesday in late-August was muggy, the air damp from thunderstorms the night before. Naomi, Tyson, and Leslie were planting portulaca and waxy begonias in the front yard. It was rather late in the season, but Naomi didn't care. They purchased the plants weeks before, which then sat in the garage most of that time, Naomi only occasionally remembering to give the things some water.

That Tuesday afternoon, the three of them started gardening, but Tyson, in one of his rare moments, had a taste for doughnuts and headed to Dunkin' Donuts with everyone's order. The closest Dunkin' Donuts shop was fifteen minutes away. Tyson left that afternoon around four o'clock.

Afternoon moved into evening as Naomi planted and replanted, paying no attention to the time. Leslie abandoned the activity around 6:30 p.m., content to watch her mother and keep her company. For sixteen, Leslie was quite the conversationalist, so Naomi didn't mind gardening solo.

It was odd, and Naomi has never forgiven herself, but at 8:15 p.m. it finally occurred to her that Tyson wasn't back. It was odd because Tyson wasn't one to take side-jaunts when he went on an errand, so Naomi should have been alarmed long before eight fifteen. But as involved as she was in the gardening, Naomi hadn't given Tyson another thought.

She started to ask Leslie to call her father, when a county police car carrying two officers pulled up. Naomi was kneeling in the dirt when the white car with its green and gold shield approached, its lights flashing silently. They didn't use the vacant driveway; for some reason that struck a chord with her. She remembers standing protectively in front of Leslie and wondering what in the world cops were doing at her house—that they might be there because of Tyson never crossed her mind.

Tyson was buried the following Tuesday.

"Why are you asking about that now, Les?" Naomi surveyed the kitchen: everything was ready except the eggs. She started toward where Ben and Vanessa were setting up trays of breakfast meats (hoping to swipe a sausage link or two), but a choked sound, low in Leslie's throat, stopped her. She turned to her daughter.

"Just am." Leslie looked down at her tray of potatoes. "I carry the memory of that day with me always. But I can never recall how I was feeling when those policemen came."

"Well, honey, that's—"

Leslie looked at her. "Ma, we're not in 'session' here, okay?"

"I know that."

"Well, I don't want you to—"

"I'm not. Go 'head." Naomi's throat dried up. She and Leslie rarely discussed Tyson's death. She didn't know why her daughter broached the subject now, but there was a reason. The psychiatrist in Naomi gave her the patience to wait for it.

"All I'm saying is, when I try to conjure up how I felt, I'm grasping at straws. I try to feel how I should've felt, but it doesn't ring true. The only feeling that does is anger. But why would I be angry?"

Naomi watched Merriam and Vanessa ready the eggs.

Leslie sighed. "So, you want me to change majors at this stage. And change it to art, of all things. This is a switch. Most parents stress studying something traditional, more 'marketable' to build a career around." Leslie shook her head.

"If I said yes?" Naomi braced for her daughter's response. She turned the bill on her cap around to the front and pulled it low on her forehead, shielding her eyes in shadow. The noise in the kitchen slackened. Yolanda Adams's "The Battle Is the Lord's" drifted from the CD player. Naomi wanted more activity, more noise. She didn't want this part of their talk easily overheard.

Leslie turned away, standing with her back to Naomi. "Don't know. But you've got to let me alone on this. I gave in on one thing by commuting to George Mason instead of staying on campus, because you asked. That should've been enough. Now you want to tell me what to study and how many men I should date."

"I don't stop being your mother because you're in college." Naomi's tone darkened, "And don't tell me what should or shouldn't be enough." She didn't like talking to Leslie's back. Even if they couldn't be overheard, Leslie's back to her surely clued onlookers that their conversation wasn't lovely.

"Theresa asked again if I was interested in rooming with her."

Naomi knew this was coming; it always did. "Meaning?" She fully understood what Leslie meant, but wanted her to say it.

Leslie shrugged. "I'm just saying."

Naomi walked around Leslie and faced her. She tilted the bill on her cap upward, taking her eyes out of shadow, and reached for a second tray of potatoes. She leaned over the tray she held, looking up at her daughter. "No, you're not 'just saying.' You never 'just say,' and neither do I. I don't like threats, Les, you know that. But if you're sending one? Take the veil off." In her peripheral vision, Naomi noted a few members of the crew paused in their actions. Some heads turned their way; others paused but then continued whatever they were doing. The smells of the kitchen were blended now, less-pungent. Naomi's hunger dissipated. She wanted her flask.

"Ma, please back off, or I'll take Theresa up on her offer. If not Theresa, then somebody, or I'll get a place of my own." Leslie only met her mother's eyes briefly. Beads of sweat dotted her upper lip.

"You know I want you with me, Leslie."

"Why, Ma? Why do you want me with you? You're busy most times with your patients and articles. Your life seems full to me. You don't spend your time sitting around the house waiting for me so that you can live vicariously through my life. Why is it so important that I be with you?"

"I have my reasons." But she didn't. Not anything concrete. Naomi turned away, heading to where Merriam and Vanessa were scrambling eggs. Leslie followed.

It may have been her imagination, Naomi didn't think so, but Merriam and Vanessa made themselves look extra-busy as she and Leslie approached. "How are we doing over here, ladies?" Naomi rested her potatoes on the counter, as did Leslie.

Merriam whisked the eggs. The muscles in her forearm bulged with each twist of her wrist. "We started these eggs a little early, so we might want to begin serving sooner instead of waiting. Ben says people have already gravitated our way."

"That okay with you, Naomi?" Vanessa was a mild-mannered woman in her late-thirties whose smile could brighten any day. She smiled now.

Naomi smiled back and pulled her Ravens cap back down. "Sure. That's fine. Did Horace's replacement show?"

"Yeah," Merriam answered. "Tammy said he was helping her and Ben set up tables out front. Said he was tall, kinda cute."

"I see. If the eggs are all we're waiting for, and they've got the tables up, we might as well get the line started."

Naomi started away, hoping her daughter would hang back with Vanessa and Merriam. She was relieved Leslie didn't follow her to meet the new guy; the last thing that girl needed was another man in the mix.

Naomi normally engaged in small-talk with a few of the visitors, but this time she made a detour. Her briefcase lay in the back of her silver BMW X5. That's where she headed, soon standing in a wide alleyway outside the door of the rec hall.

Her SUV was parked perpendicular to the building. It was bright outside, the sun beaming high in the cloudless sky. When she reached her truck, Naomi paused before opening the cargo area. She didn't give a hey-nonny-nonny about being seen inasmuch as she second-guessed taking a drink in the first place.

Naomi stood, shifting her weight from one foot to the other, taking her keys out of one pocket, putting them in another. The pull intensified. Her throat clicked as it opened and closed with the struggle between anticipation of the familiar and resistance of the ill-advised.

Detecting movement, she turned to see Leslie searching the alley, and decided against retrieving her flask.

She opened the tailgate. Realizing she didn't need it, Naomi removed her Glock-17 semiautomatic from under her shirt and tucked it in the hideaway storage space. She experienced the slightest regret (and irritation) at abandoning her initial impulse, but was proud of herself as she closed and locked her vehicle. She walked toward Leslie, who appeared relieved to see her. "Looking for me?"

Leslie nodded. "We're ready to start serving. Ben's got the line forming, but we presumed you'd want to say hi to Horace's stand-in first, since he's the only new body in the group. He doesn't seem uncomfortable, but it wouldn't hurt."

"Is he as cute as they're saying?"

"If that's your type." Leslie shrugged dismissively, but gave the smallest of smiles before returning her gaze to Naomi.

If people only knew how often the face and body betrayed itself.

"What type is that?"

"Oh, the typical: tall, dark, and handsome. Light eyes. You know—the usual." Leslie giggled.

"Is that all? Well let me greet this homely stand-in." She grabbed Leslie's forearm, pulling her along.

Naomi stood in the doorway of the rec hall surveying the place, looking for someone fitting Leslie's description. The guy sounded like he'd be easy to spot, so she didn't stay too long with any one face.

She turned to Leslie. "So, where is he?"

Leslie scanned the rec hall. "He was with Ben and Gary ..." Her eyes widened upon seeing him. "Oh, see? There he is."

"Where?"

"Behind the last table. I'd point, but that's impolite."

Naomi concentrated her gaze where Leslie directed and spotted him immediately. She should have spotted him initially—he wasn't hard to miss. Indeed, he was tall. Given her distance from him, Naomi couldn't really see his "light" eyes, but even from her vantage point, she could tell he was good-looking.

Naomi continued staring. He seemed strangely-familiar to her.

"Ma, that's embarrassing. He's not that cute, for crying out loud."

"Huh? Oh. No. He looked like a former patient, that's all." It wasn't complete fibnation. For all Naomi knew, he could've been a former patient, but Naomi didn't think so.

Leslie placed hands on hips, hinting impatience. "Are you greeting the man or not?"

"Can I have a minute first?"

"A minute for what? No, come on." Now Leslie grabbed Naomi's arm and pulled her along.

Naomi had mixed feelings about meeting him; she stopped short. "That's not necessary, Les."

"Oh. Sorry."

"Look, let's help serve the food. I can say hello later."

"Why can't you greet 'im now? We're right here."

"I can greet him now. I just want to wait. Besides, he's already spoken with a few of you." Naomi glanced over at the man again. "He doesn't seem to be feeling out of place or anything. Let it be."

Leslie shook her head. "Sometimes I cannot figure you out."

"Then stop trying. Now, let's get this breakfast served." Naomi walked behind the trays filled with piles of bacon and sausage. Her stomach growled. Staying put, Naomi donned a pair of disposable poly-gloves and stood, ready to serve.

Daylight poured in through the exit doors and high windows. The overhead lights beamed as well, making the rec hall unusually-bright. The bright room, however, didn't diminish the dimness of the situation. Most of those in the room had no home, likely receiving the only true meal they'd have for the day.

Naomi never showed pity or excess sympathy (most of their visitors resented it), but a profound sense of loneliness enveloped her when she served them. *I'm only exercising my emotional intelligence here.* She avoided bringing her psychiatry background into her world outside of work, but often couldn't help it.

As people passed through the line, Naomi made every effort to make eye-contact, to smile, to say "hello." She advised the crew to do the same. It sometimes proved a difficult task. Most of the homeless kept their eyes downcast, but at times, some of the homeless returned the greeting. They had their regulars, of course, who sporadically engaged some of the crew in light banter.

A gentle breeze blew through the open exit doors as the crew began clearing and cleaning up. Although accustomed to the low-stench of sweat and urine, Naomi was thankful for its noticeable dissipation. Only a few slices of bacon and three sausage links—rooted to their spot by droplets of congealed grease—remained in the tray in front of her. She wasn't hungry anymore, having surreptitiously downed a few pieces of meat during the serve, but she grabbed a slice of bacon anyway and took a bite.

Cold now, the bacon was rubbery; its smoky-flavor muted by the taste of grease coating portions of the slice. Naomi swallowed against her better judgment, stacked the empty meat trays, and deliberated the specifics for the topic of her next article: "Exploring Attribution Theory."

A man's voice interrupted her thoughts. "Are you Naomi?"

Naomi turned and looked up into the face of the gentleman serving as Horace's replacement. He was attractive—the contrast of his dark-brown skin and hazel eyes, arresting. She cleared her throat and extended a hand. "Yes, I'm Naomi. Naomi Alexander." Her hand swam in the depths of the man's palm, but she gripped back firmly.

"I'm Jonathan Rast. Horace Packard asked me to sub for him."

"My apologies for not saying hello sooner, but thank you for coming out. Horace didn't have to send a replacement." Naomi tried not to stare.

Jonathan tilted his head. "Is something wrong?" Concern touched his direct gaze.

"No. I'm sorry, anyone in your family involved in the medical field? Doctor, teacher, nurse?"

Jonathan shook his head. "I'm in the restaurant business. I own DeTante's downtown. And the rest of the family is sorta indirectly-involved with that. Why?"

"Well, I'm a therapist. You seem familiar to me. I thought maybe that was where I knew you. What about the volunteer stuff?" Naomi realized she sounded like an interrogator, but she needed to know who Jonathan was.

"Let's see: I help with youth-literacy; sometimes I volunteer to take pictures for my community newsletter. And, as you can see, I do on-call work." Jonathan grinned, revealing a hint of the boy he used to be. "Did that ring any bells? Jog your memory?"

"Not really, but tell you what: it was nice meeting you. Let's finish closing shop. It might dawn on me where I know you. Do I look familiar?"

"No, ma'am."

"Did you just call me *ma'am*?" Naomi wasn't really offended.

"Please don't be offended. I tend to address all women that way. Younger, older—it doesn't make a difference."

"Oh, okay. Didn't wanna hafta hurt you up in here." Naomi jokingly feigned a punch.

Jonathan laughed. "No. I'd definitely remember meeting you before. Let me know if something comes to you, okay?" He smiled and started away, whistling a tune Naomi didn't recognize.

Her smile gradually faded as she watched him go.

She hadn't met Jonathan until today, but she realized why he seemed so familiar. A knot formed in her throat. She coughed several times attempting to clear it. She hadn't met him before, but she had a hunch about him—a flash-of-truth, that didn't sit well.

It told her, quite plainly, the man wouldn't live much longer.

Naomi wasn't a psychic by any stretch of the imagination. She knew no specifics tied to his death (no date, time, place, or manner), only the certainty of its imminence. This flash-of-truth carried dread for a man she didn't know.

She wondered why she didn't get a similar hunch the day she watched her husband leave for doughnuts.

Naomi resumed assisting with the cleanup. She chatted here and there with a few of the homeless, who, having no next place to go, hung around the rec hall after breakfast ended. Done with the cleanup, Naomi said her goodbyes.

Her goodbye to Jonathan was pleasant but curt. She hoped to see him again, maybe visit his restaurant.

It was her stab at denial.

CHAPTER 6

As Luck Would Have It

Rick sat in the driver's seat of a rented Chevy Malibu, tracing a finger over the scar on his right ear, observing the sky in his rearview mirror. Sunrise approached, but it remained relatively-dark, the sky amethystine with streaks of orange toward the east.

He brooded, wondering what he was doing, or, closer to the point, what he was going to do. He was also annoyed with himself for leaving his phone in his truck. He sat parked across the street, three houses down from where Jonathan Rast lived.

After getting Dr. Alexander's info from Louise and making an appointment to see her, Rick changed his mind about meeting with Louise in person to talk about Viv. The situation with Louise could get awkward sometimes, especially when alone with her. He'd talk to her eventually.

Since Viv told him about Rast, Rick couldn't help picturing her getting busy with him. It angered him every time. But sometimes (and Rick found this most disturbing) it aroused him, too. He'd been meaning to speak his piece with Rast for weeks, but always found a reason not to. Viv was on the defensive now. He liked that. If he got into it with Rast, however, and Rast said something to Viv, then Viv would have reason (at least in her mind) to go on the offensive. Rick couldn't have that. On the other hand, he couldn't let Rast get away with what he'd done, so here he was, playing PI in Jonathan Rast's neighborhood.

Jonathan lived on LeCarton Street, west of what some referred to as the "Gold Coast," in upper northwest Washington, DC. As expected, the tree-lined neighborhood was quiet in the early-morning hour. The new-dawn caroling of birds rose intermittently from the dogwood and elm trees boxed along the sidewalks and from the park located at the end of the four blocks LeCarton Street stretched. Slowly, evidence of morning touched the detached homes of LeCarton, as here and there lights came on.

Rick wasn't certain about what he was doing parked outside Jonathan's house, but he appreciated Viv's doggedness about sending Christmas and birthday cards. Getting Jonathan's address from the kitchen laptop was easy. Catching Rast at DeTante's was not. Catching up with him as he started his day seemed easier, so Rick rose and dressed for work as usual before driving to the neighborhood near the 24-Hour Easy Rent where he parked the rented Malibu. He switched vehicles, and then drove to LeCarton Street.

He now doubted what he thought to be good, logical reasoning: no sign of activity came from Jonathan's house. Jonathan's brown Mercedes-Benz GL450 sat parked in front of his house, so Rick was content to wait. In the rearview mirror, flecks of gold blended with the orange streaks of sunrise as the purple sky moved closer to periwinkle. The trees, however, kept LeCarton Street in shadow.

Rick turned the radio on and resumed rubbing his scar. "Fairy Tales," by Anita Baker, was playing softly when Jonathan finally appeared.

Jonathan, at six feet three, appeared even taller in the low light. He stood on his front porch momentarily before descending the steps to his walkway leading to the sidewalk. Turning right and away from Rick, Jonathan headed in the direction of the park, dressed in a light T-shirt, long Jersey shorts, and running shoes. A German shepherd trotted at his heels on a leash: a good-looking dog, still puppy-like in its movement.

Rick exited the Malibu and hurried after Jonathan, staying on the opposite side of the street. Remarkably, he was cool-headed upon seeing Rast; maybe this could go smoothly.

Rick was dressed for work in a shirt and tie. His dress shoes were in the workbag in his truck; he wore hiking boots, making catching up to Rast easier.

Jonathan paused at the edge of the park and stooped to unclasp the leash from the dog's collar. Rick crossed the street and approached him from behind. He heard Jonathan whisper, "Go, Copeland!" before the dog bounded away. Jonathan turned his body, watching Rick's approach.

Rick stopped several steps away. After a beat, he extended his hand.

Jonathan rose guardedly. He grasped Rick's hand and pumped it once firmly. "Rick."

Rick gave a curt nod. "Rast."

"Oh, so it's 'Rast' now." Jonathan held Copeland's leash. The metal clasp swung like a pendulum between them.

Rick didn't reply.

"Man, you didn't come all the way over here at this hour to look at me. You got something to say, you need to come out with it."

Standing face-to-face was too-confrontational. Rick hoped to keep the encounter as peaceful as possible. He'd repeatedly gone over various things he wanted to say to Rast, but now words failed him.

Movement usually got his mental-juices flowing. "Let's walk." Rick nodded in the direction of the trees.

Jonathan turned and started along the path leading into the park. Rick fell in step beside him.

"How's Viv?"

"Don't know. As of late, contact with my wife is limited. Seems to me you'd know how she's doing."

"I haven't talked to her in a couple days now."

Small-talk was over. "Corny or not, fuck it. Why Viv, man? I mean, damn, why *my* wife?"

"Nobody set out to do this."

"No single women out here appeal to you?"

"None like Viv."

"So, you love my wife; is that it?"

"You're not going to like the answer to that no matter how I answer, so let's leave that part alone."

Rick didn't like Jonathan's attempt to direct the conversation, telling him what to 'leave alone.' "So, how long have y'all been …?" Rick shook his head, trying to clear the images. "When'd you start seeing each other?"

"The only time I'd see or talk to her was when I'd see the two of you at DeTante's, until about a year ago, when she picked up photography again and submitted shots for my opinion. Things didn't get complicated until the end of September last year."

"And by 'complicated' you mean …?"

"Exactly what you think I mean."

Rick stuffed clenched fists in his pockets.

The men walked along the path quietly. The sun was up now. Sunshine winked through the budding leafed branches overhead, creating a speckled canvas on the ground before them. Copeland darted along the path several yards ahead. Sporadically, Copeland would stop, check for Jonathan, and wag his tail before continuing his romp in the woods. So far, no one else was up and about. No morning joggers, no fellow dog walkers. Just Rick, Jonathan, and Copeland enjoying the cool, dew-dampened air.

"Rast, we've never been tight, but we've had some pretty good conversations."

"True."

"So, wasn't it you with the whole 'building up and protecting the black family' spiel?"

"That's been me on several occasions."

"And pulling up on my wife is building up the black family?"

"Not at all."

"So, again: why *my* wife?"

"The shit just happened. I struggled with—"

"Ah, fuck that, Rast! You 'struggled.' You still seein' my wife?"

"Rick, Viv is fine as shit, funny, smart—"

"You don't have to tell me what my wife is. I know what I got."

Jonathan lowered his voice. "Then why can't you keep her happy?"

Rick stopped.

Jonathan did, too.

"What're you talking about? What did Viv say?" Rick was angry but unsure of himself, knowing Viv talked to Jonathan about them—about him.

Jonathan laughed softly, shaking his head. "You know, funny thing is, Viv has said little about the two of you and your marriage. She avoids discussion of it altogether. But I figure, if she was happy with you, she wouldn't be involved with me." Jonathan checked the path for Copeland. When he spotted him, he returned his hazel gaze to Rick.

Rick relaxed some. He felt better realizing Viv hadn't been confiding in Rast; all was not lost. "Okay, fair enough. But check this." Already facing Jonathan, he stepped closer. "Since my wife hasn't actually said she's unhappy with me? I'm asking you, as a black man trying to keep his family together, to another black man who professes the importance of family, to step aside and leave my wife alone."

"The way you steppin' up to me, you got an *or else* with that?"

"Don't need one."

"Back up off me, Rick."

Rick stood his ground, gritting his teeth.

"You don't want none of this. Back up off me."

After a second or two, Rick stepped back. "I'm not trying to get into it about this. I call myself taking the civil route."

"You can be civil without gettin' in my face."

The men watched each other.

Copeland barked farther down the path.

Rick sighed. "So, what about it, Rast?"

"I don't know."

"Beg pardon?" He clenched his fists again.

"Shouldn't you be talkin' to Viv about this?"

"Not yet. I will, but not yet."

"Do you love her, Rick?"

The question surprised him. "Yes. Would I be here if I didn't?"

"Maybe."

Rick frowned. "What?"

"Maybe this isn't about love at all. Maybe you're just blown behind another man samplin' your wife's goods. Because what I was going to say earlier was: Viv is fine, funny, smart—and a man's dream in bed. So, yeah, man, I love her, and while I know the right thing is to let her go, I'm not sure I can do that now. At least, not like …" Jonathan snapped his fingers, "that."

Rick turned away and headed back in the direction they had come. He hardly heard Jonathan's last few sentences. Barely heard him profess his love for Viv. Only got the gist of him saying he wasn't leaving his wife alone. No, Rick was stuck on 'man's dream in bed,' and saw red. In fact, there were shades of black, blue, and purple, too.

He walked away from Jonathan, needing to put some distance between them. He was too angry to stand across from Rast, listening to him, so walking away was best.

Rast followed, talking about Viv, saying shit Rick didn't want to hear.

Rick walked on, trying to keep the color-flashes and images of Viv's betrayal at bay. He was losing the battle, and Rast kept babbling behind him. Rast was following and talking, and Rick really wished he'd shut up.

It was very important right now that he shut up. Silence could not have been more golden. Rast really needed to just shut the fuck UP!

Rick heard Jonathan's ribs crack, even felt them give under the force of his foot as they sunk inward, but he still didn't get it. He only turned to Jonathan upon hearing a strange gulp behind him.

Watching Jonathan fall, two things went through Rick's mind. First, he was glad Rast had finally shut up. Second, for the tiniest of seconds Rick genuinely wanted to know what the hell was wrong with him.

Seconds melted into minutes. Having studied martial-arts for over twenty years and receiving numerous master belts, Rick knew the kick he delivered could be fatal, so his initial confusion centered solely on disbelief that he delivered the kick at all.

Rick knelt beside Jonathan, gazing into his blank stare.

Farther up the path, a squirrel crossed, and Copeland, oblivious to his master's death, crossed after it. Copeland's panting and the rustle of brush echoed in the woods.

Seeing Copeland got Rick moving, but he had presence of mind to walk calmly. He didn't want to take the chance of possibly drawing attention to himself by running back to the car or cause Copeland to give chase.

Little time had passed since he spotted Jonathan leaving his house. As Rick walked to the rental, he half-expected, half-dreaded seeing someone along the way. Other than someone delivering newspapers from a small tan hatchback a block down, he saw no one. No curtains or blinds parted. Copeland barked repeatedly now, and in the tranquility of the morning, could be heard whimpering, too.

Probably found Rast.

Rick perused the neighborhood once more before getting in the car and driving away.

He drove cautiously to the 24-Hour Easy Rent. He was cautious because he was waiting. Waiting for a reaction: to feel whatever he was going to feel. Because any emotion deemed apropos took sabbatical. No remorse. No guilt. Rick wasn't scared or sad, either. Right now, he was simply happy Rast had shut up. He knew some emotion would come, so he drove in a state of passivity, waiting for it.

Rick returned the Malibu without incident, waiting to feel something.

He'd parked his Range Rover around the corner from the Easy Rent and walked there now. A knot formed in his stomach and traveled to his throat.

Here it comes.

His mouth watered. Rick paused on the sidewalk, looking around for somewhere discreet. The urge to vomit passed quickly, but the back of his throat burned and itched. Rick reached his SUV and got in, letting out a long, deep breath.

Noticing how tightly he held the steering wheel, Rick realized he was shaking. He loosened his grip on the steering wheel and checked his hands, letting them hover in a gripping position over the wheel: a barely-perceptible tremble. He closed his eyes and concentrated on the current moving through his body, recognizing the tremors for what they were.

He wasn't nervous. "Adrenaline rush." Rick opened his eyes with another deep breath. "Either that, or plain ordinary shock." He started his truck and drove off.

He took his time driving to the subway station. Once parked, he reached into his workbag located behind the passenger seat. No sign of his cell phone: he must have left it at home. He couldn't bother with that now. Rick stood outside his SUV, keys in hand, workbag on the ground beside him. He pointed his remote to set the car alarm when it occurred to him that he'd be getting to work rather late.

Rick surveyed the sky: a little after eight. He tried to think of the last time he'd rolled into the office after eight. *Viv's the one who likes getting to work on the later side. Speaking of Viv ...* He checked his pocket watch: 8:12 a.m. *Viv and Alna are already out the door.* He set the SUV's alarm with its familiar chirp, picked up his bag, and headed for the trains, whistling Earth, Wind and Fire's "On Your Face."

He tightened his tie as he walked steadily, confidently. The electrical charge, as small as it was before, was even smaller now. He figured his "rush" was ending—that the true reaction would hit him next. He was back to waiting, being cautious.

Rick walked along the underground platform, smells of motor grease and leather in his nostrils, occasionally catching the scent of someone's cologne or perfume as he or she passed. Leaning against the base of the escalator, he watched the line of round lights at the platform's edge. He waited for them to flash, to signal that his train approached.

He waited for a textbook-reaction to having killed a man.

The screeching-metal sounds of the train arriving released him from his trance. He boarded and sat on one of the solitary seats behind a glass divider and stared out the window. It didn't matter that he was underground; he wasn't seeing much in front of him, anyway.

Exhaustion set in. Rick rested his temple against the window. Someone wearing brown brushed against him, but Rick didn't look up, only vaguely aware of his surroundings. At most, he tried to listen for his stop.

Think about work.

It was an ideal diversion. His client presentation for Arrington Enterprises was a collaborative effort with Mark Dilworth. The project was a big deal, so he needed to fix his attention to it.

Thoughts on the Arrington account ("... *Then why can't you keep her happy?*") didn't last long.

That's reminiscent of my parents twenty-three years ago.

The door chimed closed with a soft zoosh.

Rick closed his eyes. Not to sleep, but to remember ...

He remembered most of all being very hungry that night, although he'd had third helpings of pork chops and baked beans at dinner. His older brother, David, slept on the other side of their room, snoring softly. David had come home from baseball practice, gulped his dinner, and was zonked out, his science book opened beside him on top of the covers. The room's only window was on Rick's side of the room, next to his bed. He remembers looking out the window at the sky for the time (almost eleven). A new moon glowed that April night ...

Richie's stomach didn't growl, but sent out a hollow feeling—a signal to his brain that got him moving. He wished Dave was awake. Usually he could convince him to sneak a snack even when Dave wasn't hungry. Richie started from under his covers, sending his Louis L'Amour novel to the floor. He leaned headfirst over his bed and retrieved his book, when he thought he heard noises from the direction of the kitchen. Probably his mother. She'd be leaving for work shortly, but Richie didn't remember her coming in to kiss them goodnight. In fact, he was sure she hadn't.

Dave stirred, let out a whistled breath, and turned over.

Richie came from under the covers and placed warm feet on the cool hardwood floor of their room. They did have an area rug, but it was rolled up against the dresser to provide a better driving surface for the small cars that littered the floor. He stepped on one as he moved toward the door. At seventeen and fourteen, Dave and Richie Phillips enjoyed the childhood game of cars (although either would die if anybody from school found out). Stepping on another car, he swore softly and paused when his brother stirred again. Initially, he wouldn't have minded if he woke Dave, but now …

The door was ajar enough for him to slide his slender frame through; he didn't want the door to creak. He stood in the hallway, listening for the noises that had gotten him up. The small hallway was dark. The light was on in his parents' bedroom across from theirs, but the door was closed. Light coming from the living room around the corner illuminated the far end of the hall. No light came from the kitchen.

This was odd for the Phillips household. Richie frowned with concern: the kitchen stove light stayed on in their house. He could hear his parents talking in the living room.

With an awareness only a child sometimes possesses, Richie moved forward cautiously. He paused, peered around the corner of the L that led to the living room and the front of the house, and listened.

"So, you're go'n say nothing to the boys?" his father, Eugene, spoke quietly. There was the distinct and familiar sound of weight shifting in his La-Z-Boy chair and of newspapers rustling.

The radio, always tuned to some talk-radio station, was on low volume in the kitchen, but was still distracting. Richie had to concentrate to hear his parents' conversation.

"I'll speak to them when the time is right." His mother, Carol, sounded tired. And at that moment Richie understood more than he cared to. He wanted his mother. He stayed put.

"There is no right time to tell a child you're breaking up a family."

"Suit yourself, Gene. Dave and Richie aren't little boys anymore."

"Where you go'n be?"

"With Betty."

"You'll be all right?"

"I'll be fine."

Another long pause. "When'd you stop loving us, Cissy?" His father's voice was plain with hurt.

Richie winced.

"This isn't about love, Gene. I love you and my boys. But love is no longer enough to hold me where I'm not happy." Pain echoed in his mother's voice, too, but Richie picked up something else as well. He just couldn't place it. Defiance?

Richie heard a match strike. "Even happiness has to be worked at."

"But you need a foundation, Gene. A basic level of happy to start from and maintain. I haven't had that in a long time."

Another pause. "When you talk to the boys, make sure they understand it ain't got nothin' to do with them." Eugene's voice was calm yet pleading.

The ever-present scent of pipe tobacco suddenly sharpened. *Dad must've lit a new round.*

"I will," Carol Phillips sighed. "I'll call soon."

More shuffling noises ensued. Richie sensed his mother moving closer to the hall. He stepped back, but not before seeing his mother approach the door with a suitcase. He tilted his head back against the wall. On the radio, WAJP's Adami Malik went on about the new struggles of urban youth.

Richie heard the front door open and close, the sound of newspapers flying, and *a single wrenching sob from his father. Richie went back to bed and crawled under the covers. He wasn't hungry anymore.*

The sound of the door chimes released Rick from his memories. The train operator announced his stop was next (doors opening on the left). Rick stood by the exit door to ride the next minute to his stop.

He waited for some onslaught of emotion: panic, fear, remorse— something, anything.

Stopping at a local deli, he wolfed-down a breakfast sandwich and grape juice before heading to the offices of Impetus Marketing, Incorporated. Although he arrived later than usual, it went unnoticed.

Rick thought about Rast twice during his run-through of the Arrington presentation with Mark.

He still waited.

CHAPTER 7

Calendar Girl

While Rick debated Mark Dilworth on the demographic strategies best for the Arrington Enterprises account, and Jonathan Rast lay dead in the park near his home (like a sentry, Copeland remained seated by his master's body, occasionally sniffing it and whimpering), Viv rose to begin her day. She sat up and looked at the clock, listening for sounds in the house.

Rick's long gone.

Viv rose to see if Alna was awake.

She decided last night to turn off both her and Alna's alarms and let the morning drive the day. If they awoke on time, it'd be work and school as usual. If they slept in, the day was theirs. This Friday was a half-day of school for Al, so Viv wasn't too concerned about keeping her out.

Viv peeped in on Alna: still asleep. She returned to 'her' bedroom and stood in the middle of it, grinning with excitement. "First things first."

A small round table stood in one corner of the room, upon which a scented candle and one of Viv's many books of inspiration rested. On the floor in front of the table lay a bright, yellow and orange pillow: Viv's "sun" pillow that she used for kneeling. The area was her spiritual-focus space; she moved there now for her morning prayer.

This prayer held a mixture of straight-talk and childlike recitation (she asked for forgiveness regarding her infidelity). Even with the stressful situation in her home, Viv treasured her quiet time; it sustained her. Viv prayed for fifteen minutes and meditated for five, when there was a knock at the door.

"Mommy?"

Viv didn't think Alna was used to her being in a different bedroom. "It's open, sweetie."

Alna stepped inside wearing a teddy-bear nightgown. She'd removed her scarf: four plaits fell just below her shoulders. "We're late, Mommy. I'll need a note for Miss Cavett." She walked over and bounced into a sitting position at the foot of Viv's bed.

Viv smiled. "Okay, but you won't be giving it to her till Monday ..." She waited for her daughter to get her meaning.

It didn't take long. "Yay!" Alna hopped off the bed with her arms wide and hugged Viv tight.

Viv guided Alna back to the door. "Now, you've got fifteen minutes to get cleaned-up and throw something on."

Alna trotted down the hall singing something called "No School Today—Hey!" that only she knew the music and lyrics to.

Viv showered and dressed, throwing on a pair of black jeans and a Philadelphia Eagles T-shirt. She'd finished her call to the office when Alna returned, dressed but looking perplexed.

"Whatsa matter, honey?"

"Mommy, how long did you say it'll be before I have my period?"

"What?! Alna, where did that come from?"

Alna sat on Viv's bed, bouncing the heels of her dangling feet against the bed frame. "Well, Ashley's eleven and she got hers last week."

Viv sat next to her daughter. Alna smelled of soap and almond-cherry lotion. She'd curled stray strands of hair behind her ears. "Honey, didn't Mommy tell you it starts at different times for different girls? For most girls, it usually starts somewhere between age eleven and thirteen. Remember? I didn't get mine until I was twelve, so you might be around the same age when you get yours. If so, then you have, what, something like two years to go. But you could start sooner. That's why we talked about it so you'd know what was happening and not be scared. Right?"

Alna nodded.

"Was Ashley prepared? Did she know what to do?"

"Yeah." Alna jumped off the bed. "Can we go out to eat?"

And just like that the subject was over.

"I guess so." It amazed Viv how children could at times simply get what information they needed and move on, and at other times pursue a subject to exhaustion.

"What else are we gonna do?"

"Don't know, but I'm sure you'll think of something. Now, busy yourself while Mommy finishes getting ready." Viv kissed the top of Alna's head.

Alna walked backward down the hall toward her room. "I'ma make you a picture."

Viv stood in the doorway. "Okay. But I like pretty colors. Lots of yellow." She'd wanted a boy (she'd lost a baby boy), but there was something about little girls.

Alna turned around and disappeared into her bedroom.

Viv closed the door.

In truth, she was finished getting ready, but her conversation with Al presented a situation needing Viv's direct attention.

Alna inquiring about getting her period wasn't a matter of concern.

How long it had been since she'd last had her own, however, was.

Viv grabbed her purse from the chair next to her bed and rummaged for her pocket calendar. No fancy-shmancy electronic thing like Louise kept telling her to get, but a plain-old calendar booklet: the two-year variety with its list of holidays, anniversary gifts, and flowers of the month.

Viv didn't know why, and she supposed most women did, but even as a married adult, she kept track of her cycle in a personal calendar. Of course, between the ages of thirteen and maybe twenty-one, Viv believed the "first day of the LMP" to be a critical piece of information during a young lady's life. After you were grown and married, you kept track of it, just not as diligently, Viv supposed, because then you were "safe." If you became pregnant, no big deal.

But if you were straying, well, that first day of the LMP reclaimed its rightful place of importance.

Viv was one of the "lucky" ones. Since day one, her cycle was regular. Without fail, every twenty-five to twenty-seven days her friend would show up for a five-day visit. She only missed her period when pregnant.

Slumping in the chair, Viv opened the calendar.

She reviewed the days of previous weeks, looking for her telltale star indicating the day she'd come on. A couple days had tiny 'JRs' written on them: days she'd slept with Jonathan. Those days were important depending on the date of her telltale star.

Finding her star, Viv counted the weeks forward. Her heartbeat picked up. She counted the weeks. The pipes made a noise, startling her. Viv counted the weeks twice more and found it possible to slump further in the chair. "Six weeks," she whispered.

She sat up and covered her open mouth with a hand, looking around the bedroom. She'd been so preoccupied with everything else, she'd obviously lost track. Keeping track of her period wouldn't have kept her from getting pregnant (she'd seen enough proof that the rhythm method had its drawbacks), but realizing she'd forgotten about it proved sobering.

"I don't believe this shit!" Viv threw the calendar across the room. It fluttered, like a wounded bird, behind the trunk stationed below the window. Viv was on the Pill (and she'd just fallen into the 1 percent fail rate). Jonathan used condoms (which broke on two occasions, so no failsafe there). Rick didn't use anything, but then he didn't have to. Rick was the husband, after all; getting pregnant by him shouldn't be a big deal. Except right now, it was a very big deal. "Dammit," she muttered.

Alna knocked on the door. "Mommy, I'm finished."

"Come on in, sweetie." *No use worrying about anything until first finding out if I am.* She was going to enjoy this day with her little girl.

Viv's calendar-check also reminded her that she and Rick had an appointment with Louise's Dr. Alexander on Monday. She didn't look forward to that at all.

"And the hits just keep on comin'," Viv sighed as Alna entered. She carried the sweetest marker-drawing of a garden Viv had ever seen. And all the flowers—from tulips to daisies to roses to some unrecognizable—were yellow.

"You like it?"

"Very much."

"Me, too."

"Let's go. Mommy's hungry, too." It was the sweetest lie.

It turned out to be a pleasant day simply because Viv enjoyed the time with Alna. And Al did come up with plenty to do. There was breakfast, followed by the Children's Museum, the park, and the toy store. Viv, of course, made a mandatory stop at the pharmacy for a pregnancy test.

The ladies didn't return until well after four that afternoon. Alna busied herself in the family room with a new DVD from the toy store. Figuring Rick wouldn't be home for at least another hour, Viv carried her latest purchase to their bathroom.

It took seconds. Viv hadn't even finished peeing before she could see the results were positive. She waited the obligatory amount of time, and reread the instructions several times, searching for the loophole. There wasn't one. She was pregnant. Of course, she should consult her doctor, blah, blah, blah. But that was all academic. She was pregnant. She now understood the recent bouts of nausea and why she was so tired.

Those "JR" days were important now.

Viv retrieved her calendar from behind the trunk. She had a good understanding of ovulation and pregnancy (having regular cycles was a bonus). There were no guarantees (she was pregnant using birth control, after all), but she still believed those marked dates would give her a good idea who the father was.

She searched for the dates. She counted and calculated twice before placing the calendar back in her purse. She picked up the test, staring at it for several seconds. She sighed and sucked her teeth.

Viv put the test back in its box, wrote the date on it, and put it in a shoebox on the closet floor. She called Jonathan's cell phone and left a voicemail message.

As she went downstairs to sit with Alna, Viv was surprised to find she wasn't all that unhappy.

CHAPTER 8

Launching Pad

Naomi gazed out the huge picture-window of her fourth-floor office, holding her Einstein bobblehead while watching the activity on the lot below. She moved into the building when the office park opened two years ago, and remained pleased with her decision. She didn't like working downtown anymore, and even with twelve minutes added to her commute, when the opportunity to move into this building presented itself, Naomi took advantage of it.

She watched the activity (people arriving, others leaving, deliveries being made), but was very much aware of the couple sitting behind her.

Richard and Vivian Phillips (now Rick and Viv) arrived fifteen minutes early in separate cars. Naomi noted that while looking through the window earlier. They entered her office as a couple, though, and then made soup of her telephone-impression of them.

The two made quite an attractive couple. Although slim for Naomi's taste, Rick was exceedingly handsome. Viv was a looker, too, though. With skin the color of butterscotch, her soft, chestnut hair had touches of auburn. She had these gorgeous, wide, round eyes and high but delicate cheekbones highlighting a dainty nose—very pretty. She was taller than average (like Leslie) but with fuller hips. Naomi noted Viv's small waist and rounded breasts in the nut-brown cotton sweater she wore.

Their daughter is probably too cute for words.

Once seated in front of Naomi's desk, making general conversation, Naomi was again reminded of how wrong initial impressions can be.

During her telephone conversation with Rick, he came across as uptight and standoffish; the answers on his pre-therapy questionnaire indicated pretty much the same. During the teleconference when Rick wanted to confirm their appointment with Viv, she came across as easy-going.

Now, after speaking briefly with them in her office, Rick appeared the calm, collected one, and Viv more reserved and uptight.

Naomi was a psychiatrist, knowing people her job; her first impression had not been far off. Sensing Einstein bobbling his agreement in her hand, Naomi watched the people below.

Something's changed since they made the appointment.

And for her own curiosity, as well as her role as family therapist, Naomi was going to find out what.

The Phillipses waited patiently behind her. Naomi turned to them and smiled. "Why don't you two come sit over here." She gestured toward a mustard-yellow leather seating-group separated by mahogany tables. "We've got work to do."

Rick rose immediately. "'Work'? Are we that bad? It's only been what, ten minutes or so?"

Viv hesitated before following her husband.

Naomi sat in the huge mustard-yellow chair, placing her Einstein bobblehead on the table beside her. She was surprised but pleased Rick and Viv sat relatively-close on the sofa: deep down, they wanted this to work. "I'm not saying you're bad at all, Rick, but you're here, right?"

Without looking at each other, Rick and Viv nodded.

"So, there's work to do."

"Because being happy takes work," Rick murmured.

Naomi nodded. "You got it."

Viv brushed a pant leg. "Don't we have to fill out more questionnaires or interpret some sketches, or role-play or something first?"

"Why? This isn't a science experiment. I'm not paying you; you're paying me. I'm about giving you your money's worth. Besides, you've completed my pre-therapy questionnaire; isn't that enough? Now, there are techniques and tools used during therapy, but I don't use them exclusively. If you're looking for perceived conventional methods of therapy, I'm not the one. Well, except for the talking-thing."

"We can do that on our own," Rick said.

Naomi didn't respond.

Viv got it. "We can, but we don't, Rick, not like we used to. We talk, but …"

"But …?" Naomi prompted.

"But it's not the nitty-gritty talking like before," Rick offered.

"Okay. My job is helping you get back to that. Back to relating with your guards down, so to speak."

"Oh boy, here we go …" Rick shook his head.

Naomi looked quizzical. "What?"

"You're getting ready to get all Zen-like, aren't you?"

"No. Look, I'm going to say one thing, and then ask one question. We'll proceed from there. Deal?"

"Deal," Rick and Viv replied simultaneously. They looked at each other this time.

"Most of my therapy is rooted in the idea that people can pretty much do anything, from creating to resolving, using good, old-fashioned common sense. True physiological impairments in the workings of the brain exist for certain cases of mental stress, but that's something else altogether. I'm talking the day-to-day stuff we end up having problems with. A little common sense goes a long way. That doesn't mean I don't use my medical background in therapy. I do, just not solely." Naomi paused. She focused on the tomes along her bookcase on the wall behind the sofa before returning her gaze to the couple. "Now, that said; shall we continue?"

Rick cleared his throat.

"Yes." Viv spoke more to herself than to Naomi.

Rick looked at his wife, seeming both surprised and pleased.

"Rick?" Naomi prompted.

Rick cleared his throat again. "Sure, okay."

"Very good." Naomi checked the clock on the bookcase behind Rick and Viv. "You have about a half-hour left, but once we get going, that time'll fly by." They had less than that, but Naomi wanted the extra time with them. For the first time in a long while, a case intrigued her.

Naomi watched Rick and Viv survey her office in silence. They truly looked good together. "Is my office suitable?"

Viv gave a sheepish grin. "Well, where do we begin?"

"Anywhere. With me, the conversation should just flow. Sometimes I'll take notes or even record. You both already understand the confidentiality aspect, so my advice is to say what you want—don't worry about my approval or opinion about what you say."

"Okay," Viv said.

"That'll work," Rick added.

Still, no one spoke. And Naomi's office again became ever so interesting to the Phillipses.

"Need me to get things started?" It wouldn't be the first time she had to get the ball rolling with patients.

Rick and Viv each shrugged.

They're in tune with each other, too—another good sign.

"Okay. Let's start out slow and easy. Viv, do you love Rick?" It was a simple question—fully loaded.

"Yes."

And Naomi could see that she did. Her eyes were direct with true emotion over him. She crossed her legs, though, so there was another level to reveal. Her trendy, round-toe pumps matched her sweater perfectly.

Naomi turned to Rick. "Do you love Viv?"

"Yes." Rick looked at his wife. "Yes."

"Is the emphasis for me, you, or Viv?"

"Her."

Viv now found the swirls in the sofa's leather upholstery something to behold.

"Did Rick need to emphasize he loves you?"

Viv kept her eyes on the sofa. "No, but I understand why he did."

"We'll address that shortly. My question now, is: Do you believe him?"

"For the most part." Viv's black eyes locked on Naomi's mud-brown ones. The look said to drop it.

Naomi ignored it. "That's a yes, then?"

Rick leaned forward. "Why are we talking about this? We're married, aren't we? We're here, aren't we? Love must be in this somewhere." Traces of Southern-dialect laced his speech.

Naomi sensed he was in the habit of protecting his wife.

Viv sighed. "Let's just do this, Rick."

Naomi sensed Viv was in the habit of calming Rick down.

Viv looked at Naomi. "Yes, I believe him."

Naomi allowed the silence to linger. She was about to go into a topic sometimes uncomfortable for her patients. Its relevance to how she approached individual therapies, however, was more important than a patient realized. Rick, however, opened the door for it. "So, Rick: what's wrong with getting 'all Zen-like'?"

Rick sat back and crossed his left ankle over his right knee. He wore heavy-duty hiking boots with caramel dress pants, matching suit vest, a white dress-shirt, and a copper silk tie with bronze stripes. He'd knotted his tie with the Van Wijk knot, creating a layered cylindrical effect. Naomi thought both his tie-knotting and boot-wearing rather cool. She gazed at the sole's pattern while waiting for Rick's answer. The sun (higher now in late-morning) filtered in, adding light and shadow to the mazes of the sole's grooves.

"I have dress shoes in the truck," Rick offered. "They usually stay in my bag until I'm at the office or at Mass."

Naomi looked at the couple.

Rick returned her gaze.

Viv looked out the window.

"Oh, pay me no mind. I was waiting for your answer, and the pattern caught my attention." Naomi added: "And please don't feel like you have to explain every little thing to me."

Naomi directed her response more to Rick, but Viv responded: "Okay." She checked her watch and sat back, too.

"Go 'head, Rick," Naomi prompted.

"Oh, nothing's wrong with it, I guess. If that's your thing and all."

"I see. And what's your 'thing'? You mentioned attending Mass."

"I'm Catholic."

"How long?"

"All my life."

"And is that working for you?" This was where things could get funky, so Naomi tensed as she watched the couple for reaction to the question.

Rick appeared totally perplexed.

Viv, on the other hand, offered Naomi something she rarely saw when she posed that question. Viv continued looking out the window, but the corners of her mouth turned up in a very knowing way.

Naomi's excitement about working with the couple increased.

Rick spoke softly: "What kind of question is that?" He looked around the office as if fearful of being overheard.

Viv glanced at Naomi before trying to read the awards, certificates, and plaques adorning the wall. She crossed her legs at the ankles. Her right foot shook rhythmically.

"It's a pretty-straightforward one, I think, Rick. If you're not sure, it's perfectly okay to say so."

"I guess I don't know what you mean by 'working.' Can you elaborate?" Rick uncrossed his leg and sat forward.

"It's a spiritual question, Rick, that's all. As a practicing Catholic, do the rituals and doctrines of Catholicism satisfy you spiritually? Again, it's perfectly okay to say you don't know."

"Why— Why are you asking about God and stuff? I mean, shouldn't we be talking about our marriage? That's why we're here."

Naomi glanced at Viv, who wasn't yet finished with the wall. She continued shaking her foot, and that knowing hint of a smile changed to a smirk. Naomi truly wanted to hear from Viv, but it was important to keep the focus on Rick. She spoke reassuringly to him: "Yes, it is, but given that marriage is an institution of most religions, isn't that a good place to start? Getting a feel for your individual religious or spiritual backgrounds gives me a clearer understanding of how each of you approaches marriage."

Leaning back, Rick laced his fingers and placed his joined hands over his belt buckle. He sighed heavily. "Man, this is deep for a first session."

"Told you we had work to do."

"That you did," Rick agreed.

"Okay then." Naomi smiled. She so enjoyed throwing people off-guard. She turned her attention to Viv. "So, you're Catholic, too?"

Viv returned her gaze to Naomi. "No. My family's Baptist but I sometimes attended Methodist services while in college."

"And since college?"

"Well, I attend my home-church whenever I can, and go to Mass with Rick and Alna as a family frequently."

"So, no declared religion?"

"Declared? No."

"And now I'll ask you, although Rick has yet to answer." Naomi looked pointedly at Rick before continuing. "Is that working for you?"

Viv looked out the window again, sans smile.

Naomi turned her attention to Rick while she waited. He tensed while waiting for Viv's response.

He faced in right profile to Naomi, and she again noted how fine he was: smooth cinnamon-brown skin, strong jawline, straight nose, and long, thick eyelashes. Naomi couldn't tell his exact eye-color, but his eyes weren't dark-brown (red?). He was clean-shaven except for his soul patch and a moustache over kissable lips. His haircut was flattering. The low-afro temple-fade, tapered at the nape of his slightly-coiled hair, had a sharp, clean lineup.

Plenty handsome men sat in her office, plenty did, but this Rick Phillips was something else altogether. She noticed, however, a small imperfection: a raised scar on his right ear curving over the top of his ear cartilage. The imperfection complemented Rick's good looks. She returned her attention to Viv.

"Viv?" Rick prompted.

Viv looked at Rick, and then Naomi. "Yes, Doctor Alexander. It's working fine." She turned back to the window.

"You know, normally, I don't mind patients addressing me as 'Doctor Alexander.' With you two, I'd prefer 'Naomi.' Okay?"

"Fine with me." Rick shrugged. Naomi noticed his cleft chin, too—a royal flush.

Viv grinned. "Okay."

"What's your 'thing,' Naomi?" Rick asked.

The question surprised her, but she answered honestly. "God."

"God?" Rick repeated.

"Yes." Naomi held Viv's attention now, too.

Rick frowned with mild-confusion. "Well, everybody's is 'God.' What kind of answer is that?"

"I agree that, to some degree or another, most people's 'thing' is God. For me, though, that's all there is—God. No rules. No mandated rituals. Just love for God and praise for God's gift of the life experience."

"So, in other words, 'no declared religion.'" Viv said.

Naomi nodded. "Right."

"But don't you think people need rules?" Viv asked. "It provides a sense of organization."

"God gave us ten simple rules and we humans reworked them and 'reinterpreted' them to death, let alone outright breaking them.

I agree that rules are needed for some things, such as laws to protect people. But rules, or too many of them, get complex, complicated, then contradictory. I just don't happen to feel or believe God is any of those things."

Viv looked thoughtfully out the window, nodding slowly.

"But what about the Bible, and Jesus, what about—" Rick stopped midsentence, clearly thrown by Naomi's remarks.

Naomi was used to it. "I believe in the importance and significance of both of those and probably, to some degree, whatever else you were about to name." She again adopted a reassuring tone. She didn't believe discussions about God should be confrontational and avoided letting talks get heated.

"The 'importance and significance'?" Rick sat on the edge of the sofa cushions now, supporting himself with forearms on his thighs. The bronze stripes in his tie shimmered. "You don't believe the Bible is the Word of God? That Jesus was the Son of God, and died for our sins?"

"Well, not all religions believe that, anyway. Your questions are central to religions of the Western world," Naomi said.

"The other religions aren't the true religions. The Bible says so."

"The Bible also says, 'Judge not lest ye be judged,'" Naomi replied.

"Matthew seven, verse one," Viv recited. Her attention remained on the view outside.

"Very good," Naomi said.

"So, anyway, do you believe the Bible is the Word of God or not?"

"I believe the Bible is the Word—but not word for word." Naomi checked the clock. This discussion could go long. She needed to get the focus back where it belonged. "Look. We have plenty of sessions going forward if you want to talk about this more, but let's—"

Rick raised a hand with a gentle wave and then lowered it. "Wait, hold up. I get your meaning about the Bible. Not saying I agree, just saying I got your meaning. What about Jesus being the Son? What's your take on that?"

"I believe Jesus to be the Son of God. However, many religions teach that we're all God's children. In that light, Rick, you, too, are the Son of God. Being gender-respective, Viv and I are Daughters of God."

"Ah, but the difference is Jesus was God also," Rick challenged mildly.

Naomi chose to ignore it. "Okay."

Viv didn't speak, but Naomi saw she paid attention to the exchange.

"Okay?" Rick sat perilously on the edge of the sofa cushions.

"Okay," Naomi confirmed. "Look, I'm not disagreeing with you, so first: calm down. Discussions about God shouldn't be combative, so I'm not arguing about it. Secondly, to be honest, I'm still working and praying on what I like to call 'the Jesus component.'"

Rick smirked. "Interesting choice of words."

"It's the best I've got for now. Can we get back to the two of you?"

"One more thing. But I'm not saying this won't come up again."

"As long as it's not in today's session."

"Done."

"Shoot."

"I got your 'word for word' meaning, but would you to expound a bit?" Rick glanced at Viv.

Sometimes, in fact, most times, Naomi enjoyed sharing her personal spiritual views; it helped nurture her spiritual journey. But not today. She wasn't trying to convince anybody of a thing, but it seemed that's exactly what Rick wanted. Naomi watched the couple. She leaned toward Rick—matching his body posture. She wasn't being confrontational, but she did want to drop the subject once she finished speaking on it.

"Actually, I'm surprised you're so interested in talking about this. I usually get a beat of silence followed by a dismissive glance, like I've just been released from a psych-ward or something." Naomi couldn't help chuckling at the irony in her statement. The idea of the shrink being released from the mental hospital struck her as funny.

Rick and Viv didn't get the joke.

Naomi continued: "Anyway, I believe the Bible was written by men inspired by God. So, yes, the Bible is from God. With that comes the understanding that those men, at that time, still relied on their individual interpretations. Many stories in the Bible are similar. I believe it's because God is sending core messages to us. Most refer to it as the Golden Rule."

"Luke six, verse thirty-one."

"Right again, Viv. Your father a minister?"

"A deacon."

Naomi winked. "Same difference."

Viv nodded. "Pretty much."

Both women shared a brief laugh.

Rick smiled. "So, you believe it's all about doing unto others."

Naomi thought his smile was one for the books. "For me? Yes. If the world stuck to that one way of living, all the rest isn't necessary. If you don't want someone backstabbing you, don't backstab anyone. Don't want people lying to or about you? Don't go to fibnation on or about anyone. Want people to love and respect you for who you are? Do the same for others. And so on."

Rick raised an eyebrow. "'Fibnation'?"

Naomi nodded with a shrug and a smile. "You'll get used to my Naomi-isms. Fibnation: land of lies."

The couple looked at each other with nods.

Rick grinned. "I like. What about envy? I know plenty people who like the idea of others being jealous of them."

"That's true. But that's where another of the Bible's messages comes through, probably the most important one: for us to love each other as God loves us."

"John fifteen, verse twelve," Viv chimed in.

Naomi gave Viv a sideways glance before looking at Rick. "If we accomplish that kind of love, I don't believe envy and all the rest would enter the picture. That kind of love cancels out the negative. If we're loving one another, the Golden Rule falls into place naturally."

Rick scoffed. "Yeah, but living up to that standard …"

"Well, we've had role models who've come close: Jesus, Mother Teresa. But okay, living up to that standard is hard by itself. Why then, add rule after rule, law after law, to make things confusing and complicated, when the One Request hits the nail on the head?" Naomi sighed. She'd already said more than she wanted. "The Bible to me is a starting point, but I believe God speaks to each of us today, encouraging us to honor simple, unchanging messages." Naomi checked the clock again.

"Well that was interesting." Rick finally relaxed enough to sit back on the sofa. "But since you're checking the clock, I guess you'd like to move on."

"You aren't paying for spiritual counseling, so, yes: I would like to talk, for a hot minute, about why you're here."

"How much time is left?" Viv's eyes held a different light, her posture less-guarded. She seemed more like the woman Naomi spoke with on the phone.

Naomi hadn't a clue what brought the change on. "Enough."

"So where do we start?" Viv asked.

"Same place I told you earlier—anywhere. Rick's Catholic and I understand you're currently undeclared. That helps. But if you need a starting point, I'll give you another one, but it's weighty for a first session. Ready?"

"Sure," Rick answered.

Viv nodded. "I guess. We don't have to answer if we don't want to?"

"Correct. I can't force anything out of you. But if it's key to what's going on with you two, it'll come out eventually."

Viv sighed. The enthusiasm in her eyes dimmed.

Naomi frowned curiously. "Is it that bad?"

Viv shrugged.

Naomi found that telling.

Rick, however, confirmed Naomi's feeling that there was at least one identifiable problem. "Oh, you know."

Naomi raised her hand in a waving-stop motion. "Wait. I haven't even asked the question."

Viv didn't acknowledge Rick, keeping her eyes on Naomi. "Ask your question, Naomi."

Naomi looked alternately at Rick and Viv. "Is a third-party involved here?"

Naomi fully expected their silence. She watched and waited patiently.

Viv did her best to keep a neutral expression. She was good.

But if this were poker, I'd be disposed to call her bluff.

Because, while Viv tried to stare ahead with a straight face, she failed on three occasions. Her eyes darted to each of her sources for emotional refuge in Naomi's office: the sofa's upholstery, the window, and the wall of plaques.

Rick, on the other hand, looked at Viv expectantly, his posture casting nothing but accusation and blame.

Viv finally spoke: "When you say 'third-party,' you mean …?"

Rick rolled his eyes upward with a sigh.

"Well, there is the obvious meaning—another lover. But third-party means exactly that. It could be anyone or anything really: best friend, vice, hobby, career, etcetera. In this instance yes, I'm asking about a person."

"I see." Viv settled on staring at the upholstery.

"Rick?" Naomi prompted.

Rick's eyes stayed on Viv. "Yeah?"

"The question was for both of you."

Rick turned to Naomi. "For me, in the past, yes. But we've gotten through that fine."

"That true, Viv?"

"Yes."

"Well, good, we won't ha—"

"No, I'm saying 'yes' to the third-party question."

Naomi glanced at Rick. "Okay. Are you speaking about yourself or Rick?"

"Me. How much time is left?"

"There's time. Want to cut it short?"

"No, go 'head."

"Is this person a lover?"

Viv focused on the far wall. "Yes."

"Male or female?" Naomi waited a beat. Neither appeared put-off by the question. Sign of the times.

"Male," Viv said.

"Does Rick know him?" Naomi watched Rick closely for reaction to Viv's answer. He no longer looked at Viv, but out the window, his jaw set. Rick moved the fingers of his right hand over the top of his ear. Not rubbing back-and-forth exactly, but moving over the place where Naomi noted the scar. Rick looked even more handsome in anger, and, oddly, sexual images of him came to her. Uncomfortable now, she shifted her gaze back to Viv.

Rick obviously grew tired of waiting. "Yeah, I knew him,"

"I see." Naomi noted Rick's use of past tense.

"Rick and I both were acquaintances of the guy we're talking about. And I say 'were' because, well, for obvious reasons Rick and he are no longer cool, although this person and I still are."

"You need a name?" Rick asked rather loudly.

Viv turned to him.

"No, I don't. How'd you get that scar, Rick?"

Rick continued fingering it. "Fight with a high-school girlfriend. I was fifteen; she was seventeen. She had a knife. I didn't."

"Rather young for relationship fights, don't you think?"

"Probably, but that's the deal." Edginess laced Rick's reply. He released his ear to pull imaginary lint from his pant leg.

Naomi sat forward as if ready to vacate her seat. "Well, black people, that'll do for today. I want to leave you with a few notions first."

Viv scooted forward, too. "A little sendoff?"

"Sort of."

Rick chuckled. "We're all ears."

"Still using 'we.' That's good."

Viv and Rick glanced at each other. And in that quick glance, Naomi saw the deep love between them still.

Naomi continued: "First, I want to say this session was a good one even if you can't see that. We may have gotten off-track there in the beginning …" Naomi looked pointedly at Rick. "But overall the session went well. Now, at the end of the sessions you may find you want a divorce …"

Rick and Viv didn't look at each other, but their eyes widened. Naomi placed another figurative checkmark in the "pro" column and responded to their wide-eyed expressions. "I'm only saying that I, as should you, take one session at a time."

Viv nodded.

Rick's face relaxed some.

"Now, I'm going to share something with you that my grandmother shared with my cousins and me. She would always remind us that a good marriage was like sweet buttermilk."

"Sweet buttermilk?" Viv repeated.

"Uh, I've had buttermilk," Rick said. "No such thing. I guess there's no such thing as a good marriage then."

"Not exactly."

"Here we go." Rick rolled his eyes upward.

Naomi chuckled. "Wait a minute, now. My Nana was on to something. Just listen. Yes, most people would agree that buttermilk on first taste is sour. But we also know many drink buttermilk like it was chocolate milk, don't we?"

Rick nodded.

Viv nodded, too. "My sister's one of 'em."

"Nana would say it was because in their mind, they somehow made the buttermilk less-sour, made it a taste they got used to and enjoyed."

"So how is a marriage like sweet buttermilk?"

"Not any marriage, Rick. A *good* marriage," Naomi corrected.

"Okay a *good* marriage then. I still don't get—"

"I do." The anxiety in Viv's eyes vanished. She smiled hesitantly.

Naomi smiled back. "Cool!"

"Is it a woman-thing, then?"

"No, Rick, listen." Naomi turned to be more one-on-one with him. "People who like the taste of buttermilk first had to change their attitude or perception of it, and they work at that every time they have some. Their taste buds still send sour signals to the brain, but somehow—"

"Mind over matter," Rick mused.

Naomi nodded.

Viv did, too.

"My Nana simply meant that a good marriage takes the right attitude and continued hard work. The two go together, or else things are sour. And, of course, there's always adding a little 'sugar' to make things sweeter."

"So, I'm supposed to convince myself that her cheating was okay? It doesn't work like that, Naomi."

Viv rounded on him. "I've done it enough times!"

There was a knock at the door.

"Pause, people." Naomi checked her watch and the clock behind Viv and Rick. She walked quickly to the door. It'd been years since needing to be interrupted for a session overlap. As a rule, she scheduled sessions with at least half-hour intervals to review the incoming patient's file and prepare for their session.

Rick and Viv's session eked into the next patient's prep time. Cathy, her resident, was at the door with the file since Naomi didn't come out for it as usual. Naomi opened the door. It wasn't Cathy, but Janet, Dr. Koenig's resident-assistant.

"Mister Rayburn's here, Doctor Alexander. Here is his file."

"Thanks, Janet." Naomi accepted Mr. Rayburn's file with relief. Mr. Rayburn was a new patient; there would be little in his session history for Naomi to review.

"You're welcome." Janet pulled the door closed.

Naomi walked to her desk, flipping through Mr. Rayburn's file. She put the file down and then turned to face the Phillipses.

Viv's foot shook steadily as she gazed out the window.

Rick focused on Naomi. He wore an expressive mixture of embarrassment, agitation, and bemusement.

Naomi folded her arms across her chest and leaned back against her desk. She didn't want the session to end, not at this point especially. Nevertheless, she proceeded to wrap-up.

"Well, as you can see, I need to prepare for my next patient. We're ending on a tense note: one I'm sure will be easily-resumed next session. What I'm about to suggest, however, may sound off, but really isn't. I want you to take a vacation, together, before our next meeting." She waited for her suggestion to sink in.

"A vacation ..." Rick pondered.

Viv's voice was low. "I don't think that's a good idea."

"It's a suggestion. Now, our next session is in two weeks. Monday, four thirty?"

"Yeah," Viv answered. "Naomi, I have a question."

Naomi hesitated.

"It's simple. Honest."

"Go 'head."

Viv nodded toward Naomi's left hand and the ring on her ring finger that wasn't a wedding band. "Are you married?"

"I *was* married."

"What happened?" Rick asked.

"See? I'll be here all night with you two." She did not want to travel this road.

Rick scoffed. "Hey, you're the one with the 'sweet buttermilk' and all."

"Rick," Viv cautioned.

"Nah, we may have someone counseling us who couldn't even save her own marriage."

Viv, probably sharing Rick's feelings on some level, turned to Naomi.

The question sat there among them.

Naomi needed to move on to the next session. She didn't want to answer Rick's question. It was a fair one. So what. Naomi decided she would need a shot of Hennessy before sitting down with Mr. Rayburn.

"My husband was murdered, Mister Phillips."

No matter how many times she said the word, "murdered" always felt cold, foreign, and heavy on her tongue. She always seemed to spit the word out at people.

Viv placed a hand to her chest. "Oh. Sorry, Naomi."

Rick's silence served his apology.

It was enough. "No problem. See you in two?" Naomi went behind her desk, the moment for shaking their hands gone now. She sat and opened Mr. Rayburn's file.

Rick and Viv made their way to the door.

Naomi found it within herself to ease the tension. "Viv, be prepared to expound on that last outburst. You too, Rick."

Viv's eyes flickered with anger before the couple nodded solemnly.

"And, guys, seriously: take a vacation." Naomi smiled.

The couple smiled back, yet Viv's smile was halfhearted. Rick let Viv out before him and closed the door behind them.

Before the door closed, Naomi took a last look at Viv's rear.

When the door closed, she opened her top desk-drawer, reaching into the back for the familiar.

CHAPTER 9

Lives

Rick sat at the table in his office, going over the final presentation for Arrington Enterprises. He'd reviewed it four times already; the presentation was fine. But he couldn't focus enough to move forward with anything else. Mark Dilworth sat across from him previewing the proposal for Donovan Industries, an up-and-coming biotechnology company, but Rick noticed every time Mark looked over the top of the folder at him.

The first session with Viv and Dr. Alexander wasn't as bad as he expected, but he couldn't concentrate on his work. He'd gotten Rast to shut up three days ago. To his surprise, he retained an adrenaline-high of sorts.

Rick closed the Arrington folder abruptly, startling Mark. "This is fine. Wanna go to Mick's? Or did you bring your lunch again?"

"I could eat." Mark Dilworth's gray eyes flashed. He was one of the few genuinely-cool guys Rick had the pleasure of working with. With his brown hair and pale skin, he looked the average Joe, but the women on their floor always had that certain-smile for him even though they knew he was married. Mark was stocky, but not dumpy; he took care of himself and it showed.

"Ah, the lunch of a single man today."

"Yep."

Rick smiled. One of the coolest things about Mark was his ability to just be. Having worked with him nearly six years, Rick never got the impression Mark tried to be anything other than what he was. When all was said and done, Rick considered him a friend.

He grabbed his jacket. Mark didn't wear one—despite it being barely-above fifty degrees outside. Even for springtime that was chilly, but Mark never seemed to mind.

Rick considered calling Viv. *Better not push it.*

He looked at Mark. "Let's go."

Mick's Carryout was a hole-in-the-wall joint, sandwiched between the new bookstore and the new super office-supply store off "L" Street. If you didn't know it was there and you weren't paying attention, you missed it. If you had a taste for something greasy, you went to Mick's.

Rick ordered a steak and cheese, while Mark opted for the turkey club and onion rings. Mick's was small, but instead of taking their food back to the office, they lunched standing at the shop counter.

Rick reached for the pepper. "So, eating out go'n be regular now?"

"Maybe. Barb and I are talking, but it's different, you know?"

Mark didn't know it, but Rick knew only too-well. He sighed. "I hear you. Hang in there, man. Never give up on your family."

"Yeah, you, too."

Rick looked up from his plate. "Beg pardon?"

"You heard me."

"What? Me and Viv?"

Mark raised his eyebrows and looked pointedly at him.

Rick leaned in closer. "How'd you know?"

"It was simple enough. You don't talk about her much. Not for weeks now. And two and two has always been four."

"I see." Rick chewed on a french fry.

"Viv find out about a new one?"

"Mark, you know I've been done, years now."

"Just checkin'. So, is it the whole baby-thing again?"

"Not really. Well, no. Given what's going on now, that hasn't even come up."

"Well, I can tell Viv's breaking your heart, not the reverse. What's up?"

Rick gestured at Mark's plate. "You done?"

"Not going to talk about it?"

"Nope."

"I want to finish my rings." Mark grabbed a section of newspaper left on the counter and casually perused it, wearing an amused grin.

"And since you're not in a sharing mood, I'll get my entertainment elsewhere."

Rick stared at him.

"It's cool, man. Finish your lunch."

For the next several minutes, Mark read and ate.

Rick just ate.

"Rick?"

Rick bit his sandwich. "Mm-hmm?"

"You knew the owner of DeTante's, didn't you?"

Rick casually finished chewing. "What do you mean 'knew'?"

"He's dead, man. His is the body they found Friday, only they were withholding the name and all. He's been," Mark read aloud from the newspaper, "identified as Jonathan Rast, owner of DeTante's Restaurant." He looked at Rick. "Didn't you and Viv know him?"

"What?! Yeah, we knew him." Rick shook his head. "I don't believe it." Having read the article earlier, he made it a point to count his french fries before continuing. "What happened?" For the first time, a hint of sadness surfaced.

"Paper doesn't say much other than he suffered from some sort of trauma. Of course, everything's all 'unofficial.'" Mark checked the article again, and then handed the folded newspaper to Rick. "Here. Wanna take a look?"

"Yeah, let me see." Rick took the paper from Mark. A picture of Rast smiled back at him. He pretended to scan the article, shaking his head solemnly.

"Think Viv knows?"

"I doubt it. She rarely follows the news on television, and she hates the newspaper. I'll call her, though. Let's roll."

During the walk back, Mark turned to him. "Some of us are headed to happy hour at Artie's Bar after work. You in?"

"Sounds good. I could use a drink right about now."

Back at Impetus, Rick sat at his desk and called his wife.

She answered on the second ring. "Systems Application and Development: Viv Phillips."

"Hey."

"Hey."

"Still configuring that new software for Werther-Grant?" Even with what was happening, he kept track of what was going on with her; they were friends.

"Final stages. And Arrington?" And apparently, she with him.

"Same here."

"Okay. You'll land 'em."

"Thank you. I uh …" He changed his mind about mentioning Rast.

"Yes?" Viv's voice was calm, warm.

"Just wanted to see how you were doin'. You know, after meeting with Naomi and all."

"I'm okay."

He didn't know what else to say.

"Rick, what's wrong?"

He briefly closed his eyes at the loving concern in her voice. "Look, um, I'm going to happy hour at Artie's with Mark this evening."

"Okay."

Rick could tell his call confused her. "Just wanted to let you know."

"Thank you," Viv said pleasantly, but still with concern.

Used to be, phone conversations ended with each saying "I love you." Used to be.

"'kay," Rick managed.

"'kay."

"Bye."

"Bye."

Rick hung up softly.

*   *   *   *   *

Seven hours later, Rick was home, sitting in the family room.

He hung out with Mark and the crew for maybe an hour, nursing a scotch and soda he didn't finish. Rick didn't care much for drinking during the workweek, but thought a stiff drink would mellow him out some.

Rick couldn't stand the restlessness. That now-familiar charge moved through him continuously. So much so, he couldn't keep still at Artie's and left early. He got home only to find the house empty. Viv and Alna were still at Louise's. He'd poured himself a glass of iced tea, grabbed a spoon and the jar of peanut butter, and now sat in the family room, in the glow of the sconces on the fireplace wall.

Having finished his glass of tea, he sulked while crunching on ice and thinking about Viv. He crunched absentmindedly, brooding over the woman at the center of his world, when he hit a cold-sensitive spot that sent him to his feet.

Rick threw his glass into the fireplace, barely hearing the tinkle of shattered glass through the haze caused by the pain in his mouth. "Damn her."

Pacing and holding his jaw, when the pain subsided, Rick loosened his tie and sat on the sofa, wondering when Viv and Alna would return. Even with the tension, he liked having them home.

He wondered about calling Louise's, but thought better of it. He wondered if he should turn himself in. It was a passing thought at best. He wondered what Viv's reaction was upon learning about Rast, then imagined her reaction if she found out he was responsible. That image alone convinced him to protect his family (what was left of it) at all cost. "I'm not losing my family." Rick paused his pacing to focus on David's picture sitting on the mantel. "I ... I can't."

Out of nowhere, his thoughts flickered to the gun box upstairs.

He shifted his gaze around the main level of their home, focusing intermittently on Viv's decorative woodwork pieces. Every piece carried a memory of either Viv or Alna. He loved them both so much. Viv's rejection of him and Alna for Rast hurt in an abstract way Rick couldn't tolerate. It infuriated him. "Damn her!"

He moved purposefully to the workroom.

Several of Viv's finished pieces lined the shelves of her homemade bookcase. She finished two figurines, a miniature rocking chair, three clock bodies, and two pieces of her latest interest: miniature shoes of wood.

Rick didn't hesitate. He crossed the workroom and pulled Viv's bookcase to the floor with a crash.

It wasn't enough. He grabbed a hammer from her Shopsmith and smashed every piece on the floor.

He was barely out of breath, so he was barely finished. Rick continued venting against Viv through her woodwork for another twenty minutes until he slipped on wood dust and landed on the floor, tendrils of shavings and small clouds of sawdust billowing around him, making him cough as he breathed it in.

His next target would've been the makeshift darkroom in their laundry room—a more-obvious reminder of Rast—but Rick didn't need that now. Besides, Alna loved photography too; he wasn't trying to hurt her.

Rick looked at his pants (dirty), his shirt (torn and dirty), and figured he looked a mess, but he felt good—better than good. He remained on the floor motionless, getting a feel for his body. The physical vent helped alleviate some of the restlessness, but adrenaline still surged.

He looked around at the destruction, unaffected.

The thrill-rush carryover from killing Rast gave him an exhilarating sense of power unfamiliar to him. "Oh yeah, I like this."

Rick sat for several more minutes just feeling the feeling, wondering what to do next.

The beep of the house security system let him know he didn't have long to figure it out: Viv and Alna were home.

CHAPTER 10

Cold Comfort

The house was dark when Viv pulled up, so she assumed Rick wasn't home yet. She parked on the driveway and entered through their front door.

Alna dragged her Cutesy-Girls backpack in behind her. "You okay now, Mommy?"

"Well, I'm still sad. Mister Rast was my good friend."

"I know." Alna spoke with an understanding that belied her years.

"Go on upstairs and get ready for school tomorrow. You should have been in bed a half-hour ago."

"Is Daddy home?"

"Alna, you walked into the house just like I did." Catching her tone, Viv paused and closed her eyes. Composed, she looked at Alna. "I don't think Daddy is home, sweetie. But I'll make sure he comes in to say goodnight. Okay?"

"Okay." Alna hesitated, but she went upstairs.

Viv locked the front door. She sighed heavily. Right after Rick called about his plans for the evening, Louise called, asking if she'd seen the paper. Jonathan's newspaper-smile echoed in her mind.

Viv entered the kitchen, appreciating the darkness and the quiet. Minimal light filtered from their workroom.

Rick must have forgotten to turn those lights off.

She had every intention of fixing a peanut butter and jelly sandwich she wasn't going to eat. They had dinner over at Louise's, where they'd spent most of the afternoon and early-evening. *Rick probably ate at happy hour.* Viv retrieved the peanut butter.

Fixing one of the easiest-to-prepare sandwiches in the world became a slow and methodical production. Spreading the peanut butter alone lasted two minutes. And the lump in her throat wouldn't go away no matter how much she swallowed.

She almost broke down at Louise's, but resisted then, too. She smoothed apple jelly to the edge of the bread crust better than any bricklayer could. *Crying was useless.* It took an entire minute to cut her sandwich into four perfect triangles. She tore a paper towel from the roll in the vertical holder and placed the sections neatly on the sheet, gazing down at her sandwich as any artist would his or her work.

A multitude of thoughts crowded her mind. She considered saving the sandwich for Alna, even entertained checking for sardines for the briefest of seconds. She wondered how Rick felt about what happened to Jonathan. *Guess that's why he went to Artie's Bar—to celebrate.* She knew she wasn't being fair to him, but having an attitude subdued the sadness. *If Naomi thought our last session ran over, wait till the next one.* Earlier in the day, she wanted to call Naomi; she had a genuine, soulful quality about her Viv liked.

Since Alna didn't come back as half-expected, Viv wrapped the sandwich in aluminum foil. Alna had to be tired. Watching a distressed parent surely wore a child out. Tired of reflecting and thinking, Viv wanted sleep. She went to the workroom to turn the lights off, and froze.

Viv saw Rick, but didn't see him. He was merely part of the canvas that was the nightmarish-painting before her. Her eyes simply could not take it all in. It was a long thirty seconds while her eyes and her brain debated what she saw versus what she wanted to accept. She knew her eyes sent valid images to her brain, but the brain insisted on sending repeated thoughts of "this is not real."

Turnabout is fair play, so in that same thirty seconds, Viv's eyes roamed Rick's relatively-untouched side of their workroom, and she wanted the Warrington hammer on the floor beside him.

Because at that moment of sadness and exhaustion, of confusion and now anger, Viv, with *gleeful* and malevolent forethought, could have easily taken that hammer to Rick's head as well as his precious cars and paints.

Instead, she looked at her husband, waiting for whatever angry words poised to come out of her mouth. *There are no words for this.*

Rick had yet to look at her. He sat, leaning against the felled bookcase, staring ahead vacantly. Fury rocked her center, but something about the way Rick sat among the destruction touched her.

Viv traversed the space between them carefully (seeing her cracked safety glasses amidst the ruin) and stopped before him.

Rick looked up at her.

Viv couldn't read his eyes. She saw hurt, yes, but also a strange element of something she couldn't place. Nevertheless, Viv kneeled and pulled Rick to her, cradling his head.

She stayed there with him, smelling his Hugo Boss cologne through the pervasive scent of sawdust, enjoying the feel of him despite herself. She wasn't entirely sure why Rick did this, though she had some idea given all that had happened (Jonathan, trial-separations, therapy).

But enough was enough; someone needed to start feeling better.

They stayed on the floor for some time in silence. Then, without speaking, Viv disengaged from Rick and they headed upstairs—to separate bedrooms.

And it was Viv after all who felt better.

*   *   *   *   *

Over the next few days, Viv settled into a routine of sorts with Rick that held less-tension, and their daughter responded positively in turn. They didn't discuss Jonathan's passing, however, and Viv understood completely when Rick declined her request to escort her to Jonathan's funeral.

Dressed in a pearl-gray suit (she considered wearing black), Viv stood at the back of St. Augustine of the Holiness Church, clutching Jonathan's obituary. The morning sun shining through the stained-glass windows of the dim sanctuary provided a hint of majestic yet serene lighting that, while appropriate for a funeral, gave Viv the heebie-jeebies. *What is it with me and Catholic men?*

Seeing Jonathan's open casket, she decided not to view his body, not wanting to remember him that way. Many attended the service to pay their respects to Jonathan and his family. Viv walked down the center aisle to the middle pews and found a seat.

Jonathan's mentee, Horace, gave the eulogy. Viv met Horace once when Jonathan subbed for him at a recent event to feed the homeless.

Viv listened to Horace, finding it easy to relate to his words about Jonathan's character and accomplishments. She loved Jonathan. She did. But it was the love for a good friend, not the profound, passionate, soulmate love most searched for.

The only person I've had that with is Rick.

But her day-to-day life with him had become so insipid she didn't know what to do anymore. Jonathan, with his entrepreneurial way of thinking, travels, and interest in photography, gave Viv an element of excitement she'd been missing lately. Nevertheless, she shared bonds with Rick that could never be broken, one of which: Alna. But having another baby, regardless of the father (and she still didn't know how to handle *that* situation), meant limiting herself even more. It sounded selfish, but so what; not everybody wanted to be Carol Brady. Viv liked the homebody-thing, too—but not all the damn time.

If Jonathan lacked anything, it was sexual prowess. Rick had that hands down. If she could combine Rick's hot lovemaking and sense of responsibility with Jonathan's appetite for adventure, she'd be hooked. In fact, if Rick simply reclaimed the man he used to be, she'd be re-hooked.

As Horace gave closing remarks, Viv shifted uncomfortably. Engaging in petty criticism at such an inappropriate time wasn't cool. *Besides, Jonathan's gone now, so several questions have been answered. Telling him about the baby is a dead issue. Pardon the pun.*

A small giggle started somewhere around Viv's tonsils. She covered her mouth, hoping she appeared to be covering a sob and decided she'd better leave. Grief aside—for whatever reason—another part of her wanted to laugh (a disservice to Jonathan's memory). The soloist began her rendition of "You'll Never Walk Alone."

Viv took that as her cue.

She excused her way down the pew to exit on the side-aisle rather than the center. A few heads turned her way, but Viv hardly noticed.

The figure entering the church captured her attention.

Viv watched Rick stand at the back of the church checking the rows. He wore his cadet-gray suit with the ice-blue tie Louise gave him for Christmas. He tied his tie with an Ellie knot—one of Viv's favs.

Rick hadn't shaved since Viv found him in the floor. He looked divine. Her body stirred just seeing him. Still, his arrival baffled her.

What is he doing here?

Rick caught her eye. Reading her expression, he shrugged sweetly.

It was such an honest and endearing gesture; Viv softened inside— and fell for her husband a little more.

*　*　*　*　*

"So now, suddenly, everything's all better?" Louise looked skeptical.

The Collinses were hosting Sunday dinner. Viv sat with Louise while Rick and Louise's husband, Timothy, visited a neighbor, and Alna played in the backyard with little Tim Collins.

With her days of nausea diminishing, Viv chanced munching on a tortilla-chip as she watched Louise move about the kitchen. She'd spent the last twenty minutes recapping events in the Phillips household, and that was Louise's response. After Rick, Louise was her closest friend, but she was glad Louise didn't know she was pregnant.

"I didn't say that, Lou."

"That's what it sounds like." Louise was born in Vietnam. When she was seven, her family moved to the United States, living in Chicago and then Washington, DC. A Howard University alum, she met big Tim at one of his Alpha Phi Alpha fund-raisers. Her straight, black hair was pulled into a ponytail. Louise possessed the same small stature as most women of her country, but her cool, laid-back manner often overshadowed her ethnicity.

Louise prepared chicken for dinner. The smell of the blood juices reminded Viv she wasn't out of the nausea-woods yet. "I know what it sounds like, Lou."

"Do you, Vivian?"

Uh-oh, she was 'Vivian' now. Louise obviously wanted to make a point. Viv did know how it sounded, but it wasn't what she meant. "All I'm saying is this was a good week, for lack of a better word, for Rick and me."

"Did he tell you why he wrecked your stuff?"

"No, but it's pretty obvious. I may bring it up in our next session with Naomi …"

"You should, but you may not have to. Naomi has a knack for bringing things out for you." Louise paused and locked eyes with Viv temporarily before returning her attention to the chicken. "Or so I've heard anyway."

"Lou ...?"

"... Two years ago. After that little girl died in my office, having an allergic reaction to the anesthetic. Remember how I wouldn't let Li'l Tim do much of anything after that? It was so stressful around here. A colleague offered Naomi's card, so ..." Louise turned on the water.

"You still going to her?"

"It wasn't just me. The three of us went sometimes. But, no, our sessions ended a year ago." Louise held the chicken under the running water for what seemed too long.

Viv and Louise were tight, so finding out this bit of info surprised Viv. But she wasn't hurt behind Lou not saying anything before. They were friends, not Siamese twins.

Besides, right now I'm guilty of withholding a few personal details myself.

Viv looked through the bay window into the backyard: Alna and Li'l Tim appeared to be racing on the swings. She never understood why going higher in the swing was considered "racing." The wave of nausea passed. Viv turned back to her friend. "She sorta reminds me of you."

Louise appeared to ponder that as she placed the roaster in a glass baking-dish. "Yeah: short and small, sharp and no-nonsense. I can see it." Louise looked at Viv a beat before both women laughed lightly. "I'm glad you like her. Lou did good. I hope she helps you guys."

"Yeah, Naomi's cool. I'm sure she'll help."

Louise walked to the stove and reached into the cabinet above it for seasonings. Rick told her time and again not to store her spices there. When Louise came back to the island counter, her serious expression returned. "But now you sound like you two don't need help anymore. What's up?"

"Well, Jonathan's gone, and I'm dealing with that. But since finding Rick in the workroom and holding him, I've wanted to comfort him. This whole thing started with me wanting to hurt him. That's part of the reason I told him about Jonathan in the first place."

"Viv, you always end up—"

"I know. But it's like Rick doesn't even need that from me anymore."

"What do you mean? It's only been a week."

"Yeah, but it's been enough for me to see a change in him, Lou. And the change isn't transient to me. It's like he doesn't care anymore." Louise's expression caused Viv to explain. "I don't mean he doesn't care

99

about Al and me. It's obvious he does. He's just … I don't know. I can't really get across what I'm trying to say." Viv paused, thinking about her husband. "I can't put my finger on what it is, but Rick's different somehow. And I like it. Fuck the dumb stuff."

Louise didn't speak. Viv watched her finish preparing the chicken. Lou then washed her hands before retrieving two bags of fresh green beans from the refrigerator. She set them and a large bowl on the table. Louise shifted a bag in front of Viv, then sat across from her and commenced picking the other bag of green beans.

Viv took the hint. She checked on the kids through the window.

"… So, you two hittin' it again?"

"No."

"No?"

"You heard me." Viv looked down at her hands as she snapped beans. It was a sound of Sundays long gone. "Not that I haven't wanted to," she added quietly.

"Oh, I know you well-enough to know that."

"Funny."

Louise looked over the bowl of snapped green beans at Viv. Her expression asked whom Viv thought she was kidding.

Viv averted her gaze.

"Thank you. Besides, that's a complication you don't need. Good."

Is that relief in her voice?

"One thing not complicated about us, is our sex life." She wanted to change the subject.

Louise moved away from the subject, but not far enough away. "So, I take it you've decided not to leave Rick?"

"I never said I wanted to carry it that far, anyway."

"Well it sure seemed like it until Jonathan died. Don't get me wrong, I want you and Rick together. Nothing against Jonathan, may he rest in peace, but you know I didn't care for you taking up with him."

"Why? Rick has—"

"Because I, too, feel family is very important. You know that, Viv."

"Yeah, but why do you take our situation so personally?"

"You're my closest friends."

"I know, but sometimes it seems like your mission in life to keep us together or something." Viv had been meaning to explore this for some time.

"I want my two friends together." Now Louise watched her own hands in bean-picking action.

"Even to my detriment?" Viv asked pointedly. "And I'm more your friend than Rick is."

"Of course not."

"Okay, so why—?"

"Because I just do, Viv! Okay?"

Lou's tone shocked her. "Okay."

The women grew quiet.

"Change the subject?"

Viv didn't have to answer. The sound of the garage-door lifting signaled the fellas' return.

Their timing couldn't have been better.

CHAPTER 11

Going Home

Rick stood by the round conference table in his office, picking up and putting down various pieces of project-related material littering the tabletop. He wanted to get a jumpstart on the upcoming presentation, but it wasn't working.

He put the papers down with a sigh and went to his desk, flipping through the pages of his schedule calendar. He and Viv had an appointment with Dr. Alexander next week.

She suggested a vacation. He and Viv were on better terms, but Rick had his doubts about Viv joining him. Reflecting on the tension between Viv and Louise at dinner the other night, he decided he and Viv would get away, maybe for the weekend, but he wanted to take care of a few things first.

On his lunch break, he visited Louise's office. Like most dental offices, hers seemed too bright; with a combination mint-and-rubber smell Rick found disconcerting—no smile could stand up to that lighting. When Louise entered, Rick noticed her give the slightest double take at seeing him.

In the fifteen or so minutes he was there, she revealed Viv thought their marriage was mending. Louise wouldn't look him in the eye. Usually, for a small woman, she could be a formidable presence, but during his visit, she seemed every bit as fragile as her slight stature would suggest.

When he thanked Louise for giving him Viv's side, there was a moment when Louise seemed ready to abandon her principles and cross the line (again). She did look him in the eye then, with a look and words of love, but she didn't try anything this time. Still, he avoided the unwanted scenario with a gentle hand to her shoulder. Louise lowered her head and apologized: to him and to Viv, explaining that her penance was ensuring he and Viv stayed together. Rick told her no apologies were necessary.

*   *   *   *   *

Six hours later, Rick sat in his Range Rover, parked in front of his childhood home. Viv sat in the passenger seat looking at him expectantly. It took little convincing to get her to come, but a trip home wasn't what Rick had in mind. Viv suggested they visit Hampton, Virginia. He didn't mind, but wished they'd brought Alna along so she could visit her grandfather.

"What's wrong, Rick?"

"Huh? Oh, nothing. Just thinking Dad's gonna want to see Al. Think we shoulda brought her?"

"Maybe, but she had two more days of school. And it's no big deal driving down here: a little over three hours. We can come back anytime."

"Then why don't we come more-often?" Rick asked rhetorically. He watched the house.

"Wanna spend the night in the truck? We can enter the house at daybreak or something." Viv smiled.

"Rim shot." Rick looked past Viv, at the house where he grew up. The two-bedroom rambler looked unchanged except for new windows installed in recent years. The front yard needed some weeding, but otherwise appeared well-kept. He admired the colorful blooms of the primrose bushes he and his mother planted decades ago.

Light came from the living room windows even with the curtains drawn. He called his father earlier and told him they were coming, so his dad was expecting them. "Come on." Rick opened his door. Weariness crept into his bones suddenly—and he had to pee.

He scanned his neighborhood, enjoying the cool April air. Years ago, there would've been more activity in the neighborhood. *We've all grown up and moved on: no one around now but the folks who raised us.*

The sound of Viv's door closing disrupted the quiet. Across the street a few houses down, dogs barked in unison. "Sorry, fellas."

Rick walked around the truck and opened the gate to the yard. "Fifth-generation Dobermans. The Henleys used to be breeders." He held the gate open for Viv. "After you."

Viv stared around her as she headed up the walk. "It's so quiet."

"Yeah, older folk like their peace." His bladder signaled impatience.

He opened the screen door and knocked. The doorbell seemed to glow with indignation. *I know my dad is right there in his chair, maybe fifteen feet away*, Rick reasoned with the doorbell. *Besides, knocking's better.*

"Well, there they are!" There was a sound of papers rustling before the door opened and Eugene Phillips stood before them.

"Hi, Dad. Scuse me, Dad." Rick hurried past his father.

Eugene chuckled. "Don't break nothin', boy. Where's your key?"

"Hi, Papa Phillips," Rick heard Viv say before he closed the bathroom door behind him.

Sounds of muffled conversation traveled to Rick as he relieved himself. He inventoried the bathroom while washing his hands. The identical wall and floor tiles were replaced recently. Rick couldn't believe his dad was able to find the same pale-blue, lavender, and white cross-stitch pattern they'd had since Rick was in fifth grade. Even after his mother left, his father kept the rooms in the house pretty much the same.

The refreshing scent of Zest dominated, but Rick thought he somehow smelled his mother's Dove. He turned out the light and stood in the narrow hallway, facing his old bedroom. Rick barely heard the radio in the kitchen, but he caught a bit of debate on how black Americans should invest their money.

His bedroom door stood ajar. Rick started to go in, but laughter from the living room drew his attention.

When Rick entered the living room, Viv and his dad were standing by the stereo console—one of those big types from the 1960s where the top lifted for access to the record player inside. Rick remembered having a good old time as a boy, with his brother, playing records on different speeds. The console was in good working order, but these days it served to display framed family pictures. Viv held one now.

Rick liked seeing Viv and his dad together. "What's so funny?"

"Your beautiful wife here is getting a kick out of your striped-shirt and plaid-pants." Eugene turned the picture around so Rick could see it. "What are you? Two, Three?"

Rick knew which picture his father meant without him showing it. "Something like that." He caught Viv stifling a giggle. "And I don't know why you think it's so funny. You were dressed the same way." Rick couldn't help grinning at his wife.

"Yeah, but it's still funny." Viv turned to Eugene. "Why on earth did you all dress us like that? I mean, dag, plaid *and* stripes?"

Eugene looked from Viv to Rick and back. He shrugged. "I don't know what to tell you."

Mild-laughter ensued before Eugene asked: "So, what brings you two down here? Where's my granddaughter?"

"Al has another two days of school left this week, so she's staying with a friend of ours. You know Louise, Dad." Without the laughter, it was too quiet in the house.

"I've known you to keep her out on a whim a time or two."

Viv removed her jacket. "Well, she and I had one of those 'whim' days recently, so another one so soon after was out. Alna's school work is more-involved now that she's in fourth grade." She handed her jacket to Rick. "We'll be cutting those school-break days out completely next year."

"Time to get serious 'bout fifth grade?" Eugene furrowed his brow with mock gravity.

"Time to get serious." Viv sat in Eugene's chair with a sigh.

Eugene looked from Viv to Rick. "That answered my second question."

Rick shared a glance with Viv. "Just wanted to get away awhile—and Viv vetoed my other suggestions."

"Why the need to get away? You two all right?"

Rick, a tad warm himself now, removed his jacket, too. He knew only too-well how probing his father could be with his questions. He shared another glance with his wife who looked grown and sexy in her Howard University cap. "We're fine, Dad. So, what'd you fix? I know there's buttermilk pie, but it smells like you've been up to more than that." Rick tossed both jackets onto the sofa.

"Who said there was buttermilk pie? Nobody said anything about that."

Rick looked at his father calmly. "Oh, there's buttermilk pie."

"The infamous buttermilk pie. I forgot all about that." Viv lifted her cap and shook her hair, giving body to the flattened style.

The move turned him on, made his heart and groin stir for his wife; he missed her. "That's because you won't even try it."

Viv poked her tongue (something she hadn't done in ages). It tickled him, but he couldn't help wondering if rebound from losing Rast triggered her renewed interest.

Rick poked his tongue back, secretly wanting to twirl it with hers.

Eugene chuckled. "That's enough now." He looked at Viv. "There's oven-fried chicken and some crookneck squash in there, but if you'd like something else …"

"Oh, that's fine, Papa Phillips, but I'm sure Rick's going to pass on the squash."

"Damn skippy."

Eugene gave a quick shake of his head. "My boy and vegetables. I made fruit-salad for him, but there's enough to share if you want, Viv."

"And …" Rick looked at his father expectantly.

"And?" Eugene responded. "And, I don't remember my son greeting his father properly when he came in."

With an apologetic grin, Rick walked over to his dad for a power-shake embrace. He loved his father greatly. Rick knew he should visit more, but this empty house … "Sorry, Dad." Rick stepped back from the hug.

"No problem, son. Like the beard."

Rick continued looking at his father, waiting.

"Pie's in the freezer now."

Rick nodded curtly with a grin.

"What is it with you and this buttermilk pie? You don't even bother to make it at home."

"It's just good."

"Yeah, but buttermilk?" Viv shook her head, grimacing.

Eugene chuckled. "Oh, don't let that throw you. Actually, it's rather sweet."

"Like sweet buttermilk," Viv murmured.

Rick shared another look, this time a longer one, with his wife.

"Pretty much. Their mother often made it for the boys, but I started making it for them after Carol …" Eugene trailed-off, evidently unable to finish.

"It's okay, Papa Phillips," Viv offered, but Rick detected her unease.

"Any who!" Eugene clapped twice. "Ready to eat?"

"I know I am." Viv turned to him, just as beautiful as the day is long. "Rick?"

Rick smiled but didn't feel like smiling at all. He wanted (needed) fresh air. He wasn't claustrophobic but experienced something very close to it. "You know what? I am hungry, but I'ma step outside, clear my head." Rick looked to the window. The drawn curtains interfered with him getting a fix on the time. He looked back to his dad and wife. "The drive down's got me outta sorts. You two go ahead. I'll be back in a minute."

Eugene and Viv looked at him, concern on their faces.

Rick picked up his jacket, backed toward the front door, and opened it. His dad and wife stared—mouths open. "Y'all go 'head now. I'm fine." He opened the screen door. "Back shortly." He closed both doors behind him.

Rick breathed deeply, primrose filling his nostrils. He enjoyed his renewed sense of power, but with it came this restlessness he found refreshing and annoying at the same time. Redirecting the surges of restless energy wasn't easy. He realized he'd one day have a handle on the altered state taking over him, but the process was slow.

His model-car collection progressed nicely, though. Before, he averaged maybe a car a month. He completed five in the weeks since killing Rast. He experienced no anxiety whatsoever. He felt more-carefree is all and wanted to do stuff. He just didn't know what stuff.

Rick let out a sigh and surveyed the sky: around 7:17 p.m. Clear except for a dark, wispy cloud drifting to his right. It was twilight time—his time. He got in his truck and started the engine, immediately opening all the windows. Driving off, he smiled to himself, mentally tipping his hat off to Viv and her penchant for opened windows.

It was a short ride. When he pulled up, Rick figured a part of him knew his destination all along. He hadn't been here in four, maybe five, years.

He loved this place.

He hated this place.

Standing outside his Rover, Rick looked to his left at the schoolyard of St. Dominic's. The playground looked relatively-unchanged since his days as a grade-schooler. Memories of playing impromptu games of football—his uniform tie abruptly relegated to his back pocket—jolted him. The playground was old; the apparent attempts at a "facelift" didn't obscure that fact. The combination concrete-and-asphalt foundation was the biggest clue (no woodchips or foam absorption-padding installed here). Nevertheless, it was obvious children still played here.

His smile faded as he turned away to look straight ahead at the small hill he approached. He saw lights glowing from the windows of the convent at the top of the hill. Trees surrounded the convent. Rick focused on the top of one particular tree: *his* tree (it still had the inner tube from David's bicycle tied to an upper branch). He started up the hill.

The tang of mulch drifted to him. Weirdly enough, Rick liked the smell of mulch. He liked most earthy, natural scents.

Reaching hilltop, Rick paused, watching the convent. He'd always been comfortable in and around the convent, but today, for some reason, he wanted to get away.

The sun dipped even lower. Cool April air grew cooler as evening moved into night. Rick zipped his jacket and watched the sky. More than thirty minutes had passed since pulling up to the school, but what he came here for waited among the trees, regardless of how long it took. Not wanting any of the Sisters to see him, Rick quickly made his way to the trees (*his* tree).

The night was quiet except for the far-off sound of traffic at the bottom of the hill. No breeze rustled the leaves. Even the crickets were taking five. He stood among the trees, inhaling the smells of mulch and dirt. Rick smiled, remembering why he loved this place.

But the choking-sob lodged at the back of his throat brutally reminded him, why he hated this place.

*   *   *   *   *

"You think he'll be much longer, Papa Phillips?"

The squash was delicious, and Viv was on her third piece of chicken. She didn't realize the extent of her hunger until she started eating. *Southern home cooking will do that to you.*

Eugene Phillips sat across from her, sipping iced tea. He'd fixed himself a plate but hadn't eaten much at all. "Oh, I don't know." He wore an odd expression.

"You know where he is, don't you?"

"I have a good idea." He went to the refrigerator. "I'd better get this pie out. I wanted it to cool, not freeze. I'm sure no one wants Popsicle pie." He opened the freezer door and retrieved the treat.

In all her years being with Rick, this was maybe her third time being one-on-one with his father. She took another bite of chicken and watched her father-in-law in silence. Although totally at ease with him, Viv knew she touched on a subject where she needed to tread lightly.

Eugene placed the pie in the refrigerator section. On the radio, Crazy Car-man Cal screamed (for the gazillionth time) about his low, low insurance rates (Got points? No problem).

Watching him, Viv could see Rick a little, but Rick looked more like his mother. David was another matter. Looking at Eugene, she saw what David would've looked like as an older man. Eugene was a few pounds heavier since she'd seen him last, but that didn't detract from his good looks. He brought to mind what a sixty-seven-year-old Sam Cooke would have looked like.

Eugene checked the clock on the wall. He went to a cabinet closer to Viv and retrieved a plate. "Guess he'll be back soon enough." He began fixing what Viv guessed to be a plate for his son.

"Where is he, Papa Phillips?"

An expression of sorrow cross Eugene's face. He placed hearty helpings of oven-fried chicken on a plate, wrapped it in aluminum foil, and set the plate in the oven. He then pulled a storage container of fruit-salad from the refrigerator, put some in a smaller bowl, covered the smaller bowl with aluminum foil, and then set both items back in the refrigerator. He returned to the table and sat, keeping eyes on her as he took a long swig of iced tea. He set his glass down with a clink. "If I know my son, he's gone to his old grade school."

"Oh. ... Why does he keep putting himself through that? It's been over ten years?"

"Mournin' has no timetable, love."

"I know, but why doesn't he just go to the cemetery like normal people? That way, he can visit them both."

"How a person deals with loss cannot be dictated by anyone, Viv." Eugene's tone held authority, but his gaze softened.

Not quite sure how to respond, she ate a forkful of tasty squash. "You know, Rick rarely, if ever, talks about David or his mom."

"Right."

"I mean, he's so dogmatic about the importance of family, but rarely talks about his own."

Eugene focused on his glass. "… When Cissy came back, it wasn't the same for those boys."

Instinctively, Viv kept quiet. She edged her plate away from her and folded her hands on the table, wondering when her husband would return.

"You know, when Rick was born, he bonded with his mother and me naturally, of course, but from infancy, the attachment to his brother was strong. We all were close, but …" Eugene stared at his glass. The ice cubes shifted, tinkling against the glass. "Did Rick ever mention his mother leaving?"

"Only in passing."

Eugene nodded. "Sounds about right, I guess." He fell silent.

Viv wanted to ask why Mrs. Phillips left. Instead, she listened to the barely-audible voices coming from the radio—and became aware of the light leaving the kitchen.

"When Carol left us, the effect was exactly what anyone would imagine. We were lost at sea for a bit, but not for the reasons you'd expect. We kept the household going. Cooking, cleaning—didn't miss a step. The boys were teenagers when she left, but they were still at an age when they needed their mother. Her leaving devastated those boys."

"Rick was pretty bad-off, huh?" Viv found the whole thing hard to listen to.

"Well, yeah, but David was hit hardest."

"David?"

Eugene sighed. "Yeah, he just …" He shook his head.

As far as Viv was concerned, Eugene didn't have to finish. His expression spoke volumes. "But she came back."

Even in the subdued light, Viv saw anger in Eugene's eyes before he spoke. "Twenty-two months, three weeks, and two days later. But the damage had been done by then, you know? And, as much as I loved her, we just couldn't get back to how it was before she left." Eugene paused

110

and took a sip of the water from the melting ice. "Then again, I'm not sure I wanted to."

"But why? Things seemed pretty good here before she left. Why wouldn't you want that back?"

Eugene Phillips finally made eye-contact with her. "Because apparently for Cissy," he said, voice rising, "it was all a lie or something." He paused, seeming to compose himself. "I'm sorry, Viv."

She rested fingers on his wrist. "It's okay."

"I don't mean to imply Carol didn't love us. She did. It's just that I didn't know she was so unhappy until the day she said so—bags packed."

"But she came back, Papa Phillips. That's the important thing." Viv's mind went to her own somewhat abrupt announcement weeks ago. The kitchen was dark now, illuminated only by light coming from the living room. Eugene covered her fingers with his other hand. She realized she was holding her breath when Eugene finally spoke.

"Anyway," Eugene continued (his voice heavy with recollection), "she came back, and we made it work for another four years until she died."

Viv remained quiet. While dating, she visited Rick's family a few times, but Mrs. Phillips died before they married. On the radio, Viv scarcely made out a discussion on the importance of health care in foster facilities.

"Three years after that, David hanged himself," Eugene whispered. The gleam of a tear trailed his left cheek. Sniffing, he removed his hand from Viv's. He got up and walked to the entryway leading into the living room, where he stopped and leaned against the archway.

Standing in left profile, Eugene looked much younger. She even saw more of Rick now. He pulled a pipe from inside his sweater and a book of matches from his pants pocket. He smiled softly at Viv while he lit his pipe.

The smoky-sweet scent of pipe tobacco wafted to her, overtaking the cooking-smells of the kitchen. Viv loved the smell; it was so grandfatherly. *Alna must visit her grandfather more.*

Eugene didn't speak, but Viv knew he wasn't finished. On the radio, the host of the WKLB Upfront Hour closed his show. Crazy Car-man Cal would be on again any minute.

Eugene took a draw from his pipe and looked at Viv once more before staring into the living room again. "Richie found him. You know that? Found him in a tree on the grounds of St. Dominic's."

"Yeah, I remember. Rick and I had been married almost two years. We got a call. Can't remember if it was you or David—"

"Me. David had come home out of the blue. He'd do that from time to time while in grad school. But that last visit, he didn't hang around and work on his model cars or putter around with his ol' man like before. This time the boy just stayed holed-up in their old bedroom writing. Thought maybe he was working on his thesis or something." Eugene took another draw from his pipe. He grew quiet again.

Viv waited patiently.

"Turns out his writing had nothing to do with schoolwork, but after four days of it, I finally called his brother home. Rick was already on his way when David came out of the bedroom saying he needed to run a couple of errands and headed out the door. Shoot, I was so glad the boy was moving about—"

"You couldn't have known, Eugene."

"He was my son. It's not like I wasn't close to my boys."

"... You don't have to finish this."

"When Richie arrived, I told him his brother had stepped out. Musta been some kind of sibling-sense, because he made a beeline to their old room." He smoked his pipe.

The buzz-whir of the refrigerator motor starting interrupted the silence, startling Viv.

"From what I could see over Richie's shoulder, nothing looked out of the ordinary. There were papers everywhere, sure, but again, I thought the boy was working on a write-up for school or something. Richie knew better, apparently, given the way he walked over to Dave's chest of drawers. Three envelopes were perched there: each had a name on it. Richie snatched 'em up and hurried past me and out of that room." Eugene shook his head. "The only thing I heard, before my son slammed the door, was him yelling 'Shit!' Pardon my language, Viv. ... My phone rang about an hour later."

"Did you ever get to read what your son wrote to you?"

"Richie handed me Dave's envelope addressed to me right after the funeral. Never read it. Still in the Bible by my bed." He sniffed. "Guess I'll look at it time enough." Eugene turned to Viv. The lighting made it difficult to read his eyes but did nothing to obscure the pain in his voice. "Your husband carries his around with him, ya know."

"No, I didn't know." But she did recall Rick's clinginess after the funeral. His obsession with family went into overdrive.

"I'm not surprised. Keeps it folded in his wallet." Eugene turned back to the glow of the living room.

"You've seen it there?"

"Yeah."

"Papa Phillips, you said you saw three envelopes."

"He'd addressed one to his mother. Of course, Cissy'd been dead for some time by then."

"What happened to her envelope?"

"Rick probably has it. No idea what he might have done with it. I've asked him about it once or twice."

"What'd he say?"

"Said for me to let my mind rest on that. That he'd taken care of it."

"You never pressed him about it?"

"Nope."

"How come?"

Eugene shrugged. He picked up an ashtray from one of the end tables and emptied his pipe. "I'ma call it a night now, Viv. You'll be all right?"

Viv understood his abrupt change in topic. She suppressed a yawn. "Sure, Papa Phillips."

As he walked toward her, Eugene Phillips reclaimed those years he lost while standing in profile. The now-heavy scent of pipe tobacco filled her nostrils as he planted a kiss on her forehead. "The Lord done real good matchin' you two. *Real* good. Don't fret about whatever's going on now."

Viv couldn't mask her surprise. "Who says anything's going on?"

Eugene scanned her face for seconds before heading into the hallway leading to the bedrooms. "Don't have to be a wise ol' female to recognize when a couple's at a crossroads. Sometimes all it takes is paying attention to the details. G'night, Viv."

"Night."

She then heard a door closing softly.

Tired or not, she wouldn't be able to sleep until Rick returned. She started clearing the table to wash the few dinner dishes. She listened to the radio while she worked, wanting to hear some Sam Cooke.

* * * * *

His head hurt, and he was exhausted, but the hollow feeling gnawing in his empty stomach dictated things. Rick knew his dad would be asleep, but as he let himself into the dark house, he wasn't so sure about Viv. He heard the toilet flush as he made his way to the kitchen. *Well, somebody's up.* He rested his keys on the table before opening the fridge.

"… Your plate's in the oven. Doubt if it's still warm. Your father put it in there a while ago. Don't forget your fruit-salad."

Rick cleared his throat but didn't face her. He stared at the contents of the refrigerator. "Thanks." He reached for the small bowl of fruit-salad.

"Rick?"

"Yeah?"

"You okay?"

He was glad Viv wasn't asleep. He closed the refrigerator door and turned to his wife.

She stood before him in an ankle-length satin gown of deep bronze, her hair pulled back from her pretty face.

Another torrent of emotion came over him. Memories of David, thoughts of losing Viv and Alna, images of Rast—all of it rushed through him. Rick wanted to go to his wife and tell her, no; right now, he was not okay. He placed the bowl on the counter and stood there, wanting to say something but not knowing exactly what. "I don't know," he said honestly. "I… I don't know."

Viv approached him tentatively.

Rick nodded.

When her arms came up around his neck, Rick struggled to contain another sob. Her body was feminine, soft, so comforting. When her lips touched his and their tongues intertwined, it would've been easy to take things further, but he didn't want that—not this time.

Rick broke their kiss. He hugged Viv tighter before stepping back. The taste of chocolate-chip cookies lingered from her tongue. "Why don't you go on to bed? Think about what you want to do tomorrow."

Her black eyes filled with concern and love. "I'll do that," she whispered. "See you in the morning." She pecked his lips gently before retreating.

It was all Rick could do not to follow her.

Instead, he grabbed his fruit, retrieved his plate from the oven (still warm), and sat down to eat.

CHAPTER 12

A Game Afoot

The articles were rarely news by the time Naomi got around to reading Friday's paper, but she sat in her study reading it nevertheless. She read Friday's paper consistently, without fail, hardly bothering with Saturday through Thursday. Friday was her day to catch up with the world. She subscribed to a few of the major newspapers and occasionally picked up copies of the more-obscure newspapers covering local interests. She believed newspapers provided psychological profiles of the nation and the world.

Naomi reached for her Belvedere vodka tonic, ignoring the bowl of lukewarm vegetable soup next to it. She had a cold and the beginnings of sinus pain, so what she needed to do was take something and go to bed, but she wanted (needed) her drink more. Naomi grimaced; the liquid irritated her scratchy-throat.

Except for a lamp and the glow from her computer monitor, the house was dark. It was quiet except for classical music playing on low from the radio on her credenza, and the occasional rustle of paper as Naomi turned the pages of the *Washington Post*. She'd been in the mood for a game of Scrabble, but when she played she usually played with Leslie, and, well, Leslie wasn't home (again).

Naomi sucked her teeth. Thinking about her daughter could be a source of aggravation. Nevertheless, Naomi paused, thinking she heard a car door outside her window. She experienced a touch of anticipatory excitement that was an endearing but sad commentary on the degree of her loneliness. When she didn't hear keys jangling, Naomi glanced at the clock on her PC. She returned to her newspaper and listened to

Antonín Dvořák's "Symphony #8 in G Major, Op.88," enjoying the short contributions of piccolo and English horn in the piece. Finished with the sports and national news headlines, Naomi opened the Metro Section, slowly sitting upright as she read an "In Brief" article.

"Death of Local Restaurant Owner Still Under Investigation."

DC police continue to investigate the death of Jonathan Rast, 41, owner of DeTante's Restaurant located in downtown Washington. Mr. Rast's body was discovered two weeks ago in Harrington Circle Park, north of Georgetown, dead from blunt force trauma. Officials are curtailing the release of information in connection with the crime, but have acknowledged that they are focusing on particulars related to an impression from a bruise on the body. The police have no suspects or witnesses at this time.

A picture stood next to the article. Naomi immediately recognized him as the gentleman who stood in for Leslie's friend, Horace, with Hardluck Rebound. The photo accentuated Jonathan's hazel stare.

That's a shame; he seemed a nice man.

Naomi's eyes flickered to her patient files for Monday's sessions. The Phillips file lay on top. Outside, another car passed by. Naomi barely heard it. For reasons she didn't understand (well, that wasn't entirely true), she reached over and picked up the couple's file.

The article's mention of the bruise intrigued her. Naomi sipped some vodka tonic. They were strange things, these hunches of hers. She didn't entertain any notion of there being anything remotely paranormal about her hunches, but given the two or three serious, dead-on hunches she'd had in the past regarding her patients, whatever the hunches were, she rarely ignored them.

She opened the Phillips file and reviewed her notes. Naomi grinned. She liked Rick and Viv and hoped, just this once, that her hunch was wrong. She thought back to the day Tyson was killed, trying to remember if she had a hunch then, too. *Even if you did (which you didn't), what help is that for anyone now?*

Naomi swiveled around to place her glass on the credenza behind her. She returned to her vegetable soup. It was cold. That was fine.

There was something about his shoes …

Although her resident transferred and prepared Naomi's notes for the file some time ago, yellow legal-sized sheets of paper stayed clipped to the inside of the folder. These sheets were her focus. By session eight or nine, one might find a doodle or three on the legal-pad sheets in a patient's folder, but never from sessions one through six. Her eyes touched on each of the yellow sheets, looking for anything she may have written about shoes. She crosschecked her notes with the typed pages, discarding them upon confirmation.

Naomi thought maybe she'd been wrong, when she found what she was looking for in the bottom right-hand corner of one of the sheets. She'd written: *Husband wore deep-tread boots rather than dress shoes. Pattern on sole interesting.*

Several lines above that, she'd written "Possibles" and drawn two lines out diagonally from the word, listing: "1- Cognitive dissonance" and "2- Cyclothymia."

Cathy transferred everything but the shoe reference. *Probably assumed it couldn't possibly have anything to do with anything.* Naomi wasn't entirely sure why she jotted it down herself. She made note to remind Cathy to transfer all her notes—regardless of perceived relevance.

Naomi stared at the notation, trying to remember what the sole looked like. Not trusting her mind's eye, she decided to make a call instead. She placed the note about Rick's shoes next to the telephone and finished crosschecking the remaining pages.

When she was done, she searched for the name and number of a forensics contact of hers who worked in the medical examiner's office: Kevin Oheneba. Kevin was single, attractive, witty, and interested in her. Three years her senior, his birthday was two days before hers. And although Naomi could easily see herself with him on a personal level, she made every effort to keep Kevin in "colleague" status.

Naomi reached for the phone. She heard another car door close outside her window and waited. This time she heard the garage being opened manually: Leslie. The garage-door remotes were relegated to the top of the refrigerator over a year ago. *I've got to get that automatic opener fixed.*

She found Kevin's business card. For the ME's office, there was no such thing as late. She didn't know Kevin's work schedule, but she wanted to try the office number first.

"Medical examiner's office." It was Kevin.

"Mister Oheneba. How are you?" She heard Leslie's key in the kitchen-entry door.

"Better now that I'm hearing from you, Ms. Alexander. What's up? Some seminar or conference you need an escort for?"

"Oh, you're cute."

"It's what my mother said, too." Kevin spoke with a faint Ghanaian accent.

"We're in rare form tonight, aren't we?"

"Nah. It is good to hear from you. How've you been?"

Naomi hesitated. "Pretty good, I guess. Not much happening."

"I could change that." Kevin's voice registered a tad lower.

Naomi didn't respond. Truth was, she didn't know how. It'd been so long since doing the male-female thing.

"Tell you what. Why don't you just tell me why you called."

"I had a few questions about the Rast case."

"Jonathan Rast, black male, age forty-one, cracked sternum, compound fractures to the left-lateral fourth, fifth, and seventh ribs, commotio cordis, punctured lung, hematoma and severe contusion on the chest and chest wall—"

"Uh, yeah, him." Naomi smiled to herself. She liked Kevin.

"What about 'im?"

"What's the bruise look like?"

"Contusion."

"Contusion. Is it … from a shoe?"

"… Appears so. A boot, actually."

"Still have the file?"

"You already know the answer to that, Naomi."

"Can I get copies of what you have?"

"You know the answer to that, too. We've only been through this once, but the same rules apply. What specifically are you interested in?"

"The bru—contusion on his chest. I'd like to see a picture of it."

"I see."

"Is the imprint that good? Someone kicked him that hard?"

"I see you've inferred a lot, but oh yeah. It's not that hard to believe. Mister Rast was tall but not hefty. He was in shape but not fighting shape, so he lived only briefly after someone's left foot smashed into his chest. The power behind the kick was hard enough to fracture several ribs and disrupt his heart rhythm. He was dead moments after hitting the ground."

"I see."

"Yeah. In those martial-arts pictures, the fighters are all toned and conditioned, and the fighting is quite choreographed. But if one is kicked square in the chest with tremendous force and it's totally unexpected? I don't care how toned you are, the kick is going to do serious damage."

"Can I get a picture of it?" Naomi wondered how Kevin knew that whatever happened was "unexpected."

"That's tame enough. I'll see what I can do."

"Slow night, Mister Oheneba? I don't hear papers shuffling."

"And you know what, Ms. Alexander? There are two other people here. We forensics people are very much into quiet, methodical research. Unlike some other professions, where folks yapping all day is the whole focus."

"Well, see, we mental-health professionals have to listen to and treat you *yappers*. Otherwise, there'd be a whole slew of folks either killing themselves or each other—creating more work than you forensics people can handle," Naomi replied, not unpleasantly.

"Touché, Ms. Alexander."

Naomi could tell he was smiling. "So, the shoeprint's the only lead?"

"Right now, yeah."

"Still determining the style and maker?"

"They've got that plus the size now."

"Yeah, but no witnesses? That makes every person who owns size whatever style shoes in the metro area a suspect. And what if it was someone from out of town? I mean, where's the help here?"

"Whoa, slow down! Did you know Rast or something? Invest in his restaurant? This sounds personal."

"No, but I met him once. Nice man."

"Okay. But why're you so worked up? Do you know something we should?"

Naomi hesitated. "No. It all just seems hopeless."

"Not really. See, not just any shoe of the established size and maker will do. People walk differently and weigh differently, Naomi. This wouldn't apply to flat-soled shoes, of course, but pressure put on certain points of soles with heavy or deep treads give them a 'signature' of sorts. So, one shoe, one sole is the key."

"I see. Still, locating that one shoe …"

"Needle in a haystack."

"Seems like it. Is that all the police have to work with?" Naomi heard Leslie in the kitchen.

"There are one or two minor points, but the shoe's the deal. My area is the body, which, other than how he died, surprisingly gave up little else. That little bit I gave you comes from the techs in the crime lab, so your information is secondhand but reliable."

"Good enough. Can I get the size and maker without bloodshed?" Naomi's attention splintered. She wanted to finish her conversation with Kevin, but also wanted to talk with Leslie.

"Naomi, I must ask again: Do you *know* something?" He paused. Naomi thought she heard papers rustling in Kevin's background this time. "You were an outstanding help with the investigation into Tyson's murder, Naomi. Outstanding."

"Thanks," Naomi practically whispered.

"You have almost the same tone and attitude you did then."

"Mm-hmm."

"That was personal, though, so I understood your pursuit of the case."

Naomi didn't reply. Tyson was not a subject she discussed. She swiveled around and finished her tonic.

"Got the detective-bug again?"

"No." It was the truth. She wasn't trying nor wanting to be anyone's "detective." She had a hunch is all. The game was afoot.

"Naomi?"

"Kevin?"

"Okay, okay. Look, how do you want to get the photo? Snail mail, couri—?"

"Meet me for dinner." The words escaped her lips before she could rein them in.

"Naomi …"

"You cannot be more-surprised than me, but I said it, so …"

"You don't have to."

"I know that. I … want to." Surprisingly, a part of her did want to.

"Well that's good to hear, but let me stress that this is not, I repeat *not*, a date," Kevin replied jokingly. "Let's make that perfectly clear upfront."

Naomi smiled. "No, not a date."

"Okay. We're just two professional colleagues meeting for the sole purpose of exchanging information. We will each find some way to write this off as a business dinner, because, well, that's all this is, I mean—"

"Okay, okay, Kevin," Naomi chuckled. She'd forgotten how sweet he could be through his humor. The kitchen was quiet now. "I have to go, Kevin."

"Okay, but we haven't set the date yet. And by 'date' I am only referring to it in its calendar-time meaning, you see."

Naomi stifled a giggle. "I see."

"What're you doing tomorrow evening? I know it's Saturday, but I'm off tomorrow."

Naomi considered his comment on tomorrow being Saturday; his assumption being, people usually have plans for Saturdays. He'd be surprised to find that she indeed was free Saturday evening—and most other evenings for that matter. "Tomorrow's fine, Kevin."

"Seven thirty? Woodward Table?"

"See you there." Naomi softly disconnected.

She stared at the Phillips folder before turning off her PC. She was tired, and her sinus pain worsened. Her next session with Viv and Rick was scheduled for Monday. Recent developments aside, Naomi looked forward to seeing them.

She paused in her office doorway. Light from the street lamps outside deepened the shadows on the main level of her home. Leslie had obviously turned in, so Naomi let her be. Besides, she needed some sleep; she, of all people, had a date later.

Deciding against taking anything for her head, Naomi went upstairs to her bedroom. She undressed, tossing her slacks and blouse across her reading chair. Placing her Glock under her pillow, she crawled under the covers in her bra and panties, the sheets cool against her skin as she relaxed deeper into them. The clock read 12:52 a.m.

She prayed before drifting off.

It was a headachy sleep, but she didn't wake in the middle of the night this time—a welcomed change.

CHAPTER 13

In a Nutshell

"Damn skippy!" Rick laughed.

"I know, right!" Viv laughed, too.

Naomi, although not quite moved to laughter, smiled as Rick and Viv teased each other about their college teams. Watching and listening to the couple for the last thirteen minutes, she wondered how much counseling the couple really needed. She realized what was on the surface could mask what was underneath, but experience taught her that by and large, the adage "what you see, is what you get" held true. Naomi treated people under that philosophy for many a year now. *Successfully* treated, she might add, if she did say so herself.

She was used to breaking the ice during the first few minutes of initial sessions with new patients. That wasn't necessary with everyone, of course, and certainly not these two. Rick radiated charm as he recapped the events since their last session. Viv appeared to hang on his every word. She smiled and flirted with her husband like a newlywed. Which was fine, but the behavior contradicted Viv's comments on her written responses submitted before session one. Rick, too, seemed different from the man on paper. Naomi decided to join the discussion (she had work to do here).

She cut to the chase. "So, did you make love while in Hampton?"

As expected, Rick and Viv looked at her—mouths open. Rick's new beard, short-boxed and cut low on his face, looked good on him.

Viv rubbed Rick's thigh. "I wanted to, but Rick abstained."

Rick cleared his throat.

"Something wrong, Rick?" Naomi asked.

"You get me sometimes with these out-of-the-blue questions."

"Out-of-the-blue to you, not to me."

Rick nodded.

"Tell me this. Why're you two here?" It was a plant question. Naomi didn't expect answers.

She didn't get any, either—just their open-mouthed expressions again.

"We're in the afterglow of a very nice getaway, Doctor Alexander." Viv looked at Rick firmly. "But there are serious issues we need to work on if this is going to be forever."

"Oh, it's forever," Rick asserted. And while those should have been words of endearment, his tone held a trace of threat.

"You said 'issues,' Viv. Care to list them?"

Rick looked at his wife. "Yeah; run those down."

Viv looked from Rick to Naomi. "Put me on the spot, why don't you?"

"Not trying to do that, Viv. Look, let me get you started. In the last session, you rounded on Rick, saying you'd forgiven his infidelities more than once, so it shouldn't be a problem for him to forgive what I'm assuming is your first and only fling."

Eyes drawn downward, Viv barely nodded.

"So, is it safe to say one of the 'issues' is cheating?"

"It's the only true issue." Viv looked at Rick. "For me at least."

Naomi turned her attention to Rick.

Rick looked alternately between the women. "What?"

"Would you say cheating is the only true problem?" Naomi asked.

Rick glanced at Viv before looking down at his indigo tie with the Cape knot. Naomi's knowledge of tie-knots came from Tyson. Until Rick, she had yet to see a man vary his tie-knots. Rick picked up his tie, studying it. He cleared his throat. "I guess."

Naomi nodded and looked at Viv; she looked at her husband with such a clear expression of both hurt and sympathy, it pained Naomi. "Do you two remember the narrative statements you provided on the pre-therapy questionnaire?"

Viv nodded.

Rick looked up at Naomi. "Yeah. What about 'em?"

"Well, it's safe to say, people in general, tend to be more honest and forthcoming in writing than in conversation. We don't know why that is; it just is. There are exceptions, of course."

"Okay." Rick said.

"I'm saying that to say your present behavior toward each other differs from what came through on paper."

Rick and Viv looked at Naomi with blank stares—mouths closed this time.

Naomi scooted forward on her seat, leaning in Rick's direction. "Rick, on paper you came across as a reserved but marginally-domineering husband and father whose only real problem with his wife was her lack of devotion to the family."

Rick looked at Viv, then back at Naomi. "Aren't those supposed to be confidential? I didn't expect you to reveal what was on those sheets."

"It's confidential to those outside this office, and I'm treating the two of you together, not separately. Secrets aren't going to help that."

Rick nodded. "So, I'm a taciturn bully?"

"Well, it's not that bad. I'd say more conventional than taciturn, but on paper—yes. But in these two sessions you've come across as quite the opposite."

"It's not possible to be conventional and carefree?" Rick asked.

"Anything's possible. It's just not likely. Anyway, let's just say there seems to be a change."

Rick gave a puzzled nod.

Naomi watched Rick closely. He feigned being perplexed, but she needed to let it be for now. She turned to Viv. "And you—"

"Uh-oh. What'd I do? I know I'm the same."

"Do you remember your written responses, Viv?"

Viv hesitated. "Not word for word, but I remember the gist."

Naomi remained silent.

Viv lowered her gaze.

Rick looked from Viv to Naomi and back again. "Well, what?"

They were silent.

Naomi and Rick watched Viv, whose eyes remained downcast.

"It's what we're here for, Viv," Naomi offered softly, surprised at her degree of compassion for the couple.

"What'd you write, Viv?" Rick's question held a mixture of curiosity and trepidation.

"I don't remember what I said word for word—"

"Okay, the gist then," Rick pressed.

Viv finally raised her head. She didn't look at Rick. For reasons Naomi understood perfectly, Viv chose to look away from Rick and out the picture-window.

Generally, experts tended to agree that direct eye-contact tied into truth-telling, but Naomi knew that some of the best lies were told while looking eye-to-eye, while some of the worst truths (the kind that hurt) were told with little if any eye-contact whatsoever.

Viv finally spoke: "I wrote that I love you, Rick. I wrote that during our dating and the first ten, twelve years of our marriage, you were lively, interesting, fun. I also said you were a wonderful father whose devotion to our daughter was inspirational. But as a husband, over the last few years, you'd become someone who only comes alive when it's the three of us doing 'family' stuff. And …" She held Rick's gaze a beat before turning to the window again.

"And?" Rick prompted. The trepidation remained, but the curiosity vanished into hurt—or anger.

Viv remained silent.

Rick turned to Naomi. "You know what she wrote. Care to finish?"

Naomi didn't like his tone and started to tell him so. "Give her a minute, Rick."

Silence again.

This time Naomi scanned her office walls and bookshelves.

Viv continued: "And who, for all his talk about the importance of family, defaces it with lies."

"What? What lies are there? I've been truthful, Viv."

"Truthful. Well yes, technically speaking, you've been 'truthful.' But have you been *true*, Rick? True to me and our marriage?"

"Viv. Viv, come on now." Rick sat back. "I thought we'd gotten past that. There hasn't been anything like that for two years now." With a sigh, Rick tilted his head back against the cushions, giving full examination of the ceiling.

"Well, Rick, seems it's one of the 'issues.'" Naomi turned to Viv, but paused at seeing the expression on her face.

Viv stared at Rick.

Three things drew Naomi's attention: the profound hurt in Viv's eyes, her quivering bottom lip, and the detail in her tightened neck muscles. A tear welled in Viv's right eye, and while Naomi could see Viv willing herself not to cry, Naomi herself willed that tear not to fall.

Don't do it, Viv. Hold it. Let it out the right way.

Naomi glanced at Rick to see if he sensed the change in his wife.

Rick sighed. He lifted his head to look at Viv. "Look, Viv, I know—" He stopped at seeing Viv's expression.

No one spoke. The only sound came from the muffled hum of a printer in the reception area outside Naomi's office.

When Viv finally spoke, she spoke calmly despite her demeanor. "Six years."

Naomi initially had no idea what "six years" meant, but then Rick lowered his eyes. His head followed. Naomi got it: Rick carried the look of a man busted.

More silence. Naomi let it ride. She wasn't pressed for time. The Phillips session was her last for the day.

Viv sniffed and tilted her head back, opening her eyes wide. Naomi easily recognized the eye-drying move. Viv faced Rick again, but the renegade tear never fell. Naomi was proud of her. "Why do you cheat on me, Rick?"

Rick's head stayed down; his body slumped. He shrugged. Except for the beard, he looked all of eleven years-old.

"Rick, that's not good enough. You need to—" Naomi started.

"You don't know? *You don't know?!*" Viv swallowed, regaining her composure. "Okay. Tell me why other men cheat. A broad overview'll do."

Naomi sat back, assuming background mode. Viv had the floor.

"I can't speak for other men; I can only speak for me," Rick said into his tie.

"Well, shit, you ain't *spoke* at all! I put the question to you, and you shrugged like some schoolkid. Why do you cheat, Rick? Why is that your go-to?"

His 'go-to'? Naomi would circle back; Viv still had the floor.

Rick studied his tie.

"You know, for years I've listened to how important family is to you. So now I'm trying to figure out whom you're trying to convince."

Naomi watched Rick. His jaw tightened, but he didn't look up. Naomi, however, had to ask the obvious: "So, Viv, why do you stay—if you've been through it more than once?"

Viv turned to her with the strangest expression—as if she'd forgotten Naomi was in the room. Her mouth opened and then closed.

"You don't know, do you?" Naomi offered.

"I do. I stay because I love him, Naomi: *deeply*. I stay because we have a young child together. Because, while I'm not obsessed about family like Rick is, I do feel family is important. Alna doesn't have siblings. Not yet, anyway. So, in a sense, we're all she has. Other family lives farther away."

Naomi noticed Viv's '*Not yet, anyway.*' She started to ask another question, when Viv continued.

"And I'm bonded to him."

Rick sat up. He gazed out the window.

"'Bonded to him'?"

Viv sat forward, facing Naomi. "See, it's like this. I'm a successful, smart, attractive black woman with a good heart who could leave her marriage and easily start a new life with my daughter elsewhere. I'm not being conceited or arrogant. Lord knows I'm not perfect. I'm just saying how it is."

"I got you. Go on."

"My point is this: I know I can just leave. But the biggest part of me doesn't want to."

"Even with him cheating?" Naomi glanced at Rick: his jaw worked.

"I know how it sounds, but yeah."

"Because you're 'bonded' to him." This was the fun part of therapy—listening to people explain themselves. Naomi found people did a fair-job of analyzing themselves more-often-than-not. Most times patients, without realizing it, usually ended up treating themselves. Naomi's job (as she saw it) was labeling the angst in big, convoluted psychiatric terms to make things interesting—and adding a prescription or two to make things more interesting.

"Yes. What I have with Rick is extraordinary, Doctor Alexander. When we interact, there's this feeling between us that is, I don't know, phenomenal. And …"

"And?" Naomi prompted.

Viv looked at Rick. He'd been so quiet; it was as if he wasn't in the room. "And our sex is unbelievable."

"I thought the sex was boring."

"No. Where we have sex can be boring. Rick has this thing about being in the bedroom when we're intimate. He'll try a new place occasionally, but overall, it's the bedroom. But now, when we're in there …"

"Good for you."

"Trust and believe." Viv closed her eyes. "When he takes me down …" She shook her head slowly, and then looked at her husband. "It's *everything* it's supposed to be."

Naomi watched Rick. He cleared his throat and cast his eyes downward in obvious blush. Nothing made a handsome man more handsome than his modesty: seeing him genuinely uncomfortable with compliments. Naomi looked at Viv.

Viv gave a knowing smile. "You believe in soulmates, Naomi?"

"No."

"I do. I don't believe there's only one per person, but Rick is mine. We have a great friendship-love-sex thing that makes it hard to just leave. It also makes it hard to understand why he does what he does." Viv looked at Rick pointedly.

"What about the sense of monotony you've been feeling in your marriage, Viv? I mean, since you're on a roll and all."

"So, Rick gets to let it all hang out next session?"

"Maybe. We'll see. You go 'head."

"Well, he lost his sense of adventure and spontaneity. He only finds a spark if Alna's involved."

"Are you jealous of Rick's relationship with Alna?"

"Not at all."

"Well, wait, think about that. I mean—"

"Doctor Alexander. Naomi. I am not jealous of my daughter. I just want my husband to keep in mind that, as much as we are a family, we are a couple first. That's all. I'm not trying to leave my marriage. I can be Miss Empowered Black America, but I want it to work with *him*." Viv gestured toward Rick. "I am not at all interested in reestablishing a relationship with someone else, when I have ninety percent of what I want," she clutched Rick's thigh, "with *this man* right *here*."

"So, if he renewed his sense of adventure and stopped cheating. I mean you have trust issues that make up a serious ten percent."

Viv released Rick's thigh. "Look, I can live with him not being Mister Excitement. I have for a while now. And anyway, since this

Jonathan situation ..." Viv sighed heavily, "Rick's, like you said, more carefree or something again."

"'Jonathan situation'?" Naomi looked at Rick and Viv. "Oh, our third-party."

Viv nodded.

"Go on. You were saying Rick's more carefree again."

"Right. Only, he's more intense lately, too—in an exciting sort of way. I don't know. Maybe it's finding out what it's like to be on the other side of things."

Naomi looked at Rick. "Maybe."

Rick looked at Naomi with sincere perplexity this time.

"Maybe," Naomi repeated. She returned her attention to Viv.

Viv viewed the exchange without comment. She continued: "I can live with the monotony, Naomi. It's not as bad as I make it sound, anyway. But I cannot live with the cheating anymore; or rather, I don't want to live with him resorting to cheating anymore. So here I am, because frankly I don't understand it. But I'm tired of forgiving it." Now Viv sat back. It wasn't a defeated posture but a tired one.

Naomi checked her watch, noting Viv's use of 'resorting.'

"So again, Rick, I'm asking: Why do you cheat?"

Rick sniffed, cleared his throat.

If he says he doesn't know again, so help me ... To help avoid that scenario, Naomi decided to guide him. "Do you love Viv, Rick?"

"Absolutely."

"Do you find Viv 'boring'?"

"No."

"Are you still attracted to your wife?"

"Extremely."

"Well, then, how do you view your sex-life? Is the sex good? Is it often enough?"

"Our sex is the best I've ever had, Doctor Alexander. And Viv wants it more than me sometimes, so frequency's not a problem."

"Okay, the ball's still in your court," Naomi replied with a touch of irritation. She centered herself. "Do you have an answer for your wife, or do you need to think on it? We can address this next session."

Rick didn't respond. He looked at Viv. With a sigh, he leaned forward, resting his forearms across his thighs. He clasped his hands and kept his head down.

Naomi waited.

Viv looked out the window. Tension lined her eyes and mouth.

Compassion for the couple affected Naomi again. "Why do you cheat, Rick?"

Silence echoed.

"… Because I can," Rick whispered. In the silence of the room, his whisper resounded.

"Fair enough." Naomi looked at Viv.

Viv continued staring through the window.

"We can end it here, guys, if you'd like. It's totally—"

"Because … you … can." Viv's voice cracked with emotion. Her brows furrowed as if trying to understand each of Rick's words individually. A single tear streamed from her right eye.

Rick looked up at her. "I know how it sounds."

Viv wiped the tear away. "No. You can't possibly know how that sounds to me."

"Look, Viv, like I said, it's been two years now since—"

"Yeah, you're right. 'Bout twenty-six months, right?"

Rick looked at Viv, mouth open.

Naomi used all resources to suppress a chuckle. "Close your mouth, Rick." She turned to Viv: "Obviously you knew Rick cheated again, although Rick apparently thought he hadn't been busted until his mess-up today with the year-count or whatever, so I'm confused. If you knew, why not confront him?"

"She was probably already planning to get back at me with Rast."

"'Rast'?" Naomi repeated.

"As in Jonathan Rast," Viv volunteered.

"Oh, no. I'm sorry." Naomi refused to view her flashes as a curse, but sometimes …

"It's okay. Anyway," Viv glanced at Rick, "Jonathan wasn't tit for tat."

"Sure about that, Viv?" Naomi asked.

"Well …" Viv hedged with an apologetic shrug. "In some ways."

"Did it end because of what happened to him?" Naomi tensed.

"Yes and no."

Naomi waited for Viv to clarify.

"I mean, 'yes' in the sense that it's obvious now that he's … he's no longer here." Viv closed her eyes, taking a deep breath before opening them. "But I'd have to say 'no' because, although I wanted to separate from Rick, I wanted to call it off with Jonathan, too. I just didn't get to end it the right way."

"Did you love Jonathan?" Naomi asked.

"Yes, but, you know, not *love* him."

Naomi looked at Rick. He gazed out the window, slowly fingering his right ear. Naomi made note of it. "You good, Rick?"

"I'm fine."

"Are you surprised Viv knew about your most recent indiscretion?"

Rick stopped rubbing his ear. The index finger of his right hand now rested on his temple in a professor's pose. "Yeah, I'm surprised … and embarrassed."

Naomi turned to Viv. "I must say I'm surprised as well, Viv, that you held on to that for so long. So why didn't you say anything until now, some twenty-odd months later?"

"Because I figured what would be the point."

"Okay, let me ask this: You were quite exact in saying how long it's been. How do you know when it ended?"

Rick shifted his gaze to his wife.

Viv looked at Rick. "I don't want to get into that now." She looked back to Naomi. "Besides, how I know isn't the issue here."

"You're right." Naomi paused to watch Rick. He seemed calmer. "So, Rick, you cheat 'because you can.' Any regret, remorse, when you do it?"

Rick shifted his gaze to Naomi. "Eventually, yeah. That was the case that last time. I was done."

Viv scoffed. "Yeah, right."

"Believe what you want, Viv."

"I want to believe I'm dreaming this shit, but that's impossible now, isn't it?"

Rick shrugged.

His response obviously hurt Viv's feelings. She sat forward and turned her body, facing him. "Do you have any idea what something as detached and unfeeling as 'because I can' says to me, Richard?"

Rick's lips parted to say something.

Viv's raised hand stopped him. "No, you don't. You can't know."

"Rick, did you or do you love any of these women?" Naomi interjected.

Rick sat straighter. "No."

It was the truth: Rick's eyes were steady, his voice strong; his answer was succinct without waffle or equivocation. Naomi was pleased.

Viv shook her head. "That doesn't help, Rick."

Rick turned to his wife. "Why? I think it should help a lot."

Viv's body tensed instantly. "How the fu—?!"

"Whoa! Wait, Viv," Naomi interrupted. Viv was obviously incensed. Naomi had to step in. "Just wait a minute."

Viv sighed heavily and rested her head in her hand.

"Before you jump in the man's chest, hear him out. It's what you're here for. You asked a question, Viv. Rick's trying to answer it."

Viv kept her head down and chewed her bottom lip.

Rick looked at Naomi with gratitude. There was pain, too, and despite Naomi's prescribed impartiality regarding her patients, she was glad to see it.

"It's getting late, though, people. If you have childcare to consider."

"Louise is picking her up today," Viv said.

"How is Alna doing?"

"She's fine," Viv answered.

Naomi nodded and turned back to Rick. "Let's continue then. Rick, why do you feel that not loving the women is important; that it should 'help'?"

"Because, I mean, isn't that what y'all get all worried about?"

"Most women, yes, do focus more on the love-aspect of sexual relations. But plenty women enjoy sex for the pure pleasure of it. It's not just a man-thing. Not every woman's heart is in her vagina."

"I hear you. But, see, for most men, or, for me at least, it's different. Love plays a part, but it's mostly about the pleasure of it." Rick glanced at his wife before returning his gaze to Naomi.

Viv lifted her head and folded her hands in her lap.

"So, you're saying it's not about love for you," Naomi stated.

"I'm saying sex isn't always about love for me. When it is, it's only with Viv."

"And your partners? Any of the women fall for you? Want more than the occasional fuck?" Naomi could tell her use of strong language surprised the couple but didn't appear to offend. "A bit unprofessional, yes, but I'm not here to impress you. My job is to help you. Being upfront sometimes makes it necessary for me to digress. Problems?"

Rick and Viv shook their heads.

"Go 'head, Rick."

"Well ..." Rick again glanced at his wife. He cleared his throat. "There was a situation ..."

"Yeah." Viv sounded tired.

"Fair-enough. No need for details. Was the matter resolved satisfactorily for both of you?"

Rick looked at Viv.

Viv nodded.

"Good."

"I always stressed I wasn't interested in anything more," Rick offered.

"Thanks," Viv said sarcastically.

Naomi smiled inside at Viv's reply. "What about STDs, Rick? Pregnancies?"

Rick's expression grew serious. "Condoms. I brought and used my own without fail. Took no chances with that shit. I ..." Rick now looked sheepish.

"Go on, Rick," Naomi prompted.

"I pulled out, too, Naomi."

"This is fucked up, but thank you," Viv expressed sincerely. She looked at Naomi. "Me? I get tested regularly." She scoffed and looked out the window.

Rick looked at Viv. He started to reply but simply cleared his throat.

Naomi spoke: "Okay. But, Rick. None of what you just described sounds particularly appealing. Doesn't sound worth it."

Rick shrugged.

Lord, he was extra-easy on the eyes.

Silence.

Naomi sighed. "Okay. Let's explore further. We've established that, for you, Rick, the sex wasn't about love at all when you were with the others."

"Right," Rick agreed.

"Where are you with that, Viv?"

Viv didn't answer right away. She stared at Rick with what at first looked like anger before her features softened. She shrugged. "I don't know. What I don't understand is, if I'm the best you've had, why do you resort to cheating whenever—? Anyway, are you trying to top our thing? What?"

"I'm not on a mission to find the Ultimate Pussy Experience." Rick looked at Naomi. "Sorry."

"Not offended. Remember: be upfront. We're all adults here."

"So, what is it then?" Viv asked again.

"I've already told you."

"'Because.'" Viv looked doubtful.

Rick shook his head and sighed. "I'm sorry I don't have a profound explanation for you, Viv."

"And you didn't fall for any of them?" Viv asked with a touch of incredulity.

"No." Rick ran a hand over his hair. "I'm not saying I didn't like 'em. I wouldn't have been bothered if I didn't at least like 'em. I'll even go so far as to say I cared a bit. I'm not a robot."

"Did you 'care' about Lynelle?"

"Not really. But see, that sounds cold. I mean, I liked Lynelle, but that's it."

"And 'Lynelle' is …?"

"The one when you asked did anyone fall for him. Lynelle fell hard." Viv offered.

Naomi noted no jealousy or anger in Viv's response. She spoke plainly: good. "Like *Fatal Attraction*, or …?"

Viv shook her head. "The stalker-craziness part: no. But the intensity of feeling for him: oh yes."

Rick looked uncomfortable with her words.

"I see. Okay, look. Viv, honey, I don't think you're going to get the answer you're looking for. You need to think about what Rick's told you and internalize it; determine if you can live with it."

"I—" Viv started.

"You can't answer that yet, Viv. Don't even try." Naomi looked at Rick. "I do have a couple questions for you, though."

"And here we go."

Naomi smiled. "It may not seem like it, but you're doing good work in here."

"If you say so." Rick glanced at Viv. He cleared his throat. "Ask your questions, Naomi."

Naomi looked at Viv. "Did you want to address anything further?"

Viv shook her head and sat back into the cushions. This time she did look defeated.

"How long did your trysts last, Rick?"

"I'd say no more than six months."

"Except that last one lasted, what, a week or so, right? So, you hit that, what, once, twice?" Viv interjected.

Rick didn't look at Viv, didn't respond.

Naomi did. "How do you know how long it lasted, Viv?"

"Same way I know when it ended."

"Which is …?" Naomi prompted.

"I'd still rather not say," Viv glanced at Rick before looking out the window.

Pressure built behind Naomi's eyes, and her temples throbbed: another sinus headache. She rubbed her eyes. "Okay. Let's leave the sex part alone, Rick. So, okay, you didn't love these women. But if you love Viv as much as you say, why hurt her on purpose?"

"I never thought of it as hurting Viv 'on purpose,' as you put it, but I see what you're saying. But that's what made me stop: realizing that I wasn't respecting or honoring my marriage to Viv, or, for that matter, our friendship. Viv hadn't done anything. Not really."

"But before this epiphany …" Naomi prompted. Perhaps the couple already explored possible reasons why Rick did what he did. There was more to this with the uses of 'go-to' and 'resort' and Rick adding, 'not really,' but she'd have to circle back. Sometimes redirected dialogue pursuits shut a patient down, and Rick and Viv were talking freely and doing good work; Naomi didn't want to interrupt progress.

"I don't know. I mean, I know it was wrong; you know, 'Thou shalt not commit adultery' and all, but I never went too deep with it in terms of guilt and Viv's feelings."

"Even after Viv found out? Didn't she let you know it hurt her? That she didn't want you to do it anymore?"

"Yeah. But now, let me say there've only been three incidents during our fifteen-year marriage."

Naomi raised an eyebrow.

"Hey, I'm not saying that like it's a good thing. I'm just saying there wasn't a continuous line of women Viv had to deal with," Rick explained.

"I hear you," Naomi said dryly. "Go ahead.

"And I'd say, really only two; that last one—"

"Counts." Viv looked at him sternly. "Don't get it twisted. I don't care how short it was, she counts." She turned back to the window.

Duly chastised, Rick nodded solemnly. "Anyway, Viv would find out, we'd reconcile, be chill for a long while until we weren't, then, well, you get the picture."

"Unfortunately, I do. Tell me this: How would Viv find out?"

"Believe it or not, I ended up telling her. Those first two times, anyway." Rick turned to his wife. "Right, Viv?"

Viv nodded slowly.

Rick looked back to Naomi. "I'd end up telling her; we'd get into it about it. Viv would be angry and tell me how she felt, how it hurt that I kept resorting to cheating whenever we— Mind you, most times, Viv is straight-no-chaser. I love that about her. She doesn't cry, get all weepy and shit."

"Would it have made a difference if she had?" It was already clear Rick didn't cheat just 'because,' but the couple kept skirting around it. Naomi would let them (for now).

"I don't know. But knowing Viv, for her to cry means she's in real pain about something. I never saw that when we'd get into it about what happened, just the anger; so I guess, somewhere inside me, I didn't believe she was really affected."

"I see." Naomi again marveled at how easily folks analyzed themselves. She noted that Rick truly analyzed his perspective instead of just rationalizing it—an important distinction.

Viv now watched Rick.

"Then today, when I saw that tear …"

"But you were done two years ago," Naomi said.

"I know. But seeing that tear made it all hit home. Hearing my wife say she gets checked regularly?" Rick paused. "That *hurt*, Naomi."

Naomi nodded her understanding.

"See, as you know, I value family highly." Rick cast a sideways glance at Viv. "And it's not bullshit rhetoric. I love my family. Will protect my family, nourish it, and be bound by it. And I will do whatever it takes …"

"Yes?"

"Whatever it takes to keep my family together. I promised myself that. I promised Dav—"

"Rick?" Viv interrupted.

Rick looked at his wife. "Yeah?"

"Get down."

"Get down?"

"Off the soapbox," Naomi offered.

"I'm not on a soapbox. What's wrong with holding the role of family in high regard?"

Viv placed a hand on his thigh. "Nothing, Rick, but you get carried away with it."

"It's okay, Viv. We may find ourselves exploring Rick's family issues before it's all over, but I want to stick to topic. Let me ask another question, Rick. How did you feel when you found out about Viv cuckolding you with Jonathan?"

Rick's eyes flashed at her with what couldn't be mistaken for anything other than pure hatred. He looked at Viv. "I didn't like it." When he turned back to Naomi, his expression was guarded.

"That's obvious, Rick. How did you *feel*? Were you more concerned about the physical or emotional aspects of their relationship?"

"Initially: the physical." Rick reached for his ear. "But that's more of a territorial thing. The idea of his hands and mouth on her, touching and—"

"I get the picture," Naomi interrupted. "You said *initially* your concern was their physical connection. What about later?"

"Yeah, later, it bothered me realizing Viv had feelings for him. While sex isn't all about love for me, I know Viv isn't going into a sex-thing unless she feels something more than a physical attraction."

"That true, Viv?"

"Pretty much. I love sex, but it still has to be about more than the in-and-out."

Naomi nodded.

Rick sighed. "So, yeah, the emotional aspect bothered me more."

"Did you say as much to Viv?"

"No. Actually, we haven't said a word about it since she told me. We've resumed being cordial, but today's the first time we've gone into how either of us felt about the whole thing."

Naomi looked at the couple. "So, you two were going to let bygones be bygones?"

"I don't know ..." Rick turned to Viv.

"No, we weren't, Doctor Alexander. Rick suggested counseling soon after he found out. Then Jonathan died ..."

"And Jonathan's dying was what? An eye-opener for you, Viv? Relief for you, Rick?"

"You could say that," Viv said.

Rick continued fingering his ear.

"Rick?" Viv pressed with concern.

"Give him a minute, Viv."

Rick closed his eyes.

Naomi recognized Rick's ear-rub as an anxiety response. "What are you anxious about, Rick?"

Rick looked at her. "I'm not."

Naomi looked pointedly at Rick's hand over his ear.

"Oh, he always does that when he's upset," Viv offered. "It's to the point now; I hardly pay attention to it."

"You should," Naomi replied, more to herself than to Viv.

Rick and Viv returned baffled glances.

"Why are you upset, Rick?"

"I'd say more agitated. I just don't want to talk about this anymore."

Naomi pressed on. "Were you relieved when you found out Jonathan was dead?"

"For the most part, yeah. I didn't wish it on him or anything, but I knew what happened to Rast would make it easier to make things right with Viv." Rick's eyes flashed with anger or hatred. Naomi, now, couldn't tell which.

Naomi turned to Viv. "So, knowing Rick doesn't love these women, where are you with that?"

Viv hesitated. "I know I said it didn't help, but it does. I guess it doesn't bother me as much now."

Naomi smiled. "Well, good." But Naomi knew better. Even in the most open marriages, there remains a degree of discomfort in knowing that one's primary partner has been with someone else. In Naomi's circle, medicine interpreted jealousy as an emotion of immaturity rooted in insecurity and low self-esteem. Naomi believed jealousy to be as common and natural an emotion as happy and sad.

Rick studied his tie yet again.

Viv shook her foot as she stared out the window.

"Have I killed the afterglow?"

Silence.

"Does your silence mean 'yes'?"

"No." Viv shrugged. "It's what we're here for."

"Rick?" Naomi prompted.

Rick cleared his throat and sat forward. He appeared relieved at Viv's answer. "Uh, yeah. I mean, no. No, the afterglow or whatever isn't spoiled."

"Very well. But you two have to talk to each other outside of this office."

"We do," Viv said.

"I'm not talking about the *safe* stuff. Being 'cordial.' I'm referring to the hard and painful, too, getting back to the 'nitty-gritty' talking you used to do. If something comes up where you'd rather have a 'referee,' so to speak, let the other know that you'd rather discuss that subject in session. Just don't rely on that 'out' every time one of you gets uncomfortable. Anyway, the point is, you've learned some things today, and hopefully you will carry good feelings home with you this evening. And, to get things off in the right direction, I want you to kiss and 'make up,' if you will."

As Naomi expected, the couple looked at her like she was nuts.

"I'm serious."

Viv and Rick looked at each other. The unspoken dialogue between them nearly brought Naomi to laughter. Their expressions said each thought maybe Naomi was the one needing counseling. That, or they thought she was some sort of secret perv.

Rick spoke first. "Doctor Alexander. Naomi …"

"Just kiss. What's the big deal?"

Rick looked at Viv again.

Viv nodded.

Rick leaned toward her.

Naomi expected a quick peck and about-face, like two child-aged siblings being forced to kiss and make up by a parent. But the kiss was much more than a simple peck. Their kiss was tender, sensual. Viv gently tugged Rick's tie, pulling him close as she tongued him delicately for long seconds. When they parted, they shared a look, and then turned to Naomi as if seeking approval.

This time Naomi did laugh.

Viv grinned curiously. "What?"

Naomi's laughter tapered to a chuckle. "Nothing,"

Rick held Viv's hand, fingers interlocked. "So, is that it?"

"For today: pretty much. There is something else, though."

"And …" Rick looked at Viv.

"Here we go," the couple said together. They looked at Naomi with amused smirks.

Naomi grinned. "It's not bad," she assured. Even with the overhead lights on, the lowering sun gave her office a somber feel.

"Doesn't sound good, either," Viv countered.

"I was just going to suggest your daughter attend a session with you."

"Why?" Viv looked concerned.

"Primarily to see where Alna is with all this."

Rick released Viv's hand. "She's only nine, Doctor Alexander."

"Still, I'd like to talk with her."

"I don't know …" Viv said.

"It's up to you, but I do think it best—even if it's not until the end. Think about it."

Rick nodded curtly. "Fair-enough." He stood to leave, offering Viv his hand.

Accepting Rick's hand, Viv stood. "So, next week then?"

"Next week, yes. You prefer mornings like last time, or was this time of day good for you?"

"This time's better." Viv turned to her husband. "Rick?"

"Uh, yeah, late-afternoon's good."

"Again, you two did good work today. I see my suggestion of a vacation did some good, too."

Viv nodded. "It did, yes."

Naomi gave them both a serious look. "But you two should talk about Mister Rast, or if not specifically about him … Well, maybe that's another session."

"Yeah, probably," Rick agreed.

"And you'll think about having Alna attend?"

Rick smiled. "You bet."

"Sure," Viv added.

"Very good."

"And with that, we're outta here, Doctor Alexander. Ready, Viv?" Rick kept smiling.

"Yep."

Still holding hands, Rick and Viv walked to the door. Mr. Phillips was bowlegged, a touch pigeon-toed.

Rick opened the door for Viv, but looked back at Naomi before exiting. He smiled. "Have a good one, Naomi."

Naomi nodded her goodbye and returned to her desk.

While closing shop for the day, her brows furrowed from time to time.

Rick's send-off was neutral enough, but it bothered her.

Ordinarily, Naomi liked Rick's smile, and he offered several as they prepared to leave. But Naomi found one thing wrong with each of them: those smiles never reached his eyes.

CHAPTER 14

Building Bridges

Viv awoke with a start, her heart racing.
She dreamed of the faceless women again.

It was Friday afternoon: four days since their therapy session. Viv rolled lazily to her back, gazing at the ceiling fan. She and Rick ended up stretching the vacation time from the Hampton trip out considerably with a series of call-ins and early-departures from work. She had plenty vacation time to cover this week and many more if necessary. Rick's firm still reveled in the success of him landing the Arrington Enterprises account, so Rick's time-off was approved with many blessings.

Viv listened for sounds in the house. All was quiet.

Before she lay down for her nap, Rick mentioned wanting to go get something—that he'd be back later and would probably pick Alna up from school early. Viv was so sleepy at the time, she didn't care what Rick's plans were; her plans involved taking a nap. She slept a lot lately, and although she knew why, Rick apparently hadn't picked up on anything.

The warmth from the afternoon sun shining through the bedroom windows didn't help her maintain the level of wakefulness she had upon stirring from the dream. Viv wanted to rouse, but drowsiness wouldn't leave her. She also wanted sex with Rick (especially since that kiss in Naomi's office), but strangely, she wasn't sure how to broach the subject.

She enjoyed the time-off with her husband, growing closer to him. He'd been talkative and more-playful than he'd been in years (much like his old self). But they had yet to follow doctor's orders and discuss Jonathan. Viv wasn't sure she wanted to, and doubted Rick wanted to, either.

Viv turned onto her stomach, resting her head on her forearms, and gazed at the dust motes dancing in the rays of sun. She closed her eyes and drifted-off again, this time dreaming of motorcycles.

A slight touch on her calf roused her.

"Mommy, wake up."

Viv kept her eyes closed. "I'm up, sweetie."

Alna walked around the bed. She reached over and opened Viv's eye with her thumb.

The move startled Viv. "Alna, I've asked you not to do that! I don't like it."

"Sorry, Mommy, but you weren't waking up fast enough."

"That's not the point, Alna."

Ordinarily, Alna's expression of earnest-innocence and sadness would've softened Viv's reaction, but vestiges of drowsiness kept her irritable. Still, she was a mommy. Viv sighed. "Alna, this is my last time telling you not to do that. If there's a next time, you'll be punished."

"Yes, ma'am."

Viv sat up. She gestured for her daughter to come around to her.

Alna looked small in her green coveralls. Four pigtails bounced in unison as she approached her mother. Without another word, she hugged Viv.

Viv relaxed with the feel and mold of Alna's body against her own. She kissed her forehead. "So, what's the big emergency?"

Alna grinned, obviously relieved her mother was no longer angry. She suddenly covered her mouth with both hands. "I'm n supzz ell ooo."

"What?"

Alna repeated herself.

Viv drew her daughter's hands down. "What do you mean you're 'not supposed to tell' me? You woke me to tell me you can't tell me something?"

Alna shook her head. "I wanted to tell you, but then remembered I wasn't supposed to."

"I see. Does this have something to do with Daddy?"

Alna giggled and nodded.

"Ooooh, mysterious. Okay, I'll wait. Got homework?"

"I'm finished; so you can check it." Alna looked crestfallen.

"Well, what's the matter?"

Alna widened her eyes. "You're not gonna try and make me tell you?"

"No. No tickle-torture this time."

"But why?"

"Well, because you're growing up, Al. Maybe it's time for you to learn what it means to be trustworthy. Daddy asked you not to say anything. And since this sounds like a happy secret, it's a good time to learn self-control."

Alna's expression? A pout, with a touch of skepticism. Priceless.

Viv laughed.

Alna joined her.

"Come on. Let's get that homework checked."

"It's in the family room." Alna tugged on her mother's wrist. "Come downstairs."

"Where's Daddy?"

"At the store. Come on!" Alna tried to get her to rise.

Viv remained seated. "You go on. I'll be down in a minute."

Alna watched her mother's face. Satisfied, she turned on a bare heel and left Viv's bedroom. Viv went to her chest of drawers. She wanted to freshen-up first.

Thirty minutes later, Viv sat on their family-room floor, her back against the sofa. Alna kneeled next to her, waiting. Her schoolbooks and respective homework lay spread over the coffee-table in front of them for Viv's review.

Routinely, she (or Rick) reviewed Alna's homework, acknowledging work well-done, and setting aside work that needed, well, more work. Geography and math looked good. Viv now held Alna's language arts homework.

Alna sighed. "I'll be glad when Daddy gets back."

"He'll be back soon." Viv handed two sheets of loose-leaf notebook paper back to her daughter. "Here. I've checked the sentences with problems."

Alna looked at the paper, scanning for her mother's marks. "Only four: that's not too bad."

"It's not, so get to it. Think you know what's wrong?"

"One of them, yeah; the rest I gotta look at again."

"Okay. But sit at the kitchen table this time."

Alna made an unhappy face but gathered her language arts materials.

Lower-back aching and thighs stiff, Viv moved from the floor to the chaise. She wondered how much longer Rick would be. He prepared dinner, and hunger no longer described the pangs in her stomach.

To shift her thoughts, Viv went to the kitchen and stood behind Al. She'd corrected one sentence but appeared to be studying the remaining three. Viv played softly with Alna's hair. It was a comforting and supportive gesture Viv wished she'd received while trying to make right all that her father had identified as wrong on her schoolwork. Or, if it wasn't wrong, then it was work "unpresentable." Viv could almost hear the creak in the floorboards as her father moved through the apartment, monitoring their progress at their established homework stations.

The door leading into the laundry room from the garage opened. In the seconds before Rick appeared, Viv's stomach knotted with a mixture of schoolgirl-excitement and a weird apprehension.

"Oh, hey!" Rick carried a canvas grocery bag in one hand and a bouquet of flowers in the other. "I thought you'd be finished by now, Al." He glanced down at the flowers.

Viv did, too. "Those for me?" She looked at him.

With a sexy glint in his eye that was part-bashful, part-flirt, Rick nodded, and Viv's tummy fluttered with excitement. She wanted her husband.

"Hi, Daddy." Alna rose and hugged her father. She took the flowers from his hand and handed them to her. "Here, Mommy."

Viv smiled at her daughter. "Thank you."

Rick set the grocery bag on the counter.

Viv looked at him. "And thank you, Mister Phillips."

Rick held Viv's gaze a beat and tipped his pork-pie hat to her. "*Sei benvenuto*." He smiled and placed his hat on Alna's head before removing his jacket.

Viv grinned at Alna. "So, what's the big surprise?"

"Alna!" Rick spoke with exaggerated alarm. "And you took the sacred-secret-dolphin oath and everything." He shook his head in mock disappointment. The dimple in his cheek gave him away completely.

147

"I didn't tell, Daddy," Alna replied blandly. She looked adorable in her daddy's hat.

Her response surprised Viv and, from Rick's expression, apparently surprised him, too. Viv looked down at Alna's homework on the table.

"Come on, Al. You have one more. The others look good, so finish this one so we can eat."

"Since I only have one, can't I do it after?"

"No." Rick checked inside a pot on the stove. "Since you only have one, get it over with."

Alna sucked her teeth and sighed.

Viv leaned in Alna's direction. "'Scuse me, young lady?"

"I wanna do it after."

Neither Viv nor Rick replied, but kept eyes on their daughter.

Alna moved back to her chair. She sat in the chair hard and snatched her pencil from the table.

"Alna …" Viv's tone signaled her nine-year-old to get her act together. She looked at Rick: he watched their daughter, an eyebrow raised in warning.

Viv smiled at him. "I see we're having spaghetti, but where's the garlic bread?"

Rick tapped the grocery bag and moved past her, smelling like a cool breeze of Artisan Black.

Viv pondered what it'd be like to rape a man.

"The stuff's in there." Rick headed toward the stairs. "I'll be back by the time the bread's done."

"Good." Viv started for the bag. "I'm hungry."

Ninety minutes later, Alna was asleep in her room, Rick sat in the family room engrossed in a Wizards basketball game, and Viv sat in her bedroom attempting to read the latest Stephen King novel, feeling foolish. Under normal circumstances, she'd be watching the game with Rick. During dinner, she did everything but drop her drawers to let her husband know what she wanted. Rick didn't ignore her exactly, but he kept his distance.

Viv didn't know what to make of it. Before talking to him about separating, Rick had plenty happening in the bedroom and little happening elsewhere. Since, though, he'd kicked it up considerably outside the bedroom but seemed disinterested in anything involving sex.

She startled at seeing Rick peeping his head in the door.

"Didn't mean to scare you."

"It's okay."

Awkward silence followed.

"Hi."

"Hi." Viv was used to the uneasiness between them, but Rick's tentativeness was sweet. "You can come all the way in, you know."

Rick cleared his throat and stepped into the room. He stood before her, muscles rippling in his wife-beater, hands in the pockets of his jeans. His slightly-pigeon-toed stance emphasized his bowed legs. Damn, he was fine!

"So, what's up? Good game?"

Rick nodded. "Pretty good." There was a beat, maybe two, before he continued: "I, uh, got something to show you."

"Would this be the surprise?"

Rick nodded again. His aw-shucks posture was so out-of-character, Viv almost laughed. Instead, she sighed heavily. "Finally." She stood, but Rick didn't move. "I'm guessing whatever it is, is downstairs …?"

"The garage."

Viv gestured for Rick to proceed. "Lead the way, kind sir."

He offered that sexy-bashful glint again before leaving her room.

The night's cool temperature somehow strengthened the smell of sawdust and car fumes in their garage. Her stomach lurched, but she was preoccupied with the sight before her: a chrome and metallic-blue Moto Guzzi motorcycle sat parked beside her Lexus.

Her first impulse was to laugh. She didn't know what she expected the surprise to be, but it wasn't this. She pictured her formerly reserved and now carefree husband on the machine. The sheer oddity of it intensified her desire to let loose with sidesplitting laughter.

"Well?"

Viv finally closed her mouth. "Well … When'd you get it?"

"Today. I started to ask you to come with me."

Determined not to crack a smile, Viv nodded her understanding. "You don't like it?"

"No. No, that's not it."

"Well, what then?"

Viv let out a giggle. She couldn't help it. "Don't take this wrong, Rick, but I can't see you riding this thing. I mean, you got your motorcycle license what, three years ago?"

"And?"

"*And* you haven't been on a motorcycle since."

"So?"

"So, this is out of left field, that's all."

Rick leaned forward, ensuring she gazed at him. "Do you like it?"

"Huh?"

"Do you like it? Forget about picturing me on it and how far out of left field it is." His voice dropped several octaves. "*Do you like it?*"

Battling the tremble his voice stirred in her, Viv stepped closer to the motorcycle and touched its black leather pillion. She knew little about motorcycles, but this machine belonged to Moto Guzzi's California Series. Up close, the touring bike seemed much longer, the Gold Series Brembo brakes in glinting contrast to the shining silver of the wheel spokes. Viv stopped trying to imagine being on the thing and simply enjoyed the look and feel of it. "Yes."

"Good. Let's go."

"What?!"

"You heard me." Rick's pleasant tone didn't match his threatening expression. Tension lines flirted with the corners of his mouth.

A tingle traveled Viv's spine. She didn't know if it was fear or excitement. "What about Al?" *Am I actually entertaining this?*

"She's been asleep almost two hours now. Besides, we won't be gone long: up the street and back. What could happen?"

"'What could happen?' They argued, charged with negligence, before Child Protective Services and a jury of their peers."

Rick twisted his lips to the side. "Seriously."

"I am serious."

"Come on."

"Rick, you can get on that thing, take a quick ride, come back, and tell me all about it. And our daughter won't be left alone in the house."

"I know all that, Viv. Tonight, right now, I want to do this with you."

It sounded like a line from a romance novel. But she wasn't reading a book. She was standing in their now downright-chilly garage (her nipples were a testament to that) and listening to a live voice. Caught up in the moment, she nodded. "Five minutes, Rick."

"Ten."

"Richard A. Phillips! We will be leaving our child alone."

"Ten."

Viv stared at her husband. Sex and danger emanated from him such that this time, her fear quashed the excitement. Rick, in his most daring moments, never came across like this. Her fear, however, didn't last. "Ten minutes."

Rick smiled.

"Not eleven minutes, *ten*. And, back *home* in ten minutes, not on the way home." She was trying to hold on to some sense of responsibility.

Rick nodded his agreement.

Viv sighed. "Where's my helmet?"

"Helmet? We don't need 'em for this. We're just go'n—"

"Be right in this house, if you don't have helmets."

Rick grinned.

He was just cute. "Come on now, stop playing."

A large duffel bag sat on the floor in front of the freezer. Rick retrieved the bag and opened it, revealing three helmets: two adult-sized, and one child-sized. He presented the two adult helmets to her: one a frosted gray, the other a deep cyan. Alna's helmet was yellow.

"Pick one."

Viv took the blue helmet. "Now what?"

Rick stepped back, checking her attire. "Now a jacket, and you may want to get your boots."

"I'ma tinkle first."

"You mean check on Alna."

Viv headed into the house. "That, too. Back in a minute."

Several minutes later, Rick parked the bike in their garage. They dismounted in silence. During the ride, Viv managed to cop a feel off her husband. She couldn't help glancing below Rick's waist after he dismounted, but she couldn't see anything: his leather jacket came down too far.

Rick checked his pocket watch. "And that was nine minutes, I'll have you know."

"Very good, very good. That was fun, Rick."

"Yeah. Al's go'n love it."

Viv stepped around the motorcycle, moving close to him. "Yes, I'm sure Alna will. But I was referring to the two of us. It was fun being alone with you like that." She took his hand.

Rick gently removed his hand and stepped back.

The lump that sprung in her throat nearly choked her. She was at a loss now: a loss for words, a loss of understanding.

Rick cleared his throat. "Well, goodnight."

"Are you going to make it one?" Being coy was over.

"And how am I supposed to do that?"

Viv looked at him, eyes direct.

Rick smiled. He looked down, shaking his head and blushing hard. He couldn't have been sexier to Viv if he'd tried.

He leaned over and kissed her forehead (a gesture reserved for nieces and goddaughters). Viv swallowed around the lump in her throat and walked past Rick toward the door leading into the house. "Goodnight."

"G'night," Rick responded quietly.

*　*　*　*　*

Unable to sleep, Viv sat in her corner chair reading. Songs by Roy Ayers played softly in the music player beside her bed. Roy Ayers or Phyllis Hyman always helped her through melancholy moods.

Viv rested the novel on her lap and tilted her head back against the chair cushion. Deep in thought, she barely heard the knock on her door. A part of her didn't want to be bothered. A much bigger part of her did.

Knowing who knocked, Viv opened the door and sat on the bed.

Rick entered and sat beside her. "Drove you to Roy, huh?"

"You could say that."

"No Phyllis?"

Viv shook her head.

Rick folded his hands and bent over, resting his forearms across his thighs. He looked at Viv, then at the floor.

Viv waited. They weren't on the outs, but it was on Rick to set it right with this particular glitch.

"It's been very good again, hasn't it? Like it was before things got—"

"Yes."

"Everything, but the one thing, that was never a problem for us."

"Well, my announcement several weeks ago affected that, I'm sure."

Rick didn't respond.

Viv ventured on. "But going to therapy has helped. We've taken steps to reignite things, and … And with Jonathan passing …"

"Are you sad he's gone?"

"Of course." Viv watched Rick's jaw tighten. "Jonathan was a good man, Rick. He was my friend. The sadness has little to do with anything else."

"But since he's gone, you might as well try again with me, right?"

"No. I love you."

Rick stared at the floor. "You loved Rast, too."

"I did. But it was different. I'm not getting into a scoring-match here: whom I loved better, more, or whatever. But it was different."

"So different, you wanted to leave Alna and me?"

"At the time, my wanting to separate had little to do with Jonathan. Honestly, I threw that out there to hurt you."

Rick looked at her. "So, what did it have to do with?"

Viv swallowed hard. Dr. Alexander suggested they get into this, and they couldn't avoid doing so forever. "Besides the cheating, these last few years, I've felt unfulfilled and dissatisfied. Your focus on Alna and this thing you have about family; it was closing me in."

"I'm never go'n discount our family, Vivian." His eyes held a disturbing determination.

"I'm not saying that. But your devotion to family, family, family gets to be too much. It made you, I don't know, boring."

Rick looked back to the floor.

"What's that about, Rick?" Viv asked softly. There had to be a reason for his fixation.

"Did you love Rast more than me?"

"Rick, I said I wasn't—"

"Viv!" Rick's tone startled her, but he looked at her pleadingly. He rarely raised his voice. Those red-brown eyes told her he needed to know. Good or bad, he needed to know.

She wouldn't have to lie to keep the peace. "No. I love you more. Jonathan's gone, Rick. He doesn't pose a threat to you. He never did."

Rick reached for his ear.

Viv gently guided his hand down from his ear and held it. "Come on, don't do that. We're talking. It's what Naomi advised us to do, right? Besides, to be honest, I thought you came in here to build some bridges." She nudged his shoulder.

Rick smiled wanly before releasing Viv's hand. He returned to his bent posture, staring at the floor. "I know how this is going to sound, given what I've done. I'm saying that up front, okay?" He paused. "It's been hard to approach you for sex because I keep thinking about you being with Rast."

"That's not fair." But empathy outweighed her anger.

"I said I knew how it sounded."

"I know." Viv looked her husband over. He'd closed his eyes. She watched his jaw muscles tensing underneath the hair on his face. Rick worked to get past his anger, but as far as she was concerned, he could stay angry; it looked good on him. Desire for him intensified. His A-shirt and jeans only amplified the situation.

He was barefoot. Viv stared at his long toes briefly before shaking her head and getting up. She'd had enough. Viv walked to the door, closed it, and locked it. She stood at the door watching him.

"Mind if we change the music? I've got more to say, but Roy …"

"No problem." Viv went to her nightstand and stopped the player.

The silence was apparently too much for him. "We can do better than that." Rick leaned over. He scrolled and reviewed titles from the music playlists. Finding something he liked, he selected it. He looked at Viv as he replaced Roy with the new music.

"I don't want to hear anything but this right now." Rick turned back to the music player and pushed a few buttons. He grabbed two Hershey's Kisses from her nightstand. He unwrapped one and popped it in his mouth before holding a hand out to her. "C'mere."

L.T.D.'s "Love Ballad" floated into the room at a low volume.

Taking his hand, Viv moved between his legs. "I thought you had more to say."

"I do. Just …" He embraced her, pressing his cheek to her torso.

She wasn't showing yet, but Viv tensed immediately. She wanted to keep that can of worms on the shelf as long as possible. Letting the moment guide her, she returned his embrace, encircling his head with her arms and holding him to her.

She massaged Rick's head, breathing in the fresh peppermint and herbal-oil scents from his shampoo, and enjoying the feel of his crinkly-soft hair under her hands as she pushed fingers through his rough, dry curls. She trailed a hand down his back, rubbing the muscles there in wide circles.

Rick soon eased his hands under her robe and nightshirt, caressing and squeezing her rear.

Viv tilted her head back in joyful relief.

Rick rose slowly, maintaining their body contact. Her clothing rose with him. His erection pressing against her hip, Rick gazed into her eyes. "I miss you, Viv. I want you so bad, I can hardly breathe. I can't take it anymore." He continued his gaze, waiting.

She looked up into the cozy fire. Everything about him, from his uneven breathing, to his intense stare, to the coiled tension she felt in his back, told Viv he awaited her affirmative signal.

Viv searched his face. "Me, neither."

Rick kissed her: his mouth hard, his tongue demanding.

Viv tasted his anger, his impatience; she returned the favor. Their exchange of breath and moan became a form of resuscitation all its own. The immensely satisfying chocolaty-sweet heat of his tongue and passion-pain of his kiss fueled her desire for him. She pulled away with a soft gasp, focusing on his lips. "Kisses … don't lie." Viv looked in his eyes.

Rick shook his head slowly, his irises firing reds and dark-golds of emotion. "No, they don't. I love you, Vivian."

Viv gazed back, listening to their pounding hearts. "I love you."

Rick pecked her lips. He unfastened her robe, and then gently guided her in a turn away from him. He stepped close; evidence of his arousal pressed against her rear.

The heat of his breath stirred her as he drew the robe off, sending it to the floor. Rick trailed soft fingertips across her shoulders, before placing his lips against her. Curving his hands around her front, he lightly grasped her breasts as he nipped along her neck, running his tongue in a tight circle at the nape.

Viv stifled a gasp as bolts of sensual electricity scorched through her, taking her breath away.

Ropes of longing left her trembling. She turned and faced him. With his fingertips at her waist (God, she loved whenever he did that), Viv touched Rick's face tentatively, wanting finally to feel the growth there. His beard lay low and even against his face, the hairs dry but smooth.

Viv paused to enjoy this masculine newness. She looked up at him, still trembling with desire. "I like this … very much." Her baby started to smile, but Viv covered his mouth with hers, letting Rick now taste the heat of her open lust for him. Her trembling fingers fumbled with the button of his jeans.

Rick gently lifted away and smiled down at her. He covered her hands with his, instantly calming her. "Hey now, we've done this before, baby." His hoarse but soothing words oozed sexily to her core.

She couldn't breathe as she nodded back, but who cared?

Rick removed his shirt.

Her husband's chest and torso formed a work of art. Viv ran her fingers over him, skimming the patches of fine hair. Tracing fingers over the fraternity brand on his shoulder, she kissed his right nipple before reclining on the bed. Viv watched her husband unfasten his jeans, focusing on that serious bulge against his inner thigh.

Holding her gaze, Rick opened the second Hershey's Kiss and placed it on his tongue before pulling his jeans off and reclining beside her. He brought his face close, looking in her eyes. "You and Me?"

Viv's insides quivered with sentiment. They hadn't exchanged their private pledge for years. She nodded slowly and cupped his cheek. "Me and You."

Jeffrey Osborne sang and Viv grooved as her husband lowered his mouth to hers. They languidly transferred the morsel back-and-forth between them. When it dissolved, her husband traced a rigid tongue over the outline of her lips with a deliciously-slow pace that ignited bursts of delight in the secret corners of her being.

With a rush of feminine power, she wrapped her arms around Rick and rolled on top, straddling him.

Passion. Desire. Lust. Viv didn't think any of those adequately described the surge moving through her. But whatever it was, it was white-hot and complete. Viv tongued her husband as if her life depended on it.

His erection was under her, lying upward along his lower abdomen and fitted between her private crevice. Her button, swollen and throbbing now, pressed against the thin fabric of her tanga panties.

Mouths locked, Rick trailed his hands to her rear and gripped her, moving her up-and-down and back-and-forth on the hardness between them.

She was at her husband's mercy, allowing him to push her headfirst into sweet oblivion. His mouth swallowed her cry as her orgasm rocketed through her, momentarily blocking out sight and sound.

Sighing deeply, Viv collapsed onto him, Rick stroking her hair and body through the aftershocks. She kissed his neck as he held her, gently nibbling his Adam's apple while he continued a subtle grind against her.

That quick surrender only took the edge off. She wanted more. Viv rolled off Rick, pulling him toward her to resume their sensual give-and-take.

Rick's fingers teased her nipple through her clothing before finally raising her shirt and bra high above her breasts and getting the real thing. Nuzzling Viv's neck, he kneaded her mounds with a fervor designed to leave her senseless. She played contentedly in his hair while he had his way, floating on a cloud of his JV Artisan Black: a heady blend that was citrusy and woodsy, with hints of jasmine and ginger.

He moaned softly and kissed down her neck, continuing his steamy assault toward her breasts where he tenderly circled each hardened nipple with his tongue, applying gentle nips with his teeth, caressing her waist and hip in time with the movements of his mouth. His hardness strained warmly against her thigh.

Savage need, hot and pulsing, clamped between her thighs. Viv bit her lip and gripped into Rick's hair, wanting him inside her. She reached a hand inside his boxers for his erection, gripping and stroking it.

Her husband let out a low, husky groan at her touch; the tremor of the sound against her skin simmered in her veins. "Damn, I'm hard …" He moved his mouth back up her body for another deep kiss.

She could've replied with some comment on how wet she was, but Rick's hand trailed toward her nether region—he'd find out soon enough. Tonguing her languidly, Rick removed her panties with quiet expertise. When his hand trailed up her thigh, she opened with welcome invitation.

With a low, gravelly moan, Rick pulled back from their kiss upon touching her. Eyes closed, his soft lips hovered above hers. "Shit, Viv." He lowered his mouth back to hers as his fingers played inside her opening.

Intense pleasure shrouded her. Feeling herself going again as he fingered her, she broke their kiss and grabbed his wrist, looking in those eyes of his. "You."

Rick tugged his boxers off and braced above her.

Viv drew her hands behind his head to play in his hair.

He eased inside as "We Both Deserve Each Other's Love" began, and Viv slowly shook her head at the sheer perfection in that timing. She closed her eyes with the feel of him filling her, the gentle pressure against her cervix reminding her how much she missed him.

He sang a few of the opening lines softly in her ear as he gyrated into her, drawing out the duration of his thrusts to allow her leisurely-enjoyment of his size. Viv rocked her hips slowly in time with him, creating a lovingly-nasty rhythm that pursued the sublime.

Rick's choked moans and low sexual grunts when the stroke was good to him satisfied her aural desires. The heat between them grew hotter. A climax beckoned. Viv rested her right hand above her head in modest submission. "Faster, baby."

Interlocking his left hand with her right, his right hand gripped behind her left knee, bringing it toward her shoulder. He lowered his head next to her and quickened the pace, thrusting his body in and out of hers while using this swirling-grind that left her bare.

She delighted in his masculinity as the scruff of his beard grazed her. Rick's hard, fast, swirling plunges ushered her deliriously toward her peak.

My goodness, this man ...

Her body exploded in bliss. She gripped Rick's hand tighter and cried out, arching upward against him, deliciously aware of her nipples pressing into his hard chest. Moaning, she rode the wave, clenching her teeth against the spasms. Rick grunted his pleasure at feeling them.

Viv grabbed his rear, driving him deeper. She experienced twinges of pain, but was beyond caring; his thrusts left her blithely-shattered.

Still holding her hand, Rick tapered his thrusts. He now alternated between tonguing her softly and gazing down at her as they continued. She whispered sexy-nothings to him as they moved together, moving her free hand over him sensuously and watching for the telltale sign of his impending orgasm.

Rick's face was calm, but then the burnt-umber of his eyes lightened the tiniest bit, as if miniscule coal-fire embers burned within his irises. Viv found the change in his eyes before he seeded her, to be something both eerily-strange and wonderfully-erotic.

His thrusts quickened, intensified, pushed deeper. "Vivian ..."

Viv caressed his head and pecked his lips and grinded back nastily, his plunges subtly-electrifying.

Her baby soon closed his eyes and released her hand. With a soft grunt, he emptied into her, punching the mattress once as he finished.

The few men Viv slept with (including Jonathan) always got that goofy, stupefied "come" face, but Rick's was different. His expression always turned painfully-angry (the way it did moments ago): beautifully fascinating. Those two things, seeing the change in his eyes and seeing his facial expression during orgasm, should've belonged only to her (his conquests before they married didn't count). Rick lowered his head, next to hers.

He felt so damn good—inside her, on top of her. Love for Rick threatened to swallow Viv whole, leaving her limp with emotion.

Rick brought his hand from behind her knee, drawing it up her body to squeeze on her breast tenderly and tease the nipple while they came down. They lay in a tangle of warm skin as she caressed Rick's head and back, kissing on him and waiting for his breathing to stabilize (hers, too, for that matter).

He lifted slightly, keeping the full pressure of his weight off her, and gazed down at her. "You okay, Lady Blue?"

Viv grabbed his head and kissed him.

Rick laughed into her mouth.

The vibration of his laughter against her teeth and tongue spurred a new turn-on. And as his laughter and feigned resistance gave way to a moan and return of her kiss, Viv wanted to go again. It occurred to her that she never cared about Jonathan immediately pulling out, never asked that he wait inside her.

Soft now, Rick chuckled as he broke their kiss and slipped out. "Hold up." He shifted to stretch out beside her. "I know your engine is still running ..." There was nothing bashful about the sexy glint in his eyes this time. He rested his head on her chest, cupping a breast and snuggling in.

Viv kissed the top of his head. "Yeah," she whispered.

Jeffrey's voice floated into the room, but she barely heard him through her high of sleepiness, emotional euphoria, and arousal.

Rick tweaked her nipple. "Want some 'in the meantime'?"

"Not this time." It wasn't what she wanted. It would be good, but she wanted the real deal.

He lifted and pecked her lips. "I can come back when Cronus rears his head again—pardon the pun."

Viv giggled. Had she really considered leaving this man? It was a sobering thought realizing that, at one point, yes, she did. Viv rolled on top of Rick and kissed him (she loved kissing him).

Sliding off his body, she rose and freshened with a moist-towelette from the dispenser on her nightstand before pulling her nightshirt over her head.

Rick propped on his elbow to watch.

Her bra fit twisted and askew above her breasts and under her arms. Viv removed that, too. She gloated inside at seeing Rick's eyes move with male interest over her body. He was naked; she noticed the muscles in his groin twitch slightly. "Come on, get up."

Rick looked puzzled, but he stood.

Viv turned off the lamp in the corner. At the bed, she turned down the covers and stopped the music player, silencing Jeffrey's serenade. "When Cronus wakes, I wanna be there to greet him."

Rick smiled.

His sweet smile weakened her. Viv guided him by the hand into bed with her, turning off the lamp on her nightstand and sending the room into darkness. Rick spooned her. The realization of just how much she'd missed her husband overwhelmed her. Viv undulated backward, trying to mold her body to his even more.

Rick chuckled against her hair. "Keep it up, hear?"

"Sorry."

"Believe me, it's not a problem."

Sleepiness descended. The clock read 11:17 p.m. She drifted off, falling asleep in the warm pocket of Rick's body behind her.

By 1:22 a.m., Cronus was indeed awake and wanting her attention. Viv was more than happy to give it.

"We'll take it extra-slow," Rick whispered as he kissed down her back toward her rear. "Like we know how to do." He lifted her leg and rested his head upon the opposite inner-thigh, his mouth wonderfully-close to her pink. "Okay?" Drawing his other hand up her body to massage a breast, he opened her wider and licked everything tenderly as he initiated round two.

Viv caressed her husband's head. She could only moan and nod her agreement. He was doing so many nice things to her …

* * * * *

The empty feeling in her bed woke her. She'd gotten used to waking alone the past several weeks, but she'd been waking with Rick for years.

Viv sat up and checked the floor: Rick's clothes were gone. She checked the clock: 10:47 a.m. Rick left the door cracked. Voices traveled from downstairs. The TV was too loud. Viv clearly heard dialogue from Alna's animated movie; she watched the same movie repeatedly over the last few days. A vase holding the lush and fragrant bouquet he bought her was on the nightstand.

Viv turned over, breathing in the side of the bed where Rick slept, breathing in his Artisan Black. Sex with him was just …

Saturday was laundry day.

Oh, this linen won't be getting stripped today.

Viv got up, brushed her teeth, and showered quickly before throwing on sweatpants, a sports bra, and a tank-top. She held prayer in her corner. Gathering the first load of clothes from the bedrooms, she headed downstairs.

Carrying a pillowcase full of whites, Viv stood in the areaway leading into their kitchen, breathing in the aroma of bacon and fried onions, and ogling her husband from behind.

Rick stood at the stove. He wore his black Impetus Marketing Inc. T-shirt and orange sweatpants; his feet clad in socks and athletic slides. Even through the loose clothing, Viv made out the definition of his muscular frame—and thought about how well he used it.

Fuck the dumb stuff: she abhorred the idea of another woman having him. Anger, rooted in jealousy, surfaced, but she let it pass and stepped into the kitchen. "Mornin', all!"

Rick turned. "Good morning. Sleep well?"

Viv made a face while poking her tongue. "Yes, I did."

Holding her gaze, Rick walked over and stopped next to her. He plucked a slice of cantaloupe from the plate of sliced melon he'd prepared. "Did I 'make it a good night,' then?" His voice was low, sultry. He smelled of soap and clean linen, and wore one of his classic fragrances: Christian Dior Eau Sauvage. The invigorating masculine scent of him made her happily dizzy.

Viv gazed into the burning-embers for as long as she could. She shook her body to ward-off the warm feelings stirring in her belly and called to Alna: "The TV's too loud, Al. Turn it down, please." Turning back to Rick, Viv tried to convey with her eyes how much she enjoyed their night. He placed the slice of melon close to her mouth for her to bite it. The cantaloupe was juicy, sweet. She blushed and slurped. "Thank you."

Rick nodded slowly and winked at her. He finished the cantaloupe with his own slurp and went back to the stove to arrange biscuits on a foil-lined cookie sheet, humming "We Both Deserve Each Other's Love."

Viv didn't know whether to hit him or take him back upstairs. She turned her attention to her daughter.

Alna pointed the remote at the TV and lowered the volume. She jumped up and bounded to her mother. "Like the motorcycle, Mommy?"

Viv smiled down at her. "I do."

"Daddy says he'll take me out later today if the weather's good."

"Well, it's supposed to be pretty nice out."

Alna clapped. "Yay!"

"Finish watching your movie, Al. Breakfast'll be ready soon." Rick kept his back to them.

"Okay, Daddy." Alna returned to the family room and plopped down in front of the TV.

Viv frowned. She didn't get why he sent her off like that. "Rick?"

"Yeah?"

"What's wrong?"

Rick turned and leaned back against the stove. "Nothing. Why?" His sweatpants jutted from obvious excitement.

Viv went flush. Her body revved for another round. Rick worked her last night, but apparently that hadn't fazed either of them. Their daughter, however, was wide-awake and about the house. And, as much as she appreciated the spontaneity of the situation, there weren't going to be any happenings right now.

Feigning indifference, Viv held the clothing-filled pillowcase up to her body (a shield of sorts) and headed for the laundry room, sensing

Rick's eyes on her as she walked past. "Let me get these started." She entered the laundry room and started the washer.

He was behind her in seconds as she bent over to unload the pillowcase. Rick grabbed her hips from behind.

The feel of his erection against her ass jolted her. Viv stood. "Rick, we can't." Her protest held no conviction whatsoever.

Rick turned her to face him, placing his fingertips at her waist. "Yes, we can."

Lord, the pressure of his fingertips ... "R- Right here?"

Rick nodded.

"Rick, Alna is right in the next room."

"I know that." He placed a delicate kiss on the mole on her collarbone, turning her bones to liquid lava and making rational thought near impossible.

"Besides, this ... isn't a bedroom."

Rick frowned. "Forget that."

"It's just—"

Rick leaned close, whispering in her ear: "I love you, Vivian. So much, baby. I need to fuck you." He placed her hand against his hardness. "Will you let me?" He was all crisp-clean-scent, loving words, and masculine goodness.

Immediately taken with desire, she whispered, "Yes."

Rick kissed her. He kissed her right, too. Kisses didn't lie. If she had other arguments, she didn't know what they were. The empty washing machine filled with hot water. Viv didn't care. Her nine-year-old could walk in on them any minute. Viv deepened their kiss, as Rick was making her not care too much about that, either. She broke from his mouth, checking to see if the laundry room door leading into the kitchen had a lock: it didn't.

Rick nibbled at her neck, sending tendrils of excitement to her belly.

"At least close the door, Rick."

He stuck a foot out to the side and pushed the door almost-closed.

Viv was relieved it didn't close audibly—that surely would have brought Alna out of her movie-stupor to investigate.

"Turn around," Rick said thickly.

Viv leaned over the dryer. Her photography supplies were carefully stacked to the side. She closed her eyes as her husband pulled her sweats down, uniquely turned-on because Rick, Mr. In-the-Bedroom-Only, Please, initiated such a risqué act.

In a move reserved only for those who know what they're doing, Rick reached under her shirt and bra, cupped each breast, and entered her simultaneously.

Viv gasped with the arousing feel of that thing overtaking her passage. "Shit, boy ..."

Rick found his rhythm.

Hot water poured into the otherwise empty washer. Viv heard the sloshing water and the drone of the washer, but concentrated more on the passionate sounds her husband made as he pounded into her. Their slow lovemaking last night and during the wee hours of the morning was beautiful, but this raw action between them now had its own beauty.

Rick worked her thoroughly but succinctly. He climaxed moments before she: hers a warm rush through her lower body (his penis was always so good to her).

Breathing heavily, Rick caressed her hip. "You okay?"

"Yes."

Understandably, he didn't wait before pulling out. Viv looked over her shoulder at her husband and grinned.

Rick grinned back. He dipped a piece of laundry from the pillowcase into the swishing water, closed the lid, and then cleaned them up quickly.

After fixing their clothes and checking them twice, they looked at each other ... and burst out laughing.

"Shhh," Viv whispered.

"No, you shhh."

Viv circled arms around his neck. "Breakfast is gonna burn."

"Nah, I turned everything off first."

"Oh, so you *knew* you were gettin' some."

Rick kissed her. Damn, did he *know* how much she loved kissing him? His tongue was warm and tasty in her mouth.

Viv grew serious when they parted. "We're making up for lost time."

"You think?"

She pecked his lips and nodded.

Rick looked toward her makeshift darkroom area. Even with the advent of digital photography, she still liked having the option of using a darkroom for developing pictures.

Viv noticed his jaw muscles working. "Rick?"

"You know, I started to trash this shit, too, that day." His voice was tight, edgy. Hearing the malevolence, Viv loosened her embrace, but Rick pulled her close. "I was so hurt, Viv."

Viv couldn't see his face, but the pain in his voice echoed. His previous tone bothered her, but she kept quiet. Rick's destruction of her side of their workroom remained a sore-topic unexplored, and, truthfully, Viv preferred they let it drop altogether. The hurt over seeing those smashed pieces lingered. She hugged Rick back. "I know, baby. Let's not do this now."

Rick stood back from her and tilted his head. His red-brown eyes sparkled. "Save it for Doctor Alexander?"

Just adorable. Viv nodded.

He leaned to kiss her again, when Alna called from the kitchen. "Daddy?"

"In here, sweetie." Viv gave Rick a look that said, *See?*

The door swung open. Alna stood in the doorway, hands on her hips. "What's going on?"

Viv tapped the washing machine. "Just getting the laundry started."

Rick's right hand was blocked from Alna's view; that hand went under Viv's shirt. He caressed the side swell of her left breast with his thumb. A tingle curled her toes.

"Everything's off in the kitchen. Is it time to eat yet?"

"In … In a minute, sweetheart," Viv stammered.

"Can I have some cantaloupe?"

His caress left Viv momentarily mute.

Rick didn't look at Alna but continued watching Viv's face. "Sure, sweetie. Daddy's coming." His thumb inched toward her nipple.

Viv made every effort to look totally-poised.

Alna watched her parents briefly; she retreated, leaving the door open.

As soon as Alna disappeared from view, Rick grabbed a handful.

Viv sighed.

Rick lifted her shirt and bra enough to expose what he wanted, and let his mouth take over the caress.

Viv's body warmed for him, but she stiff-armed Rick's shoulders, pushing him back. "You can't possibly be ready to go again." The washing machine shifted cycles.

"Not this second, no, but I'm enjoying what I'm doing to you."

The machine vibrated.

Rick cocked an eyebrow.

"Rick, no." But she allowed him to move them so that the machine vibrated against her butt. "Rick, the door."

"We won't need the door closed for this." Rick moved his body around to her right. If Alna came back, Rick's back would be to her and most of Viv's body blocked from view.

Viv swallowed hard as Rick's right hand went down the front of her sweats. Using his less-dominant hand was of no consequence as his fingers initiated their dance.

"Look at you …" He kissed her temple.

Viv closed her eyes and opened her stance, enjoying the vibration of the washer on her backside as Rick worked her front.

"That's right …"

Viv sighed deeply.

"So, what're your plans for today?"

Viv looked at him. "Wh- what?"

Rick gazed back just as composed and unaffected as if they were discussing the weather. "What's up for today?"

"Well …" She couldn't believe his attempt to have a conversation at this precise moment.

Rick leaned in, hovering close as if to kiss her. "Yes?"

"I, uh …" Viv anticipated a deep-kiss, but Rick only allowed their lips to brush.

"Yes, go on," he prompted softly. His tease of an almost-kiss heightened her desire, his breath an air of sweet cantaloupe against her lips and teeth, her tongue.

"I was s- supposed to …" Her lips skimmed his as she spoke.

"Supposed to … yeah …?"

She wanted his tongue. "Rick …"

Rick shook his head, their lips brushing. "Not yet." He kept his mouth a millimeter from hers. "I got this." Down below, her husband worked magic with his thumb and middle fingers.

Viv closed her eyes again with the joy building between her thighs.

Knowing she was close, Rick finally gave her the kiss she craved as he fingered her.

This man is just…

Viv moaned; the burst of release short but powerful.

Rick broke from her mouth. "I got you. C'mere." He nipped her earlobe. His left arm held her around her waist, supporting her as she crumpled against him.

Catching her breath, Viv reached down the front of his sweats, wanting the simple thrill of cupping the fullness of his package.

"Whew!" Rick sighed. "I'm beat. How 'bout you?"

Viv stood erect and poked him in the ribs.

"Hey!"

"Hey, yourself."

Rick chuckled. "A'ight, listen …" He lifted the washer lid, looked inside, and then back at Viv with a smirk. "Why don't you actually start a load of clothes this time, and I'll finish getting breakfast on the table. I'm sure that cantaloupe won't hold Al for long." He pecked her lips and left.

Viv stared into the empty washer, trying to gather her scattered thoughts. The laundry room smelled of dirty laundry mingled with the fresh scents of laundry detergent and their fragrances. She heard Rick and Alna talking, but their conversation echoed distantly in the background.

Giddiness and trepidation swirled within her.

Rick had certainly turned things around. And oddly, Viv knew deep down that his behavior wasn't a patch to get them through a rough spell.

He'd changed, returning to the man he used to be—but strangely different somehow.

Oh, he wanted as much family-togetherness as before, but since he'd been able to give Viv more of what she needed, she didn't mind it so much. Besides, since the in-house separation, family activities provided the only neutral ground she and Rick used to approach their husband-wife issues.

She laughed to herself as a chill trickled along her arms. After last night and this morning, she also knew Rick lost absolutely nothing sexually.

Viv restarted the cycle.

So, there it was. She could now say she had the best of both worlds (and a baby to boot). That she'd found it with her husband proved even better.

Viv stared into the washer. "So, what's wrong?"

Her mind instantly jumped to Rick's demeanor when he told her he wanted to trash her photo supplies. Replaying his words in her head, another chill went through her. Her face tightened with the worry and concern etching her features. But the chill also carried a bit of arousal.

Because, if she wanted to be completely candid, Viv had to admit she was intrigued. The intense (violent?) edge to Rick's personality captivated her.

It scared her, too.

"Stop it." Viv turned to the pillowcase and began emptying the contents into the washer.

CHAPTER 15

Table Talk

"That's every six months, Mister Phillips, not every *other* six months." Louise informed with a smile. "Now get out of here, both of you."

"Who made up that rule anyway? 'Visit your dentist every six months.'" Rick scoffed. "Why not every four or seven months?"

Tim pulled Rick's arm. "Man, please don't get my wife started." Timothy Collins's straight teeth enhanced his other features. No wonder Lou fell for him. He stood in the doorway. "Come on, frat; let's go."

"Yes, go." Viv pointed a finger at Rick. "But be careful."

Rick twisted his lips. "Ain't no fun being too-careful, but I'll see what I can do."

"Oh, I know what you can do," Viv practically purred.

Did I say that out loud?

Everyone's silence signaled she had.

Tim and Louise gave her shrewd grins.

Rick's gaze however carried provocative heat. "Yeah, I know."

"Anyway, people!" Louise cut in. "You two can get your nasty on, later. Right now, take my husband out for a quick ride on that motorcycle and get back here so we can go."

Rick turned to Tim. "Bossy, isn't she?"

"Yeah. It's funny. I always thought Vietnamese women were supposed to be quiet and submissive. Louise didn't flip the script until after the ring was on her finger." A teasing smile played around Tim's mouth.

"Same story around the world, man." Rick lowered his eyes and shook his head in exaggerated sadness.

Tim joined him.

A balled napkin lay on the table in front of Louise. She threw it at them and smiled. "Get out!"

"Back in a few." Grinning, Rick air-kissed Viv and closed the door.

"That better be a few *minutes* and not a few hours," Louise called, rising from her seat at the table.

At twelve minutes past noon, brunch at the Collins home was essentially over. Alna and Li'l Tim were in the living room playing video games. Viv and Louise started clearing the dishes, getting ready to go shopping for yet more fish for Alna.

"I don't know, Viv. When they get together sometimes ... Later, Tim'll be throwing that 'you know how it is when frat are hanging' crap at me, and I'll have to divorce him yet again." Louise giggled.

She opened the dishwasher and loaded it as Viv transferred dishes from the table to the mauve-and-cream speckled countertop separating them. The aroma of pancake batter and sausage lingered.

Brunch was over, but not surprisingly, Viv could eat again. She anticipated feeling definitive flutters in her stomach unrelated to a romantic look or touch from her husband.

"So, you and Rick are back on track." Louise wore an ao-dai of bright orange and green, one of many she sometimes reserved for their get-togethers.

"You could say that."

Louise chuckled. "Oh, that's an understatement."

Puzzled, Viv looked at her friend. "Anyway, nothing was happening, sex-wise that is, until this past Friday."

"Oh."

Viv shivered with the memory. "Girl, he sliced and served."

Louise shrugged. "You've never complained about Rick as a lover; quite the opposite." She transferred dishes from counter to dishwasher.

"I know, but ..." Viv sat at the table. Clouds passed over the sun, giving Louise's mauve-and-beige kitchen a subdued sepia effect.

Louise finished loading and started the cycle. She joined Viv at the table. "But what?" she sighed.

"Rick has this edgy, charming, assertive, but sensitive thing going on. Before, he was just working with sensitive and charming." Viv shook her head. "I don't know. I guess you'd have to be there."

"Uh, I don't think so."

"Funny. But, like yesterday: we had a quickie in the laundry room."

"Who did?"

"*We* did."

"You and *Rick*? The laundry room?" Louise sat back.

"Now you see what I'm saying. But here's the kicker: Alna was in the family room—and came looking for us!"

"Alna didn't s—?"

"No, no: we were decent when she found us." Viv sat back herself and sighed. "Girl, he did some things to me on that washing machine …"

Louise made an expression Viv couldn't place. For a second, jealousy seemed the best word to describe it. "Well, you've obviously been busy."

"But like I said, the bonus is Rick's whole attitude and approach to everything. He's like his old-self, but something's different, extra-intense. I feel sexier and bold, closer to him."

"Girl, what are you, eighteen?" That weird expression crossed Louise's face again. This time Viv thought she saw fleeting-fury. "It'll pass."

"That's just it. Since I told him about Jonathan and moved into another bedroom, Rick's changed. But I don't feel it's a temporary-thing to get me back."

"Just seems like his old-self to me: how he was back in the day." Louise waved a hand dismissively. "You're all sexed up."

"I'm serious, Lou. Rick's different."

Louise held Viv's gaze. "I guess that's it then."

Viv didn't reply.

"All is forgiven. Everything's perfect. Crisis over."

"Crisis over," Viv repeated flatly.

"You can't be serious."

"What if I am?"

Louise shook her head.

"What, Lou? I never said I wanted a divorce or anything."

"You said everything but divorce, Viv."

"So?"

"And so now, just like that, everything's back to, no wait, change that, *better* than normal?"

"I'm not saying everything's perfect. You know they're not."

"The cheating?"

Viv shrugged.

"Well, what about the monotony, his wanting so much focus on family-togetherness?"

Viv shrugged again. Except for the infidelity, the other mattered less now. And he'd said he was done when they were in therapy. Deep inside, she believed that.

"Love is not good sex, Viv."

She thought about Louise's summation. "You can't tell me what love is. Not for me anyway, or for anybody except yourself. 'Love is not good sex.'" Viv scoffed.

Louise frowned.

"What love means to someone is relative, Lou. But if I had to guess, I'd say good sex is a key part of most happy relationships. When other areas of our relationship suffered, our lovemaking sure kept things going." Viv paused, reading Louise's expression. Lou's mouth, set in irritation, matched what Viv couldn't believe she read in her eyes: envious resentment.

"So, you're going back to the master bedroom?"

"Sure. Why? Would that be a problem?" Viv didn't know why she felt defensive.

"Can I ask you something?"

Viv nodded.

"Why isn't the issue of Rick's cheating ever the focus?"

"It came up in therapy."

"And? What's he got to say?"

"I don't want to get into that now." Rick's reason for cheating (or lack thereof) still bothered her.

"Okay. But if good sex held you to Rick, where does Jonathan fit in? Was it better with him?"

"Definitely not. But Jonathan had other appealing qualities."

Louise shook her head. "Girl, you are a mystery."

"I didn't say good sex was the bottom line for a relationship. I said it played a key part. But everyone has a breaking point."

Louise grew quiet.

From the other room, Viv could tell Li'l Tim was winning at whatever game he and Alna were playing. Viv grew uncomfortable with the stillness in the kitchen.

"Well, I'm happy for you, Viv."

Viv thought she detected cynicism. "You mean that?"

"'Course I do. You and Rick are very good together. I'm always happy when a family isn't broken up."

"Okay, you sound too much like Rick now," Viv joked. She wondered what her friend would think if she knew she was pregnant.

"Well, I've always said I admired Rick's devotion to family. I know what you've been through, but I'm surprised he hasn't pressed harder for a little addition: to try again."

"He's had his moments." Viv hoped the discussion stopped there.

"Do you miss Jonathan at all?"

Viv nodded. "Yeah, but not in a lovesick-way. As I tried explaining to Rick, Jonathan was first and foremost my good friend."

Louise's eyes widened. "You talked to Rick about your affair?"

"A little bit. And can we not use the word 'affair'?"

"So, you two can discuss your dalliance, but not his?"

"I didn't say that."

Louise shrugged. "I'm just sayin' …"

Viv watched her. She clearly had some problem with Rick.

"Well this seems to have worked out well. You were unhappy, so you started seeing Jonathan. You wanted to separate from Rick and told him about Jonathan. Now Jonathan's gone, and you're once again happy with your husband."

"What are you saying, Lou?"

"Just wondering where things would be if Jonathan wasn't 'gone.'"

"I already told you."

"I know."

"No, fuck the dumb stuff: What are you really getting at?"

"I don't know. Nothing. It's just a hell of a coincidence that Jonathan ends up dead soon after you told Rick about you two."

Viv stared at Louise, mouth open.

"Close your mouth. I'm not accusing Rick of anything as awful as that. I'm just pointing out the coincidence."

"If you're not accusing, why point it out?"

"You mean you haven't thought about it?"

Viv swallowed hard. "No."

Louise looked at her. "You're right, I'm sorry."

"He wouldn't do anything like that, Lou. Come on. You know him better than that ... Whatever issues you have with him."

"What? Issues? I don't have any 'issues' with Rick. Well, I don't like that he cheated, but that's it." Louise, however, decided at that point to go to the refrigerator.

"You're not telling me something, Lou. I know you."

Louise walked back to the table with a cup of ice and sat. "Then you're getting a false signal or something."

"So why do you give me such a hard time about him?"

"Look, you and Rick must stay together. You must. But my role is to ensure you keep it real. Rick's an amazing man. I love him. You know that."

"Please. You don't have to keep anything 'real' for me. I do that on my own quite nicely." Viv turned to look through the bay window. Louise's last words stayed with her.

An instant of revelation opened her eyes to Lou's problem with Rick.

Viv turned back to Louise. She sat there, looking at her friend, feeling touched but also hurt and ... angry.

Louise spoke with uncharacteristic emotion when she said Rick was 'amazing,' and Viv was sure Louise meant for her declaration of love for Rick to come across as platonic, neutrally-caring, but it didn't. Viv heard it. She heard that special inflection on the word "love" and even "him" that was unmistakably tied to romantic love.

Although the words stayed with her, Viv ignored them. She had to. She sympathized that her dear friend experienced what Viv knew to be unrequited-love, yet she was upset because Louise also crossed that invisible but well-understood line.

"Viv?" Louise leaned across the table, peering at her.

"Uh-huh." Viv wanted to go home. She wanted to ask Lou about her feelings for Rick. She wanted her husband. Mostly, she wanted to go home.

"Is it time to go yet?" Alna paused at the kitchen entrance.

Viv stood. "As a matter of fact, it is. Why don't you and Li'l Tim straighten the living room and get your jackets."

"What about Daddy?"

"He's coming. Go on now."

Just then, sounds of a motorcycle grew louder.

Viv gestured toward the front of the house. "See?"

Alna smiled and retreated.

Suppressing the anger and hurt, Viv clapped once and turned to Louise. She pointed both index fingers at her. "Movie first, then the fish."

Louise stood. "Sounds like a plan."

It turned out to be a nice Sunday afternoon with family and friends. Viv paid more attention to Louise's exchanges with Rick, trying to pick up on any of the signs she most assuredly missed until now.

There were times when Louise's gaze seemed to linger on Rick or she smiled a little brighter at him, but Viv wasn't sure if those things were subtle indications or her imagination.

In any event, Viv found herself touching Rick more, kissing him, sharing private jokes with him …

Marking her territory, so to speak.

CHAPTER 16

Small, Simple Things

The last few weeks progressed smoothly enough. He and his wife were back on point, the sessions with Naomi were uneventful, Viv had returned to their bedroom, and talks of a family vacation were on again.

A good few weeks.

Right up to this Wednesday evening.

To begin, it was raining. Rain, in and of itself, was fine, but it limited outdoor-activity. Rick didn't like being limited. These days, he was too restless to have his options cut short, so the rain irritated him this evening.

The main problem with this Wednesday evening, however, stood in their foyer getting the hardwood floors wet: Detective Reginald Quentin Saunders. His badge read "Reginald Q. Saunders," but in the ten or so minutes he'd been in the house, Viv finagled his middle name out of him.

Rick could give a shit about his middle name. Right now, they were in the middle of dinner—family time.

Detective Saunders stood in their foyer asking mundane questions about Rast and their acquaintance with him. It was a routine part of their continuing investigation, he explained, just trying to gather information from people who knew the restaurateur. Viv, of course, was helpful and cooperative. Rick was, too, for that matter, but the fact remained he didn't like the detective.

For one thing, he didn't like cops using the term "routine." There was nothing "routine" about the police visiting your home in the middle of dinner. Second, at five feet six, Saunders was shorter than Viv, but carried seven feet of attitude.

"I must apologize again for the intrusion," Saunders repeated, directing his apology more to Viv.

"It's fine. Whatever we can do to help find out what happened to Jonathan." Viv looked at him for confirmation.

Reluctantly, Rick nodded. He wished Viv had picked something else to change into. It wasn't summer yet, but Viv, even in winter, preferred cool, comfortable clothing. She might don the occasional sweatshirt, but Viv much preferred T-shirts and tanks. She wore a tank-top now: a dark-orchid tank that popped against her skin, and black stretch jeans. She looked good. The clothing hugged her body, accentuating her slender waist, the round fullness of each breast, and the curve of her hips and ass. She'd put on a pound or two—but in all the right places.

Getting aroused, Rick instead turned his attention to Saunders, who, in Rick's honest opinion, seemed to be focusing on his baby's fine-figure as well. It wasn't blatant. In fact, Viv appeared oblivious. But Rick easily recognized what Saunders projected subconsciously. They were small, simple things, but from Saunders's slanted-hip stance and licking his lips every few seconds as he talked to Viv, Rick knew Saunders wouldn't mind having a "routine" private session with his wife. Rick's hand curled into a fist.

Bringing his fist from his pocket and resting his hand on the banister, Rick more than wanted to cave Saunders's face in. If Saunders had a sixth-sense, being a cop and all, it didn't show; he never looked in Rick's direction. *Arrogant bastard.*

Rick shifted his weight from one foot to the other. He wanted to finish having dinner with his family. Wanted the detective finished with his asinine questions. Rick checked his wife out again, wanting something else.

He partnered with the restlessness that frequently fell upon him, finding outlets for it. These days, he used his restlessness for good instead of evil, expending his energy by seeking his wife out and taking her—often. It was a new, animalistic-thing they both enjoyed, and Viv wanting him as much as he wanted her, enhanced it all.

He watched Viv's mouth move, hardly listening to her words. Focusing on her full lips, images of the superb head he awoke to Viv giving him this morning filled his mind: sucking him, getting his balls, gently using her teeth sometimes, her silky hands all over him. Lord!

Rick shifted his weight again, tightened his grip on the banister; anything to stay focused on what was happening in their foyer. Now images of him taking Viv on the stairs kept popping in his head, making concentration difficult. He kept seeing Viv, shirt raised, fully exposing those plump breasts; himself tugging her jeans down and off one leg; Viv opening for him as he placed his mouth—

"—know of. Right, Rick?"

Rick stared at Viv blankly.

"Mister Phillips?"

"Yeah, sorry. Hunger pangs. Can't keep my mind off the braised chops getting cold in the kitchen."

"Rick!" Viv looked at him with admonishing embarrassment.

"We can finish this at the precinct if you'd prefer."

Rick couldn't tell if Saunders was being accommodating or a smart-ass. He shrugged. "Right here is fine. I'm just hungry, man. You know how that is," Rick said pleasantly enough. He wanted to deliver a mawashi-geri to the detective's ass—badge or no badge.

The detective seemed mollified. "I hear you. But I'm almost done."

"It's okay, Detective Saunders."

The detective looked at Viv. He gave her this smarmy smile that was almost a pucker. "'Reggie,' please."

"Okay: Reggie." Viv turned to Rick: "Reggie was asking if Jonathan had any enemies, or any disagreements with anyone, and I told him there were none that we knew of. Right?"

Viv's question sounded unaffected, but Rick knew his wife; they were best friends. He read the subtle signal in her eyes, acknowledging that as of late, Rick had become Rast's enemy (or vice versa), but only he and Viv understood that. "Right. Rast was just a casual acquaintance. He stopped by our table to talk sometimes, worked with my wife on a few photography projects, but that was about it." Rick tensed his jaw muscles but resisted grinding his teeth. Her being with that bastard still enraged him sometimes.

Saunders nodded but jotted something down. "His phone records indicated being in contact with you, Missus Phillips. The photography?"

"Yes. We had a showing at his restaurant recently."

The detective nodded again.

"I'm sorry we're not much help, Detective Saun—Reggie."

"No, not at all. You're doing fine."

Rick already wanted the man out of his house; having his wife call him "Reggie" was pushing it. "So, you got anything at all on who might've done this?" He hoped his inquiry sounded impersonal and not too-pressed.

He didn't care about killing Rast. He didn't mean to do it, but what's done is done. He cared about Viv finding out, about being convicted of murder and sent to prison. It would destroy his family. He would let his brother down.

"We have a few leads," the detective replied vaguely, as only a cop knows how to do. "Which reminds me. Mister Rast's sister didn't recall him participating in martial-arts, but we still like to throw the question out there."

Rick waited, pretending not to get what the detective asked. He looked at Viv, who also waited—but her puzzled expression held no pretense.

Viv spoke first. "Are you asking if Jonathan knew karate or jujitsu or something? Oh, I don't know ..." She turned to Rick.

He silently prayed Viv didn't mention he practiced karate. Now was certainly not the time for her to brag about him being a fifth-degree black belt.

Rick tried to keep his hand resting on the banister, tried not to reach for the scar on his ear, but he was breathing, wasn't he?

Fingering the scar on his ear, Rick shrugged and shook his head. "Never mentioned anything like that to me." He looked at Viv. She gazed oddly at his hand at his ear. He was caught between wanting to take his hand down from his ear and leaving it there for the odd comfort it provided.

Viv turned back to Saunders. Fortunately, she didn't mention his martial-arts skills, but he didn't like her pointed look at his hand at his ear—didn't like it at all.

"Okay, well, I guess that's it. For now, anyway." Saunders flipped his pad closed.

"'For now?'" Viv asked.

"We may come through again as part of the ongoing investigation."

"I see." Viv gestured toward the front door and headed in that direction. "Well, we'll be here."

Saunders followed. "Thank you for your time."

Hands in his pockets, Rick followed silently.

The detective stepped from under cover of their portico porch and out onto their walkway into what was now moderate drizzle. Raindrops quickly peppered his tan jacket, giving it a leopard-like appearance.

Saunders gave Viv another once-over, licking his lips.

Rick almost stepped out from the doorway, but Viv put a calming hand to his chest.

"You all take care now," Saunders said over his shoulder. He got in his unmarked and drove off.

Viv closed the door and sighed.

"Well that was interesting." He couldn't pinpoint Viv's mood.

Viv stood with her back to the door, both hands on the knob. "I'll say. But will he remember anything we said? He was so busy undressing me in his mind, I'm not so sure."

"You caught that."

Viv scoffed. "Please." But she continued holding the doorknob.

Rick kissed her cheek. She wore her cinnamon and orchids body-oil: a dark, mysterious fragrance. "I'll undress you for real, later."

Viv didn't reply; instead, her brows furrowed.

Rick backed off. "Come on. Al's sure to come calling any minute. She did good to wait this long." Rick moved toward the kitchen, but Viv didn't follow. He turned back. "Viv?" Her expression as she watched him rub his scar came back to him. He tensed, waiting for her to say something.

"I don't want to start an argument, Rick."

"Argument? Why would—? What's the matter, Viv?"

"You can't get mad about what I'm about to say, or rather, I'm asking you not to get m—"

"What is it, Viv?"

Viv gave him a stern look.

"I won't get mad. What is it?"

Viv sighed again.

Rick waited, tension and worry twisting inside him.

"I don't know. Reggie's visit brought the pain of Jonathan's death back. I'm a little sad, that's all."

Fury encompassed him. If anything, these last few weeks should've made her at least indifferent to Rast being gone. Realizing his wife still carried feelings for Rast hurt, but it angered him more. At that moment, he was quite comfortable with the idea of killing Rast all over again—and not by accident. "It's cool. I understand."

Viv looked at him, trying to read his face.

Rick smiled. "What?"

"You 'understand'?" She sounded doubtful.

"That's what I said."

"And you're not mad?"

"I said I wouldn't."

"I know what you said, Rick." Viv gave him that strange look again, but this time he wasn't touching his scar.

"Look, I'm go'n get mad if we don't eat." Rick teased, wanting to clear that odd look off her face. It wasn't suspicion, but whatever it was, he didn't like it.

Rick reached for her hand.

She jumped as if goosed.

Rick looked at her questioningly.

"Guess Reggie got me edgy." Smiling, Viv grabbed his hand and headed for the kitchen.

"Rim shot. But keep that day job." Rick followed his wife. He knew Viv well-enough to know something else bothered her, but he didn't pursue it. Besides, he really was hungry.

He also figured sex might be out tonight, maybe a few nights. But that was okay—for now.

* * * * *

"I don't feel ready." Rick stood beside the conference table in his office, looking down at the presentation materials for the Donovan account.

"You'll be ready, Rick. Come on; you're ready now." Mark Dilworth sat at the conference table going over the agenda. "The big day isn't until next week. If you don't think you're ready now, you've got time to get it together."

"I don't think I'm ready now," Rick lied. He had next week's presentation down pat, but other business with Mark needed his immediate attention. Pretense about ill-preparedness provided the springboard he needed.

Mark rolled his gray eyes up in his head with exasperation. "What more could you possibly do to get any more-ready for this thing?"

Rick walked over to his desk and dialed his intern. "Candace, pull the Arrington Enterprises file for me, please."

A hesitant voice came through the speaker: "Sure thing, Mister Phillips."

Disconnecting, Rick looked at Mark, who looked completely baffled.

"What do you want the Arrington stuff for?"

"To beef up, hone in."

Understanding dawned on Mark's face. "Think that'll help?"

"Can't hurt. I struck gold with that account. They're still talking about it." Rick came back to the table. "I figure I'll go over what worked before, make sure I'm using it again, at least on some level, and I'll be set."

"Sort of like establishing a blueprint for success."

"Something like that."

The door to Rick's office stood ajar. Candace poked her head in. "I have the files, Mister Phillips."

"Great. Come on in."

Candace entered Rick's office tentatively, carrying a stack of yellow file folders. "Where do you want them, Mister Phillips?"

"Over here on the table is fine. Thanks, Candace." Rick rubbed his eyes. He was tired. He didn't get much sleep last night after Saunders's visit, but the visit prompted him to take his present course of action.

He watched Mark check Candace out as she placed the documents on the table. Rick smirked. He'd taken inventory of Candace's body months ago. She was shapely-enough, with a cute, almond-brown face, but she was too top-heavy for Rick's taste and barely-twenty: old enough, but still too young. He'd already noticed signs that Candace liked him (how many times can one get arm-touches, or compliments on ties without noticing?), so he could bed her if he had a notion. But he didn't even have the faintest notion.

She placed a hand on his upper-arm. "I'm finishing the revisions on the solicitation memo for Barksdale International." She gave his arm a combination rub-squeeze with meaning clear and succinct.

Candace was young; he didn't want to hurt her feelings by putting her in her place, so as usual, Rick disregarded it. He glanced at Mark:

all in the girl's backside. Rick looked at Candace. "Cool. That'll be ready tomorrow?"

She lowered her hand. "First thing."

From the corner of his eye, Rick discerned Mark licking his lips and choked back a laugh at the absurdity of it; the act was so unlike the unassuming-Mark he thought he knew. "Great." Rick walked back to his desk and checked his calendar. "We can go over it tomorrow morning at ten fifty a.m. How's that?"

"Mister Phillips, you and those weird meeting times. Ten fifty will be fine."

"Not weird, just nonstandard. Helps people remember better."

Mark chuckled. "You'll get used to him, Candace. I've worked with him six years now. Give it time."

Smiling, Candace shrugged.

"Have the office assistant put it on the calendar up front, would you please?"

"No problem. Your beard looks good, by the way. Missus Phillips like it?"

Rick smiled with a nod. "Thank you. Yes, she does."

"I bet. Your tie is cool, too. What tie is that called?"

"Beg pardon?"

Candace tapped her neck, where a tie-knot would be. "What do you call that one?"

Rick touched his paisley tie. "Oh. This is the Krasny Hourglass."

"Nice." Candace ran her eyes over him in such a suggestive way, Mark apparently felt the need to clear his throat and cough.

Rick glanced at Mark before looking at Candace. "Thank you."

"You're welcome." She took seconds to pull her roaming-gaze from him and proceeded to leave.

Rick watched Mark. With his eyes, Mark followed her exit.

Candace closed the door behind her.

"Damn, man!"

Mark looked at him, gray eyes wide. "What?"

"'*What?*' The way you were looking at the girl, that's what."

"I'm a man; she's a woman. I was just looking." Mark shrugged.

"Man, you were not 'just looking' at that girl. And I emphasize the word *girl*." He decided he'd ask Viv how he should set Candace straight.

"Young, maybe, but she's no girl."

"She's black, Mark."

"So?"

"Oh, nothin'. Didn't know you rolled like that."

"It's no big deal. Candace is an attractive young woman, and I like women. I know she's black; I have eyes."

"How are you and Barbara doing?"

"It's trying at times, but we're working on it. So, since you and Viv are on the outs, you banging Candace or what? It's clear she'd let you."

"Too young and not my type."

Mark smirked.

"Damn skippy."

"So, what's your type?"

Rick gave Mark a long look. "Vivian."

Mark's eyes widened. "You serious?" He sat forward in his chair.

Rick nodded. "Only Viv. Always. Forever. The end."

"Man! So, tell me: how did Missus Phillips collar this dog?"

Rick grinned mildly before growing serious. "It's not a collar, man, it's a wedding ring, and I'm going to respect that—regardless of any rough patches. The way you were licking your chops, maybe I should ask when Wolf Dilworth's go'n invite Little Red Riding Candace out for an extended lunch."

"Don't change the subject, Southpaw-with-the-Southern-Drawl. You two have worked things out?"

Rick smirked at that long-ass nickname for him Mark whipped out occasionally, and then nodded. "It's an ongoing process, but, yeah. You know how I feel about my family, man. I'm not go'n lose it. Viv is my life."

Mark stood and moved toward him.

Rick stepped back.

Mark reached him before he could take another step. Grabbing his hand for a shake, Mark pulled him into a brief hug, and then returned to his chair.

Taken aback, Rick could do nothing but blink at Mark and stare. "What the hell, Mark? You a'ight?"

"I'm fine." Mark's eyes sparkled.

Rick waited.

"I'm happy for you, man. You two have something special. Viv is so fine and such a nice lady. I never understood why you stepped out in the first place. Rough patches end, man. Anyway, I never said anything, you know, guy-code and all, but I thought you were messing with a good, and I mean *really* good, thing."

Mark's comment annoyed him, but Rick also appreciated what he said. Jokingly, he asked: "You wanna sleep with my wife, man?"

"If nobody was married, and Viv liked white men? You bet."

"Viv likes white men, Mark."

"I've talked with Viv, Rick. As a coworker or friend, we're fine, but Viv isn't sleeping with one of us. Forget it."

Rick chuckled. "Yeah, that's Viv all right."

"Besides, I'd much rather she continued working on you. Maybe calm you down."

"What do you mean calm me down? I'm calm. I may have been uptight when Viv and I were struggling, but I'm calm. Cool and calm."

"I beg to differ. Since we went out to lunch a while back and you admitted the two of you were having problems, I've noticed it. You're restless. Restless and edgy. More intense. You've got this barely-contained aggression thing going on. Shit, I don't know, I'm not a shrink, but you're different."

Rick looked at Mark quizzically.

Mark laughed. "Seriously, you've got a creative charge about you that is a plus here at the office; it's contagious. There are times, though, when you seem like you're about to pounce on somebody, do some damage. That's the part I want Viv to work on."

"I don't know what you're talking about." But he did. The recent acclimation felt good, natural.

"I think you do." Mark took a swig from his water bottle. "Like I said, maybe being on track with Viv will get you back to normal."

"I'm as normal as ever." Rick wanted to get back to the issue at hand. He picked up the topmost folder from the Arrington account and handed it to Mark. "Let's take a day or two to review this—see if I'm missing something I could use for the Donovan presentation."

Mark accepted the folder from him. "Guess we're finished talking about your restless nature."

"Guess we are." Rick pulled a chair and sat, grabbing the next folder from the pile.

The men were quiet while reviewing the contents of their respective folders.

Mark flipped through several pages. "I tell you, this was what, maybe a month ago? But looking at this stuff again, it seems ages ago."

Rick kept focus on his folder. "They're an active client. Didn't you have a briefing with them last week?"

"Last Thursday, yeah. But I'm not talking about the client being a has-been. Just looking at this file, I'm talking about how much work we put into landing them. Look at this …" Mark gestured with his hand as he continued scanning pages.

"Yeah, a lot of hard work went into them."

"We worked our asses off: you especially."

Rick couldn't have asked for a better opportunity. Mark's comments on the Arrington project provided the opening Rick was looking for. Although confident he wasn't a suspect in the Rast investigation, the detective's visit made him want to solidify things. Part of that solidification involved going over the Arrington project files with Mark, since they were working on this client when he killed Rast. The plan was small, simple: reinforce the dates and his extended presence at work firmly in Mark's mind—for whatever it was worth.

"That we did," Rick replied. "I'm curious: When did we start on this thing? You have the first folder; it should be in there."

"I know it was mid-February." Mark began flipping to the first pages in the file.

"Yeah, that sounds right."

"For me, March is a blur, anyway. We practically lived here getting ready for them."

Rick smiled. This was going to be easy.

"What?"

"Nothing. Just get the date."

Mark returned attention to his folder.

Rick pretended to review the contents of his, every so often commenting on the dates and relative scope of work involved during stages of their collaboration on the Arrington project.

He "worked" on Mark for about an hour when Mark, reviewing the last folder, suddenly put the folder down on the table and rubbed his eyes. "Have you gleaned anything yet?"

"Plenty." Rick reached for the folder Mark placed on the table. "Now, if we—"

"Come on! Let's give it a break. You said yourself we've got a couple days. We also have other clients to work on."

Rick sat back. He'd accomplished most of what he wanted, anyway. Looking out at the sky, Rick sighed. "Lunch, then?"

Mark sat back, too. "I could eat."

"Aristo's?"

"Sounds good." Mark started straightening papers.

Following Mark, Rick began organizing the contents of his folder.

Someone knocked on the door. Without waiting for an answer, Rick's office assistant, Helen, poked her head in. "Sorry, Mister Phillips. Your wife is here to see you."

"Viv's here?" A prickle of anxiety shot through him. He looked at Mark, who looked back curiously. Rick shifted eyes to Helen, who appeared somewhat irritated at his dumb question. "We're done. Send her in."

Nodding, Helen retreated and closed the door.

"Nice surprise."

Unsettled by her unexpected visit, and unsure of its purpose, Rick nodded distractedly. "Sure is."

"Well, you don't look happy about it."

"She's surprising me, that's all." Rick stood.

The door opened, and Viv entered. She stopped when she saw Mark at the table and smiled, but there was nothing pleasant about the expression she wore before seeing Mark. Rick hoped Mark didn't notice. Tension crept into his back. Viv's initial expression indicated she came to fight.

"I didn't know you were here, Mark. Helen didn't say anything. How are you?" Viv placed her blazer and leather bag in the chair next to Mark.

Mark stood. "Oh, I'm doing well, thank you. Yourself?"

"Needing a vacation—and bad."

"Yeah. Planning to take the family to the mountains Memorial Day weekend."

"That sounds nice. I'm sorry, Mark, I forgot your wife's name."

"Barbara."

"That's right. And she's well, I hope?"

"She's fine." Mark kissed Viv's cheek. "It was good seeing you, Viv. I'ma get out of your way here." He grabbed his water bottle and headed for the door.

"Nice seeing you again, Mark."

Rick finally found his voice. "Oh, yeah, man. Well, as you can see, I have to raincheck lunch."

Mark gave a "no problem" wave high over his head without looking back. He left.

Rick looked expectantly at his wife.

Viv walked to the door and closed it. As she approached him, the angry expression Rick saw when she first entered his office, returned.

"Why'd you tell him that trip to the mountains sounded nice? You hate the great outdoors," he said amiably.

Viv didn't reply.

Rick stuck his hands in his pockets and waited.

As usual, Viv looked good. She was letting her hair grow out, now freshly-styled with soft, loose curl. Her gold, button-down, diamond-neck blouse countered the grayness of his office created by the overcast lighting coming through the window. Her navy-blue suit was a favorite of his. Taking her in, looking down to her feet, he was pleasantly surprised to see she wore platform-pumps rather than walking flats. He trailed his gaze up Viv's sexy body back to her angry black eyes.

"Don't do that."

Initially anxious because he didn't understand Viv's mood, Rick now became irritated. He didn't like feeling anxious, anyway. Anger jibed much better. Working his shoulders around, Rick made effort to ease the tension in his back. "Out with it, Viv."

Viv's eyes flickered with uncertainty.

And Rick knew the outcome of this encounter belonged to him. Nevertheless, he wanted to know the reason for her visit.

"Is there something you need to tell me, Rick?" Her tone carried a hint of accusation.

Rick ignored it. "No. But you're here, all huffed up. Perhaps you have something to tell me."

She seemed to change her approach. "No, but why were you so bothered by Detective Saunders's visit?"

"It's 'Reggie,' isn't it?"

"Kiss my ass, Rick!"

Rick leaned over the table situated between them, putting his face close to hers and taking in her scent. Her body-oil blended amber with hints of vanilla: an enchanting, subtle fragrance. He spoke tightly: "I was hungry. No more, no less."

His wife searched his eyes. Her eyes flickered with uncertainty again.

Rick waited. *If she steps back from me, I'm taking her right in this office.*

Shaking her head, Viv stepped back. "No, Rick. I know you. Something during that interview upset you." Mouth set, she looked around his office. "Do you know anything about what happened to Jonathan?" She kept her gaze downward, taking in the items on his conference table.

Rick keyed in on her failure to look him in the eye. It made it easier to lie because he realized she didn't want the truth—unless the truth was the lie. He started to act offended; overreact to her even asking the question, but he had to do this right. "No."

Viv looked at him and then looked back to the table.

Rick stood straight. "Anything else?"

"As a matter of fact, there is." Viv returned her attention to him. She moved around the table, stopping before him.

Rick didn't budge. He matched her determined stare with one of his own. "I'm listening."

Viv searched his face again briefly. "Why have you been fucking me so much? Is it because you haven't been with another one?" Her voice was low but serious.

"Maybe."

No uncertainty flickered in her eyes this time. Rick saw the hurt, but anger immediately replaced it.

Viv raised her hand to strike him, but Rick anticipated the response. He grabbed her wrist, forcing it down and behind her. Viv struck his shoulder with her other hand. Rick used his other hand to grab his wife's hair at the back. He pulled her forward, smashing his mouth to hers.

The contact hurt; Rick tasted blood.

He continued kissing his wife, moving his tongue deeper into her mouth. She apparently chewed bubblegum on the way to his office. Rick held her to him, tasting bubblegum and blood, while his wife tried to push him away at the shoulder.

The taste of blood amplified the situation.

Viv's response soon changed. He realized she wasn't pushing his shoulder, but pulling it—wanting more. He gave her more. Rick broke their kiss. "Lock the door."

Rick watched his wife walk to his office door and turn the latch. His heart raced. Adrenaline rushed through him, making his ears pound. Passion for his wife stiffened an already-throbbing erection. He was restless again. Restless and agitated.

As Viv approached him, he was concerned for the first time that he might actually hurt her. He wanted her that bad.

As soon as she was within reach, Rick pulled Viv to him and resumed their kiss. He grabbed a fistful of her soft, thick hair, yanking her head to meet his kiss. He realized how hard he kissed her, but desire clawed at him; he wanted to taste their blood again.

Except for a small whimper of pain, however, Viv matched his zeal.

Rick finally had to come up for air. "Shit." He walked around to his desk, moving his leather executive chair to the side. "Come here, Vivian."

Without a word or side-glance, she moved to where he stood, facing away from him.

Stepping up to her, Rick massaged his wife's shoulders, pressing his ace-of-spades against her nice ass. The contact pained him wonderfully, but he had to gain some control now, or he would hurt her.

He spoke over her shoulder into her ear: "I'm go'n take what's mine. You have a problem with that?" He drew his hands around to the front, fondling her breasts through her blouse.

Viv tilted her head back against him and sighed, shaking her head.

Rick stepped back and unfastened her skirt. He hunkered and tugged her skirt down over her hips, breathing in the amber-vanilla encircling his head. He allowed Viv to step out of her skirt, glad it was springtime.

Springtime meant thigh-highs for Viv, which she wore now. His lowered position put Viv's rear immediately in his face—the only barrier being her navy-blue, lace boy-short panties. Her curved, shapely flesh pushed nicely against the frilly trim. Rick snatched them down. "Bend over."

Viv stepped out of her panties and bent over, throwing everything back into his face.

He enjoyed his view, taking in his wife's pussy and fine ass. Her toned ass was full, round. Rick moved his hands over the creamy-brown spheres, admiring the faint stretch-marks. He applied pressure to each globe, opening and closing—playing peekaboo with the two holes that winked at him. The delicate aroma of her sex drifted to him. "Wider, Viv."

When she did, a fog of lust shrouded him.

Rick couldn't take watching her display any longer; he bit her. Viv looked good. She smelled good. He took a bite.

Viv gave a startled grunt.

His pants were too constricting; he growled his discomfort.

"What's wrong?"

Rick stood, unfastening his belt and slacks. "My pants."

"Want me to—"

"No. Stay like that. Don't move. Shit." Rick toed-off his shoes. He unzipped his fly and removed his slacks and boxers together, feeling better instantly. His torture now stemmed from pain for a release.

Rick crouched behind her again. Licking and nibbling her sex, he tongued and slathered everything with abandon, preparing both holes for activity. Her distinct but subtle flavor and smell was intoxicating. She tasted divine. He sensed his wife's pleasure; Viv moaned and writhed above him.

"Rick …"

"Come on, baby." He continued his oral indulgence.

Somewhere above him, Viv sighed deeply as she climaxed.

Rick stood.

Viv tried to stand, but he forced her back down. "You know we're not finished. Open it back up." Holding her down, he moved to her right as she spread open again. "That's right." He smacked her shapely rear.

Rick wet the middle finger of his left hand and inserted it in his wife's anus. "When was your last bowel movement?" Tempered-steel lined his erection. He desperately wanted to rear-end her, but his office wasn't suitable for that.

"Rick, we—"

"Answer." Feeling wild, barely in control, Rick worked his finger in her, imagining the tight warmth around his dick.

"Just before coming here," Viv whispered.

"You hate going at work."

"I know ..."

Rick spit where his finger joined her. He inserted another finger. Watching himself fingering her, he barely held on to his sensibilities.

Viv tried to rise again. "Rick, that's uncomf—"

"Shut up." Rick held her down. He moved a leg around hers to hold her open. "Give it a minute, bitch." He continued watching himself finger her. He noticed Viv turning to him, but he was totally entranced by what he was doing to her. He spit again and added a third finger. He couldn't help it.

"Rick, please." Viv squirmed, but ended up giving him better access.

Rick's heart raced. He worked his fingers in her, spitting occasionally to ease the friction. He almost swooned with the smell of her. It wasn't long before he realized his wife grew quiet; that she in fact moved with him.

"Rick?"

"Another one?"

"I ... think so. It's different."

"Want me to stop?" He already knew the answer.

Viv didn't respond.

Rick brought his wife off a second time, but only allowed her moments to relax as he pulled a wet-wipe from the holder on his desk and wiped his fingers.

It was his turn now. Grabbing a fistful of Viv's hair, he yanked her up.

"Ow! Rick."

"Yeah, I know, slut. Come over here." Rick turned Viv around to face his office window. "Bend and spread it." He entered her before she could bend over good. She was wet and warm, tight. Between his saliva and her natural juices, her passage was silky-velvet. "Nice view, isn't it?" He often fantasized about sex with her at this window.

Viv ground against him, the contact of her round flesh an added thrill. "Yes, it is." She reached down between them for his balls, working them gently. It took everything he had not to explode inside her.

This was only part of what he wanted. Rick pulled out.

Viv turned, a slight pout indicating her confusion and dissatisfaction.

Rick grabbed his armless drafting chair. He sat on it and motioned for Viv to come to him. He leaned back against the wall, letting the roll of the chair push his pelvis forward: his erection an erotically-obscene protrusion.

The look of desire on Viv's face as she gazed at it was priceless.

Rick locked the chair's casters. Holding Viv's hand, he helped his wife straddle him.

She winced as she settled onto him.

"Too deep?"

"It's okay."

Rick, however, got a charge from seeing that small expression of pain on her face. He didn't want to hurt his wife. He didn't.

He looked in those black eyes. He saw lust and love, as well as leftover anger. He loved Viv, more than anything. But this? What they were doing right now? Was about wanting her, about fucking her. About pleasure: pure and simple.

She loosened his shirt and tie, initiating a slow grind.

Rick stopped her. "Not yet. Titties first."

Viv began unbuttoning her blouse.

She may have wanted to tantalize him, but he didn't have the patience for that. He ripped the blouse open, popping several buttons.

Viv looked hurt but didn't say anything. Her dark-blue lace bra barely contained her. Noticing the front hook, Rick unhooked her bra, making her shapely breasts jiggle free. He marveled at the transition of color from her lovely butterscotch-brown breasts, to the blue bra, to the gold blouse. "Take it off."

Viv removed the bra and blouse. Except for the thigh-highs and heels, she was nude on top of him. Oh yes.

"Cross your hands behind your head."

Viv gave him a questioning look.

Rick drove his pelvis upward.

Viv winced again.

"Look, bitch. It's a simple request. Do it."

Viv crossed her hands behind her head.

She was beautiful—incredibly, heart-wrenchingly beautiful. Her breasts were 'his' perfect: soft, but firm—each a little more than a handful. Stiff nipples pointed from the large, dark-brown circles forming her areola. Rick circled a thumb around one dark bud, making it harder.

Viv sighed.

She trusts me. She trusts what we're doing enough to be into it, too.

Rick however wasn't sure he trusted himself, because the desire to cause her pain excited him. *Be careful, man.*

He looked Viv over, trailing his eyes from her hair and face to the hollow spot at the base of her throat: evidence of her thudding heart pulsed there. The mole on her collarbone held his attention: he loved kissing that spot on her. He kissed her there now.

Viv sucked a wisp of air through her teeth.

Rick lowered his gaze from her breasts, which swelled with each passing second, to her stomach and curved waist. His eyes traveled from her navel, down to her sparse pubic hair, which joined his where they connected. "Keep your hands there."

He savored the look of her lovely body over his as her amber-and-vanilla fragrance captivated him. Intense love for her moved through him, but passed quickly. Rick leaned forward. Holding his wife at the waist, he suckled and slathered her breasts. The territorial and primal act of moving his tongue and spit over her bosom charged him.

Viv's moans of encouragement echoed softly in his ears.

Continuing his oral caress at Viv's breasts, Rick slid his hands down her back to her bottom. With the way she straddled him, her anus puckered nicely. Rick inserted a finger and began gently working it in her ass. Shifting from her breasts, he moved his mouth to hers, driving his tongue deep. He used his wrists and forearms across her thighs for counterbalance as he pumped into her, relishing the sensation of filling her holes: her mouth, her pussy, her ass.

Viv broke their kiss. "Rick, it hurts a little. Not so hard."

Rick barely heard her, but it was music to his ears. "Stay with me, Vivian. Give this some time, too."

"I'm trying, but I don't know if …"

Rick didn't hear the rest. He was gone. Lost in the warm seduction of her body, he forced himself to postpone climax, trying his best to prolong the sensation of possession: of having his senses consumed with the feel, smell, and taste of woman—*his* woman.

An image of Rast doing her came to him.

Rick thrust harder, deeper, faster.

He thought he heard himself say he loved her. Then there was something about the bitch belonging to him. They were words spoken from some other part of his brain. On some level, he meant them, but words didn't interest him right now. Right now, all that mattered was filling her holes. Filling her and feeling her. Tasting her. Smelling her. Fucking her. The fog of lust claimed him …

… Rick savored Viv's orgasm as her vaginal walls contracted on him. "Vivian!" He bit down hard on her shoulder as he climaxed.

Viv moaned faintly and caressed his head. "I'm here, baby." She held him through his spasms.

Rick slowly emerged from the fog. "You okay, Viv?"

She held him and played in his hair (so good). "I'm fine, sweetie."

He drew both arms around Viv's waist, hugging tightly, fearing he'd fall if he didn't. He closed his eyes, completely spent.

Rick relaxed against his wife as she stroked his hair and rubbed his back, kissing on him where her luscious lips could reach, sometimes scratching his scalp in this womanly-way of ownership: comforting him with her classic smooth-down. He loved this part with her, too.

They stayed hugged-up for several minutes, until he finally softened and slipped out.

When Viv stood, disengaging from their embrace, Rick experienced the sensation of loss his wife spoke of. He didn't like the coolness down the front of his body that replaced the warmth now vacated with Viv's separation from him.

Rick watched his wife walk to the table and retrieve her blazer. She put it on. The beginnings of a cramp pained his right leg, but Rick stayed locked on his wife's image. His loins fluttered with the view of her standing with the blazer hugging her nakedness, the thigh-high stockings and pumps accentuating her shapely legs.

Staring at his wife's curvaceous ass peeking under the hem of her blazer, he was inclined to take her again, but thought better of it. They were in his office, after all. But looking at her, as sexy as she was, he cursed practicality. Rick was dead-tired, but he wanted to fuck his wife again. She was so fine. Viv folded her arms across her chest. Her blazer rose slightly, exposing her more.

Standing, Rick knew instantly: never use a drafting chair for sex again. His leg cramped and his butt hurt. Waiting for the initial pains to subside, Rick couldn't help but stare at his wife. They had yet to speak.

His jones for her came down on him again—with a vengeance. He loved her so much he didn't know what to do with himself. The restless agitation left him. He was simply a man hopelessly in love with his wife.

Rick grabbed his underwear from the floor and pulled them on. He approached Viv.

Her black eyes regarded him calmly. She was simply stunning, shit.

Standing before her, Rick's heart raced with a commingling of elation and uncertainty. He rested his forearms across her shoulders and bent his forehead to hers. He sighed.

"I didn't come here for that."

He pecked her cute nose. "Doesn't matter now. Complaining?"

Viv looked up at him with a sly smile. She stepped back some, looking in his eyes seriously. "I do have questions about what just happened."

"Can I say something first?" Standing in his office in his underwear, talking to his wife, felt perfectly natural.

"Okay."

"I love you."

"I kn—"

"No. No, you don't. You are beautiful, Viv. Fine as shit. Kind. Intelligent. Funny. Sexy. Caring. With enough tomboy in you to be cool, too. You're my friend—my *best* friend." Rick paused. "And *you* are my Ultimate Pussy Experience, Vivian. I love sex with you."

"We are good together."

"Yes, Lord. And not just sexually."

An odd expression crossed his wife's face.

He knew what was coming.

Viv looked away. "Then why do you resort to cheating, Rick?"

The pain in her question touched his heart; a knot formed and released in his stomach. Still, all he had was the truth. "I've answered that, Viv. I don't have anything else to add."

She looked at him, the anger back in her black eyes. "So, what? You plan on continuing the shit? You can't even offer a token fake-out?"

Rick waited for eyes to soften before responding. "I don't have anything fake to offer you, Viv. You wouldn't want that, anyway." He shook his head. "No. All I have is my heart, my life to offer you. I love you, Vivian. I'm so in love with you, I can't even get my mind around it. And I am saying this to you: if you wanted to wake me up, you have.

I will not lose you and Alna. First, I'm sorry for hurting you. Second, again, there is nothing fake here: I'm all about you, Vivian—*only* you. I will never cheat on you again."

Rick watched his wife's face. Her mouth trembled, and then stiffened. Her black eyes widened, and then closed. She stayed that way for several seconds. She believed him.

Although he said as much in Naomi's office, before then, he'd never said he wouldn't cheat again. He always apologized, but never said it was the last time.

"Go ahead and cry, Viv. It's okay."

Viv breathed deeply and opened her eyes. "I'm fine." Her eyes were wet, but no tear fell.

"That refusal-to-cry thing." Rick cocked his head to the side and raised an eyebrow. "Must be from the tomboy side in you?"

Viv laughed.

Rick cut her laughter with a kiss, tonguing gently.

For some reason, Viv believed she was the one into kissing, but he genuinely and particularly enjoyed kissing Viv. With the others, there may have been a peck here and there (maybe), but that was it. He only did honest, deep-kissing with his wife. Viv's kiss took his breath away.

As if reading his mind, her kiss changed—giving him that *voodoo-mojo* joint. She took over the kiss, bringing her hands to his hair. Softening her lips and tongue, she kissed him teasingly, nibbling his lips and slowly dipping her maddeningly-soft tongue in-and-out of his mouth.

That's what drove him crazy. That lip-nibbling, slow, soft-tongue-dipping thing she did while she pressed her body to his and caressed his head. It never failed to get him hard. Never.

Cronus stirred.

The rest of his body vetoed any further activity.

Viv broke their kiss and looked at him. "I love you just as much."

He started to ask if she loved him enough to forgive him anything.

Viv lowered her head. When she looked at him again, she cupped his cheek. "I'm sorry for hurting you, too. With Jonathan, I mean. I just—"

"Shhh." Rick placed fingers against her lips. "I'm sure my actions contributed to that. That's on me, Viv." He removed his fingers. "I'm sorry for pushing you in that direction."

Still cupping his cheek, Viv shook her head. "No. I still made the decision to do it, Rick, so …" She shook her head again and looked at him seriously. "I'm sorry, too. Okay?" She held his gaze.

Those black irises had him. Rick nodded acceptance of her apology.

Viv pecked his lips and smiled. She lowered her hand. "Rick, I really need to pee and freshen-up."

"Oh, yeah, right." Rick slipped his slacks on. He left his pants opened because Viv liked it so much. Sure enough, a sexy spark passed through her gaze as she watched him. "I have something in here you can use." Rick walked over to his closet and retrieved his sports bag, feeling good.

He set the bag on his desk and fished through it, pulling out a towel, washcloth, lotion, and bar of soap. Balancing the items with his arms and hands, Rick walked toward Viv.

She wore a hurt expression as she eyed him and the toiletries.

"Nah, Viv. It's not what you think. I mean, well, yeah, it could be used in case— but no, seriously, this is for when I go for a quick workout with Mark or go to the dojo from work. Honestly."

Viv shrugged and looked away.

Rick came over to the table. After putting everything down, he gripped Viv's shoulders so that she looked him in the eye. "Honestly."

She nodded.

"Okay, then." Rick released her.

Viv looked around Rick's office again. "Too bad you don't have a powder room in here."

"Give me another two years."

"I'm sure."

"So, what were your questions?" He rested his fingertips at her waist.

Her eyelids fluttered as she let out this soft breath. "Huh?"

"Earlier. You said you had questions about what just happened …" Rick nodded in the direction of his drafting chair.

"Oh. Well, it was interesting."

"Good interesting or bad interesting?"

"Oh, quite good interesting, Mister Phillips."

"I see, I see. Continue."

"It was different for us, you know. More, I don't know …"

"Raunchy? Kinky? … Rough?"

198

Viv gazed at him. "Exactly."

"So?"

"So, where are we going with this?"

"Wherever you want to go."

"I'm serious."

"So am I. Look, as long as we're both enjoying it, let it be."

"You're enjoying it?"

Rick just looked at her.

She smirked. "I know. I mean, you're not concerned?"

"About what? A little dirty-talk, pre-school S-and-M? Child's play compared to what others are into."

"But where is it coming from?"

"What difference does it make?"

"None, I guess."

"We *are* husband and wife, Viv. *Married?* You know, committed to one another and approved by society at large? Besides, nobody knows our business except us—and probably Louise."

"I doubt I'll be mentioning any of this to Lou." She wore an expression he couldn't read.

Rick lowered his hands. "Why do you say that?" He wondered if Viv knew about Louise's feelings for him.

"It's not important." Viv reached for her bag. "Look, let me get out of here."

Rick cocked an eyebrow, looking her up-and-down. "Like that? You will be putting our business in the streets."

Viv looked down at herself and giggled. "Well, this won't do at all, will it?"

"For them?" Rick thumbed toward his closed office door, "Maybe not, but for me ..." He pulled Viv closer. "It's doing just fine. As a matter of fact, I want you to wear this again tomorrow night."

"My suit?"

"No, this." Rick gestured to her body. "I want you to walk around the house in this blazer, the thigh-highs, and heels." He kissed her cheek.

She traced her thumb along the dimple in his chin. Whenever she touched him, it was wicked-good. "And where will Alna be?"

"Isn't this the weekend for Sierra's sleepover?"

"Oh, yeah, I forgot about that."

Rick caressed Viv's round butt. "I haven't. When I seek you out this weekend, with you wearing this, I can just come up on you and take it."

"That's pretty much what you've been doing anyway, isn't it?"

"Is it?"

"Yes …" Her reply was low, husky.

"But I'm taking something different this weekend, aren't I?"

Viv lowered her eyes. Her breathing sounded more-pronounced.

Rick continued stroking her ass. "Come on, you knew it was coming. And I know we both want to. Am I wrong?"

"No—" She kissed him passionately, sending her tongue to his tonsils. The urgency and emotion in her kiss went right to his heart and nuts.

When they parted, Rick traced a thumb across her brow. "What was that for?"

"I can't get enough of you."

"Wanna knock-off early?"

"I can't. Not today."

"It's cool. Look, go on; get dressed. We'll be here until nightfall at this rate."

"Yeah, you're right." Viv walked behind his desk for her skirt and underwear. She retrieved her blouse.

"Got time to get something to eat at least?" He wanted to extend their time together.

"A quick bite, maybe." Viv examined her blouse. "What am I supposed to do about this?" She held the blouse forward, and then looked down, searching for popped buttons.

Rick shrugged apologetically. "Sorry. Is it that bad?"

Viv examined her blouse more-closely. "It's workable. I can just close my blazer for now; fix the buttons when I get back."

"Sorry," Rick offered sincerely. He embraced the mellow feeling in him now but could feel strains of agitation and restlessness creeping in.

He liked the restlessness; it rendered him charged and unencumbered. But the mellow-thing had its place, too. Apparently, he'd become a man of extremes rather than traveling the middle road he used to.

Viv walked over to him, carrying her clothes. "Hey, it's okay. Believe me, I am *not* complaining." She started dressing.

Rick picked up the lotion and other items from the table and placed them in her leather bag. He smiled as he grabbed her underwear and stuck them in his pocket.

Seeing him pocket her panties, Viv gave him a knowing smile, her black eyes full of desire. "You are so silly."

"I'm ready to eat. Chop, chop."

"I still need a key?"

"Oh, yeah." He retrieved the key from his desk.

She grinned as she accepted it. "Back in a minute."

Rick savored Viv's cool as she approached the door.

One of the first things about Viv that attracted him (other than those killer black eyes) was her walk. Her stride held this graceful saunter that was a bit sassy, too. "More like ten, but okay."

Viv poked her tongue and left.

Rick slipped on his shoes and fixed his pants and shirt. He attempted to straighten his tie (a Krasny knot wasn't friendly to readjustment). Reluctantly, he reached over to the bottle of hand sanitizer on his conference table, squirted a drop in his palm, and rubbed his hands together. He walked over to his stereo atop his credenza and turned on the radio. Leaning against the credenza, Rick mentally replayed their encounter while waiting for Viv. He closed his eyes and tilted his head back to relive the lustful experience.

L.T.D.'s "We Both Deserve Each Other's Love" came on as Viv reentered his office and closed the door. She removed the soap, cloths, and lotion from her bag and placed them in a chair.

"It's like a ghost town out there. Nobody—"

"Shhh." Rick motioned Viv toward him. "Listen."

Viv remained quiet. Her eyes softened with what Rick knew to be a memory of their lovemaking weeks ago.

Taking her hand, he drew her close. He palmed her cheek and sang the second verse to her.

Viv blushed.

Rick didn't sing the rest. Viv loved for him to sing, but he only sang when two components came together just right: the song and the feeling. And although he had both, he just wanted them to enjoy their song.

When the song ended, Rick turned the radio off and gazed into those ebony irises of hers. "You and Me."

If possible, those dark pools darkened with affection. "Me and You."
He brought Viv's mouth to his.

When they parted, Viv wore an expectant grin. "Rick? My panties?"
Rick smirked.

"You want to eat, don't you?"

Rick nodded slowly.

"Rick, no. Come on. I've got to get back."

"Well, get back. I'll hold on to these the rest of the day. You can
have them back at home."

"Rick, I'm not going back to my office commando. Now stop
playing." She held her hand out.

"God, I'm in love with you." He'd entered a zone for his wife.

The declaration apparently touched her. "Shit. Don't do this, Rick,"
she pleaded softly.

Rick quickly locked his door and came back to her. "I told you I
was ready to eat." He put his arms around her and began unfastening
her skirt.

Viv closed her eyes and tilted her head back.

Rick zeroed in on her neck, nuzzling the spot that thrilled her.

"Daaamn," she breathed.

Crouching before her, Rick inched her skirt down over her hips.
When she stepped out of it, he rested her skirt carefully across a chair.
He cocked an eyebrow and jerked his head toward his conference table.
"Up you go." He focused on his wife's ass as she moved to the table.

When Viv reached the table, she turned to him. "Rick, come on."

Rick walked over to his lady and moved a chair to the side. "You're
the one who's going to be coming." He kissed her.

In moments, Rick had Viv supine on the table, breasts exposed.
With his elbows, he held her legs wide as he licked and nibbled his
wife's slit, her taste so mild it was practically-nonexistent. He played
with her nipples, taking in the view of Viv's body splayed before him.

She lifted her head to watch him work. Their eyes locked. Rick
watched her arousal build until she gripped the edge of the table and
threw her head back. Other than a quick gasp and slight puff of air
through her lips, she remained quiet through her orgasm. He let up,
licking very lightly now as she came down, her body pliant and fully-
reclined as he finished.

Giving Viv pleasure, satisfying her body, welled in him a tenderness for her that was humbling.

He quietly rose to his feet and looked down at his wife. She'd crossed a hand over her chest and closed her eyes. He concentrated on the rise and fall of her midsection, her legs still spread in relaxation.

Staring transfixed into his wife's sex, Rick stepped forward. The bulge in his pants touched her where it mattered. Viv shifted a bit, causing her spread vulva to rub against his crotch, and the sensation rocked him. He hadn't dry-humped anyone in decades. He'd forgotten the innocent pleasure of it.

Viv propped onto her elbows. "That … was lovely."

Grinning at her, Rick initiated a seductive grind. Practicality and exhaustion be damned. He unzipped his fly.

"Rick …"

"Viv …"

She smiled a sexy smile as he freed Cronus, and laughed lightly when he pressed the head against her. "What in the world …?"

Rick entered her. Gripping her thighs, he closed his eyes seconds after Viv closed hers.

Finding their rhythm, he centered on the feel of her sheathing him in snug warmth. Rick didn't know Viv's secret, but her passage remained tight despite having children, despite their frequent sexual exploits. Head back in nasty splendor, Rick focused on the delicious friction against his length and the primitive, bestial sensation building low in his belly, between his legs. Viv had some dangerously-good—

He looked at her. His wife gazed up at him as they did the deed, with this look that held his trifecta: sexy, whorish, loving. Those juicy tits bounced sweetly with his thrusts. Viv's hair lay spread beneath her in a halo of chestnut with touches of auburn as her beautiful black eyes conveyed that she owned his shit. To demonstrate, she 'milked' him: combining this rolling-move with her hips while working her vaginal muscles on him in this way that almost sent him to his knees.

He let go inside her forcefully.

A depth of feeling rose in him that surpassed anything he'd ever known. And this time his connection to her was *solely* about love. He stayed inside her, not wanting to break contact.

They held each other's gaze.

"You okay?"

She nodded with this knowing-grin (so damn sexy).

Without question, she was the best he'd ever had. Sex with those others wasn't even in the vicinity.

Finally slipping out of her, Rick used what strength remained to reach for one of the cloths Viv placed in the chair. He continued holding his wife's gaze while he cleaned them up. When he was done, he reached out to Viv and helped her off the table. They fixed their clothes.

Rick pulled her into his embrace, holding her for quiet seconds until she stepped back from him, her expression unreadable. "What's wrong?"

She looked down. "Nothing."

Rick lifted her chin. "What's wrong, baby?"

"What positions did you use with the others?" Her black eyes looked vulnerable, as if she didn't want to ask the question, but needed the answer.

He sat on the edge of his conference table. "Why do you ask?"

"Answer me." She plucked a LifeSaver from the bowl of candy on the table, unwrapped it, and popped it in her mouth.

Rick sighed. Women wanted to know some of the most painful things. "Doggy-style or reverse cowgirl."

Viv raised an eyebrow. "That's it?"

"Yeah." He could tell she wanted to ease her mind of something. "Lyn—" Rick sighed again. "Lynelle wanted to face me, but ..." He studied the materials on his table.

"But ...?"

Rick looked at her. "But I avoided it."

Viv looked at him questioningly.

"Not facing was better, Viv. It made it easier to ..." He looked away again. He really didn't want to talk about this.

"Easier to what, Rick?"

Rick focused on a draft brochure for Donovan Industries. "Easier to fantasize about you." There, he said it. He figured the admission would piss her off: why would he think about her while being with someone else? Rick looked at her, readying himself for her anger.

Viv drew in an audible breath. She went quiet, looking around his office and sucking her LifeSaver. She turned to him. "Wow, that's ... I mean, I wasn't expecting—"

Her reaction surprised him. "It's the truth, Viv."

Viv gave him an examining look. "So ... So, they never got to see how your eyes ...?"

His eyes? What did his eyes have to do with anything? "How my eyes what, Viv?"

Viv just kept looking at him. "Or see your facial expression when you ...?"

Well, that one was obvious. "When I come? No, Viv." He paused. "If you've seen one man's face, you've seen them all, right? Let's see. I've heard our expressions described as 'goofy concentration,' 'goofy surprise,' 'goofy intensity.' I'm guessing the key word here is 'goofy.'" He smiled.

Viv smirked, but then she scanned his face dreamily. "So, only I've seen how your eyes ... How your expression turns ..." She trailed-off and looked toward his crotch, then shook her head and smiled softly.

Normally, Viv was straight-no-chaser, but presently she was in one of her rare "girly" moments. Rick didn't mind. He liked seeing her mysterious feminine-side. But she mentioned his eyes again. "How my eyes what, Viv? My expression turns ...?"

She looked at him, and her soft smile turned secret. "Don't worry about it, baby. I'm glad those things still belong to me. They're still mine."

"Huh? What's still yours?"

"It's a woman-thing."

"Obviously."

She cupped his cheek. "Yours isn't, you know."

This discussion was all over the place. He had no idea what she was talking about.

"Your expression, when you ... There's nothing 'goofy' about it." She looked at him with nothing but love.

Rick cleared his throat. "Oh. Okay."

Viv lowered her hand. "You are so cute. A little uncomfortable talking about what you look like when you climax, Mister Phillips? I thought we could talk about anything."

"We can. We do. Apparently, we just did." He shrugged.

Viv chuckled.

In their seventeen years of gettin' it in, they'd never discussed their facial expressions during orgasm. He wondered what other topics remained unexplored. "There's nothing 'goofy' about yours, either."

Viv laughed (a pleasing, throaty sound).

Rick joined her.

When their laughter died, Viv gazed around his office again. She turned to him, her expression humorless. "You are mine." She whispered it earnestly.

"I'm yours, Vivian."

Her expression remained serious. "And I'm yours, Richard."

Rick pulled her to him. Her body molded perfectly to his as she leaned onto him. He whispered, "Yes, Lady Blue," and kissed her.

They kissed slowly, softly, teasingly. He kissed her for solid minutes; Viv's mouth a haven of juicy tangerine flavor. Before they parted, she transferred the dissolving circular sliver from her mouth to his.

Rick crunched the candy and finished it. "Kisses don't lie, girl."

The erotic black smoke of her eyes held him captive. "Not our kisses, anyway."

"So why—?"

"Don't, Rick. That's done."

Rick nodded agreeably; she had a point. "Come on. You gotta go."

Viv kissed his cheek and stepped back. "Oh, now you realize that."

Rick stared at her, breathing in her amber-vanilla fragrance and thinking dirty thoughts. "Your pussy tastes and feels so good, baby. You have an absolutely-divine cunt. I think I'll have meatloaf with a side order of my wife's pussy for dinner tonight." Licking his lips, he reached in his pants pocket. "Maybe for dessert, too." He handed Viv her panties.

"You've got the dirty-talk thing down, huh? Like back in the day."

"You don't like it?"

"I didn't say that." Viv stepped into her panties and readjusted her skirt.

Rick drew Viv close again. "So, you do like it."

She played with his tie. "It always added a certain something. I wouldn't want to hear it all the time. But you can be gentle and sensual, too, so it's fine—long as you mix it up."

"Don't I always?"

"Here lately? Even more so."

Rick understood what she meant by "here lately." Especially since ... "Think you'll be able to?"

"To what?"

"Talk dirty to me again. You know, like we used to."

Viv stepped back. She trailed her gaze over him seductively, pausing at his crotch before meeting his eyes. "Oh, it won't be much of a stretch. I sometimes talk dirty in my head, anyway. I thought you'd become too prudish for it." She moved close again, standing between his legs and leaning against him, their alignment always subtly-arousing. Her amber-vanilla fragrance embodied her femininity and pervaded his senses, making his head swim with feeling.

Rick encircled her waist. "Me? Prudish? I wouldn't say prudish."

She gently scratched in his beard. "What would you say?"

The coarse sensation turned him on. "Reserved, careful maybe, but not prudish." He wanted nothing more than to go home and lay down with her. Snuggle in, get some more of her classic smooth-down, and fall asleep.

"Whatever it was, let's just say there's been a change for the b—"

"Was Rast better?"

Viv looked at him for solid seconds before stepping back from his embrace. "You were real truthful when you explained your feelings for me and all, so I must but be real truthful with you."

Rick's heart skipped several beats. His throat dried-up. Swallowing did little to help it. He clenched his jaw in preparation for her next words.

"No, Rick, Jonathan wasn't better. He was okay, but nothing compared to you. Your dick is bigger; you command your fuck-stroke way better; you last considerably longer; and ..."

"And ...?"

"And, if it matters to you, I didn't have him wait inside me: only you. I never ... I never downed his flow: only yours."

Rick didn't realize it until she'd said it, but it did matter to him. He avoided dwelling on Viv being with Rast because it hurt too much. Yet knowing she didn't completely give of herself to Rast assuaged some of the pain. "It matters, Viv."

Viv nodded solemnly. "I know it does." She stared at him. "Did—?"

"No, Viv. They didn't swallow mine, either. And I've only waited inside you." Looking at his wife, he was glad he could answer honestly.

Viv's eyes looked thankful before she gave him a small, sexy grin. "Rick, you work your cock inside me better than any other man I've been with. So, you can have a big head about that, because that shit in your pants ain't nothin' but the truth for me."

Rick didn't know if her words relieved him or turned him on. He figured a little of both, but mostly the former. "No, talking dirty again won't be a problem for you." He smiled.

Viv, however, didn't smile back. "I'm so in love with you."

Rick looked down at his wife's hands: they were clenched. He brought his eyes back to hers. "That word isn't it, is it? It's not enough." He took her hands in his.

She shook her head. "It really isn't."

"Love doesn't adequately express my feelings, either. I'm glad it's reciprocated." He kissed her hands. "We can come up with another word."

This time she did smile. "You can be so silly. I'll let you handle that assignment."

Rick looked out his window, checking the sky. "You've been here over an hour. We'll have to pass on that quick bite."

"I know. I'm getting ready to go."

"You don't wanna go, do you?"

"I really don't."

"Then don't." The afternoon was shot for him.

"I have to."

"Come on. We can go home, get in bed. Listen to some EWF. I can talk more dirty-stuff, spank that ass …"

"See? Already. I've had my fill of being called a bitch and a slut today, thank you. And where was that coming from?"

"Just role-playing." It was half-truth. His wife was by no means a bitch or a slut. But today, as he fucked her, the words felt good and right to him. Role-playing suggested pretense, and it was—to a degree.

Viv stared at Rick.

Rick stared back.

Viv giggled and covered her mouth.

Rick couldn't help chuckling himself.

Finally, they both laughed.

When their laughter died, she tugged on his tie. "Know what I wanna do with you?"

Rick looked at her suggestively.

"Always and all the time. Every day."

"Whoa!"

"But seriously: let's rent an RV and take off."

"You want to rent a camper …?"

"Yes."

"And go where?"

"Anywhere."

"What for?"

"Who cares?! Come on; it'll be fun. You've been Mister Spontaneous lately. Now it's my turn."

"We have an SUV, a car, and a motorcycle. Plus, you hate the great outdoors. Why rent an RV?" Rick tried to get on one accord with his wife, but something troubled him.

"For the sheer adventure of it!"

"I see. Okay, when? Is Alna a part of this road-trip fiasco?"

Viv punched his arm.

"You like hitting me, don't you?"

"Gets me hot," she deadpanned. "Anyway," she continued excitedly, "of course our child is included. Al would be heartbroken if we didn't."

"That's fine. Thought you were talking about our slow-motion getaways, some four-twenty fun. We're overdue for one of those."

Viv seemed to ponder that. "Hmmm. We are, aren't we? Still have some BSB left over, too."

"See? You can do brownies."

"Why me?"

"Yours turn out better than mine."

"Hmm. Now you got me thinking. But for this trip, no; it'll be the three of us."

"Okay, so now we're back to when."

"Not sure yet, but soon. It'll be during the week, not the weekend, so I need to check my calendar at work first."

"Me too, for that matter. Look, go! Get out of here."

She kissed him lovingly, pressing against him and playing in his hair with one hand while running her other hand over him teasingly. The way Viv touched him was everything. She fondled his junk skillfully with possession, adding these delicious rakes of her nails over his semi-hardness to full effect before pulling back. She looked at him, black ardor in those eyes before she tenderly pecked his lips and headed away with that walk (that ass) of hers. Jesus. "I'm gone. What's for dinner?" She paused at the door.

Remnants of her expert-touch ghosted his groin. "Meatloaf, remember? And I'm having a special side-dish ..."

Viv smiled.

Rick's heart melted. She smiled that smile that'd been so long in coming: her "best present" smile.

That did it for him. He had his wife back. Looking at that smile made him goofily-giddy inside. "I love you. Get outta here."

She blew him a kiss and left.

Rick missed her already.

He stayed put, feeling the emptiness of his office around him. He slowly got his office back in order. He put the damp cloths in a spare plastic-bag and repacked the soap and lotion. He pushed chairs back into place.

As he moved about his office, a nub of apprehension curled in his stomach. He realized what bothered him when Viv talked about renting a vehicle.

It was a small thing. Minor. A simple thing, really.

But usually the small, simple things tripped a person up.

The rental car agreement and receipt.

Rick tried to remember what he'd done with them.

He'd thought enough to get rid of the clothes and shoes he wore that day (actually, Viv was taking care of that once she dropped the box off at the donation center). He didn't know if he'd left any traceable evidence, but he'd seen enough crime shows to use some precaution at least, and destroying the perfectly-good clothing and shoes seemed a sacrilege.

But all his work on Mark (and Viv, too, for that matter) would be for naught if Viv somehow came across those papers. He could easily lie about it, but apparently Viv already had questions in her mind. Rick didn't want to spark any more. The date of the rental alone could lead to more questions than he cared to answer.

Finished with getting his office in order, Rick untied his impossible-to-readjust Krasny Hourglass and retied his tie with a Half-Windsor knot.

He sat at his desk, thinking. There were only one or two places the papers could be. Short of that, Rick had no idea where to check.

He needed to go to the men's room to wash up, but Rick sat back and scrunched his lips to breathe Viv's various scents around his mouth. He closed his eyes. He'd worry about the rental-stuff later. Right now, he wanted to think about Viv's visit. About that smile she gave him before leaving.

He had his wife back. He had his family back.

Rick's cell phone emitted a whistle-chirp tone: a text message.

It was Viv: *"Damn, baby ... Find that word, okay?"*

And he'd die before ever letting anything threaten that again.

CHAPTER 17

A Sour Aftertaste

Naomi sat at her desk, unable to concentrate. Hunger persisted. The only thing she'd eaten all day was a piece of pastry. She did have a glass of chardonnay around noon, and so far, a second glass of chardonnay, three-quarters gone, rested on the table by sofa. Naomi eyed the glass sporadically as she reviewed the Harris file. Giving up, she went over to the table, picked up the glass, and drained it.

What she wanted, though, was food. But she needed to finish the Harris profile. It was due Monday, which was why she was in her office on a sunny Saturday rather than at home. Not that she'd be doing anything special at home. She'd probably be working there, too, but most of her research materials for the Harris case were housed here in her professional office.

Her stomach rumbled as she returned to her desk. Sighing, she turned the volume down on her radio and reread the last portion of her work on Bernard and Deirdre Harris: a patient file with meat. The Harrises were an older couple with a college-aged son, Bernard Jr. Their daughter, Grace, was abducted and murdered sixteen years ago at age seven.

The Harrises exhibited generalized anxiety disorder throughout their six sessions so far. At least a year of work lay ahead for this family. When she came across real family dynamics (as with the Harrises), she was encouraged. As fed up as she was with patients with superficial issues, Naomi enjoyed helping families with real problems. That wasn't to say she didn't like the "quick fixes." She met her fair-share of nice or at least interesting people when they came to her for what Naomi considered "drive-thru" therapy.

Drive-thru cases usually involved patients resolving problems early in the sessions but continuing to see Naomi for the comfort and reassurance it provided, or just to vent from time to time. Naomi didn't mind that—until the visits were a waste of time for all involved.

She smiled to herself. The Phillipses were transitioning into that drive-thru category. Unable to focus on the Harris file, Naomi rose and silenced Beethoven's oft-overplayed "Für Elise." She walked to the window, thinking about her reigning favorite couple. Her sessions with Viv and Rick were routine but not static, so Naomi continued seeing them. Besides, she genuinely liked them (sanctioned neutrality be damned).

Rick represented a wildcard, though. Charming and incredibly sexy, Naomi understood why those women said yes (even with Rick's minimal interest in them). He was also deeply committed to Viv and to working through their sessions (although he remained highly-guarded about his family-life in Hampton). And while Naomi liked Rick, her suspicions about him hindered liking him too much.

Rick manifested Cyclomythic behavior with signs of Intermittent Explosive Disorder. This raised Naomi's caution flag. Still, she suspected that it could all be tied to Rick experiencing a brief psychotic disorder. And because of her flashes-of-truth, Naomi checked in with Kevin periodically for progress regarding the Jonathan Rast investigation. So far there was little.

Naomi wanted to be wrong about Rick. Viv and Rick made a remarkable couple. From her perspective, anybody paying attention would recognize how good they were together. Clearly BFFs, the couple exuded intimate dynamics of friendship, love, and fun (not to mention sex). That came across increasingly with each session. Occasionally during their sessions, she became too preoccupied imagining their sexual escapades to pay attention to the exchange of dialogue.

Naomi sighed, hoping she was wrong about Rick; she didn't want Viv hurt.

She briefly entertained leaving the whole thing alone. If she was right about Rick: so-the-fuck-what. She could put herself in a place of understanding why Rick might have killed Jonathan. Given his mania regarding family, Rick would do whatever necessary to save his. But, laws of society aside, killing someone was innately wrong. She looked in the eyes of her Einstein bobblehead. "God put us here to create and enhance life—not destroy it."

Other than the two absolutes of God and death, everything else held shades of gray—including Jonathan's murder. Naomi was resigned to find out if her suspicions about Rick were correct, but she wasn't clear on motive anymore. If anything there had to be "justice" for Jonathan's family, but even that reasoning seemed tenuous.

Her stomach rumbled again. It was going on two o'clock. "Enough on the Phillipses. I need to eat." She gazed through the window, trying to decide what she had a taste for.

Deciding on a burger, Naomi went to her desk for her wallet. She pulled out a ten-dollar bill when the phone rang.

"Hello?" It was Saturday; formal greetings were reserved for Monday through Friday. Besides, who'd be calling her?

"Doctor Alexander?"

"Yes?" Naomi thought she recognized the voice.

"Hi, Doctor Alexan— Naomi. This is Viv Phillips. I didn't expect you to answer. I was prepared to leave a message."

Naomi guessed right (speak of the devil). "Well, you don't have to; you got me. What can I do for you? Everythi—?"

"Everything's fine. Great … Things are fine, but I just— I don't know, I—"

"Well, you'll be in here in a couple days."

"I know."

"… You need to talk, but you don't want to wait for the session because what you really need is to discuss things you may not necessarily want Rick to hear. What you'd like is a little one-on-one counseling."

"… You're good."

"It's what they tell me. When did you want to talk?" Naomi glanced at the empty glass and the paperwork on her desk. "Can you meet today?"

"Well, I was all prepared to leave a message requesting either some time Monday or later in the week, but today is fine. Rick is out with Alna. They probably won't be back until late, so today actually would be perfect."

Looking at the paperwork, Naomi approximated how much more work she needed to do. Not much.

"Naomi?"

"I'm here. Sorry. Trying to get a game-plan together."

"I'm sorry; I don't want to interrupt your work or anything."

"I suggested today, didn't I? I can use the break. When and where? And your 'where' needs to be someplace food is served: I'm hungry."

"Hungry-hungry, or just hungry? Upscale, middle-of-the-road ...?"

"Doesn't matter."

"... DeTante's?"

Naomi wasn't surprised. It meant more of a commute, but she didn't mind. "What time?"

"Whatever time it is when we're there at the same time. Can you leave now?"

"Sure can."

"Okay, see you shortly. I'll wait outside for you."

"You don't have to do that."

"I know."

"Okay, then."

"Bye!"

"Bye." Naomi hung up. She'd work on the Harris case at home.

Protocol dictated therapists severely limit interaction with their patients outside the office.

Naomi packed her briefcase and headed out.

Viv wanted to talk about Rick. But why?

*　　*　　*　　*　　*

The two women were relatively-finished with their meal and pleasantries when Naomi finally commented on Viv's preoccupation with the entrance to DeTante's. Viv stared in that direction intermittently throughout the meal, obviously drawn to Jonathan's memorial plaque and photograph patrons saw immediately upon entering the restaurant. They dined at the front of the restaurant. The memorial stood several feet behind Naomi.

Naomi forked a last remaining bite of her smothered lamb chops. "I've got two questions for you. One, how long do you plan to stare at Mister Rast's memorial plaque? And two, now that our bellies are full and the small-talk has served its purpose, are you ready to discuss why you called this meeting?"

Viv carried her gaze around DeTante's. "Nice crowd."

"For a Saturday, it sure is." Naomi ate her bite.

Viv sighed. She put her head in her hands, and shook it, making her chestnut hair bounce. Her manicured fingernails, polished a dusty-rose, complemented the diamond-accented platinum bands with the three-carat round-cut solitaire diamond on her left ring finger, and the white-gold band on her right thumb. She wore no other rings. Naomi wasn't into jewelry, but Viv's wedding-set screamed expensive. The ring was classic and stylish—much like the woman wearing it.

"Let's start with question one. Do you want to switch seats?"

Viv looked up from her hands. "You'd do that?"

"Sure. Why not?"

"I don't know. I thought you'd be more like: 'Look, he's dead. You're with your husband; get over yourself.' It would be voiced tactfully of course."

"Well, that'll come only if you decide not to switch seats but continue to obsess over the plaque." Naomi smiled. "Just kidding."

Viv smiled, too.

"I know I can be a bit frank, but I'm not the tin man. I have a heart." Naomi ate another bite.

Viv nodded. "Well, no, I don't need to switch seats. And I'm not sure I can help staring at Jonathan's memorial." Viv turned her attention outside their window.

"It's okay if you loved him, Viv. It doesn't compare to what you feel for Rick."

Viv continued looking through the window. "It's not even close."

"I know."

Viv looked at her. "How do you know?"

"I am your therapist. I see the two of you on a regular basis. You two are very much in love; that's obvious. And it's a good, *deep* thing you two are showing me. Sometimes I wonder why you're coming anymore. Although I can see where some work still needs to be done."

"Such as?"

"Uh-uh, Miss Lady. You called me, remember? You're supposed to be doing the talking."

"I know. But this is helping me warm up."

Naomi nodded. "Okay. Well, Rick has a borderline-obsession regarding family that apparently stems from trauma in his past. I'll get more out of him when the time is right. And you, well, you're working on putting closure to Rick's past infidelities. You still want a reason why."

Viv shook her head. "You really are good."

"So you've said. But this is what I do for a living."

"But you're not all mumbo-jumbo, grow-within, etcetera about it."

"I don't do mumbo-jumbo well."

Viv nodded.

"Having said that, I'm also going to say this: there is no reason, Viv. Rick cheated because he could. He cannot validate your worth with this one."

Viv's eyes widened with indignation. "Validate my worth? I don't need him to validate me. You're the last person I'd expect t—"

"I don't mean validate in the strict-and-domineering sense you're going-off about. All I'm saying is, you feel, that Rick not having a reason for cheating somehow makes you nothing. And by 'nothing,' I simply mean by your not being considered in his actions—not any other way. If he had a reason, say, he didn't love you, or the sex wasn't good, then at least on some level, even if it was negative, you mattered to him when he initiated cheating. Rick saying he didn't have a reason suggests that you didn't matter to him, which isn't true, but it's the 'not mattering' that's hurtful and hard to accept—so you're still wanting a reason to validate your presence in his heart and mind." Naomi paused. "Understand?"

After a pause, Viv nodded. "You bordered on mumbo-jumbo for a second there, though."

"I know. I'm officially sworn to use mumbo-jumbo at least once a month." Naomi sipped from her glass. She ordered one of the restaurant's specialty drinks, DeTante's Peach Passion—a blend of peach and passion fruit flavored liqueurs too fruity for Naomi. She took her time finishing it.

"Well ... What if I believe there're reasons he cheated, but Rick's just not acknowledging it?"

Naomi looked at her for calm seconds. "Then that's something requiring discussion in therapy—with Rick. Next week?" Perhaps this was what their uses of 'go-to' and 'resort' and that 'not really' were all about— and that they had yet to explore in session (she'd get there).

Viv paused, staring at her plate. She shook her head. "It'll keep."

"I'll leave it up to you, and thus my conclusion still stands."

Viv took a non-sip from the glass of Merlot she nursed. Naomi noticed that she barely touched it. "So, in other words, you're telling me, tactfully, to get over myself with needing Rick to give me a reason—any reason, for why he cheated."

"Pretty much."

Viv looked serious. "Done."

Naomi watched Viv for several seconds, reading her. "Good for you. Now, if only all my patients were this easy to treat."

Both women laughed.

"I'll have my moments, but overall, I'm cool." Viv sighed. "I have a question …"

Naomi nodded.

"Do you believe in hell?"

"Is this question in light of Rick's adultery—and yours?"

Viv nodded.

"Well, the real question is, do *you* believe in it? It doesn't matter what I believe."

"I know. I just—"

"Not really, no. No, I don't."

The relief in Viv's eyes made Naomi uncomfortable. She was Viv's therapist, not her conscience. "Want to tell me why?"

"Not really, no. No, I don't."

"Come on, Naomi. I know you're not trying to convert me. Just share your point of view, that's all." Viv's black eyes were direct but beseeching.

Naomi sighed. "Okay, here goes. For me, it just seems that in the grand scheme of things, given poverty, disease, homelessness, etcetera, 'cheating' on a spouse, even for the 'wrong' reasons, is small potatoes. I'm not saying infidelity is okay or right, although sometimes, shit, maybe it is. But considering the big picture, there are bigger things to worry about and try to change."

"And hell?"

"Christian Bible scripture emphasizes Faith—not works or actions. It seems to me that that would apply to both good and bad actions. To that end, I believe God wants us, through our faith, to impact the big picture. This world given us: keep it beautiful. So, no, I don't believe God will send us to some eternal damnation because we make mistakes.

I believe there is an accounting for the choices we make, but not in the grand and excruciating measures many religions prescribe." Naomi sipped her drink. "How was that?"

Viv nodded slowly. Her gaze was intense without being impolite. "Just fine, Naomi. Now, since I'm cured, now all you have is my husband."

"Who is not here, thus making any discussions moot. But enough with the warm-up, what's on your mind? I know it's about Rick, so, again, out with it."

Viv picked up her water glass and stared down into it. She swirled the glass, sending the water and ice into a gentle spiral. "... It's very good between us again. Not the sex; that's always been good. I'm talking about everything."

Naomi said nothing.

"It's almost too good, ya know?"

Although Viv prompted her for an affirmative response, Naomi remained quiet. She'd come in when needed.

Viv continued, gazing into her glass. "We'd sort of settled into a routine in our marriage; I guess we both grew overly-complacent. But Rick has become this practically-new person overnight. You mentioned it in one of our earlier sessions. There's this edge and tempered sense of danger about him now that is sexy and intoxicating to me. On top of that, and pardon my language, but I know you like keeping it real, but on top of that, Rick is fucking me so thoroughly and so right, I'm at a loss for words." Viv waited.

"Go on, Viv. I can't help you yet. I don't know where you're going."

"Have you ever tasted buttermilk pie?"

Naomi was unfazed by the left-field question. "When I was a girl."

Viv looked surprised. "I remember you telling us about your grandmother's view of marriage, about it being like sweet buttermilk, but I thought buttermilk pie was an obscure recipe few knew about. I'd never heard of it till I met Rick. Anyway, it was a specialty of Rick's mother, but his father made one for Rick when we went down there recently. I tasted buttermilk pie for the first time—delicious. But me with my discerning tongue, I thought I could still taste the subtle sourness of the buttermilk. Maybe his dad missed a step, but I have no point of reference, so maybe it was fine. Rick loved it, though, so ..."

Naomi knew Viv's rambling had a point. She let Viv get there.

219

"Initially, I didn't get the idea of there being anything sweet about buttermilk. After you explained your grandmother's view, I've tried to use it in my relationship with Rick, but it's held a different meaning for me. Our renewed love and commitment is oh-so-sweet, Naomi, it really is, but there's this sour element underneath it all …"

"And it has to do with Rick?"

"I think so."

"You still don't trust him?"

"As far as other women? Oh yeah, I trust him. Rick's said and done crucial stuff to re-earn my trust with that. But as much as I like this semi-new Rick, I don't trust where it's coming from."

"Where do you think it's coming from?"

"I used to believe it was sparked by my announcement to separate and him wanting to win me back. But like I told Louise, I think the winning me back was more of a byproduct rather than Rick's intent with the change in him, so I don't know where it's coming from. But it's not just that; it's …"

"Take your time."

"Louise pointed out a coincidence to me weeks ago that we both shot down, but then a detective investigating Jonathan's murder stopped by our house recently and …" Viv sipped her water. "And now I think I'm paranoid or something."

"Paranoid?"

Viv returned her gaze to the window.

Naomi did, too. The sun dipped low. Rays of gold and yellow-red bathed the sky, giving the streets of downtown DC a mellow atmosphere that blended well with the putty-white lighting in the restaurant.

"How do you feel about intuition?"

"We all have it to some degree or another."

"And what if your intuition is telling you something you don't want to believe?"

"You act on it or you don't."

Viv looked at her. "Everything is not black and white, Naomi. Act, don't act. It doesn't work that way."

"I believe it does. You do something or you don't—that's the black and white in life. The shades of gray come after that initial decision."

Viv stayed quiet for a long time, returning her gaze to the window.

Naomi waited. When their table-attendant approached, asking if they wanted dessert menus, she nodded.

"… You know what I'm thinking about?"

"From your face, I'd say something sexual about you and Rick."

Viv glanced at Naomi before turning back to the window. "That obvious, huh? Rick surprised me at my office the other day." Viv looked at her. "He did a bowling ball and then went on his way." She turned back to the window with a blush.

"Talented man."

"You don't know the half." Viv looked at her, her black eyes conveying happiness. "We now meditate and pray together."

"Good, Viv. Hold on to that."

Viv nodded. She then grinned warmly. "He makes me laugh …" She closed her eyes with a deep breath before looking serious. "Rick fills me up, Naomi. Emotionally. Spiritually. Intellectually. Sexually. I love him so much. I know: fantastic sex isn't love, but …" Viv trailed-off. She lowered her head and looked away.

"Well, love is determined by the individual, Viv. You just named several reasons why your love is so deep. No one can dictate or define what love is for anyone except himself or herself."

Viv jerked around, surprise on her face. "Thank you, Naomi. Thank you. It's weird, but I said something similar, to Louise recently. The thing is, I love Rick beyond the sex. This shit between us is extreme, profound. I will feed him, wipe his ass when he can't, all of that. But this man has me turned so inside-out sexually, I can't think sometimes. We've even …" Viv hesitated.

"Go on, Viv. There's little I haven't been exposed to in my line of work."

Viv took a breath, leaned forward, and continued: "We've even tried scenarios where Rick rapes me." Viv watched Naomi, waiting.

"What are you looking like that for? What did I just say?"

Appearing relieved, Viv sat back. "I know, Naomi. But this wasn't some fake-out role-playing. I mean, it was in the sense that we planned it, but, well, it played out very real, that's all." Viv shook her head with the memory. "My, my shoe came off; Rick dragged me back behind our house; my skirt was torn. I just— It was just—" Viv stopped, looking at Naomi. "A second or two, I thought I was being raped by a stranger— being raped for real."

Naomi waited a beat. "Did you like it?"

A hint of a smile quickly vanished before Viv replied. "I had a strong orgasm, so I guess so."

"Not necessarily. The body can and will respond even when the mind or heart doesn't want to. It's something real rape victims have to contend with."

Viv nodded slowly.

"So, did you like it?"

Viv returned her attention to the window. "Yeah. Yeah, I did, Naomi."

"Cool. No one was hurt, and apparently a good time was had by all. You guys are married. Do your thing." Naomi stopped short of adding: *but be careful.*

Viv looked at her. "And you know, with all the new things we're exploring with sex, the most important and beautiful thing about it for me is that it's with my husband. I'm not out here trying to find it with anyone else; I don't have to. I have it all with Rick. Like I said, it's almost too good."

"You two don't fight?"

"Of course. Can get really pissed-off with each other. But we've never been big on arguing, most times agreeing to disagree."

"I see. Okay. So, I understand that you are unequivocally into your husband. I got that. I'm happy for you. Where does the negative intuition, Louise's coincidence, the detective's visit, and your paranoia come in?"

Viv looked at her strangely.

"I'm sorry. I can only go around Robin Hood's barn once or twice. After that, I'm about opening the door."

"No shit."

"Yeah, shit." Naomi had an idea where Viv was headed. She doubted she could give concrete guidance on it, but she'd try.

Now Viv searched Naomi's face. "… I think Rick had something to do with Jonathan dying."

"Is that the sourness you alluded to earlier?"

Viv nodded.

Here we go. Naomi's thoughts wavered on how to pursue this with Viv. "So, what if he did?"

Viv sipped more water. "Then I'm fucked."

"Kinda sorta."

The two women were quiet for some time. Their attendant returned with dessert menus.

Naomi asked: "Have you said anything to anyone else?"

"I asked Rick if he had anything to do with it."

"He denied it, of course, but you have your doubts."

"But I don't have any proof, either, not even anything circumstantial. All I may have is a possible motive."

"Too much crime TV, Viv?" Naomi smiled (although there was nothing humorous about what they were discussing).

Viv offered a semi-smile.

"Does it matter if he had a hand in it or if he did it himself?"

Viv shrugged. "I know it sounds bad, but if he is involved, I'd prefer that he didn't actually do it—makes it easier to swallow that way. But no; no, it doesn't matter. Either way it's wrong." A hurt expression crossed Viv's face. She picked up a dessert menu, and then put it down again. "The main problem, though, is I don't know anything for certain. But I don't know how long I can take having this question of whether Rick did or didn't go unanswered."

"Now I'm back to my original question. What if Rick was involved? Say you find out something you could go to the authorities with. Given all that you've said about your feelings for him, what will you do?"

"I couldn't let Rick get away with something like that, Naomi."

"You're sure?"

Viv hesitated before answering: "Yes." Naomi noticed, however, that she replied into her dessert menu. "It's not like I have much choice, anyway."

"Please. Black or white, remember? Shades of gray come later."

"I hear you. But, again, I don't have anything, and my name is not Easy Rawlins or Nancy Drew."

"I understand." Naomi's heart went out to Viv. She couldn't let Viv in on her own semi-detective work. And trying to explain her flashes-of-truth was out. Hell, she hardly understood them herself. "I'm sorry, Viv."

"So, I guess I'm in wait-and-see mode, huh?"

"I guess. Can I ask why you wanted to talk to me about this?"

"Well, my main reason was to talk about Rick's personality change. I wanted to get your ideas on what could have caused it. To be honest,

I think he's changed in response to what happened to Jonathan—but because he had something to do with it, you know? Since you're our therapist, I'm guessing you'd be the best person to answer that for me."

"You're asking if Rick's sudden 'personality change,' as you put it, could be caused by him taking part in or committing murder?"

"Yes, that's what I'm asking. Could it?"

"Well, yes—without the mumbo-jumbo."

"Thank you."

"You're welcome."

"Guess I have my first clue, huh?"

"Maybe. Rick's change could have also been brought on by the threat of losing you and Alna. Given his obsession with family, a threat to its foundation would be just as traumatic as having killed someone, triggering the behavioral response he's exhibited lately."

Viv nodded her understanding.

"Will your feelings change, Viv?"

Viv hesitated but shook her head.

"That must be some sex you're having."

Viv closed her eyes briefly before responding. "Girl, it's always been good, but *this man* ..."

Viv's use of girlfriend-talk touched Naomi. She didn't get to hear it on such a personal level that often. She smiled.

"Can I ask you something? It's kind of personal."

Naomi tensed. "Sure."

"Do you ... have someone?"

"You mean am I gettin' some on the regular?"

"Well, that, but you know, just ... someone."

Naomi thought about her few dates with Kevin. Their last date or two indicated they'd moved from colleague status, becoming friends. Their kiss the other night wasn't magical but held promise. Naomi, however, needed to resolve other issues before moving on to anything more. Fortunately, Kevin was in no rush. "I guess I have someone."

"I'm glad. Even loners need people they can get interpersonal with."

"I see. And you consider me a 'loner' because ..."

"I can just tell. Don't need a psych degree to see that."

"Just remember, 'loner' doesn't mean 'lonely.'"

"Oh, I know."

"Good. Now, can I ask you something?"

"Go ahead."

"It's two questions, actually."

"Okay."

"Several sessions ago, the one where we delved into Rick's infidelities, you were adamant about knowing when he'd been with that last one."

"Yeah?"

"How did you know with such certainty?"

Viv signaled the table attendant. "They give these dessert menus, you think they'd want to take an order the same day you had dinner."

"I want the crème brûlée."

"I want the pineapple-crush cake."

Their attendant returned, and Viv ordered for them. She waited for the attendant to be out of earshot. "I have an associate who's an ex-cop. She works as a private investigator on the side. After Rick's second incident, she periodically kept tabs on him for me."

"You pay her?"

"Surprisingly, no."

"The sisterhood lives."

"It lives."

"So how could you not let it be an issue? What—"

"Please don't. Louise and Patrice have badgered me enough. Besides, that's over."

"You sound positive."

"I am. That shit is dead. Like I said, he's said and done major stuff to convince me."

"Pro bono PI, huh?"

"Yep." Viv took another sip of wine. Only, it wasn't quite a sip.

"Sweet. Now question two. And this one's personal."

"Oh, so we're just girls hangin', are we? Cool. What's up?"

"How long will you be ordering glasses of wine as a front?"

Viv's eyes flickered. "What? How's that personal?"

"You've ordered this wine, but you haven't touched it. Not really. You've brought the glass to your lips and wet your lip with wine but not much else." Naomi paused. "Even with all that's going on, having a baby is a good thing, Viv. I take it Rick doesn't know."

Viv shook her head. "Maybe your name should be Nancy Drew. Shit."

"Have you remained tightlipped because there's a question of who the father is?"

"I know who the father is."

"Then I'm going to leave that right where it is. So where are Rick and Alna?"

Viv checked her watch. "Right about now, they're probably leaving her martial-arts class. He'll probably run a few errands before stopping to get ice cream and take-out to bring home. We've been on an ice cream kick lately."

"What discipline does she practice?"

"Judo. Rick will probably move her into his discipline, karate, later on."

Naomi ears pricked. "Oh, Rick's into it, too?"

"He's a fifth-degree black belt. I think it's kinda neat, but he says I brag too much, so I try to keep my adoration to myself."

"He's that good?" Kevin's description of Jonathan's injuries echoed in Naomi's mind.

"Yes." Viv looked at her watch again. "I'm sorry, Naomi. I'm going to have to cut this short. The donation center closes a little earlier on Saturdays, and they're closed tomorrow. Rick's been pressing me to get some stuff to them. I have time to drop it off if I leave now."

"It's cool. We can doggie-bag dessert. You guys doing some spring cleaning?"

"No. Rick's getting rid of this box of shoes and clothing he had in the garage."

"Why doesn't he take it himself?"

Viv shrugged. "You know how husbands can be some— Oh, sorry."

"What?"

"I mean … your husband …"

"Was exactly that—my husband. He's dead. But he was a husband before he died, so I can relate."

"I don't even know why he's getting rid of it. He's barely worn some of that stuff."

Intuition was a bitch sometimes. "I'll take it for you."

"Oh, you don't have to do that. Although … I would prefer to go home and try to get a nap before they return."

"Well, there you go." An excited anxiousness stirred in Naomi's belly, but her heart twanged with sadness.

"I guess. Sure you don't mind?"

"I wouldn't have offered. A center is on my way home. I can give you the receipt when you come for your session."

"Works for me. Thanks, Naomi."

"No problem."

The women said little as they walked to Viv's car. The fairly-light box Naomi accepted from Viv contrasted Naomi's heavy heart.

Before getting in her car, Viv surprised Naomi with a hug. The gesture reflected an understandable conclusion to their meeting. And although Naomi hugged Viv back, tension and emotional resistance hampered her response. She wasn't particularly comfortable with public displays of affection.

Driving home, Naomi listened to her favorite classical music station, happy the announcer included Pachelbel's "Canon in D Major" in his set. She thought about Viv, Rick, and the box in her trunk.

She'll search it, of course.

It may hold nothing or it could hold everything.

Naomi wasn't sure which she wanted.

CHAPTER 18

Recollections

Viv sat back, sipping her Sprite, watching her husband and daughter play tic-tac-toe on a napkin resting between them at their table.

Rick suggested they resume their family-night-out ritual, and Alna, tired of Zibby's, suggested everyone dress up. So, Viv found herself eating at DeTante's for the second time within a week, and although she loved the food and the atmosphere, she would've preferred to dine elsewhere.

They sat in a booth on the second tier (Viv made it a point to sit out of view of Jonathan's memorial), having a nice time. The kind of quality family-time Rick thrived on.

But Viv was tired. Tired, wired, and uncomfortable. The first and latter were due to her residing in the final stages of the first trimester. Her energy returned for a few weeks, but waned again. Her clothing, too, caused mild discomfort—especially tonight with the form-fitting midnight-blue dress she wore.

Tired and uncomfortable, yes. But she was wired, too: unable to fully relax since her one-on-one with Naomi.

Viv watched Rick purposely put his O in a square that would allow Alna to win the game.

"I don't like when you let me win, Daddy." Alna put her X in the appropriate square and drew a line through her row of Xs to signal tic-tac-toe. She wore an expression of defeat, not victory, and put her pen down. "I'm turning ten. I don't need that anymore."

Viv remained quiet, cheering inside for her daughter. She kept her attention on Rick, waiting for his reaction.

Watching him, the flutters started. He sat across from her in a tailored midnight-blue Everett Hall suit and crisp white shirt, accented with a tie and kerchief of Baker-Miller pink. He'd tied his tie with the Fishbone knot; an intricate, visually-appealing knot that gave Viv delightful goosebumps whenever he wore it. Before ordering dessert (which they waited for now), Rick loosened his tie and unbuttoned the top button of his shirt; something she found profoundly sexy.

Rick smiled at their daughter, and Viv's heart flew. Tired or not, she was having him tonight. They hadn't done anything in three days.

"I know how old you are, daughter of mine. Who said I let you win?"

Alna rolled her eyes upward, looking pretty in last year's Easter dress.

Rick laughed. "A'ight, a'ight. You're right. I'm sorry."

"No more cheating?"

"But you won. How can I be cheating if you won?"

"Daddy ..."

"Okay, no more cheating." Rick gave Viv a conspiratorial wink.

Viv smiled down into her glass: his simply being a daddy turned her on. She returned her gaze to her husband.

"Promise?"

Rick's jaw dropped. "Dag! I gotta promise and everything?"

Alna doodled on the napkin. "Uh-huh."

Rick glanced at Viv.

Her expression apparently telegraphed her mood. Rick looked at her and did a double take before holding her gaze. The warmth in his eyes told her he, too, wanted something more-intimate later.

"Daddy, promise."

Rick returned his attention to Alna. "I promise."

For some reason, Alna gave her mother the biggest grin.

"And desserts are on the way." Rick reached for his spoon.

The attendant served Rick and Alna their ice cream. Opting out this go-round, Viv had a spoonful of Alna's fudge-brownie sundae to satisfy her sweet tooth. Rick and Alna ate their desserts in peace.

Alna scooped a last bite. "When is Aunt Louise coming for me?"

Rick checked his Movado pocket watch. Viv was a 'hand' girl: Rick had some nice hands. She admired the hand holding his watch as the diamond accents in his wedding band glinted. He repocketed his watch. "Soon. Why? You ready to ditch us already?"

Alna nodded.

"So, it's like that."

Alna smiled. She eyed his bowl. "Can I have the rest?"

Viv shook her head. "You've had enough, Al."

"Aww ..." Alna whined. She looked at her father.

Rick raised an eyebrow, his face serious.

Viv knew it was time to go; even that expression got her hot.

"Hey, fam!" Louise approached from behind Viv.

Rick stood. "Hey, Louise." He leaned to kiss her cheek. "Whassup?"

"Nothing much." Louise glanced around at everyone. "You guys look special." She looked at Viv. "Hey, stranger."

Viv didn't know how to interact with Louise since her revelation regarding Louise's feelings for Rick, so she hadn't talked to her much over the last few weeks. In fact, Rick coordinated Alna sleeping over at Louise's. "No stranger than you. Hello, love."

Louise leaned over and hugged her.

Over Louise's shoulder, Viv read Rick's expression. With his eyes, he asked what the deal was between her and Louise. Viv closed her eyes and shook her head slightly, telling him, *not now.*

Lou pulled back from the hug. "Hello, Miss Alna. Finishing up?"

"I'm done."

"Get your bag, honey, and switch places with Daddy."

Alna scooted out of the booth and grabbed her overnight bag from under the table. She handed her bag toward Rick. Rick pointed to Louise for Alna to give the bag to her. Alna turned to Louise, who shook her head and pointed back to Rick. Alna turned to her mother. Viv pointed to Louise.

"Thank you, Mommy."

The adults laughed. Viv noticed Louise resting her hand on Rick's back. Until recently she wouldn't have given the gesture another thought.

Rick slid back into the booth opposite Viv. "Take a load off, Louise. We're not ready to release her yet."

Although not standing immediately next to Rick, Alna was still the closer of the two, but Louise slid in next to him. Alna sat next to her mother.

Viv wondered again if she'd missed these cues all these years, or was just supersensitive to everything given her hormones, and what she recently discovered about her friend. Nevertheless, pangs of jealousy surfaced with Louise's proximity to him. As much as she wanted to say something, what could she say?

Rick innocently rested his arm behind them across the back of the booth (the idiot). Viv tensed. Did Louise move closer to him? *No, just stop.*

"I'll meet you at judo practice tomorrow and pick her up." Rick sipped his water.

She trusted Rick, but the idea of Rick and Lou alone still didn't sit well. "I'll pick her up."

Rick and Louise looked at her oddly.

"Oookay." Rick turned to Louise. "Tim getting his bike?"

"Are you kidding? He's still in the talking stage."

Looking at Rick in profile, Viv newly-realized how long his eyelashes were; they belonged on a girl. And that cleft, still noticeable through the hair on his chin. The man was just … Oh yeah, Lou and Al needed to go.

"Tell him to stop talking and get the doggoned thing."

Louise turned her body toward Rick (Viv didn't imagine this one). "For what? He isn't certified to ride yet." Her eyes roamed Rick's face.

"He's in the class though, right?"

Viv needed a connection with her husband. She recognized her insecurity as silly and petty, but she didn't care. Taking her shoe off, Viv slid her foot along the inside of Rick's leg.

A soft, knowing-grin eased across his face as he kept eyes on Louise. Viv carried her caress upward.

Louise nodded. "Yeah. He's waiting until he finishes before buying."

"See, if he got the bike now, he could be practicing. Besides, it'd be incentive for him to get certified."

"Mommy, would it be rude if I read my book?"

"Yes, but you're allowed since you asked first. Go ahead."

Rick shifted his body to face Viv more. He slid his hips forward and opened his legs. To anyone else, he appeared to be simply relaxing against the booth cushions.

Viv stared at Rick's Adam's apple. It bobbed as he spoke; she wanted to run her tongue over it.

She sent her caress higher. The feel of his erection under her toes created all kinds of good feeling inside her. Love and lust combined almost-painfully.

Rick continued small-talk about motorcycles with Lou. She appeared thoroughly engrossed in Rick's discussion of the new Kawasaki series, while Viv gave her husband a tender foot-job under the table. His eyelids dropped slowly a time or two as he spoke, indicating his aroused-pleasure to Viv, but Louise either didn't notice or paid it no mind.

Perfectly content in her covert activity with the beautiful man sitting across from her, Viv was glad no one tried to include her in the conversation. She needed to stop, though; this wasn't doing anything but making them crazy, but their mutual excitement made stopping difficult.

Viv was ready to go home. Ready to have her baby on that African-print rug and feel his long, thick inches plunging inside her. Ready to see those eyes lighten right before he—

Rick sat upright unexpectedly, making it harder for her to reach him. He likely sensed the need for them to disengage as well. Disappointed over returning to neutral corners, Viv slid her foot back into her pump.

Rick's hand rested on the table.

She imagined it spanking her before curling her fingers around his.

Rick winked at her and turned back to Louise.

Louise looked from Viv to Rick. "What are you two up to?"

"Huh?" Rick looked at Viv again, brows furrowed.

Viv opened her eyes wide for effect, trying to look as dumbfounded as Rick. She shook her head and shrugged.

Alna lifted her head long enough to regard the adults at the table mildly before lowering her eyes to read again.

Louise sighed. "Never mind."

Viv became spiteful. With her finger, she beckoned Rick to lean across the table. Rick looked at Louise, who shrugged noncommittally. He wore an expression of baffled amusement, but he leaned over.

Viv leaned forward, too, and gazed into her husband's eyes. He wore Burberry Touch cologne.

Rick's puzzled-gaze turned serious. He spoke softly. "That dress, Viv. You're killing me, you know that?"

"Thank you. You're killing me, too." Viv didn't take her eyes off him. "Excuse us, Louise." She cupped Rick's cheek and kissed him. His tongue was soft, warm, inviting. As worked up as she was, she didn't give him a raunchy tongue-down (she did have some class, and Alna was present), but she put enough tasteful sensuality into it to let anyone watching (Louise) know that she and Rick were together—and rubbing Louise's face in it.

When they parted, Rick's confused look returned, but Viv could tell he was turned-on, too. "Okay ..." He sat back.

Viv looked at Louise openly. She understood Louise's strange look in return. Louise didn't know Viv knew about her feelings for Rick. No one knew what Viv was doing but Viv.

Rick looked alternately between the women.

Louise frowned. "What was that about?"

"Nothing. I've kissed Rick in front of you before."

"Yeah, but ..."

Viv waited.

"Are you angry about something, Viv?" She sounded truly in the dark.

The genuine concern in Lou's question made Viv instantly sorry. She sighed. "No."

Alna now kept eyes on her mother.

"Then what—?" Louise started.

"Not now, ladies," Rick interjected quietly.

Louise continued looking at her.

"It's nothing, Lou. Pay me no mind. I'll call tomorrow if I'm really picking Al up. Rick will probably do it."

Looking hurt, Louise turned to Alna. "Come on, sweetie. You and Li'l Tim won't have much playtime if I get you back too late." Louise slid out of the booth and started helping Alna. She turned to Rick. "I'll be sure to tell Tim you called him a wimp."

Rick laughed. "See, you ain't right."

"I know." Louise leaned toward him for a hug.

"I, uh, I'd stand, but, um, Viv's got me kinda ... you know."

Louise's eyes flitted downward before she averted her gaze. "I got you." She gave Rick a leaning, sideways-hug. "Well, see one of you tomorrow."

"Yeah, one of us," Rick confirmed.

Louise grabbed Alna's bag. She looked awkwardly at Viv.

Viv slid out of the booth and hugged her friend. "It's cool," she whispered in Louise's ear, "maybe we'll talk tomorrow."

Louise hugged her tighter. "I sure hope so."

Viv turned to her daughter, giving her a hug and kiss. "Be good, Al."

"I will." Alna squeezed by Louise and her mother to crawl into the booth and kiss her father's cheek. "I like your hairy face, Daddy."

Rick kissed Alna's forehead. "Yeah, your mama does, too. Love you. Have fun."

"Okay." Alna joined Louise on the floor.

"Bye, guys." Louise waved behind her as she and Alna left tier 2.

Viv sat. If she could have a glass of wine, now would be perfect. She looked at Rick. "You ready?"

"Don't even try it. What was that about?" Rick folded his hands on the table.

She trailed a finger over a hand, caressing it. "You're wearing Touch tonight."

"Don't dodge, Viv. Tell me."

Viv inferred sincere friendship from his words; his sensitivity warmed her. "I don't know if I should say anything. It involves you."

"Me?"

Viv nodded. She wasn't sure she wanted to get into this.

"What'd I do?"

"Be you." She tried hard not to stare at his beautiful mouth, imagining his lips and teeth moving over her nipples.

"Beg pardon?"

Viv sighed. "I found out recently: Louise has feelings for you that she shouldn't have."

"What? She wants to get busy with me?"

"I'm sure that's part of it, but she's actually in love with you."

Rick lowered his eyes to look at his hands. "Did she tell you this?"

Viv noticed his lack of shock. "No, but did she tell you?" A sense of betrayal, all-too-familiar before recent events, surfaced.

Rick looked at her squarely. "I have not been with Louise, Viv."

Viv held in a sigh of relief. "Thank you for that. Now spill it."

Rick sighed. "New Year's Eve party, six years ago."

"Yes …?"

"She kissed me."

"Kissed you?"

"Kissed me."

"You mean …?"

"Yes, Viv: *kissed* me. Not some special-occasion platonic-kiss, either."

She was surprised to hear it. "It was a party, maybe she—"

"Louise wasn't drunk, Viv. Not *that* drunk, anyway."

"Did you kiss her back?"

"Yes and no. I mean, yes at first, because, well, it was Louise in friend-mode, you know, so I let her kiss me because, I don't know, I was being nice, but then, almost-instantly, she put her hands to my hair and parted her lips. I pulled away and pushed her back. I looked at her, hoping she *was* drunk."

"Where was I? Where was Tim?"

"On the front porch, saying goodbye to guests."

"Did she say anything?'

"Just that it was New Year's. That she'd made a resolution to be more-forthright or something. She said that she had a confession, something that she hated herself for because of you, but she couldn't help how she felt anymore, either. She then told me she'd been in love with me for years; that she loved me more than she ever loved any man."

"And kissing you? What was that supposed to do?"

Rick shrugged.

"She probably figured, since you weren't faithful anyway …"

It wasn't her intent, but Viv could see her comment bothered him.

"What'd you say?"

"What could I say?"

"That it wasn't mutual. That you wouldn't, couldn't, stoop—"

"She already knew that, Viv. I don't think she expected reciprocation. I think she just couldn't keep it in anymore."

"Oh, you like this, don't you?"

"Not at all." He sipped his Elijah Craig 23.

"How come you never mentioned it to me?"

"One, it wasn't my place. Two, what good would it have done?"

Viv thought about that. No-longer feeling betrayed (not by Rick anyway), she asked: "So, how was it?"

Rick's eyes changed; the smoldering embers burned at her. "I enjoy kissing only *you*." His tone held a mixture of lust and pure resolution.

Sex and danger emanated from him again, making Viv tingle. Could she ever get used to this about him? Her heart softened at the implication of his words, realizing her kiss alone brought him pleasure no one else could. "Is that so?"

"Without question," Rick replied warmly. "Is that what the foot-action and that damn kiss were for: as a message to Louise?"

"'Damn kiss'?" Viv didn't know how much longer she could take looking at him and talking.

"It's a good thing, believe me. Well?"

"In a way. The foot-action was because I didn't like her sitting so close to you. The kiss? Well, yeah, that was an in-your-face thing. A message of sorts. I kinda felt bad afterward."

"Well, I'm sure she ..." Rick looked around tier 2, "and everyone else got the message if they saw us." He returned his gaze to her. "And you should have felt bad. That wasn't necessary. Louise hasn't tried anything since that kiss at New Year's. Talk to her about it."

"I can't."

"Then let it go."

"I can't do that, either."

"Well, you can't keep making me hard and shit all out in public whenever you're feeling threatened around Louise. You shouldn't feel threatened, anyway. It's a one-way thing, remember?"

"Yeah, but who knows, she might—"

Rick's mellow baritone dropped lower with reassuring compassion. "What have I been telling you, showing you; in as many ways as I know how?"

"I know."

"No one else ever again, Vivian. I never will."

"Pretty strong words, Rick."

Rick simply looked at her: reasserting his words without speaking.

Viv sighed with a nod. "I'll talk to her about it. One day. Doesn't mean I won't take opportunities to mess with you sometimes."

Rick smiled. "Aw, come on now!"

His smile was simply to die for. "You know you like it."

"A hard dick usually indicates liking something. Yeah, so?"

"So, work with me. I won't be doing it a lot. Now, enough: I want to get you home. Fuck the dumb stuff: it's been three days, dammit."

"Listen to you. Countin' days and carryin' on." Rick looked at her curiously. "Which brings me to something I need to ask you. I've been doing a little counting myself …" Rick finished his practically-melted ice cream.

Viv's heartbeat quickened. Rick was no dummy. "What do you mean?"

"Viv?"

"Yes?"

"We've been pretty hot-and-heavy without fail for weeks now."

"Except these last three days: a girl's been left high and dry."

Rick's lashes lowered with a blush. "Except these last three days, okay. Still, is there something you need to tell me?"

"There will not be a fourth day."

"Come on, Viv. I'm serious."

"What, Rick?"

"Okay, let me try this again. One, we've had sex frequently at whim for over a month now, and two, I haven't seen any feminine-hygiene stuff in the trash for longer than that. So again, what's up? Is there something you need to tell me?"

Viv closed her eyes. Here it was. "… Shit."

"So, you are?"

Viv opened her eyes and gazed at Rick. As serious as this discussion was, looking at this handsome man, who was hers, sitting across from her, all Viv wanted was to make love to him, because she did love him so. "Can we not talk about this now?"

"No."

"Rick …"

"How can you think we're not going to talk about this?"

"I don't, but …"

"No, Viv. Answer me."

"Yes. Yes, I am. Happy?"

"Given recent events, that depends on the answer to the next question."

Truth stood proud; she never wavered. The issue had to be addressed—unfortunately sooner rather than later. Viv just didn't want her pregnancy to affect what was happening between them. It would eventually, inevitably. But if she could put it off awhile longer …

She loved and wanted the child growing inside her, but it was also important that she and Rick reestablish their relationship. Not only that, she was too horny to focus anyway. "That, I am not going to answer yet."

"What?"

"You heard me."

"So, it is Rast's baby!?" He sat back, reaching for his ear.

"Don't do this, Rick. We'll talk about it. We don't have much choice, do we? But not tonight. Please? Let's finish tonight like we both want to."

Rick signaled their server to bring the check and then reached for his wallet.

Viv noticed the folded letter in one of the slots: David's letter to him that he always kept close. She absolutely could not ask him about it now, but intuition told her the letter was important. They were silent until their server returned with Rick's credit card.

He finished his bourbon. "Ready?"

"Isn't that my line?" Viv wanted to lighten the mood.

Rick smiled weakly before getting up to help her out of her seat. He smelled so good.

Silence escorted them for most of the ride home. Rick didn't bother to turn on music, and Viv left well-enough alone. She thought about the letter in her husband's wallet. Unable to take the quiet, Viv ventured: "Why do you carry David's letter around?"

"It's important to me." Rick's tone held little emotion.

"Will you ever share what's in it with me?"

"Yeah. Eventually. Why?"

"Because it's important to you." Viv wanted to be his friend now. They rarely discussed what happened to his brother. When they did, Rick stuck to the basics.

Rick shrugged. "Not much to share. Just a letter telling me how much he loved me even though I was a pain-in-the-ass little brother."

Viv believed him, but even from the side, the pain in his eyes told her there was more to it. It hurt seeing that pain in his eyes. She rested a hand on his thigh. Rick's leg tensed but then relaxed. Her reticence about the baby's paternity still bothered him. Regrettably, Viv realized there might be a day four (or five or six) after all.

Aside from opening her door for her when they arrived home, Rick avoided interaction with her.

Viv understood. She didn't know why, but she waited at the bottom of the stairs as Rick moved about the main level of their home, checking doors and turning out lights. He stopped when he saw her waiting for him. In the dark, Viv made out his gesture for her to proceed. They climbed the stairs and entered their bedroom.

Rick tossed his keys on his nightstand and entered their en suite. Seconds later, Viv heard him peeing. Trying not to feel too disappointed, Viv headed for her lingerie chest (pajamas were definitely a part of the picture tonight). She listened to Rick wash his hands. When he left the bathroom, she stiffened as he walked past her. The silence and darkness added to the tension between them. In her peripheral vision, Rick disappeared into his closet.

Sighing with disappointment and frustration, Viv wanted to slam her drawer closed—anything to disturb the awful quiet. Standing next to their bed, she began undressing.

It dawned on her that no sound came from Rick's closet. It wasn't until she removed her last piece of clothing that she sensed his eyes on her. Nude, she looked toward Rick's closet, seeing that he indeed watched her.

Rick stood in his closet doorway. Even in the dark, she saw he remained fully-clothed down to his shoes. His hands were in his pockets.

Viv turned back to the bed. His menacing (alluring?) posture made her nervous. She picked up her nighttime-bra.

"No."

Viv hesitated but lowered the bra to the bed. She turned to him.

"C'mere."

She walked toward him, feeling vulnerable but sexy. Trepidation mixed with anticipation moved through her. She stopped before him.

"Kiss me."

Viv stepped up to her husband and drew her arms around him.

Rick didn't move.

Bringing her hands to the rough, dry curls of his crinkly-soft hair, she touched her mouth to his. Viv wasn't sure what was going on, but they weren't role-playing. Rick's demeanor scared her, but she was drawn to him.

He didn't resist as she eased her tongue into his mouth. Rick's soft lips and warm tongue merged with hers. His mouth tasted of bourbon and traces of cream from his dessert—heavenly. The scent of Burberry Touch enveloped her: an intoxicating blend of violet leaves, cedar wood, and white pepper elements that titillated. Viv brought a hand from his head to caress the smooth hair on his face. The tickle of his moustache as she moved her mouth with his, made her crazy. Rick didn't embrace her, but she detected a more-obvious sign of his arousal. Viv broke their kiss and stepped back.

Rick removed a hand from his pocket, wiping his mouth. "Yes, Lord. Kisses don't lie."

Viv remained quiet, not knowing what to say. Her body, however, had a soliloquy ready for him.

Rick reached out and fondled each breast, making already-stiff nipples harder. "Turn around," he whispered.

Viv turned, feeling like property being inspected (but it excited her). She trembled as Rick's hand caressed her backside, gentle squeezes accenting each caress.

"Very nice. Face me, Vivian."

Viv faced him.

Rick stared at her through the gloom. She watched Rick unzip and release his erection. His swollen organ jutted from his suit pants with authority. It turned Viv on immensely, but she remained wary of his disposition.

"On your knees." His tone was as dark as their bedroom.

Viv lowered to her husband's crotch. Additional instruction wasn't necessary. She mouthed her husband's stiff flesh, tasting and smelling the usual fading but pleasant flavor of the lotion he used.

Rick's tone was dark, but he caressed her head lightly. "That's enough. Get up."

Viv stood.

Rick leaned against the doorframe. "Touch me."

Viv encircled him with a hand, stroking gently. He was unbelievably hard. A soft sigh escaped his lips as she stroked his length.

"Three days is too long for me too, especially now. I— I can only control it for so long on my own before … I must do something. Fucking you helps me keep it back. Keep it … Keep it under control. It's a simple outlet, but effective."

Viv had no idea what "it" was or why he needed to rein it in. She was confused by his words but afraid to speak up. At the same time, her desire to have him inside her grew steadily.

"But what's different tonight is I'm pissed, and anger doesn't mix with it well. Not well at all. It's scaring me, Viv."

Viv continued stroking him, desire and anxiety each vying for position within her.

"I want to lay you down, do a soft, slow thing. We need one of those. But, Viv, right now I need to just fuck you. Because anger is in this now, and I don't know how—"

Viv found herself lifted against the wall, pain shooting through her upper back from the force of impact. Rick held her leg open at the knee with his right hand, gripping her throat his left. He entered her, ramming thoroughly while grunting something. She listened more-closely.

"Mine." He repeated it, the gruff chant low, animal-like.

No longer startled, Viv allowed lust to take over, oddly moved by his need to possess her. Given her position against the wall, Rick thrust deep inside her, but it was a good deep, the friction deliciously amazing.

Her haze of passion, however, cleared abruptly: Rick's hand tightened at her throat.

"Rick!" Her croak wasn't even a whisper. She tried again: "Rick, stop!" She pushed against him futilely. Rick was lost—and strong as shit.

"God, I love you. Beautiful bitch! You're mine dammit!"

She couldn't speak.

Air was suddenly scarce.

Panic set in as a thin border of gray mist outlined her vision. Her throat burned horribly. She mentally screamed and prayed for him to stop, refusing to believe he would kill her.

His grip tightened.

The gray border of mist thickened with the pressure in her head. Viv closed her eyes, waiting and praying, thinking her throat seemed so small in his hand, the term 'hyoid bone' suddenly critically important ...

Rick must have "heard" her: he suddenly loosened his awful hold.

But Viv was shocked to find that even with the terror happening, her body reached a powerful and wrenching orgasm.

Hell above, heaven below.

Viv coughed and gasped through the conflicting pleasure traveling through her. The gray mist slowly retreated, but her throat throbbed painfully with the air now rushing down it. Despite herself, the contrast of her nudity and Rick being clothed still aroused her.

Finding something erotic in what was happening, given that her husband nearly strangled her, blew Viv away. She closed her eyes as Rick continued thrusting, his hold to her throat much-lighter now. Warm semen bathed her insides as he emptied into her.

Dizziness claimed its post in the melee.

She thought insanity was close behind.

Thankful for life and not knowing what else to do, Viv wrapped Rick in her arms and held on as her dizzy-spell passed.

Rick's chanting stopped, but he breathed heavily as he fucked her, his erection never subsiding.

Overcome by love and concern for her husband, Viv guided Rick's mouth to hers, kissing him deeply. He moaned into her mouth; Viv tasted salt. She opened her eyes.

Rick's eyes were closed, but even with what little light there was, she saw tears glistening on his face. She closed her eyes, tonguing him softly now. Rick's thrusts were deep but gentle.

Something was very wrong.

On one side, her mind screamed this wasn't good, shrieked and bellowed dire warning.

On the other side, as Rick's hand now slid down from her throat to massage her right breast and thumb the nipple while they kissed and he gently drove into her with this slow, deep, grinding-swirl that was always uncommonly-good, the parts that made her female told her, oh yes, it was all very, *very* good.

Her body betrayed her again, sending a second wave of thrilling spasms through her.

Rick moaned into her mouth again as he, too, somehow reached a second release.

Her heart, beating rapidly in indecision, rested on the fence.

* * * * *

She awoke to the pleasurable-warmth of Rick spooning her. His pubic hair and soft penis nestled comfortably against her rear.

Rick slept soundly behind her, his left hand holding her left breast.

After that encounter, he carried her to their bed. He undressed and snuggled beside her, where they fell asleep in the spoon they were in now.

She didn't say anything about him choking her. She doubted Rick had a clue. She couldn't let it happen again though, so she had to do something—what, she didn't know.

Viv thought their spell would be broken with his hand clamping on her evilly, squeezing her breast painfully. That fear passed instantly as Rick's hand simply cupped her lightly before relaxing. She detected the slightest movement against her butt as Cronus stirred.

Rick slept.

Viv smiled to herself. Regardless of what happened last night, she wanted him again.

She initiated subtle movements against her husband. Not enough to wake him, but enough to stir his subconscious and wake that certain part of him she needed.

Soon enough, Cronus stood at attention. She could tell Rick didn't sleep as soundly as before, but he was still out of it. Viv positioned and inserted Rick's penis from behind, cherishing their intimate connection, and appreciating his dimensions. Why they couldn't stay in bed this way for the rest of their lives, she didn't know. Initiating a sensuous grind against him, she'd reached her zone when a warm hand closed gently on her breast, messaging the nipple.

Viv tilted her head back with a sigh. "God, yes."

"Good morning," Rick greeted quietly.

"Shut up."

"Yes, ma'am."

"I'm— I'm taking what's mine. Got a problem with that?"

"No, ma'am."

Viv shifted them so that she straddled Rick in reverse cowgirl and then began varying her movements. She briefly lifted her hands behind her head, feeling a sexual freedom in the open space of their master bedroom.

Rick repositioned, giving her what she needed better (goodness, the man could fuck). He reached around and cupped her right breast, tweaking the nipple, while his left hand moved lovingly over the rest of her, making her skin sizzle from his touch.

She settled into a rhythmic-grind with her husband, sometimes grasping his shins and leaning forward, allowing Rick direct view of their intimacy to satisfy his visual desires, and giving him opportunity to lightly tease her anus to entertain his other carnal desires.

Their moans of pleasure, passionate breathing, and X-rated commentary provided a beautiful, sensual soundtrack to their lovemaking that fulfilled Viv's need to hear their sex as well as feel it.

"Damn, baby. Is it … just as good … to you … as it is to me?" Moaning deeply, he spanked her ass some.

Instead of words, Viv used her body in answer, undulating her hips and working her pelvic muscles on him to his enjoyment, accompanying her movements with a gentle toying of his sac. A sense of erotic possession, of them belonging to each other, descended on her. She focused on the sensation of his hands on her body, of her hands on his body, as they did what they knew to do so well.

It didn't take long for either of them.

Lord, have mercy. This man …

Viv reclined onto him. *There's just something about early-morning love.*

Rick grunted at the awkward angle of being inside her. "Uh, sweetie?"

"Sorry, baby." Staying connected, Viv shifted to her side, guiding Rick with her; they relaxed into a spoon.

"You okay?"

Viv smiled to herself. "I'm fine." The Staple Singers' "Let's Do It Again" popped in her head.

Rick hugged her tighter against him and kissed her hair. "That was wonderful." He hummed some of the chorus to "Let's Do It Again." Their synched-vibe didn't surprise.

"Very." Viv swallowed painfully.

"What time are the carpet people coming?"

"Not until eleven. What time are we picking up Al?"

"One thirty, two o'clock-ish."

Viv lifted her head to look at the clock: 7:36 a.m. She dropped her head to the pillow. "Shit."

Rick lifted his head to look at the clock. "What? It's still early."

"You forgot the landscaper's scheduled for nine thirty."

Rick dropped his head next to hers. "Shit." Fully soft, his penis slipped out.

"Tell me about it," Viv groaned, perfectly content in bed—wet spot and all. Secure in Rick's arms, she closed her eyes. Nothing and no one else mattered. If time could stop, now would be perfect.

"Want breakfast?" Rick started rubbing her belly, but stopped.

Understanding his hesitation, Viv grabbed his hand and pressed it against her. "Regardless of who the father is, we will raise this child as ours." Not facing made talking about it easier. She waited.

"… I know."

Viv breathed easier. Any other response would have made things more-difficult. She needed to know it didn't matter to him. They stayed that way awhile, Rick warmly touching her belly.

"Taking care of yourself?"

"Yes. I've had my initial visit. Taking my prenatals. I have an appointment next week."

"Can I come?"

"Yes." They went silent. "Rick?"

"Mm-hmm?"

"It's yours." Viv turned in his arms and cupped his face, the hairs tickling her palms. "Now, you need to understand something." Viv peered into those long-lashed eyes. "There is no guesswork here, not even a smidgen of room for doubt. This is your— *our*, baby. I am not speaking figuratively here, okay? There were no 'JR's during that time."

"Beg pardon?"

Viv smiled. "Never mind."

Rick held her gaze. "I love you." He pecked her lips.

"I know. And fuck that. C'mere." She kissed his sour mouth without reservation.

When they parted, Rick emitted childlike excitement: "How far along are you?"

"Twelve weeks."

"Due date?"

"November seventeenth."

"Our anniversary. Sweet. You want a boy, or a sister for Al?"

She hesitated. They'd lost two babies …

He pecked her lips. "Don't, Viv. We have to believe, this time—"

Viv nodded. "This time will be different."

Rick nodded slowly, his eyes locked on hers. She saw the pain of their past losses reflected in the fire, as well as happiness and hope for a different outcome this time around. She loved him so much.

He pecked her lips tenderly. "You want a brother or sister for Al?"

Viv drew from his strength. "I said what I wanted when I was pregnant with Al, and had the opposite. Let's say I want another girl."

"Cute."

"That's my story, and I'm sticking to it. How about you?" Her emotional connection to him deepened. She'd forgotten how special this moment was.

"I ain't fakin' the funk: another hardhead boy." He was much better than she was about accepting certain sad events in their past.

"Typical," Viv teased, still drawing from his strength and optimism.

"Damn skippy. I gotta pee." Rick rolled out of bed and padded to their bathroom.

Once he finished, Viv reluctantly padded in after him. He stood at his sink brushing his teeth when she entered. She had to pee, too.

"Yow nef dmoph ou s'fast?"

Viv finished wiping herself. "What?"

Rick removed his brush and spit. "You never said about breakfast."

"I'm not hungry." Viv walked to her vanity and rinsed her hands. She retrieved her toothbrush.

"You've got to eat."

"Rick, don't start," Viv warned, squeezing the tube of toothpaste.

"Sorrwy," Rick said around his brush.

Viv brushed her teeth, eyeing Rick in the mirror.

"Sorry," Rick repeated, wide-eyed. "I'll do better this time. I'll try to be less-protective, but you know how I am, Viv."

Viv lowered her eyes and finished brushing. When she finished, she reached for Rick's hand and held it. "Yes, I know. But our family is good, Rick, strong. Please tell me why you are so compell–"

Rick pulled his hand back. "I just am, Viv." He seemed in pain again.

Viv thought about David's letter. "Look, we'll both be better this time around. Besides, it wasn't that bad before, just at times."

Rick lazily ran his eyes over her.

In the cool bathroom, his gaze sent warmth through her.

"Will you at least have toast and a cup of fresh fruit, if I make it?"

With the look he just gave her, food was the last thing on her mind. She smirked at him. "Fine. But what I'd really like, is for you to take me back to bed before these people come bothering us."

"Horny, are we?" His body was ripples of cinnamon-brown yes.

"Horny was last night. This morning is something different …"

"But we just finished—"

"*And*?" She traced fingers over the branding on his shoulder.

"*And* nothing, apparently."

"Thank you. You don't have to play all four quarters. If you must know, I just want you to go bowling …" Viv turned to leave the bathroom.

Rick pulled her to him. "I haven't come up with a word yet, but I'm feeling that thing beyond love for you." Rick leaned in to nuzzle her but stopped. "What happened here?" He touched the side of her neck.

Viv knew what he had to be pointing out. Her heart raced as she turned and craned her neck to see in the mirror better. Viv didn't bruise easily, but a circular spot of purplish-blue stood out on the left side of her neck from the pressure of Rick's thumb.

"I'm sorry, Viv."

"You know what you did to me?" It was much better thinking he had no clue.

"Well, you didn't have the mark last night at dinner. You now have it this morning. And I know our sex was kinda rough last night. It had to be me. You wouldn't do this to yourself."

Viv was relieved. He knew (through deductive reasoning), but he didn't *know*. As she assumed before, Rick was lost for a spell last night as he went at her. Softly, but with an injection of humor, Viv offered: "You damn-near strangled the shit out of me."

"What?!" Rick was clearly upset; the red in his irises deepened.

Viv watched him, looking for a hint of deception. She found none. "Well, last night, you were bothered about not knowing the father."

"Yeah, I know." He leaned toward her, eyes piercing.

"But you still apparently wanted sex. Or should I say, *needed* sex. At least that's how you put it last night. You said something about keeping 'it' back or in control or something. You said fucking me helps you do that."

"Go on," Rick urged.

"I don't know, next thing I know, I'm pinned against the wall, and you're banging the shit out of me. It was so good at first, baby." She looked at Rick affectionately.

He stared back at her, obviously waiting to hear the rest. As he looked at her, a modest but sexy grin formed as he digested the meaning behind her words. He tried not to blush at her compliment. "I'm listening."

"Well, you were grunting 'mine,' and your hand was at my throat. It kept tightening. You were choking me and fucking me, Rick. I tried to get through to you, but then I couldn't breathe, and I was fading. I thought I was gone when you finally let up."

Rick searched her eyes and face. "Motherfuck!" He turned and punched a hole in the wall behind the toilet.

Viv jumped, but she wasn't scared.

Rick gathered her to him. He inspected her neck again, kissing it all over. "Aw no, no," he groaned. "No." He then kissed her mouth, dipping his minty-tongue into her mouth. He pulled back and sat on the commode.

He held his head in his hands. "No need worrying about anyone else destroying my family. Shit. Evidently I can do that my damn self." He looked at her. "I'm so sorry."

"I know." There was nothing left to say.

Rubbing his ear, Rick rocked to-and fro, looking all of five-years-old.

Viv went to him. "I'm fine, Ricky." She hadn't called him "Ricky" in forever. She stroked his back, calming him. First the choking, now this rocking. She'd never seen these extremes in him before. "You were crying, you know?"

He looked at her. The red in his irises softened again, the flame now a warm flicker. "Really?"

"Uh-huh." Now she felt like a little girl.

"Did I say anything else?"

"No. After we came—"

"You still …?"

"Amazingly, yes. Shocked the shit out of me. Anyway, we came, but you kept going. You slowed it down, made your thrusts more gentle and sensual, but you tongued and moaned into my mouth while you fucked me. As awful as that choking was, you were damn-sure making up for it." Viv paused suggestively again. She needed to see that sexy blush again.

She got it. Rick's modesty was always a serious turn-on for her.

"We both reached a round two. The messed-up thing is, they were probably two of the strongest orgasms I've had recently: including the 'rape.'"

"The rapes! Damn, Viv. You're preg—" Rick started to stand.

Viv stopped him. "I'm— *We're* fine."

Rick looked at her doubtfully.

Viv looked back squarely.

"You're sick," Rick teased.

"No, just honest. But don't do that shit ever again."

"I— I won't."

But Viv knew they were thinking the same thing. He didn't know he'd done it this time. How can he know he won't do it again? Still, Viv reasoned, it was better with him at least being aware of it.

"Come on. We're wasting all this nudity. The people will be here, and a girl needs her hook-up." Viv pulled Rick by the hand toward their bedroom.

Rick held back. "You can't possibly—"

"I told you what I wanted, didn't I?" She felt sexy, powerful. "And now someone has to repair the wall. But not today."

"Viv, I don't—"

She cupped his cheek. "Rick, no. Don't let last night interfere. We'll deal with it. You're not angry now, anyway." She led him into their bedroom.

"Angry?"

"Never mind."

"No, Viv—"

Viv pressed two fingers against his lips. The feel of his moustache under her fingers got her going. "Shhh." She kissed him. She played in his hair and kissed him the way she knew would bring results.

Rick, relenting, stroked her back and ass. Once he was hard, Viv lowered and indulged in what made him male.

His hands went into her hair. "Damn, girl …"

Satisfied, Viv got on with her plans for the morning.

* * * * *

At quarter-past-ten, Viv decided she'd lost her mind.

Only beginning-dementia could explain her present state of mind. A week ago, she was trying to determine how to deal with believing her husband a murderer. To that end, here she was, holding the letter from Rick's dead brother. Rick was outside with the landscaper, so she plucked the letter from his wallet, intent on finding a clue to what was going on with him.

Viv sat on their bed holding the letter. The windows were open. The sun finally burned off an early-morning fog. Rick's voice trailed to her, and she closed her eyes. She didn't even know if she wanted to read the letter now. Why open doors she may want to keep closed?

She listened to her husband's voice, missing him.

And that's where the problem came in. One minute she was playing Sherlock, wanting to rest her mind of worry and confusion. The next, she was wanting Rick—period.

Viv swallowed. The soreness was dissipating fairly-quickly, but it prompted action. She unfolded the letter:

> Hey, Richie:
>
> You probably think you've outgrown "Richie," but if you're reading this, I know I can get away with anything right about now. I wrote Dad, too, ya know. I even wrote Mama. I know she's gone, but, well, I had some things I wanted to say to her. Soon enough, I'll be able to tell her face to face …
>
> Anyway, little brother, I'm writing to tell you two things. One: I love you. You were a pain-in-the-ass when we were kids and now that I think about it, a pain-in-the-ass as adults, too (just kidding), but we've never had a problem with the love thing, so I wanted to get that out there. I love you, man.
>
> Second, and this is vital, Richie: hold on to your family. You and Viv haven't started one yet, so Viv is your family. Well, Viv and Dad, but you know what I'm saying. Me and Mama are your family, too, but both of us will be gone soon. It's you and Viv right now, Rick, but when you and Viv have kids, you make sure you

do whatever it takes to keep your family together and thriving.

I know you're reading this, working through your pain, wanting to know why. I'm trying to put it down here so you'll know (Dad's letter doesn't address any of this. I'd appreciate you keeping your letter to yourself).

Honestly, Rick, I don't know how else to stop feeling sad.

When Mama left us, I almost lost it then. We aren't momma's boys, but our family, for me at least, was everything to me. Mama, Daddy, you, me. It fit well, you know? I felt I could do and be anything with the family I had. Isn't that how it's supposed to be? But then Mama left us, and even though she came back, our family life was never the same. And neither was I. Don't get me wrong. I loved Mama. Still do, with all my heart. But, I don't know, her rejection, her leaving, fucks with me—even now (and I'm a grown man).

You never told me what you heard Dad and Mama talking about the night she left, and I'm guessing that's a good thing. It helped not knowing what the real deal was. For a long time, I made up my own justification for why she left. In the end, there wasn't justification enough for me—even after she came back.

I've carried a hole filled with sadness in my heart ever since.

So again, I'm saying, Rick: hold on to your family, okay? Work through the hard shit together, not apart. You never know what impact a broken family can have on the members—from the oldest to the youngest. Some people are stronger than others; I know that. I believe you to be the stronger between the two of us.

You know I ain't no punk, Rick, but I can't carry this hole around anymore. It's getting bigger with time, little brother, not smaller. Remember, before Mama left, how we used to plan our lives sitting in our tree at St. Dominic's? We had some of the best times in that tree. I still go over there sometimes to try and recapture that time. Every once in a while, I succeed.

I gotta go. Your letter is the last one, but I have a couple loose ends to tie up. Take care of Dad (I know you will), and take care of my sis, Viv (she's truly lovely, Rick, and perfect for you)—I know you'll do that, too.

And promise a dead man you'll hold on to your family—no matter what.

Peace and love always,
David

Below David's signature, in red ink, it read: "Whatever It Takes!" It was Rick's neat handwriting.

He'd signed it: "Richard Alden S. Phillips"

A brown thumbprint, Viv recognized as old dried-blood, stood next to the word "takes."

Viv reread the letter, focusing on Rick's signature and thumbprint. She tried to swallow around the lump in her throat but couldn't. A drink of water from their bathroom helped. She refolded the letter and put it back in her baby's wallet.

It was none too soon. She'd just stepped away from his dresser and headed for her closet when she heard him coming up the stairs.

"Viv?"

"In here." She breathed slowly, trying to settle her nerves.

"Hey," Rick said breathlessly. He stood in her closet doorway, his T-shirt a mess with smudges of dirt and grass stains.

Viv looked him over. "What could you possibly be doing to be so dirty? And grass, too? I thought the landscaper was repairing the sprinkler."

"He is."

Viv looked pointedly at his shirt. "So, what: you're his apprentice?"

Rick smirked. "Rim shot. Look, the carpet people won't be here till eleven, right?"

"Right." Looking at him, she smiled inwardly. *I crazy-love you, boy.*

"Cool. I'ma run get a haircut. I should be back, if not before they get here, then soon after. Okay?"

"Okay." This was the happiness from seventeen years ago, nine years ago, from as little as four, maybe three years ago.

Rick lifted his shirt over his head.

Viv took in his ripped abdomen. His jeans hung low. His happy-trail, that midline of hair down his torso that disappeared below the band of his boxers, enticed her. Heated memories of the shower they shared earlier came to her. She grunted her approval.

"Quit it. You must be worn out." Rick tossed his shirt toward the basket next to his armoire.

"Are you?"

"In a way, yeah. Put it this way: I need at least until tonight. You're telling me you aren't tired?"

"A little," Viv replied honestly. Still, him standing there like that …

"See?" Rick grew quiet, watching her look him over.

She thought about David's letter. "C'mere."

"What?" He asked quietly.

"Just c'mere."

Rick moved closer. He lifted her chin. "How's your neck?" He kissed the bruise and looked at her. "I'm sorry, Vivian."

"I know you are. It's gradually getting better. Let it go, okay?"

Eyes somber, Rick nodded.

Viv caressed his jaw. "Talk to Candace?"

Her husband nodded, still somber. "Yeah. Went like you said."

Viv nodded. "Good." She pecked his lips, treasuring the idea of his baby growing inside her. "You done knocked me up, mister. Now what we *go'n* do?"

Rick smiled softly at her tease. He touched her belly, lightly kissing her cheek. "Wanna go to the movies later?"

Viv trailed fingers along his abdomen. "Alna's seen everything."

"I don't mean with Al. Just you and me, and well, baby boy Phillips."

"Claiming that boy, aren't you?"

Rick nodded. He left her closet and came back with a fresh shirt. He sniffed under his arms. "I'm good, aren't I?"

"You're fine."

Rick put the shirt on.

Viv couldn't imagine the man standing before her as a murderer. The man at her throat last night was a different story. Now that she'd read David's letter, she didn't know what to think. David's letter, however, did give her a more-sympathetic perspective. She wondered about sharing her discovery with Naomi, and decided she would. "Why don't we stream something to watch? With Mother's Day close, I kinda want all of us spending the time together. Alna's been under the care of others a lot lately."

"Yeah, but only so her parents could get their act together."

"Which we've done."

"Definitely." With a look, Rick took her hands and bowed his head. Viv bowed hers.

Their quiet prayer finished, Rick looked down and then brought his eyes to hers. "You and Me, Viv."

"Me and You, Ricky."

They grew quiet, speaking with their eyes.

Rick parted his lips to speak.

"Shhh. Don't say anything." Viv kissed him. Although their tongues danced, passion yielded to something much deeper.

"I gotta go," Rick whispered when they finally parted.

"I need candy."

Rick stepped toward her door. "What kind?"

The hold of his kiss lingered in the space between them. "Chocolaty, nutty. You know what I like."

Rick surveyed her closet before looking at her suggestively. "In here, real soon."

Viv couldn't help looking toward his package before quickly lifting her eyes to his face. "Let's stream something scary."

Rick raised an eyebrow. "Because, that's perfect for Mother's Day?"

Viv just looked at him.

Rick chuckled. "Okay. Two horrors, one animated feature."

"We let Alna watch horrors—with us, anyway."

Rick grinned. "I know. The animated movie's for me."

"Well, why not add something to watch in the privacy of our sitting room …?"

Rick shook his head. "You just nasty. Those hormones have taken what was already there and amplified it."

"Complaining?"

"I'll answer that tonight." He turned to leave.

Viv tapped his tight butt, loving him hard.

Rick left her closet but poked his head back in. "Think we should have Al sit with Doctor Alexander?"

Viv thought a second. "No. But we should talk with her. She's happy things are back to normal, but she's old-enough to understand a little of what happened to know that not-so-good things happen in life sometimes."

"Okay. When are we telling her about, you know …?" Rick used his head and eyes to indicate her pregnancy.

"Tonight, if you want. Al's learning to keep secrets."

"You don't want to say anything yet?"

"Not yet."

"My dad?"

"Oh, sure. I didn't mean Papa Phillips. Of course, we tell him. Whom would he tell anyway? I meant, you know, the local crew."

"Gotcha. You'll be showing soon, anyway."

"I know. Go! Bye, boy! And don't forget my candy."

Rick air-kissed her and was gone.

Viv stood in the silence of her closet, having forgotten what she'd come in there for. *The memory loss begins.*

Unable to remember, Viv left her closet and lay across their bed. The carpet people would arrive soon—not enough time for a nap.

She reflected on David's letter and Rick's apparent blood-vow. The childlike-simplicity of it moved her.

Another question, though, nagged her.

She now understood Rick's odd devotion to family.

But was killing Jonathan part of "whatever it takes"?

CHAPTER 19

1½ Cups Buttermilk

Naomi sat at her desk in her home-office, wincing. Something close to a gag tickled the back of her throat. She hated martinis. Gin in most any other form was fine. Leslie made one for her, though, so she was duty-bound to finish it. Les was on a bartending-tip lately; she considered martinis her specialty. Naomi, however, was not the ideal point-of-reference.

She glanced at the phone. Her mood needed improving and a martini simply didn't cut it. A Fuzzy Navel was best for spirit-lifting. Fuzzy Navels (with a splash of Belvedere) were an old stand-by, a favorite.

Naomi thought about her discussion with Vivian Phillips thirty minutes ago and smiled. Her smile faltered with thoughts of her conversation with Kevin, with whom she'd just finished speaking. Right now, she stood knee-deep in shades of gray. She held on to the hiking boots with the unique pattern for several days before deciding to turn them over to Kevin for analysis.

During a recent session with the couple, she had the audacity to steer the dialogue toward discussion of Jonathan Rast. She commented on the nice boots that she hadn't seen Rick wear anymore. His reaction: a raised eyebrow and nothing more—he didn't even touch his scar.

Naomi hoped she hadn't played her hand too soon, but she wanted Rick to know he'd fucked up. She wasn't at all comfortable with this sleuth shit, but anger for Viv and annoyance with Rick at his stupidity motivated her. Naomi directed some of that anger internally for having to rip them apart. But then, did she have to?

That was her point of contention—and why she was none-too-happy about her conversation with Kevin. As it stood now, the "signature" of the sole matched the contusion on Jonathan's torso perfectly. Kevin now pressed Naomi to give up the owner, or at least give up what she knew in connection with the boot, but Naomi begged-off, claiming doctor-patient confidentiality. It was her crutch, and it kept Kevin at bay for the time being; even though he expressed his discontent with her offering such a prize if she planned to cop-out at the end. The issue strained their budding romance, but that was neither here nor there.

She'd be giving Rick up, of course, but she wanted to help the couple. Viv's info on David's letter was a good start. If necessary, serving as alienist, Naomi could modify Rick's psychological profile to help his case.

Eating her olive (she did love olives), Naomi paced in front of her desk. She heard Leslie on the phone, moving about in their kitchen. A semi-truce existed between them now, but Naomi had every intention of broaching an otherwise-buried topic. She picked up her martini-glass and drained it, not wanting to worry about Les. Figuring out how to deal with the Phillipses: that's what she needed to do.

Naomi stopped pacing and approached the far wall, pausing before her favorite lithograph: a gift from Tyson for their fifth wedding anniversary. She often gazed at it when troubled; the art soothed her mind.

When Tyson first presented it, she didn't understand. It was nice enough as far as art goes, but Tyson's excitement at the time far exceeded hers. He insisted she hang it in her study. Naomi and Leslie moved shortly after Tyson's murder, but by then she'd grown attached to his gift, so she made a spot for the lithograph in her new study. She enjoyed the company of it. Its diverse patterns rarely presented the same image consecutively.

Turning her Ravens cap backward, Naomi concentrated on the flow of etching in the upper-left corner. Her thoughts returned to Rick and Viv.

Viv didn't acknowledge the technical name for it, but she experienced erotic-asphyxia from Rick choking her. The couple came upon the experience by happenstance, but it was a dangerous sex-game many pursued frequently. Going over the event, Viv acknowledged that on some level the experience was pleasurable; she did not, however, want to repeat it.

Viewing the lithograph, her thoughts focused on Rick and Viv from an analytical perspective. Naomi concluded that, if anything, Rick exhibited signs of Intermittent Explosive Disorder, but that was such a controversial catch-all category, Naomi was hesitant about putting all of Rick's eggs in that basket. She stiffened her posture. "Fuck it."

She needed more time with Rick, obviously, but Naomi realized she might not have time: she couldn't take that chance with Viv's life. Rick being totally unaware of what he'd done to Viv was the only saving grace—or maybe it was the wildcard that could prove fatal (for Viv?) if left unchecked.

Besides, if she served as an expert-witness, Naomi could help regarding Rick's defense. Decision made, Naomi called Kevin back.

* * * * *

Early Monday morning, Naomi sat in her professional office recompiling the Phillips file. Her eyes kept cutting to the box sitting next to her yellow counsel chair. Now that she had the boots, she had no reason to hold on to the box. She did check the box to see if she could discover anything else important from it, but the search proved pointless. In any event, she had to get the box out of her office today; their session was tomorrow.

Sighing, Naomi removed her eyeglasses and rubbed her eyes.

When she called Kevin back last night, she gave as many additional details as she could without giving a name. Kevin, however, wanted exactly that. She promised to give the name, but wanted another day or two first. Kevin hedged. Naomi changed the subject, moving more into talk of their relationship. She sweet-talked him a little, asked him out. Not unwise to her MO, Kevin agreed to another date—but gave her until Thursday to give him the name. He'd have to acknowledge receipt of the evidence and give her name to the authorities otherwise, and it would be hard to bring the shoes into evidence without her. The defense would easily blow it apart. Besides, he'd asked her, how could she purposely let a murderer go free?

She countered that she was sure the murder wasn't premeditated. Kevin believed her but said his job mandated he examine the evidence;

the rest was up to legal. It was a cop-out if Naomi ever heard one (much like her doctor-patient-confidentiality one, she guessed).

Naomi closed the Phillips folder and walked over to her office window. The sun beamed high and hot already. The Harrises were scheduled for 8:30 a.m., so she had another hour or so. Naomi walked back to her desk, deciding she'd better grab a bagel before Monday officially started.

She didn't know why Mondays posed such a problem for folk; Mondays were fine for her. Tuesdays, however, weren't good. Naomi chose Tuesdays for charitable work, and since Tyson's death, it served as a counterbalance for the sadness that often wanted to descend. She shifted her thoughts, not wanting to think about Tyson. With their wedding anniversary approaching, she thought of him more as it was.

She no longer wanted a bagel, but couldn't decide what she wanted.

A knock on her door interrupted her thoughts.

Naomi frowned. Who'd be at her office so early? She hesitated.

"I know you're there, Doctor Alexander. Saw your car on the lot." It was Rick Phillips.

She ran a hand over her hair. "Just a minute ..." Her voice shook. She briefly rested her hand on her gun at the small of her back.

Naomi quickly walked to the door and opened it. It wasn't until she opened the door and stared into Rick's chiseled face that she remembered the box—in plain view several feet away.

"Surprise, surprise." Rick grinned. He wore jeans, a throwback Washington Bullets #41 Wes Unseld jersey over a T-shirt, and a pair of well-maintained retro Air Jordan III's. His haircut was now a low, blended-fade.

"That's for sure. What can I do for you? Anything wrong? You guys are scheduled for tomorrow afternoon ..." Naomi trailed-off, cursing herself. She hated being caught off-guard. She hated her anxious reaction even more.

"Whoa, slow down. I know that." Rick frowned. "Can I come in, or ...?" He smiled hesitantly.

"Oh, yeah. Sorry." Naomi backed up, allowing Rick to enter.

Rick furrowed his brows at her as he entered. "Everything okay?"

"Yes." She didn't want to close the door behind him, but did anyway. Grasping the doorknob, she turned to find Rick staring at the box. He looked back at her and then walked toward the window, his pace slow, musing. Naomi gave him the once-over. Rick's hands were in his back pockets, making his shirt ride up. He filled his jeans nicely: tight butt, bowed legs—great combination. "Not working today?"

Rick turned to her. "Beg pardon?"

With a nod of her head, Naomi gestured toward his attire. "Unless it's dress-down Monday …"

"Oh. Nah; I'm debating on taking the day or going in late."

"I see."

"Do you?"

Naomi gripped the doorknob tighter before walking to her desk.

Rick looked at the box. "Viv told me she passed this on to you, but I see you can't seem to get it to the center, either." He looked at Naomi and smiled a tight smile that drew his lips taut. He shrugged. "If you want something done … Right?"

"I guess. But it's okay. I'm definitely dropping it off today."

"Find anything you could use?"

"I'm not following." She silently berated her stupidity for bringing the box to her office.

Rick scoffed with a smirk. "Well, for one thing, I can tell the box has been opened. For another, the box is here—not at the donation center."

She swallowed hard.

"So, did you?"

Naomi held his gaze.

Rick slowly moved toward her. "You know, I've paid attention to a lot that's been said and unsaid during our last few sessions. I know Viv talks to you outside of therapy, too." Rick paused to run his hands along the back of the chair, studying the movement of his hand. Beneath the hem of his T-shirt sleeve, Naomi noted the lower-portion of some type of branding or scarring on his right shoulder.

"Why are you here, Rick?" She wasn't frightened (not exactly).

"I'm here to find out what you plan to do about what you know, or rather, what you *think* you know."

"Oh, I know what you did, Rick. The guessing's over."

That tight smile crossed Rick's mouth again, but didn't touch his eyes. He looked at the box again and then back at Naomi. "You seemed more than interested in the shoes I wore to our first or second session." He nodded toward the box. "Are they in there?"

"No."

Rick nodded slowly, accepting her response. "So again, what do you plan to do, Doctor Alexander?"

"Honestly?"

"At this point, what else is left?"

Naomi heard pain rooted in uncertainty beneath his question. She relaxed, but not completely. "I don't know. I've started the ball rolling, but I'm not sure how it'll play out."

"My shoes?"

Naomi hesitated before nodding.

"Shit." Rick sighed and tilted his head back. "I started to burn 'em."

"Probably would've been better-off."

Rick looked at her. Something passed through his eyes she couldn't place. Knowing his newfound propensity for violence, Naomi raised her guard again. He moved toward her. Small as she was, with Rick taller than six feet, he towered over her.

Naomi stood her ground.

He stepped up to her. "You know, people often compliment my ability to deal with obstacles head-on, with control. No doubt it helped me get where I am professionally." Rick paused, searching Naomi's face. "But there was a threat to my *family*, Doctor Alexander … and I lost it. I dealt with it, yeah, but control was nowhere to be found." Rick cleared his throat. "Killing Rast was an accident, pure and simple."

"I believe that, Rick. What—"

"Funny thing is—accident or not—the shit gave me a high you wouldn't believe. I walked around edgy and excited for weeks. It's only recently that I've gotten a better handle on it. Don't get me wrong, it's still a high. There is a magnified sense of power and control that you can't help being on a natural-high, but it's contained."

"And choking your wife? Is that 'contained'?"

"No. No, it's not." Rick lifted his left hand slightly, gazing at his wedding ring. "You remember how we met …?"

"Economics symposium: professor from Howard lecturing at George Mason …"

Rick nodded slowly, his eyes still on his band. "There's something about her love, Naomi. What I feel for Viv … is indescribable. So that won't happen again. I live for her." He looked at her. Another odd expression, softer and more-reflective, crossed his face.

"You're not insane, Rick, but you do need help."

"I take it that's where you come in. And I know I'm not insane."

"Where I come in? Maybe."

"So, how long do I have before there's a knock on my door?"

Naomi didn't answer.

Rick stepped closer. "Look, Doctor Alexander, killing Rast was an accident, but understand that my awakening stemming from that experience makes me unafraid of doing it again."

Naomi looked at him, took in his *unbelievably*-handsome face and the subtle, warm scent of his cologne, and stood taller, looking up at him. She'd had enough. She moved her hand to the small of her back. "Don't threaten me, Rick. Mind you, I know I can help you and Viv get through this. I've taken a liking to you both, Viv especially, so whatever I do, my primary focus is her. But don't threaten me. Because I will shoot you. I'm a small woman. I carry a gun. I will shoot you. Shoot you and watch you bleed, 'pure and simple.' Don't threaten me."

"That ... does not bother me."

They stood toe-to-toe.

Finally, Rick smiled a genuine smile that touched his eyes and it was a beautiful sight. Up close, with the morning light hitting them, Naomi saw that his eyes were uniquely-pretty, with irises the reddish burnt-umber of autumn. "How long?"

"Another day, maybe two."

Rick stepped back. "Should I just turn myself in?"

Naomi relaxed but kept her hand in place. "No. They'll treat you the same either way. Let them come to you. Spend time with your family."

Rick tilted his head. "Two days?"

"Bargaining, are we?"

Rick shrugged. "I guess. Need to take care of some things. Talk to Viv. Try to at least prepare—for whatever that's worth." Resignation and concern filled his reply.

Naomi nodded. "I'll call your house first, regardless." She paused. "It'll be all right, Rick."

"Oh, I know."

Naomi brought her hand from behind her back.

Rick headed for the door. He paused before opening it, his hand resting on the knob, and looked back at her. "You know, I probably wouldn't have hurt you. But I feel the surge, you know? Anyway, just wanted to tell you that you were a good therapist, so thank you. Never been to a psychiatrist before, but I'd guess your style borders unorthodox."

"So I've heard."

Rick gazed at her. "... As good as you are though, Doc, you might wanna chill with the drinking."

Naomi couldn't move or speak.

"Hey, we're all human. I'm sure shrinks have their share of problems. But this time, listen to a patient: nothing can be solved with alcohol. Muted maybe, but not solved. Try treating yourself, Doctor Alexander. But if nothing else, leave the alcohol alone. Try drinking iced tea instead." He shrugged. "I don't know. It's just a thought." Rick opened the door and left, closing the door softly behind him.

Naomi stared at the closed door, trembling. Tears welled.

Quaking like she was, Naomi was glad he didn't wait for a response. Rick's menacing behavior and threats were nothing compared to the impact of his parting words. They unnerved her.

Rooted to the spot, she breathed deeply to calm herself. It wasn't until the tears fell that Naomi moved to action.

Fisting away the streaks, Naomi spun on a heel, walked to her desk, and picked up the phone.

CHAPTER 20

Coming Together, Falling Apart

Late Tuesday morning, Viv sat in her family room getting over the guilties. She left work early yesterday and didn't bother making the effort at all this morning. Her workload didn't cause her guilt; she was on top of that. It bothered her realizing that, come November, she'd be taking even more time off.

Viv reclined on the family room sofa and sighed. Her favorite music station, WMZZ, played softly from the stereo in the entertainment center. The deejay was on a roll. The station often featured nice rotations of classic R&B hits from the sixties and seventies, but this morning, the set proved especially potent. She closed her eyes, grooving to New Birth.

The idea of going in late crossed Viv's mind, but work didn't fit in with how the morning began. Rick was in an odd mood yesterday, keeping pretty much to himself. Viv was concerned, but gave him his space.

Rick didn't want space this morning, however. While she showered, he joined her. He lathered her body completely, and then made love to her against the stall. After her climax, he carried her soapy body to their bed and continued his efforts, moving over her at an exquisitely-slow pace. His oral caresses and gentle finger works were more than enough to keep her body warm despite the coolness from her damp skin, the contrast itself erotic.

He bound her wrists to their headboard (he was increasingly into bondage), and then loved her slowly, gently, completely. Her bindings ensured she didn't reciprocate with her own caress or touch. "Let me love you, Viv," he'd said. "Let *me* love *you*." His gaze had been so intense, all she could do was nod (and give in to sweet surrender). Rick covered her mouth with his then, with a kiss so fervent …

By the time he finished with her, taking off from work was a foregone conclusion.

Rick took off, too.

Is love fun? Oh, hell yes.

Her body roused with the memory of him thrusting into her; how he held her gaze as he climaxed (those irises lightening right before he looked sexily in pain and angry with her). The lovemaking was incredible. But Viv couldn't help feeling apprehensive. Because although he more than pleased every inch of her, she sensed it was, well, a goodbye or something.

Jonathan's face appeared in Viv's mind unexpectedly. *So, what if he did?* Viv breathed deeply, trying to shut out Naomi's question. *Would your feelings change?*

Viv sat upright. Naomi's questions nagged her when she just wanted to relax. She didn't want to think about her responsibilities or any emotional consequences right now. To that end, she was glad Naomi cancelled their session.

She glanced at the clock. Rick dropped Alna off over two hours ago. He told her he had an errand to run (he'd been on many errands lately), but he should have been home by now. Viv reclined again. She listened to a Delfonics double-play, allowing the groove of music to soothe her.

She rose and tidied the family room. The room didn't need much attention at all, but Viv wanted to stay occupied (she wasn't exactly sure why).

When Brainstorm's "This Must Be Heaven" began, the music evoked crushing waves of sentiment she didn't expect. Viv paused in the middle of her tidying, overcome with loving thoughts of Rick.

She rubbed her belly soothingly.

The song ended, and the station rolled into a series of ads. Viv, however, didn't move for several seconds. Naomi's question (*So, what if he did?*) nagged at her again. Viv gazed around the rooms before focusing on the clock again. With what she wanted to believe was resolve, she said: "Then I have to let him go."

She went to the kitchen and opened the fridge. Her appetite fluctuated over the weeks, but she stayed thirsty. Looking at the contents, Viv shook her head with a smile: jugs of orange juice crammed the second shelf. A note stuck to one of them: *"Good source of folic acid (don't be mad). Love, Ricky."*

Viv grabbed the jug with the note on it and set it on the counter. Still smiling, she plucked a clean glass from the cabinet. She removed the note and reread it. He signed it "Ricky." She started calling him Ricky again, especially during their lovemaking. She poured some juice and downed it. Viv checked the clock again.

She wanted him home.

To get her mind otherwise occupied, Viv walked to their workroom. Standing in the laundry room entranceway, she sighed. Although not the mess it was on the original night of destruction, plenty work remained to get their workroom back in shape from Rick's tirade. Both she and Rick avoided the task to avoid the memories tied to it. She missed her woodwork, though, and wanted to get back to it as soon as possible. Rick would want to handle the major cleanup, but she wanted to get the ball rolling. She looked around the room, trying to decide where to start.

She moved to the windows and opened them. With all the dust likely to be disturbed, she'd need as much ventilation as possible. The smell of rain permeated the air. She opened the window connected to the garage, but closed it immediately as thick, warm air bathed her face. The quality of air in the workroom was cooler, less-stuffy—no sense ruining it with the code-orange air of the garage.

Viv stood at the window looking in their garage, focusing on Rick's motorcycle. It did look nice sitting there. She'd been on it twice since that first time, and both times she and Rick ended up getting nasty. Of course, Rick reminded her, she only had a few weeks to ride with him before (he felt) she'd have to stop. His overprotective-side surfaced on occasion, but it was nowhere near his behavior during her other pregnancies.

Turning back to the workroom, she surveyed the floor, finding several good pieces strewn about, some close to being finished. Rick already righted the bookcase and picked up her tools. Viv glanced over at Rick's side, and again, although fleeting, the urge to trash his side surfaced. She noticed he'd finished quite a few cars in recent weeks (since Jonathan died?), but many were in various stages of completion.

Admiring his work, she decided to get him a display cabinet for Father's Day.

With that, she began picking up the salvageable wood pieces and placing them on the empty bookcase shelves.

Viv moved about the workroom purposefully. She'd picked up all that could be saved, and now began the sad task of sweeping up the dust and wood splinters of what remained. Papers and tool parts littered the floor as well. She couldn't just sweep everything up. She'd have to go through the papers; many held good design ideas.

Lightning flashed.

A sudden breeze lifted dust and papers into a swirl. Thunder rolled in the distance. Looking out the windows, Viv watched the blowing branches and darkening sky, glad she'd taken the day off. She preferred being home during thunderstorms. She again wished Rick home when she thought she heard the garage door lifting. A light rain started. Hurriedly, Viv grabbed an empty box from the corner and began picking up papers and tossing them inside it. She performed a perfunctory review of the sheets before tossing them in the box; so far, they'd been keepers.

Viv was pretty much on autopilot with the task of picking up, scanning, and tossing, so she did a double take and dug back in the box when she came across a few sheets having nothing to do with woodwork design.

Thunder cracked in the background, but it was closer.

Viv sat the box of papers on the Shopsmith with one hand, while staring at the papers clutched in the other. Her mind screamed with doubt and denial as her body tingled with certainty. Viv reread the rental car receipt and agreement repeatedly—hoping for an inconsistency in the dates. Any inconsistency would do: wrong month, wrong year, different day. Finding none, Viv's chest tightened and then relaxed. The papers shook with the trembling in her hands.

Rick rented a car the day before Jonathan died and returned it the day of his murder. Circumstantial, yes, but with all that she'd discovered, analyzed, and been through, she didn't need much else.

"So, you found it?"

Viv startled. She turned to Rick and stared.

"What I wouldn't give to have found that before you."

Viv could only stare.

* * * * *

She simply stared at him. And although his mouth was dry and became drier still with anticipation of her reaction, Rick couldn't help noting Viv's beauty. The glow was starting. In the leggings and tank-top, their 'baby-bump' was more-apparent. Soon, she'd be beyond description for him.

She was, forever, the absolute love of his life.

Standing in the laundry room entranceway, abstract pain jabbed his insides with the thought of not being with her. He'd never fainted before, but the dizziness and cool feeling shooting through his head indicated he might. Rick closed his eyes to steady himself. He swayed and closed his eyes tighter until the vertigo passed. Viv still hadn't spoken.

Rick opened his eyes.

She continued staring. "... Rick?"

He nodded and started down the steps toward her.

"No."

Rick stopped. His throat hurt.

They stared at each other for what seemed a slice of eternity, as the wind and rain picked up outside.

"Why, Rick?"

His heart ached for her, for himself. Nevertheless, anger, keen in its depth, rushed through him before swiftly being replaced by the heartache again. "Storm's coming, Viv. Let's take this inside."

Viv didn't move. "Why?"

Rick wasn't sure of his answer.

He moved to the open window nearest him. He had to walk past Viv to get to it. He felt her eyes on him as he passed, and the stiffness in her posture told him her guard was up. Lightning flashed as he closed and locked the window. He headed for the other window, but Viv stopped him with a raised hand.

Thunder boomed, startling them both.

"I'll do it." Keeping an eye on him, Viv moved guardedly to the other window. Her demeanor hurt him more than anything.

With his eyes, as Viv watched him, Rick tried to convey she was not in any danger.

Her eyes remained guarded, but she turned her attention to the window and closed it. She turned back to him. "Answer me."

Faint strains of music from the family room floated into their workroom, but the sudden loss of sound from outside, of the wind rustling and the rain pattering, made the near-silence too loud.

"I love you, Vivian." It was weak—he knew that—but it contained the whole of it.

"Ri—"

"It was an accident, Viv!" He felt like a six-year-old apologizing.

Watching her, Rick felt a glimmer of hope. The guarded look in her eyes softened. Viv lowered her head and shook it solemnly before suddenly bracing herself with a hand to the window.

He approached her, but Viv waved him off. "No. I'm all right. Just give me a minute." She closed her eyes, breathing unsteadily.

Rick ignored her. He went to his wife and positioned under her outstretched arm. He wrapped his arm around her waist. "Let's take this inside, Viv. You need to sit down." Thankfully, she didn't resist his efforts to get her into the house.

As soon as they reached the kitchen, however, Viv disengaged and stepped down into the family room, establishing the distance she apparently needed. She kicked off her slides, but didn't sit.

"Viv, sit—"

"You say it was an accident. Renting a car the day before someone is killed doesn't sound 'accidental' to me."

He hesitated. "It was an accident, Viv." He repeated it without the childlike-plea for understanding.

Viv sighed heavily. "What happened, Ricky?"

Rick cleared his throat. He could use something to drink but was reluctant to get it. He didn't want the act to be misconstrued as a move for extra time to think of a lie. Keeping his eyes on Viv's, Rick moved into the family room, hoping she wouldn't step back from him.

She didn't.

So as not to press his luck, however, he kept several feet away.

An old Stylistics cut came on; the music louder now that they were in the room with it. The edginess, the restlessness, crept through him. And while those feelings now gave him a sense of power, Rick had to admit he wasn't ready for this. Wasn't ready to answer to Viv for what he'd done. Feeling trapped, Rick gazed at Viv, fighting the urge to strike out at something—wanting only to dance with her.

He nodded toward the entertainment center. "Would you turn that down some, please?"

Showing no emotion, Viv turned and lowered the volume. She turned back to him—waiting.

Rick sat in the big leather chair closest to him. Surprisingly, Viv sat on the chaise. It seemed a good sign. Still, he reached for his ear (the scaly texture of his scar soothed him instantly). "... I wanted to talk to Rast, and that's all I wanted to do. *Talk*."

Viv remained motionless and seemingly emotionless.

"I wanted to catch him in the morning, before folks started milling about. If we got into it about you, I didn't want the world knowing our business, you know?'

She nodded her understanding.

Encouraged, Rick continued: "I even started to forget the whole thing, when he came out to walk his dog."

"Copeland?" Viv sounded wistful.

"Yeah. Anyway, I got out and caught up with him. We headed into the park and started talking." Rick paused. This was where it got fuzzy before clearing again. This was the hard part. He stopped rubbing his ear.

"Go on, Rick."

He cleared his throat, again wanting something to drink. "Well, like I said, we were talking about you. About you and him. About you and me. It was pretty tame at first, then ..." Rick sighed and paused again.

"Finish it, Rick."

Rick closed his eyes, remembering what details he could from that morning. The same raw anger from that day rose in him. A part of him would kill Rast again if he could. It was a small part of him now (he'd gained a much better perspective on things), but a part of him nonetheless. He used the rising anger to finish it.

Standing, he approached Viv. She watched him calmly, but Rick noticed her hand grip the chaise cushion. He bent down, bringing his face close to hers. A magnetic-whiff of her jasmine body-oil drifted to him. "Then the conversation shifted to what it naturally would. And when that bastard mentioned his relationship with you sexually? Viv, I lost it. It's as simple and as real as that. I lost it." Straightening his posture, Rick walked back to his chair. He crossed his hands behind his head and looked at his wife.

Lightning flashed.

Viv glanced through one of the windows, before bringing her eyes to his. "So, what? You just—"

"No. Believe it or not, I walked away from him, Viv. There was no way I could continue listening to him and visualizing the two of you. I walked away."

"Are you telling me Jonathan came up on you? That he attacked you or something? You're saying it was self-defense?" She stood.

Rick sighed heavily. "No. I'm saying that what happened to him wasn't intentional. That I did not go there with the purpose of killing Rast. I went to ask him to back off so that I could save my family."

Viv's eyes flashed with something Rick couldn't decipher. "So, you walked away?" She sat again.

Rick nodded. "But Rast followed me. I was trying to get a grip on my emotions, but Rast kept talking about the two of you as he walked behind me." He swallowed. "I just needed him to shut up a minute ..." Rick paused again. He'd reached the fuzzy-hard part.

"What, Rick?"

"I don't know. Next thing I know, all was quiet, and I could think again. When I turned around, Rast was falling to the ground. I went to him, but it was too late."

"It was suddenly quiet, and Jonathan was on the ground? What the fuck are you talking about? What happened to him?!"

Hearing the pain in her voice, Rick sat again. "From what I could tell, my best guess is, I delivered an ushiro-kekomi to his chest."

Viv shook her head. "You're talking that karate shit. What does that mean exactly?"

"It's a driving back-kick. It's not deadly per se, but under the right circumstances, and if the person catches it unprepared ..."

"It can be fatal," Viv finished.

Rick looked at Viv solemnly. He nodded. "It was an accident, Viv," he repeated yet again, determined to make her understand that. "But given the shoes I had on ..."

"The damn boots! Were you wearing the hiking boots you've be trying to donate? The ones in the box?"

"… Yes."

Viv stood. She walked to the window and watched the rain.

Rick took in his wife's body, her beautiful, pregnant body—and wanted her. He knew better than to go there, but he couldn't help it: the woman owned him.

Cronus stirred.

Rick willed him back to sleep.

Finally, Viv spoke. She kept her back to him. "You know, Rick, you keep emphasizing it was an accident." She paused. "But you rent a car the day before he is killed, and are hiding or getting rid of evidence shortly after." She turned to him. "I'm not getting the 'accident' part."

With impatience bordering on anger, Rick stood. "Renting the car in advance was because I wanted to *talk* to Rast, Vivian, *talk* to him. I've said that. I just didn't want to go in my car to do it. Kicking him was an accident born out of rage and confusion. Getting rid of my shoes and clothes is exactly what it looks like: covering it up. I was shocked at first, then determined not to lose my family. And while I could have gone to the police, I— I just didn't."

"And then the cockiness set in," Viv mumbled.

"Something like that."

His baby looked at him sharply.

"I'm being straight-up, Vivian."

Rick took a chance. Holding her gaze as thunder sounded above them, he approached Viv. On the radio, "Stay in My Corner," by the Dells, began. He stopped before her.

Viv shook her head. "Rick …"

"What?" Rick spoke softly to her. He'd explained all there was to what happened with Rast. He was done with that. All that mattered now was Viv.

"Shit, I don't know. I mean, I can't … We can't—"

"It's obvious we can't keep this here, between us. I know that. You wouldn't be able to if you tried." Rick thought of Naomi. "Besides, it's out of our hands now, anyway."

"What? Why?"

"Shhh. Doesn't matter." Rick paused, listening to the song. "Hear that?"

"Yes, Rick. I hear it."

"That's what I need. I can handle whatever the future holds, if I have you in my corner."

"I understand what you're saying, Rick. But you killed a man."

Rick returned her gaze without speaking. He wasn't explaining about it being an accident anymore. As it was, the Dells were doing his pleading for him. He waited: wanting her, needing her.

She was his family.

CHAPTER 21

Saving the Last Dance

Stay in his corner. Have his back. Breathing was near-impossible. Viv gazed into her husband's eyes-of-fire, listening to the Dells. She resisted the pull of the song's lyrics as Rick's eyes calmly implored her, knowing she had to be practical and not let emotion sway her.

Jonathan was dead.

Rick killed him.

It wasn't that simple, but …

"Dance with me." Taking her hand, Rick brought her close.

She didn't resist being pulled into his embrace. The ebb and flow of her emotions rendered any intended reactions inert. She moved with Rick easily, but thoughts of Jonathan kept her from molding her body to his.

As they danced, Viv attempted to regard Rick objectively, to see him as something horrible. She pictured Jonathan on the ground dying. An ache for his suffering resonated deep within, and fleetingly she hated Rick.

But Rick was no killer (at least not the old Rick). And even though he'd changed, Viv didn't think this "new" Rick was, either. The point was, Rick was the old-Rick when he met with Jonathan that day, and Viv absolutely believed Rick killed Jonathan by accident. Still …

Viv stared over Rick's shoulder. She'd forgotten how long the song was. Rick's abrupt disengagement as the song ended surprised her. Moving to the stereo, he lowered the volume more.

Rick held a hand out to her. "C'mere, Viv."

Viv shook her head. "Rick, I can't do this now. I need time t—"

"You don't have much of that anymore." Rick went to the kitchen. He poured himself some iced tea, drained the glass, and came back.

She looked at Rick, finding him extremely sexy despite the situation at hand. He wasn't trying to be, the hurt in his eyes told her that, but then Rick never tried to be sexy—he just was—because he wasn't trying.

Viv regarded her husband, figuring this to be the last time she'd see him this way before letting him go.

She blatantly looked him over: from his nice haircut, to his long lashes and low beard, to the natural swell in his jeans, that bowlegged, slightly-pigeon-toed stance. She wanted him. Searing his image in her mind, her body stirred with an anticipation that would never be satisfied again. With this once-over, she began her goodbye.

"Viv?"

"Yes?" Viv shifted her gaze to meet his eyes.

Rick cocked an eyebrow. "You're looking at me like you want to fuck, not fight. I'm— I mean—"

Viv sighed heavily. "I know. It's okay." She walked to where Rick stood and sat on the sofa.

A lump of sorrow lodged in her throat; her chest grew heavy with the impending loss of her marriage. Her body beginning to slump with the weight of emotion, Viv straightened her back and swallowed—hard.

Rick sat beside her. "It's over, isn't it?"

Viv hesitated but then nodded slowly. "It was an accident, but ..."

"I understand."

"I'm sorry."

"It's okay, I'm sorry, too ... For so many things."

They grew quiet. Rain and soft music accompanied their thoughts.

"I came up with that word, you know?" He offered reflectively.

Viv smiled a small smile. "Doesn't matter now, does it?"

Rick reached for his ear. "No. No, I guess not."

Silence again.

Rick looked at the floor.

Viv stared out the window, listening to Rick grinding his teeth. The lump returned. She swallowed again. "So, what now?"

"Not sure. But I've taken care of a few things. You and Al and ... and the baby should be set. No red tape, you know?"

Viv nodded. She wasn't sure what he was talking about, but she didn't have the mental energy to devote to it.

Thunder rolled.

"Rick?"

"Yeah?"

Viv turned to him. "What did you mean by it 'being out of our hands'? About there not being much time?"

Resting his forearms across his thighs, Rick looked intently at her before looking at the floor. "Naomi knows. She gave me a day or so first. I'm guessing my time's up. She said she'd call before the authorities showed up."

Again, Viv could only nod her understanding. She didn't know whether she was relieved or irritated that Naomi knew.

The steady downpour signaled the storm had settled in their area. On the radio, WMZZ probably played some good stuff, but Viv barely heard any of it. Her vision seemed hazy at best. Weariness set in. And it got harder and harder to keep the lump in her throat down.

He gently took her hand. "We can't sit here waiting for the phone to ring. Dance with me. They're playing some nice cuts today."

Looking at Rick, Viv wanted to speak, but was afraid to. There were words in her brain—calm, coherent ones—but somehow Viv knew that if she allowed herself to speak, the words in her brain would not be those coming out of her mouth.

Viv followed Rick to the center of their family room. Before, during the Dells, she only saw the dancing's purpose as one-sided—as Rick's attempt to persuade her to stay with him. This time, as the deejay played a lesser-known song by L.T.D., the dancing served a different but common purpose.

She slipped her arms around Rick's neck, this time fully-molding her body to his in a painfully-familiar way that felt right as rain.

"Sounds like a B-side of L.T.D.'s. But it's nice."

Viv regained the power of speech within the comfort of his embrace. "Yeah, Jeffrey can make damn-near anything sound good."

Moving with him, Viv felt better as the seconds passed. She could do this. Viv caressed the back of Rick's head, gently pulling him closer as they danced. Saying goodbye to him this way flowed with her mood. Viv closed her eyes, letting the music and dancing pacify her. She paid the insistent lump in her throat no mind; she would dance until the phone rang. She was in a good place. She could do this. She was fine.

The 'B-side' rolled into "We Both Deserve Each Other's Love."

Viv's eyes popped open.

And like that, she was broken down to the least-common-denominator. An emotion, masquerading as heartache but exponentially worse, seared her.

Closing her eyes again, Viv danced with her husband as tears accompanied the memories flooding her mind.

She thought about the day they met and the smell of his Creed Green Irish Tweed. About his aversion to vegetables and his fondness for iced tea. She thought about the first time she learned he cheated on her, and the look in his eyes when he told her he'd never do it again. About his PB&Js with a side of sardines, and the orange sweatpants he wore that Saturday—that blessed Saturday—when he fucked her in their laundry room. She thought about his country breakfasts. About their long talks in the middle of the night when neither of them could sleep. She thought about motorcycles. About Alna, and about their children lost. About big fights over pet peeves and little fights over big stuff. She thought about tender foot-jobs under the table and about sexy fun with vanilla yogurt—or peanut butter. She thought about their chess games that could last weeks. JV Artisan Black. His varied tie-knots. His smile. His kiss. His ear-thing. His wonderful morning-love. She thought about Rick: her friend and husband—her life.

Viv rested her head on Rick's shoulder as their song ended. She heaved and held Rick tighter.

Rick cushioned her head. "Let it out, Viv." He sniffed.

Hearing him, Viv pushed back.

He was crying, too.

Viv kissed him. She kissed him with everything she had, trying to reach his larynx with her tongue. His mouth tasted of salty-sweet iced tea as tears mingled in their joined mouths.

Passion and Sorrow worked together.

Rick stopped their kiss. "Shit." He moved his lower body off her and smiled an awkward smile. "Sorry. I know this is a messed-up time for us, but kissing you like that ..." He looked away and down.

Viv lifted his chin and turned it to her, looking in his eyes. "I know how I'm kissing you. Your response is exactly what it's supposed to be." She moved up against him, feeling his erection. "I'm aroused, too. Kisses …"

Rick's gaze locked on her lips. "… don't lie."

Viv nodded. "I wanted to taste and feel *us* again. You know, just …"

"One last time," Rick finished softly.

Viv nodded.

Her tears gushed anew. The idea of him locked away in prison made her even weepier. But she had to let him go. She couldn't put Alna and their little one through the ordeal of having a father in prison.

Rick turned the music off. He retrieved a box of tissues from the end table and brought it to her.

"Thank you," Viv heaved, taking several from the box.

"Welcome." Rick grabbed a few tissues, too, before placing the box on the circular coffee-table behind them. Instead of wiping his face, he helped Viv dry hers. He held a tissue over her nose as if she were a toddler, coaxing her to blow. "Come on …"

Viv blew her nose and smiled shyly.

"Better?"

"A little." Her head felt better, less-congested, but her chest tightened with feeling. Crying never brought on any supposed release. It only compounded things. It was why she resisted doing it.

"Can I kiss you again?"

The unassuming innocence of his question touched her. "Please do."

"Okay, but you can't, you know, *kiss me* kiss me. I mean—"

"Shut up." Viv pulled Rick to her with an odd sense of urgency. Going about their goodbye this way—this playful-discussion thing—was strangely comforting.

"Can I tell you the word first?"

Viv wasn't sure she wanted to go there, but she nodded.

"Live."

"What?"

"Live. L-I-V-E. Live."

"Live?"

"Yep."

"As in, 'I *live* you'?"

He placed a gentle hand to each side of her face, looking in her eyes with desperate intensity. "As in, I *live* you, Viv, yes. As in, without you, I do not live. You are my life, Vivian Elaine Williams Phillips. I *live* you."

Viv stood there, transfixed by his gaze, the reds and dark-golds of his irises firing passionately. The power of Rick's emotion emanated from him into the air around them.

She turned away, giving Rick her back. The power behind his feelings proved too much for her to take head-on. At the moment, it was simply too much. As it was, it was too late.

Holding back a full-fledged crying jag, Viv spoke quietly: "Yes. Yes, that is the word. You did good, Ricky. I— I live you too. But …"

Rick turned her to face him. "Just kiss me, Viv."

Viv did. Taking her time to explore and rediscover (for the last time) the contours and textures of his mouth, she focused on the taste and feel of Rick's tongue as its rigidity shifted with the demand of her kiss. She'd kissed him thousands of times, but every time her mouth touched his, it was something warmly-familiar and tantalizingly-unique all at once. Touching his lips and tongue with her own, consistently sent a bolt of heat through her that melted her insides.

Feeling his erection against her made her moist. Viv sighed into his mouth, wanting to fuck him right there on their family-room floor. She reached for his erection and kissed him harder, squeezing and stroking him.

When she raked her nails all over it, Rick moaned harshly with arousal and broke their kiss. "Viv, we can't."

Viv pressed a palm against his master-of-ceremonies. "This tells me we can." She began a rubbing motion as she looked at him.

Her baby's eyelids lowered with a breath of arousal. "B- But, Viv …"

She whispered, "C'mere, Ricky," and pulled his head close, bringing their mouths back together.

The phone rang, interrupting their momentum.

It rang again.

Rick, breaking their kiss, nibbled her lips teasingly before stepping back. The phone rang a third time. "The answering machine'll kick in if I don't get that."

Painful boulders of sadness, anger, and defeat crowded her middle.

Moving to the phone, Rick mouthed, "I live you." He turned and picked up the receiver. "Hello?" Looking at Viv, he nodded: it was Naomi.

Viv, rooted to the spot, tried desperately to hold on to her composure. The moment was here. Time, essentially, was up. Her marriage was over. Dancing and kissing didn't stop it.

"Yeah, I know. Uh-huh …" Rick's eyes stayed locked on hers. "She's right here … Yeah … I think so … Maybe."

She could hear strains of Naomi's voice through the receiver.

Rick surprised her by smiling and saying: "She cut me loose. But she was nice about it." His eyes held Viv's. "Well, Doctor Alexander, I'ma go. I have one last thing to take care of before they get here so … Yeah. Thank you … You, too. Here she is." Rick handed the phone toward her.

Viv shook her head.

Rick put the phone in her hand and held her gaze. "Do you know how much I love your eyes, Lady Blue?" He placed his lips to her temple and kissed her. "I *live* you, Vivian." With that, he left the room. Viv heard him dashing up the stairs.

It seemed hours before Viv finally brought the phone to her ear.

"Hello?" Naomi called.

"I'm here."

"… I'm so sorry, Viv."

Viv didn't speak. She couldn't.

"I'll be able to help Rick's case, Viv. He'll have to do time, but, well, you get the picture. Does that help at all?"

"Rick killed Jonathan."

"Yes?"

"And I— I …"

"Yes? Come on, Viv. What is it?"

"But he killed him, Naomi," Viv said in a rush, her tears flowing freely again. She listened to near-silence from the other end. "Hello?" Viv grabbed the box of tissues and hugged them.

"Does it matter?"

"I …"

"Rick said you cut 'im loose. I take that to mean what he did does matter. But listening to you now, I'm asking: Does it *really* matter?"

Viv trembled as lightning flashed.

Iced tea, orange sweatpants, Burberry Touch, model cars, unzipped jeans, and the graze of his moustache, raced through her mind. She thought about how his tickle-torture always leads to hot, sweaty lovemaking, and about warm cuddles on the sofa as they spooned while watching TV or in bed while reading. Christian Dior Eau Sauvage. About long nights studying for their graduate-school exams—and the pillow fights that cleared their heads. She thought about dances together in the family room whenever a good cut came on the radio. About how sometimes their innocuous conversations brought them closer. Guerlain Vétiver. His kiss. About the crinkly-soft feel of her fingers moving through his rough, dry curls when his hair is longer. About triannual steal-away weekends getting a gage up. She thought about the closing lyrics to "We Both Deserve Each Other's Love," and about quiet moments meditating and praying together. Showers together. His sky-reading thing. About playing Mastermind, and the quirky way he'd twist his mouth whenever he'd lose, came to her. His kiss …

Her love and trust were utterly with him.

Viv sniffed and heaved again.

"Let it out, Viv." Thunder boomed, almost drowning out Naomi's voice.

Viv shook her head. "No."

"You need to let it out, Viv. Even though you've ended it, the coming months are going t—"

"No. No, it doesn't matter," Viv interrupted. Her knees buckled, and she sat on the coffee-table. Her sobs came from her toes. "I— I *live* him, Naomi!"

"I know you do. Tell 'im, Viv. I don't know what last thing he has to take care of, but you may want to …"

Viv didn't hear the last of Naomi's words. *Last thing. I've got one last thing to take care of … As in without you, I do not live …*

"Rick, *no!*" Viv dropped the phone and raced for the stairs.

Lightning flashed as she entered the spare bedroom.

Rick's back was to her as he pointed the gun at himself.

"Rick, *no!*"

Rick turned.

The gun went off.

Or was it the crack of thunder?

To her left, the wall exploded. Drywall dust and whiffs of sulfur assaulted her nostrils as the sound of sirens drew nearer.

Rick trembled as he stared at her. "Viv?"

The gun fell to the floor with a muted metallic-clunk that sickened her and flooded her with relief simultaneously.

"Yes, Ricky. I'm here. It's going to be all right. Naomi says she can help, okay? We'll get through this, baby. I love you. I … *live* you. It doesn't matter what happened."

There was a knock at their front door.

"I'm scared," Rick admitted.

"I'm not."

There was a second knock, much harder this time. The doorbell rang.

"I can't," Rick uttered.

"I can." Viv watched her husband, thinking about what lay ahead for them. "You and Me."

The vulnerability and pain in Rick's eyes lessened with her words to him. "… Me and You."

From downstairs: "Richard Phillips? Police!"

Rick's gaze softened. "We'd better get that, huh?"

Viv nodded—and offered him her hand.

CHAPTER 22

Reconnections

Naomi finished the interview summary for her new patient with a sigh. Placing the folder to the side, she laid her hand across it, drumming her fingers. For two o'clock in the morning, she was wide-awake—and bored. Her date with Kevin ended nicely enough; she now wished she'd gone ahead and invited him to stay the night.

She could finalize her work from her exit session with Vivian Phillips, but she wasn't ready for that. She'd spoken with Viv several times since their exit session a month ago—three months since Rick's arrest.

Things could have turned out much worse. Naomi often wondered why she didn't get a "flash" about Rick's suicide-wish. Hell, she was their therapist; why didn't she see that coming?

Rick was charged with first-degree voluntary manslaughter.

Naomi indeed helped with his case. With a plea down to second-degree manslaughter, he was sentenced to sixty months with continued psychiatric counseling.

She counseled Viv through the initial proceedings until both concluded she'd be okay. Besides, having a baby provided plenty diversion.

Naomi reached for her glass of sweetened iced tea and took a swig. She could have used a tad more lemon, but the tea was good. Who knew?

She went to her bookshelf, hoping to find a good read (or reread). Most of the books were medical, certainly, but she kept other genres on her shelves, too. Naomi retrieved a book exploring history of African spirituality. She pulled down a favorite Connie Briscoe novel as well, figuring she was so bored, she'd read them both.

Keys rattled, and the front door opened as Naomi perused pages of the spirituality book.

Leslie was home.

Naomi froze.

Low voices, one distinctly-male, drifted to her. Their conversation, muffled by the walls through which it traveled, was difficult to make out. Naomi's grip on the book tightened. There was a brief period of silence before she heard the front door close and the lock catch.

Placing both books on her desk, Naomi left her office, seeking her daughter. Sounds of cabinet doors opening and closing came from the kitchen. Naomi paused in the arched doorway leading into the kitchen and watched her daughter prepare a peanut butter and honey sandwich.

Leslie didn't look up. "No one's here but me."

"How was your date?"

Leslie focused on a slice of potato bread. "Good. Yours?"

"Very nice, actually. I'm encouraged."

Leslie finally looked at her. Surprise mixed with a sardonic twist tinged her expression.

"What?"

"Nothing." Leslie returned her gaze to her task. "You're up yet again." She gestured toward the counter, where slices of bread were spread with peanut butter. "Want one?"

Naomi nodded. "Yeah. Make mine with crunchy, would you, please?" She folded her arms and leaned against the archway.

Leslie rolled her eyes upward before turning to retrieve the jar of crunchy peanut butter from the cabinet. Before Leslie turned completely away from her, Naomi saw a hint of a smile.

The tension in Naomi's back and arms relaxed. Maybe it wouldn't be so hard after all. She'd truly had enough of the unspoken but minimally-expressed antagonism between them. Leslie was grown; it was time mother and daughter related to one another as adults.

"I'm sorry, Leslie." This had to be said first; otherwise, the rest would be pointless.

Leslie, in the middle of spreading honey on a slice of bread, dropped the knife to the counter. The clang of the knife against the countertop resounded in the early-morning stillness of the house, startling both women.

"Sorry," Leslie said, referring to the noise. "Please stop saying you're sorry, Ma. I know, okay?"

Naomi eyed her daughter. Leslie's hair was longer. "Letting it grow out, I see. So much for like mother, like daughter."

"No; just a change in style. Look, I know you're sorry, Ma. And I know you love me. Please let this go. If you can't, I'll have to leave. It's been over three years now. This has to end."

"I'm trying to let it go, Les. It's funny. I'm a psychiatrist, and I can't figure out my own issues."

"I don't believe that for a minute. Simple fact is, if you'd let what happened between us go, there wouldn't be this, so-called 'issue.' I've moved on, Ma, feeling no shame, but you have to, too."

"You sound like me."

"And the drinking has to stop, too." Leslie's eyes were direct, angry.

"Now you sound like someone else ..." Naomi replied softly, thinking of Rick Phillips.

"Who? Doctor Oheneba?"

"No," Naomi said, feeling sad. "It's not important. Anyway, I'm already working on that."

"Self-rehab?"

"When's the last time you've seen me with a drink?"

Leslie opened her mouth, and then closed it.

"Come on. We haven't been best-buds in this house, but you know when I've been drinking. I've never been flat-out drunk; I can say that. But even through a mild-high, I could detect your disdain. So again, I ask you. When's the last time?"

Leslie looked at her mother for several seconds. "It's been awhile, I guess."

Naomi extended both hands, palms up. "That's all I'm saying."

"Well, good for you. One down, one to go."

"You're sounding like me again."

"Well, apple doesn't fall far and all that. Let it go, Ma. The incident happened a long time ago. Daddy's death had us both messed up. It was one, *one* night between a mother and daughter who needed each other and who had no one but each other. Like I said, I'm fine with it—feeling no shame. I love you, Ma, and believe it or not, what happened helped me. I'm not some damaged, fragile woman. I believe I've shown you that."

"You have."

"Yeah, but you gotta do something on your side. Something to make it right for yourself. Something—"

"I will. It helps knowing where you are with it." Naomi paused. "'A night between a mother and daughter …'"

Leslie cocked an eyebrow.

Naomi ran a hand over her hair. "I know. It was what it was. But when it's said aloud …"

"Uh-huh. So, the mighty Doctor Naomi Alexander isn't so no-nonsense after all. Even the formidable doctor has points of sensitivity and experiences discomfort at some of life's base moments." Leslie wore a small grin.

"I'm human, too, Les." Naomi moved further into the kitchen and stood beside her daughter.

"I know you are. Problem is, you forget that fact all too often." Leslie hugged her.

Naomi hugged back tightly. It'd been so long since really hugging her child.

Leslie let out a few fake coughs. "You're holding me too tight, Ma. I— I can't breathe."

This was much better. Naomi released her daughter. "Cute."

Leslie reached for the knife. "I'll finish these. Get the milk. We can laugh at infomercials while I tell you about how it's going with Scott." She started spreading the honey.

"Scott? Who's Scott? I thought—"

"See? That's what I'm telling you. My life is moving on, but I can't share it with you because you're back in—"

"Okay, okay. Fine. We'll critique, *Scott*, is it?"

Leslie nodded.

Now Naomi cocked an eyebrow. "Serious?"

"Not yet."

"That the deep-voiced gentleman saying goodbye at the door?"

Leslie nodded, barely suppressing a grin.

Naomi opened the refrigerator and looked at her daughter. "Well, he gets major points for that voice alone."

"I sure as hell think so."

"What's he studying?"

"Ma, don't start."

Naomi laughed. "I'm not. Seriously, what?"

Leslie arranged the sandwiches on a plate. "Art history."

Naomi held a straight face for as long as she could before pushing an underhanded fist out and pulling it back. "Yesss!"

"Get the milk, Miss Crunchy Peanut Butter. I'm hungry. And by the way, I'm sculpting again." Leslie grabbed several napkins and left the kitchen.

Naomi grinned to herself as she poured two tall glasses of 1 percent milk. She figured she looked silly grinning all alone in the kitchen, but she didn't give a hey-nonny-nonny. A great deal of weight had been lifted from her heart and mind. Traces of guilt remained, probably always would, but this, this was much better.

There's nothin' like family—no matter how big or small.

Naomi's grin faded with thoughts of Rick and Viv, but she shook it off. She was hungry, too—and a peanut butter and honey sandwich had her name on it in the next room.

EPILOGUE

Viv Phillips sat at the table sipping iced water, studying the box for a five-hundred-piece puzzle that was now more-than-halfway complete. "Finish getting the rest of the blues together, Al. We'll finish the sky first. I'm sure the trees will give us a run for our money, later."

Alna pointed a freshly-polished nail at a completed section of puzzle. "We did a pretty good job on the creek and rocks."

"When do we paint it, Mommy?" a small voice asked.

Viv leaned over and tapped a small brown nose. "We don't 'paint' it, RJ. We shellac it."

"Well, when do we shlak it?"

Viv kissed her son's forehead. "That's 'shellac,' RJ. *Shell-lack*. And we don't do that until the puzzle's finished."

"And putting the sealant on is my job, bubblehead," Alna added.

RJ poked his tongue at his sister.

Alna returned the favor.

"All right, that's enough, you two." Rick took the puzzle box from Viv with a grin. "Here, let me see."

Viv quietly observed her family.

Alna, almost fifteen, had Rick's nose and complexion, but otherwise looked like her. Their four-year-old son, Richard Jr. ("RJ" for short) was a miniature Rick. He resembled his dad so much it was pitiful. They couldn't call him Little Ricky; that was so *I Love Lucy*. And Little Richard, well, the world already had one of those.

When RJ was born, Rick wanted to give him the middle name Jonathan. Viv admired how much of a man he was for that, but she vetoed it. Rick was already paying for what he'd done. What happened wasn't intentional; Rick didn't have to pay for the rest of his life, by naming his son after Jonathan.

RJ selected a puzzle piece that fit and smiled at his father.

Rick smiled back. Twins: thirty-eight years apart.

Alna rubbed her brother's head. "Good job, man."

The phone rang.

"That's probably Olivia for you again, Al. Why don't you get that?"

Alna made a cross-eyed face, laughed, and picked up the phone. "Phillips residence."

RJ looked at his parents sharply. "Hey! We don't live here. That's what we say at home."

Rick palmed his son's head. "It's okay, man. It's our summerhouse; where I lived as a boy, remember?"

RJ shrugged. "Can I have an ice-pop?"

Viv nodded. "Eat in the kitchen or go outside with it."

Alna, deep in adolescent conversation, headed for the bedroom area. RJ hopped up and went into the kitchen for his treat.

Viv removed her reading glasses and went to the window. Holding her glass, she trailed a finger along the bottom rim.

"Viv?"

"Yes?" Viv looked at her husband and smiled. "I'm good, sweetie."

Rick paused to read her before grinning with a nod. "Just checking."

She air-kissed him and turned back to the window.

Rick's imprisonment was the longest, most-painful period of her life. Her friendship with Naomi helped get her through. Rick was released on good behavior after serving thirty-two months. And although their family had been whole for some time now, Viv still experienced moments of thankfulness and humility. Rick was everything to her. *Everything*. Their separation strengthened their deep bond.

She was wholly-uninterested in a life without him.

Viv enjoyed their mini-vacations to Hampton. Eugene had a fatal stroke a year ago, and the house went to Rick. Rick added her name to the deed. After his release, Rick still had a job waiting for him at Impetus Marketing. She didn't exactly struggle when Rick was away, but major saving took a backseat to other financial needs. Given the job market, Rick's return to Impetus was more than a blessing. He didn't return to the executive position he once held, but in the years since his return, he worked his way back to upper management, with talks of an executive position once his probation was over. His probation was ending in a matter of months (they planned a getaway tree-climb for shortly thereafter). So, yes, she remained thankful and humble.

Rick cleared his throat. "Hey, RJ, wanna go outside with Daddy?"

"Yeah!" RJ called back. Viv heard him slurp. "Can we read the sky?"

Viv turned to Rick. "You have not been teaching him to tell time by surveying the sky!?"

Rick smiled with a wink. "To within the hour."

Viv smirked incredulously.

"I think he got it naturally, Viv. It didn't take much 'teaching.'" He called back to his son: "Yeah, little man, we can if you want."

"Yay!" There was more slurping.

"Rick, he's not yet five-years-old. He's just starting addition concepts. Telling time is a ways off, no?"

"It's a matter of assigning a number with the position of the sun and moon, Viv. Overcast days involve a little more, but ..." Rick shrugged. His reading glasses rested midway down the bridge of his nose. He looked over them at her—just as cute as he wanted to be.

Viv walked over to him. She put her glass down and moved between his legs. The woodsy, spicy-tobacco scent of Guerlain Vétiver teased her nostrils. Whenever her baby wore it, she was ready.

She took his glasses off and hugged him to her. "'Got it naturally,' huh?"

Rick looked up at her, those red-brown eyes sparkling. "I think so, yeah." At forty-three, he looked amazing. He did. Over the years, his chiseled features changed little. He needed reading glasses now, and strands of gray flecked his temples and neatly-trimmed Balbo, but that was it. His loose-fitting khaki-colored cargo-shorts and forest-green Polo shirt only masked his cut physique underneath.

Viv bent down, touching her lips to his. His lips were so soft. She kissed him tenderly, enjoying the graze of his moustache along her upper lip. Viv pulled back and looked down into those eyes of his. "I miss you."

"There was this morning."

Her mind touched instantly on the delicious oral-pleasure Rick administered during the 4:00 a.m. hour. "And that means what, exactly?"

"Nothing." Rick stood, pulling her into his embrace. "It means absolutely nothing." He dipped his head to brush his lips against the mole on her collarbone, sending tendrils of desire through her. He looked in her eyes. "I love you, Vivian." He kissed her with a soft, quick dip of his tongue. "Decades in, I'm still learning how much, Lady Blue." His gaze was soulful.

"*You* are a gorgeous man, Richard Phillips."

Her husband simply did not readily-accept compliments; such an endearing character trait that had its sad roots here in this house when he was a little boy. Rick lowered his eyes with a hesitant grin. "Where is that coming from?" He looked at her with this expression of bashful confusion—sexy as hell.

Gazing back at Rick, Viv held an unspoken conversation with her husband neither Alna nor RJ needed to hear. Loving heat moved between them along some invisible, private current. Gazes soon shifted to each other's lips; the desire for a kiss that was deep and slurping and leading to something necessitating nudity, drawing Rick's mouth closer to hers …

They smoothly shifted to neutral corners, however, as Alna returned from her phone conversation and RJ returned from his snack.

RJ made a beeline to his father. "Let's go, Daddy!" He looked up at her. "Wanna go, Mommy?"

Viv smiled down at her son before returning her gaze to her husband. "Not this time."

"Go?" Alna stood by the table. "I thought we were finishing the puzzle?"

Rick held Viv's gaze. "That, too."

Viv looked in the eyes of the man she'd made children with—and wanted him immeasurably. Still looking at Rick, Viv spoke to their daughter: "We are, honey."

Alna sighed heavily. "Oh boy."

Everyone looked in Alna's direction.

Viv rubbed RJ's head. "Whatsa matter, Al?"

Alna wore a perceptive smirk. "Nothing. I'm fine." She looked at her brother. "Come on, RJ. Let's go to the rec center for a little while."

"I'm goin' with Daddy."

"You can go with Daddy, later. Let's let Mommy and Daddy work on the puzzle some by themselves, okay?"

Viv exchanged a glance with her husband. It dawned on her (and Rick too, apparently) that their daughter recognized sexual tension between her parents. Viv didn't quite know how to feel about that. Yes, Alna was weeks shy of fifteen. Still …

Rick picked up his son. "Yeah. We'll read the sky a little later, man. Okay? I wanna work on the puzzle with Mommy."

Viv tingled with anticipation.

RJ's small pout changed to an inquiring smile. "Can we get a car to put together?"

"You bet." Rick kissed RJ and put him down, RJ hugging his legs.

"Come on, bubblehead." Alna took her little brother's hand. "We'll be back in a few hours." She looked at her parents warmly. "Have fun with the puzzle."

Rick cleared his throat. "Um … right."

Viv was speechless.

Alna took her brother to the rec center.

They were quiet after the door closed.

Rick spoke first: "Well, that was …"

"Interesting."

"Yeah." He turned to her. "C'mere." His soft command carried an extra-something in that mellow baritone of his.

"No. You to me."

Rick raised an eyebrow.

Viv softened her gaze, but didn't move.

Rick came to her. "So?" He rested his fingertips at her waist.

The man had no idea what that move (simply placing his fingertips at her waist) did to her. His gentle but masculine power calmly claimed her.

Viv breathed in the coriander, nutmeg and cedar in his scent as she circled her arms around his neck. "So … handle your business."

"Don't I always?" That edge of sex and danger crept into his voice.

Viv still wasn't used to it. "Without fail," she whispered.

Rick's soulful gaze returned. "You and Me."

Viv caressed the back of his head. "Me and You: always."

"Fuck the dumb stuff?"

Viv smiled warmly at her friend. "Damn skippy."

With this sexy smirk, Rick lowered his mouth to hers. Their tongues danced in a soft, pliant way that made her wetter by the second.

As usual, the radio played continuously in the kitchen. Instead of political talk, classic R&B hits played on low. Right now, "Look at Me (I'm in Love)," by the Moments, was on.

Without breaking their kiss, Viv slowly guided Rick in the direction of the remodeled master bedroom. This time, the proclivity for the bed was all hers.

Once in their bedroom, they paused long enough for Viv to close and lock the door. As she approached Rick, she wanted to do something to him that—in their twenty-plus years together—it had never occurred to her to do.

When she reached him, Viv pressed her body to his and kissed him. She nibbled his lips and dipped her tongue in and out of his mouth very softly while she caressed his head—something that drove him crazy.

She broke their kiss and watched his face.

He gazed back with smoldering curiosity.

Viv reached for Rick's right ear and caressed the scaly texture there. She'd never touched him like this before.

Rick's breath caught. He closed those long-lashed eyes. "O- Oh, shit." When she drew her right hand down to stroke his hardness, Rick moaned and looked at her. Desire and love leapt from his eyes as she caressed him, the reds and dark-golds blazing. His breathing grew ragged.

She drew close to kiss him again, but Rick stopped her. "I'ma shoot in my pants if you kiss me, too, baby." He spoke low and hoarse with arousal, the sound speaking directly to her female; Viv loved it.

Viv gently rubbed his scar. She gazed into the fire and stroked his erection, feeling it pulse with what she was doing to him. His excited-breathing melted her heart.

She watched her husband do his level-best to maintain control of himself. At his most vulnerable, he was absolute masculine.

Viv wanted his tongue. She tried to kiss him again.

"I'm— I'm serious, Vivian."

Holding his gaze, Viv slowed her caresses. She lifted Rick's shirt over his head and trailed fingers over his torso, before resting her hands at his belt. She unbuckled, unfastened, and drew his zipper down.

Viv stepped back slowly, alternating her gaze between his eyes and the view of his opened pants. She removed her strapless maxi dress.

He watched as she slipped her sandals off, took off her bra, and stepped out of her thong. Viv moved closer to the bed. She'll be forty-five soon, but since taking up martial-arts with her husband, she knew her body was tighter than ever; she worked hard at it. Viv turned back to him.

Rick's eyes deepened with desire. He toed-off his shoes and smiled at her.

She didn't smile back. "Ricky ..."

Rick crossed the room and drove his tongue deep into her mouth. It was Viv's turn to moan as he pulled her close and caressed her body. Rick softened his kiss. He teased her tongue with his as he teased her right nipple with a gentle pincer grasp. Her hands were everywhere on him: his butt, his strong back, his hair, his face.

Viv went back on the offensive. Mouth locked with his, she turned them around, backing Rick to their bed.

Rick broke their kiss to lie back on the bed, his eight-pack and happy-trail calling to her as he air-kissed her and whispered, "You." He raised his hips and drew his boxers and cargo shorts down to his knees before reclining and propping on his elbows.

The sight of his imposing shaft pointing at the ceiling got her moving. Unless he was returning to flaccidity after orgasm, his shit didn't lean or bend—it stood tall. He didn't like her saying his dick was "pretty," but it was. She pulled his pants and socks off, tossing them atop her clothing.

Viv kneeled between her husband's legs. She leisurely ran her tongue over his heavy sac and beautiful length, listening to Rick's sighs and moans of pleasure and getting-off on his dirty words of encouragement, before climbing on top and straddling him. She sank onto him slowly, ignoring the usual twinge from internal pressure and relishing the feel of him filling her.

She interlocked her left hand with his right. Resting her free hand on his hard torso, she held his gaze and commenced with handling *her* business.

Her breasts soon ached for his touch.

Rick reached up and fondled them, alternating between sensual squeezes and thumbing her nipples in wide circles. He then put his left thumb down between them and massaged her button as she rocked her pelvis with his. The carnal pleasure of their intimate connection seeped through her bones.

Rick mouthed, "I love you." Sunlight coming through the windows highlighted the simmering molten fire of his burnt-umber irises, and Viv wanted to cry. She was so in love with this man, her soul belonged to him.

She grabbed Rick's wrist. He was sending her over, and she didn't want to go yet. She whispered, "You."

It was Rick's turn to be dominant. He gently repositioned them, placing her head on their pillows. He pulled out and gazed down at her.

He was about to do that "thing"; something they now called the "Rice and Gravy." She wanted to cry again—for the pleasure awaiting her.

Rick took both her wrists in one hand and put them above her head, then leaned in and kissed her, allowing her to suck his tongue; a thrilling turn-on they discovered the night of his release. Sucking Rick's tongue was a fiercely-intense, personal thing, more personal than giving him head; she experienced a closeness to him that was feral, dire, visceral. She sucked hungrily.

When he broke from her mouth, Rick rose to his knees and looked down at her, bringing her hips toward him before bracing over her again.

Viv reached down and gripped him, stroking slowly. She worked her thumb over the tip, circling the droplets of fluid there, making him close his eyes with a moan.

"R- Ready?" He looked at her.

Viv held his gaze before releasing him with a nod.

He entered her again, but allowed only the head to penetrate. He gently worked just the head back-and-forth, long-ago recognizing how sensitive her opening was to this type of friction. When he first did this to her, Viv wanted to hurt him, he felt so good.

Viv closed her eyes with her own moan. *This man ...*

"Uh-uh. Look at me ..." Rick urged softly.

She gazed up at her husband as best she could under these most marvelous of circumstances. Slowly, back-and-forth: Ecstasy.

Pushing in just a little deeper, Rick sometimes lowered his gaze to watch their sex, his breathing more-pronounced as he grew closer to climax with the friction against his spot.

The pleasure at her core steadily increased, too.

Wanting to climax with her husband, Viv gripped and pushed his rear, guiding him all the way inside, and then wrapped him up, bringing his entire body down to her.

Rick shuddered as his body lowered to hers, and Viv's heart went out to him. The angle of his penetration changed, sinking deeper.

Feeling his thudding heart as he moved against her, Viv swirled her hips upward in time with Rick's thrusts, her body soaring with the passion overtaking her.

Using her muscles on him, she turned his head to her and tongued him deeply, caressing the scar on his ear.

That sent him over.

Viv went with him.

As they came down, Rick shifted his upper-body to the side, leaving his hips resting in the intimate cradle of hers. He spoke through ragged breaths into the crook of her neck: "I'm so in love with you, Vivian. Damn."

Viv responded with a caress to his head and nip to his earlobe; his feelings were reciprocated.

When Cronus slipped out, Rick shifted off her completely. He lay on his side beside her, tracing a finger over her breasts and navel. "You okay?"

"Yes. I live you, Ricky."

"... I live you, Viv."

That declaration floated in the space around them, as birds chirped outside the open window.

Viv pulled the sheet over them, the wet-and-sticky secretly pleasing.

"C'mere." Rick shifted to his back and gathered her to him.

She rested her head on his chest, listening to his heartbeat and playing with his pubic hair. "That was intense."

"Truly. Gimme kisses ..."

Viv shifted to tongue her husband down a little before settling back on his chest. "Is it ever just 'blah'?"

"Nope. You've got some powerful stuff, girl: my kryptonite."

Viv smiled (and blushed). "Why don't you do that more-often?"

Rick chuckled. "It's my secret weapon. Don't wanna overuse it."

The Rice and Gravy felt so good, Viv didn't think overuse was possible. "I see. And now I have a secret weapon," Viv purred, thinking of her husband's response to her caressing his scar.

"You sure do, shit …"

Viv hugged him. "I won't overuse it. I'm calling it the Sweet Cornbread."

"The 'Sweet Cornbread,' huh?"

"Yep."

"Cute. … How long did Al say they'd be gone?"

"You mean our too-wise-for-her-own-good daughter? She said a few hours, but I'm sure it'll be less than two. Why?"

Rick chuckled again. "Yeah, that was something, wasn't it?" He yawned. "Need a nap."

"Me, too."

"Where's your cell?"

Her body strumming with satisfaction, Viv gazed lazily around the room. "In the living room. Why?"

"Mine is in my pocket, on the floor over there, but I don't want to move …"

Viv cupped Cronus and the boys and played lightly. "For …?"

"To set the timer for an hour." He kissed her hair. "You wore me out, Missus Phillips."

"No such thing." Viv looked up at him. "Okay, if I leave the coziness of this bed to get your phone, you owe me one."

"One what? And I usually give you more than one."

She resisted blushing; so true. "I'll let you know what."

Rick's smile was both sexy and loving. "If I gotta pay, I gotta pay."

"Oh, you'll pay," Viv replied suggestively, turning away from him. She leaned from under the sheet, across the floor, trying to reach Rick's shorts. "Hold my legs."

Rick grasped her thighs.

With a final lunge, Viv reached his shorts. She hurriedly backed into the comfort of their bed. She felt for his phone, retrieved it, and handed it to him, dropping his shorts to the floor. "Set it for fifty minutes—just in case."

Rick unlocked his phone. "You could've done this."

"I know." Viv got a little more tongue from him before snuggling back onto his chest.

"… There. I set it for forty minutes. I only need about a half-hour anyway, and we need to at least attempt to work on that puzzle."

Viv giggled. "That's fine."

"… Wow."

"What?"

"You're beautiful, and naked, and in my bed." Rick let out a relaxing sigh. "Life is good."

"You can be so silly."

"Feel like a game of chess later?"

"Maybe. Or some Mastermind …"

He trailed long fingers along her lower spine, her waist, her hip. "Know what I have a taste for?"

Viv resumed light play with his lower-abs and personals. "No idea. Hopefully nothing involving peanut butter, jelly, or sardines." She yawned.

Rick chuckled. "Buttermilk pie."

She shifted, gazing into the molten-fire of his irises. "Seriously?"

"Yeah."

"We can all make one tonight, if you want."

He pecked her lips tenderly. "Sounds like a plan."

Viv rested her head back on his chest. They went quiet. She closed her eyes, drowsy now.

"… Viv?"

"Mm-hmm?"

"… Marry me."

She snuggled in deeper. "You want to renew them for our anniversary, over the Thanksgiving holiday?" She imagined dancing with him to "We Both Deserve Each Other's Love" in front of their guests.

This time, she did shed a tear.

"Lucky number twenty-one," he mused with a sigh. "Yeah, that's cool."

Rick's left hand rested on his abdomen.

Before drifting off, Viv rested her fingers across his, purposely touching his wedding band.

He was hers. She was his.

Perfectly simple.

Simply perfect.

ABOUT THE AUTHOR

S.F. Powell grew up in the Washington, DC, metropolitan area, where she lives with her husband and their children. Her submission of *Like Sweet Buttermilk* won first place in the Black Expressions Fiction Writing Contest.

For more on her stories and the characters in them, she invites readers to visit her website, www.sfpowellbooks.com.